OBSESSION 101

OBSESSION 101

A novel by
Michelle McGriff

Q-Boro Books
WWW.QBOROBOOKS.COM

An Urban Entertainment Company

Published by Q-Boro Books
Copyright © 2006 by Michelle McGriff

ISBN 0-9777335-4-8
First Printing December 2006

10 9 8 7 6 5 4 3 2 1

This is a work of fiction. It is not meant to depict, portray or represent any particular real persons. All the characters, incidents and dialogues are the products of the author's imagination and are not to be construed as real. Any references or similarities to actual events, entities, real people, living or dead, or to real locales are intended to give the novel a sense of reality. Any similarity in other names, characters, entities, places and incidents is entirely coincidental.

Cover Copyright © 2006 by Q-BORO BOOKS all rights reserved
Cover Layout & Design – Candace K. Cottrell
Editors – Stephanie Wilkerson-Hester, Candace K. Cottrell, Tee C. Royal

Q-BORO BOOKS
Jamaica, Queens NY 11431
WWW.QBOROBOOKS.COM

Prologue

In the back of the warm, darkened parking lot of Moorman University, she was grabbed from behind, her mouth covered by a huge gloved hand.

Muffled, growling, angry words were said in her ear as the man lifted her from her feet and carried her a few feet away from her car before slamming her to the ground.

Barely holding on to consciousness, her mind soared as she used what was left of her strength to kick and flail her arms in an attempt to rip the ski mask from his face. All the while, the man's large hands ripped at her clothing.

A plethora of thoughts went through her mind as she felt her underwear leaving her body. God, this can't be happening, she was sure she said aloud.

She felt her voice rumble in her throat, but upon opening her mouth to scream, she felt his fist—slugging her quick and hard, stunning her into silence.

The beast of a man rolled her over onto her stomach, pinning her to the gravel with one arm, daring her to move, or to breathe, as he readied himself to take from her what he had no rights to—what was not his.

"Don't fight me or I'll kill you," was all she heard him say.

Maybe he said something else. Who could remember such details? It was so long ago, yet she revisited time and time again.

Prying her legs apart and forcing her to expose herself to the night air, she felt him rip into her dry and unreceptive body. The pain caused by him tearing through her as if she had no feelings, as if she wasn't even a person . . . The sound of him grunting and sucking for air through his teeth as if he were truly receiving some kind of pleasure from this act of violence—it all sickened her. As he rode her for what seemed like hours, she tried hard not to vomit.

Surely she would wake up before she vomited.

The helplessness of it all.

A warm tear ran down her cheek as she suddenly felt him releasing his demons inside her.

"This can't be happening to me all over," she pleaded, as she looked up to see Reggie, her son, standing in the darkness watching the violent acts of his father.

"Say his name, Reggie. Call to him so I'll know who he is!" Rashawn called out. "Say his name. Make him stop," she screamed, only to find her sister, Rita, shaking her awake.

Chapter 1

It was cold and wet outside today. The weatherman had predicted that it would be the coldest day of the year. Of course, he had said the same thing about the day before.

A change of scenery was always welcoming after another rough night of sleep had left her drained for most of the morning. Rashawn ordered a refill of her usual, a mochaccino-half-caf-sumatra, and then took a seat in the nearby restaurant where she had gone to sort out her life. Sitting there was better than her tiny office any day of the week.

Moorman University may have had the reputation of a great curriculum and some of the best teachers in Northern California, but Rashawn Ams had decided that they didn't know a thing about office space.

"Speaking of space," Rashawn went on in an undertone, "I need to get back to looking for a place to live." She nodded her head in confirmation of that fact.

Rashawn lived with her sister, Rita. It had been their arrangement for years. However, Rita had married Terrell nearly two years ago, and with that marriage had come twins—all of seven months later.

But who's judging? Rashawn thought now, unconsciously shrugging. *I'm sure that wasn't the reason they got married. Maybe he really does love her.* Rashawn sighed heavily, unable to explain the feelings she was having.

"And as if the house isn't small enough, Rita is pregnant again," Rashawn fussed on, still in a barely audible undertone, rubbing her forehead, trying to force the negative thoughts to go away.

Rita's pregnancy was supposed to be a secret. Rashawn was sure of it, especially since Rita had all but shredded the letter that Kaiser had sent, announcing the test result. The letter read as if it was a congratulatory proclamation, as if another baby this soon after having twins would be something any woman would want. Rita had both spindled and mutilated the notice—apparently attempting to toss it in the trash. It had missed and landed on the floor behind the receptacle. That's where Rashawn had found it, anyway.

"But I know she won't abort." Rashawn sighed again, sipping her coffee. *She loves Terrell too much to do that. How can that be love, expecting Rita to give up her whole life like that? She gave up her career and everything for him and those boys. What about her needs?* Rashawn went on in her mind, over-analyzing the subject. Teaching Ethics often had Rashawn 'over-thinking' things, things like family, love, and friendships.

Lately, however, Rashawn was trying to distance herself from all of those things that required so much thought.

Rashawn knew that it was her 'give-a-damn' attitude toward everyone that had Rita analyzing her a lot, too. She was always labeling Rashawn with titles and couch phrases, blanketing her feelings with statements like, "You're just afraid of commitment, afraid to be loved, afraid of closeness," and things like that.

"Whatever," Rashawn would respond, mumbling under her breath.

Rita would never understand how the return of Rashawn's nightmares kept her nearly paralyzed when it came to relationships. Rita, even though she was a school psychologist with a sharp mind and well-rounded grasp of human nature, would never understand how much Rashawn wanted to go on with her life, but still felt stifled by the past.

A rape isn't something you just '*get over*'.

Shows how much you know, Ms. Psychologist, Rashawn thought to herself, admitting to herself for the first time that she was not '*over it*'.

Rashawn reached into her purse to pull out a mint. The purse went with her shoes, which she hadn't worn in a while either.

She had left so many of her things in storage when she'd left for Georgia after the attack, before her son came into her life. Now that she was back, it was like going on a shopping spree every time she opened a box. She was pleased with how well everything still fit, considering how big she had gotten while pregnant.

Her pleasant thoughts wandered for a moment and then settled again in a dark place, the place that held the hardest things for Rashawn to face.

There was not enough strength inside Rashawn to tell Qiana, her best friend, the truth about her son, Reggie or the rape. Heaven forbid Rashawn would find the bravery to tell anyone, especially Qiana, that there had never been a lover, that Reggie had been conceived from a vicious rape, a rape committed by Qiana's ex-boyfriend.

So instead, Rashawn lived a lie, and with each day *she* deepened the riff between her and those who cared about her.

Rashawn knew in her heart it had been Qiana's ex who had raped her. He was a pig of a man and perhaps it was the furtive knowledge that the very man who had murdered Qiana's unborn child in a vicious attack was possibly the same man who had fathered Reggie.

Maybe Rita was right about things. Maybe a renewed closeness with Qiana was scaring her. Perhaps rekindling their relationship would force her to admit just one too many bad things, to face one too many bad memories and realities.

"Like what a lousy friend I am?" Rashawn uttered under her breath, thinking of the way she had abandoned Qiana during her recovery from the attack on her life. Sure, Qiana had a strong support system, her husband.

"But still . . ." Rashawn sighed, shaking the negative thoughts from her mind. She had changed . . . a lot. Gone was the strength she once possessed. Gone was the depth in character she used to be so proud of. Where was the Rashawn she used to know?

And I thought I had fully recovered; maybe I haven't even started.

Rashawn continued digging deep into her purse for what she hoped to be at least one strip of gum; even a fuzzy mint would do.

Why was it that every time she ate garlic she would find herself unprepared to at least freshen up her breath? Even her back-up toothbrush was back at her office, and there was no way she was going out in this hurricane!

"Shoot," she growled, giving up the search.

Suddenly from over her shoulder, she heard the clearing of a throat. She turned, only to see Davis, a math professor from the university, standing there.

Shocked by his sudden presence, and without forethought, she looked him over from head to toe.

In the five months since being back, she'd been seeing a lot of familiar faces at the university, and Davis was one of them. He was divorced and attractive, but a bit on the '*unusual*' side in Rashawn's opinion. Yes, Davis was very different. He didn't carry himself like most divorced men. He seemed settled—old, different—yet he was somewhat sexy. He reminded Rashawn of a smoldering flame, so she wasn't sure how close she wanted to get to him.

Of course, it wasn't like she had her mind on that kind of thing lately anyway.

"Sorry," was all he said. She shook her head, not even feeling the goofy grin creep onto her face.

"For what?" she asked.

"Didn't mean for you to think I was stalking you," he answered.

"I was sitting over there," he pointed behind him, toward an auburn-haired woman sitting alone at a table. The attractive woman waved at Rashawn.

Without control, Rashawn's face tightened while she waved back, smiling diplomatically.

Yeah, it figures. He's old, sexy, and involved. Nothing different about that, she now assumed of Davis.

"I thought it was you sitting over here, so I asked . . ." He turned to the woman again. "You must know, Sam's wife. You know, Sam Thorton Business Law. He's on a couple of the same committees you're on. Well anyway, we all usually come here for lunch on Fridays," he volunteered, answering her unasked question.

Of course, the big guy with the booming voice. How could she not know him? His points are always made at the meetings. Perhaps Sam's presence had kept her from noticing his timid-looking wife, let alone meeting her. Who could get around him?

Rashawn, now more than a little self-conscious of her breath and embarrassed at her incorrect assumption, fanned her hand over her mouth. Davis waved Sam on, who had joined his wife, and invited himself to Rashawn's table.

"What's good?" he then asked her, as he began looking over the menu handed to him by the waiter. Rashawn nodded, saying nothing. There was no way she was ready to share her garlic breath with this man.

Davis held back his smile, causing a deep crevassing dimple to come to his cheek.

"Ahhh," he answered himself while looking up at the waiter, handing back the menu.

"Just gimme what she had," he requested.

The waiter took his menu with a smile, but before he walked away, Davis tugged at the waiter's apron. "Oh, and don't forget my Tic Tacs," he smarted off. Rashawn burst into laughter. Yes, Davis was different—interestingly so.

The man searched for the passkey, hoping not to jingle the other keys that hung on the large ring too loudly. He wouldn't want the strange woman in the office next door to come out.

Surely her concert music was too loud for her to hear any noises.

It seemed to him that the professors on this campus were among the most obtuse people on earth. He would wager that Rashawn Ams would probably not even notice if things had been moved around in her office.

While inside the office, the man looked around at all of Professor Ams' personal things sitting on her tiny desk. He smiled at the familiar faces in the pictures. He fondled her trinkets, tossing one of the smaller shiny objects into his pocket.

It had been a year and a half since he'd seen or touched her. He found it hard to believe how excited he was that she was back. Somewhere in his sick mind he had even reasoned that she had returned on his account.

"Just couldn't stay away from me, eh?" he asked the picture of her, holding it up.

Finally he turned to the small refrigerator and opened it. Inside he found three bottles of water, two yogurts, and a box of raisins. He had an occasion to examine the contents before. As usual for her, one of the bottles of water was open.

"Hardly enough to keep anybody going," he said with a disappointed sneer. His judgments over the contents of the appliance almost made him forget his purpose for being there.

"She just never drinks enough water," he said, removing one of the new bottles of water and replacing it with another one that he himself had brought.

"Oh well, a little dabba do ya," he snickered wickedly, thinking about the tainted liquid he'd put in the bottles.

"This is gonna make things a whole lot easier," he said, closing the refrigerator.

Watching Rashawn over the last five months, he studied her every move while there on the campus. So far he found her to be a creature of total habit. He liked that in a woman.

He'd been intrigued by her since the first time he saw her over two years ago when he first started working at Moorman. She was smart—real smart—and sexy beyond belief. It wasn't a wonder why so many men craved her.

Or maybe it's just me, he thought now, subconsciously licking his lips, remembering their last time together.

The scent of perfume in her hair . . .

Too bad she had to fight me, he thought now, feeling only a subtle hint of remorse over his actions that night in the back lot of Moorman University. He looked at the open palms of his large hands, remembering how hard he had hit her.

That had been a long time ago.

"Things are different between us now, baby," he whispered, touching his fingers to his lips and then touching the picture of Rashawn and her five sisters that sat on her desk. In his mind, her smile was for him and him only.

"I'll never take you by force again. I love you too much for that. You made me love you," he said with a wink of his eye and a tune forming in his words. "I didn't wanna do it," he added with a wicked chuckle coming out.

Locking the door, he made his way out of the building; unseen.

At the small coffee shop across from the campus, Rashawn had sought solace at the end of the day. A familiar face entered the coffee shop. Rashawn knew the massive, menacing man. It was Blain Tollome, the campus cop. She hadn't seen him in a long time.

By the looks of him, she could have sworn that he'd gotten bigger, if that was possible.

"Hey, Rashe," he said to her, grinning wide.

"Rashawn," she corrected. "Actually, Professor Ams to you, Officer Tollome," Rashawn added.

The comment had been a private joke between them once, but somehow, the reason it had been funny was hard to remember, and she could tell that he hadn't remembered the reason either.

Blain sat down across from her.

Broad-shouldered, with an arm span that stretched the length of the sofa, his features were ethnic, though his skin was white. His narrow, chiseled, angular face sitting on a thick neck gave him an almost superhero-like appearance. His bulky, muscular upper-body, tight rear end, and thick thighs could surely turn heads, but there was something unsettling about Blain. Something that Rashawn did not like, and frankly couldn't pinpoint.

Although she had attempted dating him once, that

was enough to know she would never make the mistake of getting too close to him again.

"Missed you," he said. Rashawn looked around for escape.

"Yeah," she mumbled.

"How long has it been?"

"A while, I was on sabbatical," Rashawn answered, giving in to the fact that she would have to talk to him.

"Maybe we could try going out again," he said, apparently unable to get the smile that began to curve his full lips to stop coming. Rashawn's golden eyes shot hot beams at him, causing him to turn away slightly and lick his lips, showing discomfort.

"I don't think so," was all she said. Just then, Blain's pager went off. He glanced down at it and then back at her.

"Duty calls," he said.

"Goodnight," she snipped.

He looked down at her.

"Yeah, you have one too," he said before strolling out.

The Session

"I'm glad you could see me on such short notice."

"Well, you sounded very agitated."

"I am."

"Why?"

"The woman I told you about."

"Yes, the woman. You don't believe that she's got a thing for me, do you?"

A slight chuckle.

"I never said that, nor implied it. I have no idea—in reality—who this woman is, beyond assumption. Therefore . . ."

"And you don't need to know her."

"All right, all right, agreed. We agreed we would not say her name."

Heavy sigh.

"Anyway, she came back—as you know."

"So you think she came back for you?"

"I know she did."

"What makes you think that?"

"I can tell by the way she looks at me, or doesn't look at me. You know how coy some women can be."

"Maybe she truly doesn't realize how you feel about her? Maybe she has her eyes on someone else?"

"Oh please, it's more than obvious how I feel about her. And if she's not sure, then I guess I'll have to change that."

"And how do you propose to do that?"

"Perhaps I'll just tell her to her face. I'll tell her."

"Tell her what?"

Silence.

"*I don't want to tell you.*"

"*Why?*"

"*Because it's private, what I need to say to her.*"

"*Our visits are confidential. You can say whatever you want here. Perhaps you could practice what you want to say to her.*"

Silence.

"*What? So you can laugh at me.*"

"*I would never laugh at you.*"

"*Good thing. I don't like to be laughed at.*"

Chapter 2

Davis surrendered this room over to the night classes at the end of the day, so he was used to seeing his students still meandering in and out, even after his class period was over. His was the last class of the day, promptly ending at 4p.m.

However, this was Friday so there were no classes tonight.

A petite blonde sat in her seat long after the rest of the class had walked out. Davis noticed her after gathering his things together.

Setting his heavy briefcase on his desk, he asked, "Yvette, is there a problem?" It had begun to rain again. It was a cold rain, and Davis couldn't wait to get back to his apartment. He lived on the coast, outside of the city. He loved how the rain looked falling over the ocean. He loved how the air smelled—salty, with a hint of the day's catch lingering. He loved living in his small community. Everyone knew everyone in Pacific View.

"Yvette," Davis called again, noticing the girl's trembling bottom lip. He hated it when women cried. Suddenly, tears streamed down her face. He walked over and sat on the desk in front of her. Davis was a compassionate man—kind, easygoing, gentle even. Perhaps that was what his ex-wife had really meant when she left, after calling him temperate and boring. Maybe his ex had never met a man who was truly gentle. Because in his heart, Davis knew, boring he was not!

"What's the matter?" he asked Yvette, getting his ex off his mind.

The girl looked up at him with her nose red and glowing from the onset of her crying jag, one which Davis hoped could have waited until she got home before releasing. "You're such a nice guy, Mr. Davis. I just, I just need to talk to someone," she began.

Davis looked around, hoping they were alone. This had all the makings of a confidential conversation, and he would hate them to be interrupted or misunderstood.

"Why don't you go see Professor Roman? He's a counselor," he suggested.

"No, I want to talk to you because, well . . . because—" She stopped abruptly. "Because I'm pregnant," Yvette whimpered.

Davis's heart jumped. Why was she telling him this bit of news?

"Yvette, why . . . ?"

"You don't understand. I've never had sex," she cried, shaking her head, her eyes widening and taking on a crazed look. She was nearly hysterical.

"Yvette, what do you mean?" Davis asked cautiously.

"I mean that I don't know how it happened. I went to this frat house party at the end of last semester and now . . . now I'm pregnant," she went on.

Davis almost found the comment funny—a woman, disclaiming involvement in the conception of a child. That usually was a man's line.

"Now, Yvette, if you went to a party, weren't there guys there? Did you have too much to drink?" Davis began questioning. "Party, drinking—I may just be a math teacher, but that starts to add up real fast, if you pardon my pun." He chuckled overtly now.

"You don't believe me either, do you? I thought I could talk to you, Mr. Davis. I really thought I could," she yelled, bursting into full-on emotions now. She jumped up from her desk. Davis reached for her.

"Yvette, it's not that. It's just—well, I mean . . ." Davis stumbled badly.

Yvette's glare told him his efforts were now a waste of time. She had trusted him, and he had failed her. He had been the one man she could look up to. He had been the math teacher from heaven for her, but now he was nothing more than just 'that old guy who teaches remedial studies.'

"I only had a soda. That's all I remember. I had a soda. I don't want to talk about it anymore," Yvette growled behind jagged tears.

Chance Davis. What an interesting guy, Rashawn thought, reliving their pleasant luncheon encounter from a few days ago. But then again, they had been passing each other in the halls and happening upon each other a lot more frequently since.

"Surely it's just a coincidence," Rashawn reasoned, once again fighting the truth. Rashawn had no boyfriend. And with her gossiping sibling, Rita, just the mention of a man in her life could easily become the scuttlebutt of the year since she was the only Ams woman who was still single. Just the mention of a man's name, and her sisters would have her married off within the month. That was not how Rashawn planned for either her life to go, or her son's.

"I've got things to do and places to see. Me and my boy don't need nobody!" she said aloud while strolling across the campus toward Davis's class. It wasn't like she wanted to ask him out, or vice versa. Dating Davis hadn't even crossed her mind as a matter of fact. He was just a nice guy—funny, witty—and she needed the laughs right now.

Starting over did have its drawbacks, although Rashawn could not think of them right now, considering change had done wonders for her mental health, and though she would never say it out loud, her physical health, too. She knew she looked great!

A lot had changed in her life since giving birth, and that was okay because she was doggedly determined to keep a close tab on those 'changes'. Sometimes negative changes could come upon a person before they knew it, and Rashawn was looking at experiencing only the positive.

Moving would be the first of those positives.

Terrell and Rita were getting her down with all their 'lovey-dovey-we-are-family' stuff. She'd had enough!

Reggie didn't need to be getting all those 'Daddy thoughts' in his head.

With Rita's boys calling for their father all the time, Reggie had taken to calling Terrell 'Daddy' sometimes, too. And that had to stop.

"There's never been a 'Daddy' for Reggie, and there will never be one," Rashawn huffed, shooing the thought from her mind.

Though the house they all lived in belonged to both herself and Rita, Rashawn would gladly let Terrell buy her out—anything to get out of that 'Love Shack'.

What was even worse was that Rashawn couldn't even turn to her best friend, Qiana, for comfort and association. Whenever she did buy out the time to spend with Qiana, all she did was talk about her perfect marriage. She was wearing Rashawn's nerves thin, too.

"What was up with these broads, mannn?" Rashawn asked, letting out a huff. She was fighting all possible thoughts of jealousy over the women in her life. She didn't want to let herself feel disturbed by how much in

love they both were. She didn't want to think about relationships and loneliness. Rashawn wanted content-
ment in her decision to live with anger.

Anger is good.

Even some of her coworkers, those diehard single,
successful women Rashawn could always count on for a
little male bashing from time-to-time, had succumbed
to the dreaded "M-word."

"I'll never give in," she told herself.

Just then, Rashawn noticed a young blonde girl all
but running from Davis's classroom, with him following
close behind. Soon the girl, gaining ground, left him
standing at the edge of the lawn.

What was that all about? Rashawn wondered.

"Grading kinda stiff, aren't ya? Leavin' dem students
in tears?" Rashawn called out to him jokingly. She got
Davis's concerned expression in return.

Upon turning to her, he squinted as she got closer to
him, and then suddenly his face straightened.

Blind as a bat, she thought.

"Hey, Shawn," he said, abbreviating her name the
way only her family did. But it sounded good coming
from him, so she didn't correct him.

"No, I uh. . . ." he stumbled, looking around to see
which way Yvette had gone. "She, uh. . . ." He caught
himself, as if quickly deciding not to betray Yvette's confidential talk.

Besides, Davis figured, *Yvette might eventually get herself
together and come back to talk some more—or not.* As upset as
she was tonight, if he ever saw the girl again in class,
he'd be surprised.

"She's got some personal issues going on," was all
Davis said.

Rashawn chuckled.

"Looked like it." She smiled. Davis looked around
again, and then apparently gave up with a heavy sigh.

"Well, what's going on, kid?" he asked, again getting

friendly. Rashawn kept smiling. Just then, the campus lights came on. Rashawn loved when that happened.

Money well spent, she thought to herself.

"Nothing, I just thought you might like to get out of the rain and grab a cup of coffee?" she asked, pulling her jacket close in around her. Davis smiled now, causing that cute crease to show up deep in his cheek again. Rashawn noticed freckles dotting his light skin.

She hadn't noticed them at lunch. At lunch, she had only noticed his dimple. "Sure," he answered, pulling his fedora down on his head.

At six foot, Rashawn was sure she topped Davis by at least four inches, even in bare feet, although he seemed confident walking with her in the light, misty rain through the parking lot to the coffee shop just across the street. When they went inside, Davis assisted her with her coat. He had impeccable manners, unlike any she'd seen in a long time. It suddenly felt good to be with him. She almost leaned back into his embrace, but she caught herself.

That feeling had never before come over her so quickly. Rashawn was immediately transported to another time and place—a time when 'Rashawn and a man' were said in the same sentence—oh so long ago.

Davis fanned his hand for the young man to come over to where they were about to sit on the comfortable looking sofa near the blazing fireplace.

Rashawn liked this place—Cecile's Cultural Bookstore and Kettle House. Sometimes there would be readings, or even a little jazz guitar, played by a local artist who was hoping to get a following. However, tonight it was quiet except for a few of the college kids trying to get warm before heading home. Rashawn noticed a book on the table. It was one she had wanted to read for a while—*Healing the Breach* by Rosalind Stormer.

"You ever read this?" she asked Davis, who shook his head.

"Looks like a chick book," he chuckled, taking the novel from her and looking it over, noticing the references to possible spiritual awakenings the story could cause—*far from what was awakening in him.*

"Where do you call home, Davis?" she asked him.

"Pacific View. I grew up there and just stayed," he answered, quickly putting the book down. He then ordered their coffee from the young man standing over them. "But my family is from Louisiana. That's where I was born," he went on. Rashawn had thought she noticed just a little 'back-home' diction in his speech.

"Maybe I didn't want Sumatra Mandheling, Davis," Rashawn commented on his taken liberty in ordering her coffee. He looked confused for a moment, and then smiled.

"Oh, sorry, but you look like a rainy-day-Sumatra-Mandheling kinda woman," he chuckled.

"I am, but taaa."

"Well, there we go," he laughed. "And it's, Chance," he interjected quickly.

"Yeah, you took a chance all right," she chortled.

"No, my name—it's Chance Davis," he corrected.

She looked at him for a moment, digesting his words.

"Ohh, your name," she said, grinning wide in her embarrassment. "I knew that." She giggled.

"You have a beautiful smile," he said. Rashawn leaned back, looking him over critically as if his words had broken the spell she was now under.

"I know, you don't like to hear junk like that," he said, pushing on the bridge of his glasses. It seemed as though that might have been a nervous mannerism for him, since he pushed them up even before they slipped.

"No, I don't like to hear come-ons. I hate them," she

answered, sipping her coffee the young man had placed on the table. Davis nodded knowingly, and sipped his too, smiling all the while.

Just then, Blain Tollome strolled in. Seeing them, he came over. Clearing her throat, Rashawn looked him over from head to toe as he sat down across from her and Chance, completely uninvited.

As he spread his arms over the back of that small sofa, Rashawn caught a glimpse of his gun in the holster, under his leather jacket. She could tell he wanted her to see it, and suddenly both he and it became even more unimpressive. Blain smacked his full lips, curving them into a confident smirk. It was almost as if he could read her mind.

He called out in a loud voice to the young man working there, "Hey, buddy! How about something strong over here to take the chill off?"

"Sorry, sir, we don't serve alcohol," the young man called back, his voice sounding weak and shaky in comparison to Blain's booming baritone.

"Shit—aw well," Blain was grinning now, looking straight at Rashawn with an odd sparkle appearing immediately in his dark eyes.

"So gurl, 'ow ya been?" he asked.

Rashawn was almost catching an accent of some kind.

"Long time, no see ya," he added.

Davis cleared his throat, and Blain then turned his attention toward him, looking him over sort of the way a bulldog looks over a small, vulnerable rabbit.

Of course, Davis returned the observatory stare, viewing Blain the way a carpenter would view a big, thick piece of brainless wood.

"What brings you out on this wet night, Tollome?" Davis asked, showing Rashawn that he was ready to take on the obnoxious intruder, "I've noticed you're back on campus. You were at Danton for a while, correct? So what's up with all this drug stuff going on? Do you guys really think you can do any good with stopping the problem here?" Davis went on firing questions.

Blain gave Davis only a sideways glance. And then, in a mannerism that Rashawn had hoped was unconscious, Blain licked his lips while looking back at her. He reminded her of someone about to bite into a greasy burger. She set down her coffee, as it had backed up in her throat.

"I've got to run," she said, hoping her eyes were not widening. Her face was a dead giveaway. It always told on her.

The panic was building.

Not here, Shawnie.

Not here, girl.

Hold it together.

Damned panic attacks! Rashawn hated them, having fought them for a long time. She thought she had 'em licked. However, there was something about Blain Tollome—he had the power to drive her nuts. One moment longer in his presence and she'd have to break out of there screaming into the night.

Davis, noting the sudden change of expression showing on Rashawn's face, grew instantly irritated. There was always some jerk interrupting him when he finally found himself in the right place at the right time with her. Over the last few months he had been trying to talk to this woman. *Actually, over the last three years,* Davis thought.

Well, maybe not a full three years. She had been gone for a while, and before that, he was preoccupied with his divorce from *that woman.*

The scowl left from *that* memory covered his face. Rashawn noticed.

"You don't have to walk me to my car," she commented while both men were busy displaying their bursting egos. One could almost hear them pop.

"Oh no, no, sure, I'll walk you back," Davis offered, standing now.

"Goodnight, Blain," Rashawn said, with a forced smile on her face. Davis shook hands with him. It was the least he could do before the symbolic bell rang and they both came out fighting.

Rashawn's silky nylons rubbed against Blain's leg as she moved between his large trunks in an effort to get by.

"Excuse me," she said, seeing that he had noticed the slight contact they had made. He smiled up at her, winking ever so covertly. She could no longer control her face. She knew her lip was curling into a snarl and she couldn't stop it.

"Goodnight, Officer," she said, her voice just above a whisper.

"Yeah, whatever," Blain said, sucking his teeth while watching as Davis slid her coat onto her shoulders and then shrugged into his own, carrying his hat in his hand.

Outside, the rain came down in a light, steady flow.

"What was with that guy?" Davis asked.

"I'd rather not talk about it," she answered.

"Good," Davis said, becoming aware of Rashawn's uncovered head. He playfully placed his fedora on top of her head. She giggled, pulling it down tight over her mass of thick locks.

The move was a natural one when Davis put his arm around her shoulder. She felt so much better now. Maybe it was just her imagination again, but suddenly Davis didn't seem so much shorter than her as she nestled into the crevice of his embrace.

By the time they reached her car, they were soaked, but laughing. In those ten minutes together, they had managed to get acquainted faster than they would have at the coffee shop. That much was clear.

"So, dinner?" he asked her, confirming the date they'd alluded to in their strolling conversation.

"Dinner?" she asked, shocked at how smooth he had been in asking her out.

Had she missed the offer somehow? She was slipping for sure. It had been a long time.

"How about tomorrow? I'll pick you up," he offered.

Suddenly, Rashawn thought about Rita's ol' nosy behind. It would be her first date in forever, and there was no way she wanted Rita involved. Rashawn then thought about Reggie. No, she didn't want Rita on a Daddy-Hunt for Reggie, that was for sure.

"No! I mean, I'll meet you there. Where do you want to eat? I mean, I like Benny's Chinese Palace," she said, not sounding as smooth as she intended.

Rashawn climbed behind the wheel of her car; he closed her car door for her. She quickly rolled down the window, leaving Davis in the rain without his hat. He reached in and snatched the fedora from her head.

"It looks better on me," he winked playfully. Rashawn felt the heat rise under her Hershey-brown complexion.

Thinking of candy now, Davis reminded Rashawn of a piece of homemade divinity. His coarse, bristly looking, short cropped hair was a sandy brown. Rashawn had to wonder about his parents. She wondered if his mama was a white woman.

It was only one of the many questions she hoped he would answer during the 'date.'

Of course, she had no such answers planned for him. She didn't intend to give up any of her personal business.

"OK?" he asked, bringing her back to the now.

"Huh?" she asked, her mind running through the possible things he could have asked.

"Where did you go all of a sudden?" he asked her.

"Sorry, what did you ask me?"

"Nothing." He winked as he turned and walked away. Rashawn sat watching him for a minute as he got into his car. Then suddenly, she realized he was just sitting there watching her.

It came to her what he had said.

"I'll wait until you take off."

Nothing more.

In an apartment on the south side of town, Andy Simmons and one of the prettiest girls in school enjoyed pizza and beer in front of the fireplace.

They had been going out for weeks now, but nothing was going on in the 'get-it-on' department. The girl was shy, and Andy didn't want to scare her off. She was pretty, smart, and most important to him—virginal. What a catch!

When Andy's roommate shared his own personal dating success secret with him, Andy couldn't wait to try it out. If it didn't work, nothing lost, right? If she had a bad reaction, they could always blame it on the pizza, right?

"Want some more beer?" Andy called from the kitchen.

She stretched out on the blanket. *Andy is so sweet,* she thought to herself. He had been nothing but attentive all evening.

And a picnic, too, how romantic, she thought.

"Sure," she answered.

Plop, plop, fizz, fizz. *Now for the secret,* Andy thought now, the old commercial coming to mind. It was time for a relief, that was for sure. He'd not had sex in months. He was tired of this dry spell and, if all went well, it would end that night. When he handed the beer to her, she chugged at it and then sat the mug down on the floor while waiting for Andy to sit next to her on the blanket. When he did, she wrapped her arms around his neck and planted a big kiss on his cheek.

"What's that for?" Andy asked, surprised at her willing show of affection.

"You are so sweet." She grinned.

Andy was shook, for a moment, by the look in her eyes. Was Sharon coming onto him?

Boy! That stuff is WAY fast.

Slowly, he moved his hand onto the front of her thick sweater, letting his fingers tighten around one of her small breasts. Her eyes closed as if the feeling sent pleasure throughout her entire body. Andy then squeezed the other. She arched forward, giving in to the groping. Andy grew excited, unintentionally pushing her too firmly. She fell backward onto the blanket.

"Wait a minute, Andy," she gasped. But Andy wasn't listening to her. He was all over her, kissing her neck and face. He covered her mouth hungrily, sucking on her tongue, biting her lip teasingly. His hands moved quickly down her body to her jeans, on which he now tugged. She moved his hands away.

This wasn't going to be as easy as he had hoped. Maybe she hadn't drunk enough. Maybe it didn't work.

"Andy, wait. I wasn't trying to go all the way. I wasn't," she pleaded now, attempting to roll over onto her stomach in order to get away. In her efforts, she spilled the beer.

Seeing the remainder of the potion pouring out, watching the last drop of 'easy sex' trickle from the glass, Andy scrambled to save it. "The beer!" he yelled out.

"Jeez, Andy, it's just a beer," she commented, apparently noticing his desperate tone. She stood up and adjusted her clothes.

"I needed that," he said.

"I thought the beer was for me," she said with a nervous laugh.

"Anyways, look, I don't mind making out, but I wasn't planning to, *ya know*," she went on. Digging deep into the pocket of her tight jeans, she pulled out a strip of gum. After refreshing the piece she had in her mouth, she tossed her long, blonde hair. Andy stared at the soaked stain on the blanket.

"I was," he mumbled under his breath.

"What did you say?" Sharon asked, noticing Andy's pained expression and overly disappointed attention to the spilled brew.

"I said . . ." Andy began and then caught himself, "Nothing."

This girl wasn't stupid. She'd heard about the date drug, 'Ass Get' or 'Get Ass,' or something rude like that. Everywhere, it seemed, college girls were slipped something in their drinks, and, come morning, none of them remembered what they had done the night before, or with whom. It was getting very popular up and down the peninsula, and even more so at Moorman U.

Surely Andy wasn't one of those guys? Surely he hadn't tried to drug her. Had he?

"What was in the beer, Andy?" she asked. Andy said nothing. His head was buried in his hands.

"Andy, what was in the beer!" she yelled, kicking him hard in the leg before, suddenly, she dropped like a sack of potatoes to the floor—unconscious. Andy didn't hesitate, he quickly began to shimmy her from her Levis.

The Session

"I'm glad you could see me on a weekend."

"Did I have a choice?"

"You always have a choice."

"Very true, I'm in control of my own actions."

"Unless you relinquish that control."

"I would never do that."

"Maybe not intentionally, but there are times when we lose more control than we are planning to."

"I'm sure there are times, and there are people who allow that to happen. I'm not one of those people, and so there is no time when that occurs."

"What if someone had control over you—your mind, your thoughts? What if a person could control what you did and how you acted?"

"What do you mean?"

"I mean, what if a person could control your mind, make you think what they wanted you to think?"

"I don't know . . ."

"You understand my question. Don't play dense."

"They would have to have me under some kind of influence, like a drug or something."

There is a chuckle; it's more of a snicker, a mocking outward sign of disbelief.

"I'm sure it wouldn't be so hard to control you."

"Why, because I'm weak?"

"No, because I'm more powerful. That is the problem many people have. They always look to themselves and their own *strengths and weaknesses when sizing up their adversaries, when in fact they need to be looking for the weaknesses and strengths in their enemy."*

"You sound like you're going to war."

"Life is war."

"I see. Am I the enemy?"

"My, aren't we jumping to delusions today?"

"You mean conclusions."

"I mean what I said."

Chapter 3

Rashawn thought the day would never end. She couldn't wait to meet Dav—er, Chance.

She would have to get used to calling him that, having only referred to him as Davis since meeting him over two years ago.

After a somewhat rough morning in the house, Terrell and Rita—along with their boys—had decided to take off for the weekend. Terrell's grandmother was not feeling well, so she was calling all her 'cheerins' to her side. It wasn't the first time, but Terrell always went. They knew he would never forgive himself if he didn't go one of these times and she really did pass away. She lived across the bay in a big old house that easily held all her loved ones, so usually Terrell and Rita stayed overnight.

Between folks sleeping in and otherwise tending to their own business, even the phone didn't ring until late in the day.

So this Saturday morning, Rashawn found herself with a little quality time for her Reggie.

While Reggie napped, Rashawn dug out her favorite

Stevie Wonder CD and hummed along while making cookies. When he woke up, they snuggled together on the sofa under a heavy throw and ate. Watching Reggie playing alone with his toys, Rashawn had to admit that she hadn't given Reggie much else other than herself. Now that she was back teaching at the university, she wasn't even giving him much of herself anymore.

By evening she realized she no longer wanted to go out.

What was she thinking, sharing what little time they had together with Chance Davis?

Rashawn watched her little man for a while as he toddled around the living room. Reggie was nearly two years old. He was big for his age, and many people thought he was already three. He stood much taller than the twins did, but then again they were early.

Rashawn was also a little surprised at how much he didn't look like the man she felt in her heart had raped her—not really. Nor did he look much like her—actually. She was shocked he hadn't gotten her eyes.

Rashawn and her sisters had their mother's eyes—exotic almond-shaped eyes the color of copper, Rashawn and her sisters all had a unique look about them. With rich brown skin tones, they were all shapely and tall with thick heads of hair, ample hips, and thick, pretty legs. Although they were big-boned women, sometimes brash, sometimes even kinda loud, many men found them quite beautiful. There was no vanity needed. It was a fact.

But looking again at Reggie, Rashawn once more faced his looks head on, trying with all she had to accept his differences—his dark eyes, nearly black, and his hair—what Auntie Ams called 'good hair,' growing in long, soft ringlets.

Reggie, with his crooked grin and bowed legs, looked unlike anyone in her family. Although Rashawn found him beautiful, and often pretended that she knew why he looked like he did, in her heart she wondered where his looks came from. *Who was his father?*

"And then they fight . . .ohhh my gaad, like cats and dogs they fight," she said to Davis, telling him all about the women in her life, and their husbands included.

She had called and canceled their dinner plans, asking Davis to meet her at the house instead. Why waste a nice, big, quiet house? Besides, Reggie was sound asleep by eight thirty, and always slept like a stone. There would be no need to cross her two worlds if she played her cards right. She had Davis come at nine.

"I find them painfully humorous," she added while handing Davis a dessert plate.

"Why?" Davis asked, accepting it.

Rashawn sat next to him on the sofa.

"Because, I mean, think about it. They're all so pathetic. And they call that love," she explained, fanning her hand in disgust. "Sounds to me like a bunch of trouble for the askin'." She chuckled now.

"But when one of them leaves, do they come back?"

"Of course," she sighed. "They don't really leave. They just like go for a drive or something."

"Sounds like love to me." Davis laughed, filling his mouth with a big bite of the cherry pie. Out of reflex, Rashawn playfully slapped his arm. He noticed.

"Men. You would say that," she joked.

"What do you think love's supposed to be like?" he asked, sounding serious now.

"I think loves s'pose to act righteous, not childish."

"Righteous?"

"Yes, real, you know—right," she answered, sounding very full of conviction.

"Right?"

"No games, Davis. You understand what I'm sayin'?

You should be able to meet someone and, if it's love, you should know it right off, and show it right off," she answered, her words intended to end the conversation.

Suddenly their eyes met in a longing gaze. Rashawn studied his face, the smoothness of his complexion dotted only by light freckles and the crease of his dimples. Just then, Davis leaned in for a kiss, breaking the spell. Rashawn reared back quickly.

"What?" he asked, taking on a joking tone, showing his embarrassment, and then masking it over by copying the mannerisms Rashawn had used at the restaurant that day.

"Now I need a Tic Tac?" he asked. Rashawn giggled nervously, glancing toward her bedroom. Her mind was on Reggie.

"No, it's not that. I . . ." she began, only to be interrupted by his lips and mouth invading hers. She pushed him away.

"Davis, I'm not into this," she said, showing her firmness. He smiled again, his dimples on full display now.

Was he smiling to cover a building rage?

Rashawn's heart began to pound. She looked for a change in his attitude.

He had only two ways to go.

And she was ready if he chose the wrong one.

She had a resolve. No man would violate her again. She would kill 'dead' the next man who tried. She would not be taken against her will again, not in this lifetime. This mathematician would be counting bullet holes if he decided to get froggy with her.

No one forgets rape, no matter how long ago it occurred.

Rashawn's mind swiftly formulated and calculated how quickly she could retrieve her loaded .22 from the locked roll-top across the room. She had locked that weapon away before leaving for Atlanta with the result of her vicious attack in her belly—Reggie. And despite how she had tried to make the best of it, how hard she had worked to get over it, how much she loved Reggie and felt he was a blessing, she would kill the next man who tried to violate her.

Davis sat back on his side of the sofa and went back to eating his pie.

"I'm just not into that," she said again, keeping her mind's contents out of her tone and her expression. He looked at her.

"I heard you the first time. So, what are you into, my beautiful friend?" he asked and then filled his mouth with the last bite of his pie. He then eyed her piece. "Cuz if you're not into your pie, I sure am," he said, smiling again, showing off those cute dimples of his. Rashawn laughed, relieved.

The man could barely stand the pain. It was getting worse with each passing day, week, month. At first he wanted to blame it all on the winter and getting old, maybe a little arthritis settling in. But of course, he was wrong. It wasn't that cold and he wasn't that old.

"Thank God I'm still fit," he told the bartender who was barely listening.

"Look man, you gonna nurse that drink all night or what?" he asked, pointing to the one drink the man had ordered nearly a half hour ago. The man's smile was his answer and he slid from the barstool and through the crowd in search of a table.

Watching the gyrating bodies on the dance floor, he found himself taken back to a good place in his mind. To a time when he would have been out there, moving to the club beats of Chic and Kano. The memory brought a smile to his face.

Just then, a tall, thin, ebony princess joined him at his table. He couldn't help staring at her.

"Hey, wanna dance?" she asked, sounding young and foolish, ready for anything.

There was a day he would have taken her up on— *anything*. There was a time when he was challenging, youthful, bold. But tonight he patted the table instead. "Sit, let's talk a minute," he offered.

Wrinkling up her nose, she giggled at him as if his words were not spoken in English. "Sit for what?" she asked.

"Talk, sweetie. Let's talk, you know, with our mouths," he added. With that comment the girl quickly turned to the dance floor, regretting the ticking seconds she was wasting now while her favorite song played.

"Never mind," she said before starting to walk away. The man grabbed her hand. She pulled against him slightly, trying to show no fear, although he could feel her pulse quickening. Her fear actually caused him to react. It had been a while since a woman had responded this way—intimidated, submissive.

"Go on, go play," he acquiesced, as if granting her permission to do what she no doubt was planning to do anyway.

Rashawn Ams filled his mind as he watched the young girl saunter to her next prey, landing a young man with just a smile. The two of them moved to the dance floor, quickly entwining themselves in their musically led copulation. He thought about how Rashawn's body would feel next to his, how she would feel in his arms.

Discreetly taking a small plastic pouch from the slot in his wallet, he opened it, slid his pinky finger in quickly, and then put it away. Sliding his finger along his gums, he then gulped down the drink. The forbidden poison on his fingertip was not enough to alter his mood or affect his performance. It wasn't like an average street drug, it was more than that and he had mastery over it, feeling as though he was in total control over it. His mind filled with thoughts of his day, and what an unfulfilling day it had turned out to be.

The Palemos on a Saturday night was a surprisingly quiet place, he thought while cruising through the small neighborhood. He missed cruising along these streets while Rashawn was gone for those seventeen months, three weeks, and two days. At first he had still driven through here, but without the tall beauty undressing behind her thin shade, without her beautiful silhouette moving about against the flickering candlelight, the Palemos was a pretty boring place.

He now thought back to when this all began, the night he'd first parked in front of the house after seeing her car. He'd only come to leave a note there, stuck perhaps in her windshield wiper to maybe mess with her head for a while—a secret admirer of sorts.

He always enjoyed playing head games with his prey before closing in and conquering them.

"Now if that were true, that would make me a monster, now wouldn't it?" he asked under his breath, remembering the women in his past, the rejections, the results.

Rashawn Ams—a woman bent on refutation, thriving on a man's humiliation.

Just like Jasmine.

Women like that deserved to die.

The night this all began, he'd arrived around midnight. Pulling in front of the house, he'd noticed she had left the shades up. Out of curiosity, he'd gone up to the window.

Looking in on her, he'd seen her sleeping. The thin white linen barely covered her in the flickering light of the scented candle.

He had fallen in love with her that night. How he

had wanted to hate her, but instead she'd astounded him. The more he watched her, the more he grew lovesick.

When the night came to take her life, he took her body instead.

How feminine she was, he thought now, remembering that night, his body reacting instantly to the memory of her lying there, vulnerable—open. The smell of her fear nearly drove him mad.

There wasn't a moment that he had ever believed she didn't want him.

He could almost hear her pants and grunts, even now.

How easily she could make a man want her. How easily she could make a man act out of character. How desperate she could make him feel—primal.

After he had taken her, he couldn't get her off his mind. He found himself watching her, following her. Soon he found himself truly infatuated with her. Even after all this time she was a full-blown obsession. There wasn't a minute of the day he didn't think about her.

Shaking his head, he freed the memory, returning it to the dark recesses of his mind.

He sat staring at the house.

Now she was back.

How she'd changed over this last year, how stunning she had become. It didn't seem possible that a woman could top perfection, yet Rashawn had done it. She was more beautiful than ever. He wasn't sure what she'd done to herself while in Atlanta, but it had been worth the wait to see her now. Rashawn was beautiful from her head to her feet. Her copper-colored eyes sparkled— called him, urged him to touch her.

And how badly he wanted to touch her.

How could he have ever thought he hated her?

Of course, now, now she was messing things up. She was seeing Chance Davis. Didn't she know he was no good for her?

Doesn't Chance Davis know Rashawn is taken? It seemed to him that both of them had some lessons to learn.

He drove off angry, ending up at the club where he sat now, nursing his melting ice cubes.

Just then, the sound of a loud siren outside the club snapped him back to the now. He fanned the waitress over to refill his glass. He would have to get back to Rashawn and his fantasies another time.

Maybe tomorrow.

Chapter 4

Sunday came in with church bells ringing in the Palemos and rain pouring down all over the world, or so it seemed. Everyone knew that only in this plush green strip of Northern California— just a few miles from the Pacific Ocean—it could rain this hard in October.

Many of the residents in the small community had lived there since the area's conception. It had started out as a tract of homes all named after different breeds of horses. The equestrian-named tract had developed in hopes of bringing in middle-to upper-income residents. With prices bottoming out during the recession of the seventies, it had instead enabled many lower-and fixed-income families to own their first homes and raise their large families. Many of these families still lived in this tract, referred to now as the Palemos—misnamed after the mispronounced Palomino horse.

Rita and Rashawn had inherited a home on the third street from the main drag. The main drag separated the Palemos from the next small community called Sandiville. That tract was named for its seaside theme-named streets. Their house sat between and across from relatives. It was quite a convenient setup, if you liked that sort of thing. Of course, Rashawn wasn't sure if she did or not—not anymore, anyway.

Having cousins across the way and next door, well, it could put a cramp in your style as far as Rashawn was concerned.

"Saw yo' boyfriend last night. He's kinda on the light side, doncha think?" Auntie Ams yelled through her screen door. Rashawn froze in her steps. She had hoped to grab the paper and get back in the house without having to speak to the 'whole' neighborhood, especially before coffee. It was bad enough that her sister, Carlotta, had already called and 'informed' everyone she was cooking dinner that night. So, of course, everyone was to come to her house to eat.

"Shelby and 'that boy of hers' are in town and so we need to feed them," she had barked.

Rashawn's kid sister, Shelby, was star center this year, and 'that boy of hers' was forty-two pointer, MVP of the year, Bishop Stokes. However, that didn't mean Rashawn felt like dropping what she was doing every time they came into town. So what if Carlotta had a gorgeous home in the Richmond Hills? That didn't mean that Rashawn always felt like driving all the way up there when it came time to socialize. As if that wasn't enough, here was Trina, the sister married to the writer, Jason— The One-Book-Wonder— pulling up now, no doubt to talk about Jason's movie.

Terrell, being an entertainment lawyer, had assisted him with his book and video deal. That contract was a great wedding present. They were still living off it. The video was having problems in the production phase, and though Terrell could do nothing about it, Jason loved to talk about it.

Rashawn could barely stand Jason, with his big blue eyes aided by colored contacts. He was getting pretty phony these days, and taking Trina along for the ride. It was hard to watch.

"No, Auntie, I don't have a boyfriend," Rashawn answered quickly, hoping Trina wouldn't hear—too late.

"Boyfriend! What boyfriend?" Trina squeaked, using her '*Hollywood*', voice, the one that didn't suit her stature. It was too light, too girlish for a big girl like Trina to have naturally.

"It's about time you got that boy a daddy," she remarked, as if she knew anything about the needs of children. It wasn't like Trina had any, and with her knuckles tapping on forty's door, it wasn't likely she was ever going to.

Trina was a bit overweight, even for five foot nine. She was thick and had large features like their father, and unfortunately, Jason's small movement among the 'in crowd' hadn't convinced Trina to get a professional makeover. She was still using the colors she had favored since high school—frosty gray eye shadow and that '*oh my god who got stabbed in here*' blood-red lipstick. Her clothes were tight in places where they needed to be loose, and vice-versa. She was a mess.

Maybe I'm being too hard on my sister, Rashawn thought for a moment, watching Trina rush toward her—jewelry clanking, large hoop earrings swinging, hair wild about her head.

"Naw," she said unconsciously, as she felt her eyes rolling back during the overly affectionate hug from her big sister.

"No, Trina, I'm not dating," Rashawn assured her.

"Who was tha man up in thea lass night?" Auntie asked.

Trina glared at Rashawn, holding her at arm's length, daring her to lie right to Auntie's face.

"No, no boyfriend, Auntie. You've got your facts incorrect," Rashawn insisted firmly. Auntie then noticed Trina.

"You gaining alotta weight, girl. You pregnant?" Auntie blurted without exercising a bit of diplomacy. Jason joined them then. Joining in on conversations uninvited was one of his favorite things to do, and he was getting pretty good at it, too.

"No, Auntie Ams, my baby's just been enjoying the good life," Jason said, giving Trina a flirt-filled slap on her ample rear, which she reciprocated with a squeeze on his pink cheeks.

Jason was fair enough to be white, but he wasn't, not with that nappy mess on his head.

Rashawn wondered why Auntie had no comments about Jason's color.

Please don't pop those contacts out of his head, Trina, Rashawn inwardly pleaded, watching her sister pucker and make kissy noises close to Jason's lips that were now pushed forward in her grip.

"Oh my God," Rashawn sighed while heading back toward the house.

"Well, alls I can say is, he looks better than that other man creeping around here," Auntie added before slamming the screen. Rashawn paused from her words.

What other man?

Everyone was more than comfortable in Carlotta's house.

The men milled around while the women busied themselves in the kitchen. The children were upstairs in the playroom under the watchful eye of Carlotta's daughter, who just loved kids.

"I don't know what you mean. I think Jason looks totally fine with those contacts," Trina defended, tossing the salad high in above the bowls edge, showing her growing agitation.

"He looks like a damn freak!" Rita blurted.

Trina's lip curled disdainfully. She was hurt, but knew it was the truth.

"Well, he looks good to me," she pouted.

"Good. You keep him," Rashawn said, glancing toward the open doorway to make sure Jason wasn't eavesdropping. He had been wandering around all afternoon. The men had abandoned him, he'd been shooed out of the kitchen, and when he went upstairs, the twins started screaming.

"Why you lying about having a man?" Trina asked abruptly.

"I don't have a man," Rashawn denied.

"Please, Auntie saw him," Trina divulged.

"What man?" Rita asked, sounding immediately as if she'd been left out of the loop and was planning to get back in. Rashawn shook her head adamantly.

"I don't have a boyfriend and especially one that Auntie Ams would have seen creeping around in the middle of the night, or whatever she implied he was doing. I'm not like some people who can't make it through a day without the male species in their sights," Rashawn snipped.

Trina snarled her lip, knowing that Rashawn was referring to her '*for better or worse, mostly worse,*' relationship with Jason.

"At least I'm not the one who had to lie about my baby daddy because I didn't know who he was," Trina said, bringing up Rashawn's personal life as she saw it.

Everything and everyone went silent, except for the hum of the ceiling fan. Trina's words seemed to radiate throughout the large, tiled kitchen, ricocheting off the pots and pans that hung overhead, literally turning Rashawn's head as if slapping her hard across the face. She turned back to her sister, her eyes glowing with anger. Trina knew that apologizing to Rashawn would only make things worse, so she said nothing at all, and made it worse.

"Trina you're . . ." Rashawn raised her finger to tell Trina off in the worst way.

"Hold on now. Let's not get started," Ta'Rae said, as she stepped in now to end this before it began.

"No, let her talk. Let her get all up on that high horse of hers and say what she thinks she needs to say to me," Trina defended, putting on a brave front that everyone saw through.

Just then, the front doorbell rang, taking the edge off the tension.

"Aunt Shawnie, something came for you," one of the kids called out.

"For me?" Rashawn asked, thrown completely off kilter now.

Just then, Carlotta's daughter brought in two red roses tied together in an elaborate ribbon.

"The card says 'Ms. Ams', and so I figured they were yours. You're the only Ms. Ams around," Carlotta's youngest daughter explained.

"Oh, honey, we all go by Ams. They are probably for your mother," Rita explained, taking the flowers and putting them quickly in one of Carlotta's vases in the kitchen.

"Oh, well sorry, Aunt Shawnie. I thought you was get-n da hook up," she teased.

Why the thought of someone delivering her flowers had instantly sat her on edge, she didn't know. But it had.

Rashawn sighed with relief, accepting that she was the mistaken recipient of this delivery.

The Session

"So since we met last, how have you been feeling?"

"I've been okay. I had some issues come up, but I worked them through. I started to cancel this meeting with you."

"Really? What's happened? Has she . . . ?"

"Why do you think my mood is always reflective of that woman?"

"Well . . . whether you know it or you are willing to admit it, everything you do seems to be reflective of 'that' woman."

Silence.

"What if I tell you that she and I have . . . "

Silence.

"You have what?"

"Nothing."

"No, tell me. I think whatever developments there are in your relationship with her, I need to know."

"I don't."

"You are being stubborn."

He smiles.

"I can tell you like that about me."

"How I feel about you on a personal level has nothing to do with why we are here."

"Sure it does."

"I think our session is over."

"Whatever. One day you will admit how jealous you are."

"Jealous?"

"Yes. You're jealous at how much I love her."

"You mean how obsessed you are."

The smile fades quickly.

"Obsession is for the weak-minded. It's for someone who can't fill their brain with more than one thought at a time. That's not me, and you know that. I'm a man with many sides, many ambitions and interests. I'm diverse and my life is full. If you don't know that about me by now, then you haven't been paying attention."

Silence.

"I don't care for the tone you're using with me tonight."

"Am I scaring you?"

"Are you trying to?"

"I think fear is very sensual."

"Sensual?"

"Yes. On a woman, the smell of fear is a very arousing."

"Well I think . . ."

Pregnant pause.

"What?"

"Never mind what I think. This is your session, not mine."

"If that be the case . . ."

Standing.

"Goodnight. I have somewhere I need to be."

Chapter 5

It was a busy morning. Allen Charles Roman, Ph.D., rubbed his head. It was part of his contract to keep a tight assessment on the university staff. He'd had another session with Blain Tollome.

What a troubled man he is, Roman thought to himself, looking over his notes from the session.

"Blain is enough to send the doctor to the couch," Roman admitted, glancing at his own schedule to see when he too would fit in his next therapy hour.

Tollome was a man in need of control all the time.

"But yet, he's so weak, so malleable," Allen Roman said out loud, stepping from behind his desk and looking out the window, down onto the campus below as the big man strolled from the building toward the administration office.

"And his feelings for Rashawn Ams . . ." Roman muttered, shaking his head pitiably. "How could he figure a woman like that would even be remotely interested in him, especially after what happened?"

* * *

Maceba Baxter was a good agent.

She was determined to get over any obstacle in her way. She had even gone back to doing undercover work for the agency, despite the incident that sent her to the hospital barely two years ago. She'd been following news out of Moorman U. and she didn't like what she was hearing.

Her thoughts on the Moorman University case were as follows:

Dirty cops and the conspiracy to sell drugs on the part of the faculty, assaults, and from the information given to her by an informant, rape and homicide were now a strong possibility.

She wanted to get to the bottom of it, not just to make a name for herself, but to end it once and for all. Moorman was not the only campus being hit with this plague, but it was surely the one being hit the hardest.

Taken completely out of the jurisdiction of the local authorities, the Bureau for International Narcotics and Law Enforcement had planned on breaking up this drug ring, cleaning up the universities, and keeping the learning environment safe for students.

Maceba wanted to clean up Moorman U. She felt driven to do it. Perhaps it would end her nightmares.

Danton campus, the big man, the dark parking lot.

It took nearly six months for Maceba to walk without support, and even longer for her to sleep alone in her own house.

After many months of investigating, she'd found few facts, the main one being that the man who had beaten her to a pulp, and tried to kill her was called Doc. She believed that man was now terrorizing Moorman University, peddling drugs, and, working in cahoots with someone on staff or in some other position of power and presumed innocence. She believed that with all her heart, and she was determined to get to the truth.

"I'm on your ass now, Doc," Maceba said aloud, closing the folder on the mysterious and once nameless campus terror.

Due to the drug's international transport, the Moorman University case had gone to the next phase, touching many levels of the police force—here and internationally.

The INL had hoped that once Doc was in custody, he would face a grand jury for his alleged crimes in the United States, as well as on the island of Jamaica where the drug currently plaguing Moorman had originated.

However, Maceba was removed totally from the case. Her superior had told her that she was too personally involved.

"You aren't going to be any good to this unit or to yourself by continuing on this case," he explained on her first day back on the job.

How could he know that this case was what helped her recover, that finding the bastard who had put her in the hospital was the main reason she fought so hard to get back on her feet?

"What are you saying?" she yelled upon getting the news of her change in duties.

"Now Maceba, I don't want to argue with you on this," her boss said, standing in order to increase his authoritative appearance.

"I don't believe you are doing this to me. Do you know what I've been through?" She spat and cursed obscenely.

After her diatribe, he simply sat down at his desk and ignored her, giving her the silent treatment, letting her know that their meeting was over. She had been given her orders.

Trying to block it all out, Maceba stepped from the administrative office and onto the quad of Moorman Campus.

Just then, from across the way, she recognized the big man heading toward her immediately. It made sense he would be here. She had seen the faculty list. Allen Roman worked here, so seeing Blain Tollome's name on the security list shouldn't have surprised her.

Blain had been a source of irritation and nuisance when she worked at Danton. Both he and Allen Roman seemed to tag team her nerve endings, both trying hard to drive her to the couch.

Of course, each of their reasons for getting her there were very different.

"What are you doing here?" she asked, hiding any residual feelings she had for him.

"Working," he answered, recognizing her immediately.

"Seems like you are always working on a troubled campus," she stated.

"Maybe . . . maybe that's why they call me. You see Danton is cleaned up now, right?"

"Yeah, but I'm always gonna wonder though, what came first, the chicken or the egg," she remarked with a smirk. He rolled his eyes.

"What brings you here?" he asked.

"Taking a couple of classes."

"You're taking a couple of classes?" he asked, pointing at her.

"And why not?"

"I don't know, I guess I just figured after what happened to you, you'd never want to step foot on a college campus again."

"How do you know what happened to me?"

"I know about what happened to you and why you left the Feds. I even came to the hospital," he said.

"How could you know that?" she asked, avoiding admittance or denial of her current agency status.

"Ceba, I cared about you."

"Cared?"

"Look, you set the rules. I can't help that I couldn't win a cheater's game."

"Yeah well, okay."

"Yeah, it is okay. I'm seeing somebody else now—someone more . . . compliant."

"Compliant? That's an interesting word to describe a girlfriend. How does that translate in 'real people' language? Easy?"

"Well, it just sorta came out. But, you know what, Ceba? I think you've got a case of sour grapes."

"Perhaps, but it's better than being a rotten apple."

"Touché."

"I better get to my new class. Don't want to be tardy. I'm already running late."

"What you taking?"

"Ethics—believe it or not, with Dr . . ." Maceba read her form, "Ams."

"Good teacher," was all Blain said.

Maceba took a deep breath as she passed him, trying not to take in his scent, trying not to get infected by his aura. Blain Tollome was a drug and she was sprung—always had been.

Dr. Roman was a colleague, and well-respected on campus. He taught abnormal psychology and sometimes subbed for the philosophy professor. It was those few times, while subbing in his minor field of study, that Rashawn and Professor Roman would encounter their differences.

In Rashawn's opinion, he was haughty and flamboyantly vain—a know-it-all. Sure, he was intelligent. That was obvious, but that wasn't the problem. The issue she had with Dr. Roman was that he had no qualms about letting her, the students, and probably his own mother know when he was right and they were, as was his common phrase, "unequivocally wrong."

A couple of times Rashawn had taken sessions with the great Dr. Roman, right before her abrupt exodus. He was acting in the capacity of Moorman's on-campus shrink, and possibly this was the biggest problem Rashawn had with the man.

After the first visit, she had given him far too much information. She had allowed him to come into her life way too far.

In her severely shattered emotional state, she had told him all about the rape—the pregnancy—the nightmares, and then, like a crazy wild woman, she left his office—*ran out was more like it*. She felt compelled to go back again to make sure he knew she wasn't truly crazy. The sessions never got better, so she ended them.

Rita had called her a couple of times while she lived in Atlanta to let her know that the eager doctor had even come by the house to '*check-in*' on her.

How dare he, Rashawn remembered, growing angry all over again.

Since returning to Moorman, she had done all she could to avoid him. It seemed like around every corner there he was, offering her a 'session'.

I don't need a session, she mentally fussed. *Just leave me alone. You think you know everything about me. You know nothing.*

Nevertheless, Roman had put the buzz out around campus about his condominium being for sale. And Rashawn had told herself to ask a few questions about it, but only about the condominium. As much as she wanted to avoid him, this offer to buy his condominium was one she could not pass up.

He's such a know-it-all pain-in-the-ass, she thought to herself.

"But I need that condo," she admitted to herself, picking up her phone.

*   *   *

It was the start of a miserable work week, and it was only Monday. Allen Roman sat at his desk staring into space, his mind once again filled to capacity.

"Why did she have to come back?" he asked himself aloud, as the vision of Rashawn Ams' shapely hips, long legs, and intoxicating laughter filled his brain again. Although the last time they were together, she was far from happy. He remembered her tears. How he had wanted to wipe away those tears, hold her close, comfort her.

Dr. Roman admired Rashawn. She was a confident woman, one who was always up for a good debate. He respected her. True, the physical attraction was there, but that was something he could control, most of the time.

He wasn't weak like some men.

At his age, many would find it laughable that he desired a woman like Rashawn. But desire her, he did. Yes, he would have to admit it eventually. He desired Rashawn Ams, and now that she was back, he was going to have to let her know it. He was going to have to step up to the plate and take on his responsibility to her, and to Reggie. Oh yes, he had a responsibility to Reggie. If it were not for him and his foolish infatuation for her, Reggie wouldn't even be here.

For now, the business with this condo would have to suffice.

He was practically giving it to her. He would have given it to her outright, no problem, except that she surely would have figured him out if he had, and he couldn't handle her reaction to that revelation. Surely she would have some kind of breakdown upon finding out his role in her life, and in the life of Reggie.

Roman was dying to get to know the boy. He'd tried everything, everything short of the direct approach.

He rubbed his temples firmly and glanced out his office window down onto the campus.

"The direct approach. Yeah, sure, that would get me in the door," he mumbled under his breath. "I can see it now, 'Hello there, Ms. Ams. I need to talk to you about your son, Reggie. I have information regarding his father. I'm . . .'"

Just then, the phone rang.

"Hello," he answered.

"Hello, Dr. Roman. It's Rashawn Ams, Professor Ams," she announced.

His palms became sweaty, and his heart began pounding in his chest. She was completely unaware of the reaction he was having to the mere sound of her voice.

Rashawn was pondering over her life while sitting in her office later that day. She had to wonder what would be worse—dealing with the 'infallible' Dr. Roman, or continuing to deal with her family.

"Here I am, back at Moorman University, hiding out in my office. I never thought this would be my fate," she complained to—no one. "What happened to ya balls, Shawnie?" she asked herself before bursting into macabre laughter.

What a terrible day.

She looked around her desk for her favorite stress relief toy. It wasn't sitting in its usual spot. Glancing beneath her desk, she cursed under her breath.

What a terrible day.

And to make it worse, she'd soon have to meet again with the one man she'd wanted to avoid the most since her return. For some reason, the more she tried to avoid him, the more circumstances threw them together. And now she had called and made a 'date' to talk to him about his condo.

"See, you get yourself into messes like this," she growled, reaching into her tiny fridge and taking out a bottle of water.

The clock ticked loudly. She looked at her watch, comparing the time. She took another swig.

"Chance Davis," she mumbled, turning the bottle up again.

"What am I thinking," she went on, her brain now filling with garbled knowledge. "I've got a headache," she said, reaching for her aspirin stash.

Rashawn could hear the sound of someone coming up the stairs.

It's probably just my office-neighor's husband. He usually meets her here on Mondays, Rashawn deduced.

She took an aspirin and closed her eyes to rest them for a moment. Maybe she could doze off for a couple of minutes before heading home. Before she knew it, she was sound asleep.

Perhaps to dream?

"Hello there, Professor Ams. Can we talk?" the man asked, his voice was very low, almost a whisper.

Rashawn attempted to return to a fully awakened state. She looked at her watch and then back at the man.

"My door was locked. How . . . ?" she asked. Her mind was scattered.

Oh, that's right, I'm dreaming, so, never mind.

The small quarters were tight for the two of them, as tall as they both were. The man looked almost hunched over as he sat in the small chair beside her desk. It was the chair her students occupied when explaining how they couldn't possibly accept a C on their mid-term.

Alice in Wonderland, Rashawn thought now, as the vision of Alice squeezed into the rabbit's little house brought a smile to her face.

"You're in the hot seat," she heard herself say, and then giggle.

"Yeah, hot," he replied.

His words caused her to sneer. He was coming on to her. She hated come-ons, even in her dreams.

"How can I help you tonight?" she asked, wishing she

could take those words back immediately. She didn't want to help this man. She wanted him to get the hell out of her office—Creep!

The clock ticked loudly.

Oh wow, do I ever need a new clock.

"I just think when someone fights you, it makes it all bad," he said, standing and taking off his jacket.

He then locked the door while Rashawn, in silence, watched him.

"Ridiculous," she then heard herself say.

"When a man and woman are meant to be together, there isn't a need for fighting," he went on.

"Ridiculous," she heard herself say again.

I know I said it this time.

And . . .

Get the hell out of my office!

I always thought people in your dreams did what YOU wanted them to do.

He lifted her from her seat and sat her on her desktop. She felt herself falling against his chest and then falling back against her desktop, her head resting on his balled up jacket. It smelled like leather mixed with a hint of light cologne.

"Love is love, no matter how much time passes, or who else you think you love. I love you, Rashawn. And you . . . you love me," he said, sounding flat and artificial.

"Yeah, right," she chortled, covering her mouth to keep from bursting out laughing at the cornball dialogue he was feeding her.

Who does he think he is, coming into MY dream this way? He could at least have some better lines.

She then looked into his dark eyes, those familiar dark eyes. She turned away and started to make her way off the desk. Her hand knocked over the water bottle, which she heard fall to the floor, the water spilling out with a splash. The man turned her back around and began to hike up her skirt. It was then that she realized this dream was getting ugly . . . and she wanted it to end.

"I don't want . . ." she slurred, only to be shushed by the man who now hovered over her.

She looked at him.

"Davis?" Her question pleaded. She was not even sure if her thoughts were audible.

She then saw him unzip his pants and expose his engorged member.

Yes, this is a dream, because I would be fighting him if it weren't.

She felt her underwear being removed, and in the deepest part of this delusion, she didn't mind at all when he orally pleasured her. She even gave into the pleasure a little, closing her eyes and verbalizing her feelings.

What a naughty dream. Sex with Chance Davis in my office. Shame on you.

"Yes, shame on me," she heard the man say in a half whisper.

Is he reading my mind, or have I been talking aloud all this time?

She opened her eyes as the man crept upon her.

Of course, no one could read her mind like Allen Roman. Of course, that's who this man was—Dr. Allen Roman.

Had to be.

"Shame on you, Allen," she said, giggling in embarrassment at the thought of Allen Roman climbing all over her this way. Sure, he was handsome, robust and all, but surely sex on a desktop was not his style.

She would have to remember to share this fantasy with Qiana when she woke up. Qiana always used to get a good laugh at the men she would have sex with in her wayward dreams. Once it had even been the mailman, old Mr. Crawford, and he was at least a hundred and ten. In that dream he had chased her three blocks before catching her and having sex with her right there on the sidewalk, on top of everyone's mail. Qiana had told her that she would never look at her electric bill the same way again.

"I never want you to fight me again," the man whispered in her ear as he pushed himself inside her.

She could say nothing.

What a vivid dream. It almost hurt. It almost hurt for real when he filled her body with long, deep thrusts that felt so real, so real.

"Now, isn't this better, my queen?" he asked.

His dark eyes, his familiar dark eyes stared deep into hers as, suddenly, he began to sound more and more familiar. Inside her he felt familiar. Yes, she remembered this. The sound of the air through his teeth, the look of pleasure in his eyes, the smell of his cologne—yes, she remembered this.

But how? The man she knew to be her rapist—Russell Thompson, was dead.

Could this be a ghost?

This dream was getting out of control. She placed her hands on his chest and pushed slightly as suddenly her belly rumbled with building orgasm. She could feel the rolling sensation coming over her and she couldn't stop it.

She cried out, "I don't want it . . . I don't . . ." and then moaned aloud as she gave in to the intensity of her orgasm.

"That's it, baby, take it all and give it back," he said between primal grunts, thrusting harder and deeper, faster and faster.

"Yesss," he suddenly roared.

Then she woke up.

Rashawn looked around her office, and then at the clock, and then her watch. It was nearly ten p.m. She examined herself sitting there in her swivel-back chair.

Everything seemed intact. Even her hair was as she had left it.

"How weird," she heard herself say as she looked around for something to explain what had happened in the last three hours of her night.

"The water," she gasped, looking around for the spilled water bottle. There wasn't one, only her half-filled, opened bottle sitting where she had left it on her desk.

She opened her little fridge to find the two water bottles she had left sitting there as before. One opened and one closed, just as before.

All the way to her car she wondered about the time in her office, and the odd dream.

Davis. That's who she needed to talk to.

Suddenly she felt a strange release come from below. She clicked on her inside car light and realized her period had come.

Chance Davis walked the campus late that night. His comfort level was low. He was having a hard time with his thoughts.

Just then, he noticed Blain Tollome heading toward the cafeteria. Blain stopped short when he saw him.

"Hey there, what's got you out so late, Dr. Davis?" Blain called to him.

"I was about to ask you the same question," Davis answered.

"Look, I'm security. I'm supposed to be here," Blain snipped.

Davis was caught off-guard by his defensiveness.

"Touchy, aren't you?" Davis chuckled.

Blain stood tall and lean with his hands on his waist, irritation showing now as his open jacket exposed the handle of a hunting knife hanging from his belt in a leather holder. Davis recognized that type of knife. His father had one. As a boy, he would admire it while they sat on the creek banks, fishing.

"What's up with you people, staying out here so late at night? Don't you have lives or anything like that?" Blain asked.

"Yeah, actually, I'm about to go get me a beer or something right now," Davis answered, loosening up a bit. Why he felt so tense around Blain was a mystery to him.

Blain was all right—just really tall, and that was a little intimidating. But other than that, he was pretty average in Davis' opinion.

Just then they both noticed Dr. Roman heading out to his car. Blain snickered.

"See what I mean," Blain said, pointing in Roman's direction. Davis chuckled.

Blain then looked at his large watch.

"Well, shit," he groaned, stretching and letting out a wide yawn that ended in a loud, roar-like groan.

Davis thought about asking Blain to join him. Being '*social*' with Blain Tollome had never been on his list of things to do, but then again . . .

Why not?

"Hey, Tollome, how about joining me?" Davis offered; it was easier to attempt civility now since he wasn't with Rashawn. "I need to get my mind off some things, and company would be good," he went on.

"Naw, I don't fraternize," he said with a straight face. For a second Davis couldn't tell if he was joking or not, but then he noticed the slightly crooked curve of Blain's lip.

Just then both men noticed Rashawn's car in the distance, leaving the parking lot. They turned back to each other and laughed.

"No life," Blain said before the two men bumped fists in a manly agreement.

"Well, I hope to change that," Davis divulged.

"Is that right?" Blain said slyly.

"Yeah, it is," answered Davis quickly, before pushing up his glasses.

"I don't see how. She's seeing Allen Roman," Blain said, pointing off toward the direction he had just seen the two of them go. Davis looked puzzled for a moment before taking a defensive stance.

"Pardon me?"

"Didn't you just see them leaving together?" Blain explained flatly.

"Actually, I didn't," Davis answered curtly.

Blain took a toothpick from his breast pocket and tucked it in his cheek.

"Well then, you need to open your eyes," he said, bluntly. "Sorry to burst your little bubble, dude, but ahh, that's how it is. I know everything that's going on on this campus, and those two are doing the nasty big time, up in her office, on the university dollar," Blain explained before he then ended their conversation with a simple goodnight.

With the urge now to drink something stronger than a beer, Davis decided to forget the whole thing and go home to sulk.

Rashawn got home and dashed into the bathroom to square things away with her monthly visitor before she gave attention to the small gift box and a bouquet of red roses waiting—along with Rita's nosy behind.

"What's this all about, missy?" Rita said, holding up the unopened gift card. Rashawn snatched it from her hand.

"Why aren't you in the bed?" Rashawn teased. Rita rolled her eyes as Reggie's laughter could still be heard coming from their bedroom.

"So who is this all from?" Rita asked again.

"Let me read it and I'll let you know—maybe," Rashawn answered, opening the card.

So glad you're home was all the card said.

"Must be umm . . . a student," Rashawn said, inhaling the roses. She grinned at Rita.

"A pretty nice student," Rashawn added, noting the address on the gift card was that of the most expensive flower shop in the city.

"Girl, you need to quit," Rita said, shaking her head and heading back into the kitchen. "Somebody's got a serious crush," she called over her shoulder.

"Apparently," Rashawn agreed, examining the flowers a little closer. She couldn't help but hope that they were from Chance Davis. The catnap in her office had put Davis at the forefront of her mind.

"Makes me think those flowers that came to Carlotta's were really for you," Rita said, reminding Rashawn about the afternoon and the strange delivery—one that Carlotta had no clue about either. The rest of the evening they all sat around guessing who the roses could be from, finally deciding on a happy customer of Carlotta's—someone who really had enjoyed his or her meal.

Having forgotten about the gift box, Rashawn now opened it. When she lifted the lid, her heart began to pound and her legs buckled slightly beneath her. She couldn't breathe. Fighting the urge to faint, Rashawn rushed the box to the kitchen, shoving it deep down inside the trash.

"What the heck is going on?" Rita asked as Rashawn began hurriedly ridding herself of the roses as well.

"Stop, Rashawn. Stop!" Rita gasped, while attempting to keep Rashawn from destroying the beautiful gift. "Don't do that. Stop! What's happening?"

Rashawn took a deep breath now, rubbing her forehead. Her hands were shaking, and although she attempted to speak calmly, her voice was trembling.

"The gift was very inappropriate," was all she could muster before quickly heading into her room.

Rita lifted the roses off the box. Inside the small, satin-lined gift box that bore the label of Rashawn's favorite lingerie store—Beatrice Drawers—there was a single pair of black lace panties. Rita looked for a card, but there was none, except for the one that came with the flowers. Confused, Rita placed the box and crushed roses back in the trash.

It was "Frat House Party" night. The music banged from the speakers. It was anyone's guess how much louder it would actually get before the night was over.

No one was complaining on the inside. It was all about the party.

One good thing about Moorman University was its racial equality. A white kid drinking until he passed out was no more or less accepted than any other kid— Black, Mexican, Asian or Jew.

Moorman University definitely had a racial mix. In fact, it could be considered quite diverse. Especially with the exchange program they had instituted a few years back. That program had brought many kids from all over the world to study at Moorman. The only problem was that the exchange had also brought drugs — drugs that these American kids had never even seen before. And even more disturbing was that they surely had no idea of their potency.

It's not to say that the drug problem at Moorman University was supposed to be completely blamed on the foreign exchange students. Nevertheless, they had, no doubt, exacerbated the problem—a problem which had now become out of hand.

The music was hot and everyone was having a good time. Rogelio and his friends had danced on stage that night, and everyone was hyped after their performance. Rumor had it there were scouts there, and that rumor was all it took for Rogelio to shine, to spark, hell, to damn near burn that mutha up!

Suddenly, through the crowd, Rogelio saw one of his

friends talking with one of the guys who did security on campus. They were talking kind of covertly, and by the looks of it, this security guard had other things on his mind than the safety of Rogelio's friend as the two of them drifted outside.

Although Rogelio hadn't been raised on the streets, he had been raised streetwise. A drug deal was going down. He was sure of it.

Rogelio was tired of all the drug-shit at these parties. He was there to have a good time—to dance, to flirt, maybe even to get '*safely*' laid. All these drugs were ruining the vibe. Now his buddy from the dance crew was outside buying some Get Ass.

That's what was on all right. What else could it be? This big redheaded guy was showing up at a lot of campus parties lately, peddling his wares. Nobody dared to turn him in, maybe because they were scared of him, or maybe they were his customers. It didn't matter, as Rogelio was neither.

"Naw. See, this shit's gonna stop," Rogelio said, stomping outside to break up the buy.

Stepping outside, the cool air hit Rogelio like a wall, but he couldn't give into it. He was on a mission.

"Hey pawdna!" Rogelio yelled, hoping to stop the exchange before the money went from one palm to the other.

The large redhead glared now, his eyes like green diamonds glistening against the lights.

"Rogelio, stay out of it, man," his friend said, holding him off, urging him not to interfere. Rogelio continued to step forward.

"Stay out of what? We're just talking . . . pawdna," the redhead said now, sounding innocent of all wrongdoing, shoving his hands deep in his pockets. Rogelio's buddy sighed heavily, noting the change in the action. Rogelio smiled, victorious.

"They want us back on stage," Rogelio lied, standing his ground until the redhead walked off.

"Hey, I'm just lookin' out for you," Rogelio began, as soon as the redhead was of out of earshot.

"You're not my damn daddy," his friend growled, pulling his fingers through his matted afro.

"Why you buyin' that shit, man? It's nothing but glorified Ecstasy. Why do you need it?"

"Look, I'm not you, Rogelio. I'm not you, aiight," he said, showing embarrassment in his voice.

"True. As you know, I do not need a drug to get that ass," Rogelio joked, attempting to lighten the mood.

They were both into break dancing, a very strenuous and physical type of dancing. Rogelio, who took it on as more than just a pastime sport, was stronger than his friend—toner, more fit.

Puerto Rican and African-American by race, his face was smooth, his eyes light, and his hair was long and curly. These features, coupled with his strong, youthful body—no, Rogelio did not have to drug a girl to have sex with her. However, his friend was not so blessed.

"Well, I'm not you. I guess nobody can be you," his friend snipped, sounding sarcastic and full of jealousy.

Shocked at the attitude he received, Rogelio stood watching his lanky friend disappear back into the crowded frat house.

Why do I even try? Rogelio thought now, feeling stupid for attempting in a small way to keep things cool among his friends. All he wanted was to get through college intact, but it seemed like he was the only one who wanted that.

Hearing the music in the distance, he now felt put out and ready to go home. He was no longer in the mood to please the crowd. He started for his car.

"Forget that dumb guy. Just forget him. Let him do an unconscious girl. What is the point in that?" Rogelio huffed, pulling his keys from his pocket. Suddenly they slipped from his hand and dropped to the ground. As he bent to pick them up, he was shoved into the car door.

Before he could yell out or turn to see his assailant, Rogelio was lifted from his feet. Rogelio knew from his own size, his attacker had to be huge. Just from the sheer ease in which he was hoisted off the ground and thrown onto the car, he could tell.

"You wanna break something up, huh?" the attacker growled. Rogelio, catching his wind, swung at the hulking figure.

"Yeah, I do," Rogelio challenged, showing no fear.

"Well, so do I," the man answered the challenge, slamming his fist into Rogelio's face.

Pain surging through his body, Rogelio put up the fight of his life.

Like a rag doll, the large man slung Rogelio from the car and onto the ground, pummeling him, yet Rogelio refused to give in and soon found himself on his feet, dancing lightly with fists balled up, jabbing quickly, ducking and swerving. Finally seeing an opening, he threw two well-landed punches that bloodied the lip of his contender. It was just enough to give Rogelio a little confidence that maybe he could hang a few rounds with the giant.

Jack and the Beanstalk came to mind.

Rogelio took two hard hits to the head.

Things were getting hazy, but still he felt the need to get to his feet. He wouldn't go out like this.

Staggering, Rogelio attempted to swing on the man who now appeared to be twins, that is before the large mitt-like paws swatted him to the ground again, causing him to writhe in pain.

Before he could get to his feet, the man was on him. Rogelio kicked and squirmed in his attempt to break free from the vice-tight grip of Doc, whose lips curved into a demonic grin.

Rogelio had heard the rumors about this crazy maniac named Doc, but didn't believe them . . . until now.

Rogelio thought about his mother. She'd be waiting up tonight, but he knew he'd not be making it home.

The Session

"The last time we spoke, you said something about fear being a turn-on for you?"

"No I didn't."

"You most certainly did, and I want to address that with you."

"If I'd said it, or even implied it, I would discuss it. But since I did not say such a thing, I would rather spend my time and my session on something else."

Silence followed by a heavy sigh.

"Okay, but I worry about you."

"Why? You think I'm up to no good?"

"How are you handling your issues with that woman?"

"I'm handling them just fine. We've um . . ."

He flashed a wicked smile.

"What is that look for?"

"I guess I'm feeling embarrassed to expose so much to you."

"You've had sex with her?"

"Jealous?"

"No. You keep asking me that, and I don't see why I would be."

"Whatever."

"It just puzzles me that she would consent, considering last year and the problems the two of you had in that department."

"We never had a problem per se. I just think I didn't clearly communicate my feelings clearly to her, and now I've resolved that."

"How?"

"I've gotten into her head, her dreams, you could say. She's a lot more compliant now."

"Compliant? What a strange word."

"Really? How so?"

"Never mind. It's semantics, I'm sure. Tell me, how has she become more . . . compliant?"

"Trust me, I'd tell you, but then I'd have to kill you."

Wicked laughter.

"Again, you think you're scaring me?"

"Are you scared?"

"No."

"Now I think you're trying to scare me."

More laughter.

Chapter 6

Thursday morning came and Rashawn headed to Allen Roman's office as soon as she got to the campus. Meeting with him was something she was ready to get over with. She reached his office only to meet his secretary sitting at his desk.

"Where is Roman? I mean, Allen, I mean, Dr . . ." she stammered, showing her frustration.

The secretary acted as though she hadn't noticed Rashawn's discomfort. "He's out for the morning, Ms. Ams. But he left me the message to tell you that he'd like to put your meeting off for a couple of days," she said. Rashawn sighed with mixed emotions.

"Fine," she said, spinning on her heels and leaving without anything further.

On Rashawn's way out of his office, she spied Chance Davis, talking with the young girl she had seen running from his class before. He noticed her and motioned for her to stay put until he finished up with the young girl.

"Hey there, kid," Davis said as he approached. Rashawn smiled at the familiar expression.

"I've got class," she said, before he asked. He nodded with full understanding.

"Figured that, but how about lunch?" he posed. Rashawn hesitated only a moment before agreeing.

"Oh shoot, I just forgot an appointment I have with my wife." He snapped his fingers over his head.

Davis nearly swooned at the sound of his own words. "My ex-wife," he corrected. Rashawn made no change in expression. "Tomorrow?" he asked now.

"Perhaps," she answered vaguely. His brow furrowed. "Perhaps?"

"I'll call you," she answered, moving past him and heading on to her next class.

There was no way she was even going to address Davis's faux pas about his ex-wife.

"Not even going there," she told herself, as the students began filling the room.

Around noon, Rashawn had finished up with her morning classes and headed back to her office to grab her purse. When she walked in, she noticed the red rose on her desk. For some reason it didn't startle her. It was almost as if its presence was expected. There was no note with it; it just lay on her desk—fresh and waiting.

Surely her office-neighbor had let him in; she was the only one with the extra key to her office.

Rashawn picked up the phone and called Davis's cell phone. He answered on the first ring.

"Davis."

"Rashawn," she said, sniffing the rose. She could tell the smile on her lips could be heard in her voice, "Lunch tomorrow, Davis?" she asked. There was hesitation.

"Dinner tonight?" he asked.

"Lunch tomorrow," she answered.

"Dinner tonight and lunch tomorrow," he said, flirt filling his voice. Rashawn sniffed the rose but said nothing about it to him.

Apparently, he was attempting to be her secret admirer, and so why end the game? It was kind of fun in a way. Sure, she was frightened at first—the underwear and all, but he had been a married man until recently. Intimate gifts were probably the norm for him. She would forgive him this time.

"Alright," she agreed and then hung up, still smiling. She headed out toward the cafeteria carrying the rose.

The man thought Rashawn would be in her office. Tomorrow was Friday. She always planned quizzes for Fridays and she always worked on the test the night before—in her office. That way no one could get their hands on the questions.

You see, the man knew everything about Rashawn and he had to admit that he loved her dedication to teaching.

After being gone so long, many teachers would have lost their touch in the classroom, but not Rashawn. She was born to teach.

He'd read her questions once. They were very thought- provoking and he had an extremely high IQ, so he should know.

He was disappointed when he arrived. She was not there. He expected her to be there, asleep.

The man had thought about his actions the last time and he promised himself to be more controlled this time. However, how could he prove it if she wasn't there?

"I was just so happy to be back together with you," he admitted, speaking to the picture of her that sat on her desk. He so loved that photo. She looked so carefree in it. He picked up the picture and held it for a moment while he lingered. Just being where she had been felt good to him. He fondled her desktop items while sitting in her soft swivel chair.

Nice leather, good taste.

He noticed her open planner and began to glance

through it. That was when he noticed her social plans as well as her curriculum.

That lunch date tomorrow with Chance Davis.

Trina thought about Rashawn. She knew she would have to make peace. Even if it was for no other reason than the fact that she knew that soon she would be leaving Jason, and where would she go but to Rashawn and Rita's house?

Ta'Rae was just too perfect to understand what it meant to fail at something, especially something as important as marriage. Carlotta, well, Carlotta was just too bossy. Surely she would insist on 'getting to the bottom of everything' and surely Trina was at the bottom, of this marriage anyway.

Her marriage to Jason had failed. In just these couple of years, it had failed big time. She looked over at him, sleeping like a baby.

That's fine, because he sure acts like one, she thought now, shaking out the last of the ginger snap cookies from the large bag, and shoving it deep into her mouth.

She stared at her phone, debating how she would ask Rita to come stay, especially after what she had said to Rashawn. How could she ask?

Just then, Jason turned over, his mouth dropped open, and he began to snore. She shoved him hard to move him away from her.

"Yeah, baby, I like it like that," he mumbled. Trina's stomach tightened.

"Like what?" she whispered close to his ear, changing her voice. Jason's hand reached out to grope, but Trina moved away slightly.

"Amy . . . you know I . . ." Jason began before his eyes popped open and he met Trina's.

"Who the hell is Amy?" Trina screamed, hitting him over the head with the empty box of cookies.

"Trina, I . . ." Jason stumbled, still half-awake.

Trina jumped from the bed and began emptying the bureau of Jason's clothes.

"Trina, what are you doing?" he asked, rushing over to her to stop her, grabbing her arms.

"Get out, Jason. Just get out. It's over," she insisted.

"I'm not going anywhere. This is my house!" he snapped.

"How the hell do you figure that?" Trina asked, slamming her hands on her hips.

"Look, Trina, come back to bed. Come on, baby. Let Daddy make it good to ya," Jason purred in her ear, only to receive Trina's long acrylics across his neck.

"Damn it, Trina, what the hell is wrong with you?" Jason said, grabbing at the scratches and rushing into the bathroom to look for blood.

"It's only good to you, Jason," Trina yelled, grabbing up her robe, slipping into her house shoes, and storming out the bedroom.

Giggling like a schoolgirl, Rashawn rambled on a mile a minute while Chance watched her mouth move.

How beautiful a woman she was.

He'd have to admit that he'd not felt so stirred in a long time. Sure, his ex was a total sex kitten, still purring. But Rashawn, she was different. She was someone he could feel more for—above the waist.

"And what about you?" she asked, bringing him into the conversation.

"Me? I'm just a guy . . . looking for . . ." He paused, remembering the rest of the stupid line. "I remember how you feel about what I was about to say, so I'm not gonna say it." He grinned, causing his dimples to show.

"There's not much about me to tell," he said, sipping his wine. "I'm divorced after years of struggling to make something that was wrong—right. I've got no children, thank God, and um . . ." he went on, not realizing that Rashawn had left the conversation with his last statement. Her eyes all but glazed over.

Rashawn's mind went to Reggie and his needs. Again, she felt like a bad mother, sitting in this expensive restaurant sipping Château St. Michelle and wasting time with a man who didn't even want to be a father figure.

She wondered if Reggie was asleep.

Chance noticed Rashawn glancing at her watch.

"You ready to go?" he asked, hoping she would answer no. She nodded. He couldn't help but wonder what he had said or done to change her mood so quickly. Truly, she was a mystery and he was only half sure if he was up to the challenge.

Blain entered the gym. He could feel the eyes of several women turn on him.

"That's cool . . ."

It wasn't as if they could help themselves.

His frustration had warmed him up before arriving and so he jumped right on the weight equipment, loading it up—three fifty.

That would be good for starters.

He knew he had to get Rashawn off his mind. She was a waste of good energy, and he knew this. Maceba was more his type. However, the force that fed his heart and drove his passions desired Rashawn, beyond his reason, beyond his control. He hated not being in control.

He fought the thoughts of Rashawn; however, lying down under the bar, with each rep, he thought about her more and more.

She's so stubborn, he thought. *You'll never get her,* he told himself.

Don't be so self-defeating. You haven't even tried.

Five . . . Ten . . .

What's it gonna take before she realizes how much she needs you? he asked himself.

Just a little persuasion.

Twenty . . . Twenty-Five . . .

What do you want me to do?

She's got to see one day that I'm the only one who really cares about her, his inner man reasoned.

Forty . . .

She's got to see one day that I'm the only real man around.

You're so full of shit. He chuckled, laughing at the arrogance of his inner voice.

"Whoa, boy," a woman said, breaking his concentration, interrupting his private conversation.

He sat the weight bar in the groove that held it securely, and looked at the woman who'd come into his personal space.

How rude is she? his inner voice asked, angry at first, but then, focusing on her shapely thighs, he quickly regrouped.

"You got things to burn off, I see," she flirted.

"Yeah, maybe," Blain mumbled, not particularly interested in her.

His low voice must have affected the woman as Blain could see her body react instantly to just the sound of it.

She's easy, he quickly deduced, his inner man nudging him. *Go for it, I could use a little.*

The woman was tall and red-headed, strong, and lean—fine. *She'd be a much more enjoyable way to burn off some steam,* the inner man reasoned.

Blain's lower anatomy could fight his loud thoughts no longer. One conversation quickly led to another and together they left the gym.

Chapter 7

Friday—the week had finally ended.

Blain walked into the office. Dr. Roman felt his presence before even seeing him. There was something about Blain Tollome that sat his senses on edge, put him on constant ready.

Roman knew what it was about the young man that bothered him so much, but facing it, accepting it, admitting it, was another issue.

"I wanted to talk about this woman I think I'm going to have a problem with," Blain began without hesitation or a formal greeting. Roman turned from the window where he had been enjoying the view.

"These sessions are not designed to be your 'fix a date gone badly' dating service," Roman smarted off.

"I'm not expecting you to solve my dating problems, like I have any," Blain guffawed.

Roman cleared his throat and smirked at the haughtiness of the tall, boorish, yet deadly handsome man sitting in the chair with it teetered back, while resting his feet on the desk. Roman glared at the heavy shoes and then back at Blain.

"I'm talking about my job here on campus and a person who may start to cause me some problems in that area."

"Perhaps you should change jobs."

"You of all people know how impossible that is for me to do," Blain explained, snapping his words out quickly and with a cutting edge on them that Roman nearly felt.

"I'm merely suggesting that perhaps the problems with this woman, as well as the conflict you have with the . . ." Roman paused allowing his hands to fall open as if finishing his sentence for him, ". . . may all be in your wild imagination."

Blain quickly sat upright in the chair. "I don't even know to what you are referring, doctor, would you be so kind as to clarify that statement?"

"Rashawn Ams. You act as though you are not following her, stalking her."

"And how, my good man, in the hell, have you managed to deduce that scenario?" Blain asked, his inner man taking over the conversation.

"She's told me that you're following her."

"Oh, so you're seeing her?"

"I can't tell you that."

"Sure you can. I'm not stupid. I know you see the entire staff at one time or another. But my wonder is if you are seeing *her*," Blain volleyed, "or are you just lying to me, trying to piss me off?"

"Ohhhh, you mean professionally? Am I seeing her professionally?"

"I sure as hell didn't mean socially," Blain said, bursting into loud laughter. "I've already told you what I would do to you if you even tried to 'go there.'"

"Oh yes, you've threatened me, Blain. I even taped that conversation."

"Good, that way you can play it over and over after I bust your ass. You won't have to ask yourself why. When your mouth is busted and they ask you 'boy, what the hell happened to you'? You can hold up that damn tape recorder and play it." Blain stood, and with his fist he pushed Roman's head hard.

Roman stood quickly, steadying his stance, ready to defend himself against the man who he probably matched inch for inch, if not pound for pound. He grabbed Blain's collar, pulling him close. The two of them grimaced at each other before Blain shoved Roman back, freeing himself from the grip.

Blain was a muscle bound bully with an Achilles heel, and in Roman's opinion that made him a weak opponent, easily conquered. Yet getting to the point of victory with Blain would come at quite a physical expense, one Roman wasn't ready to wager just yet.

"Your time is up. Get out of my office," Roman yelled.

"Here I am, again, trying to help you, and what do you do? Throw me out. It's always Blain who's thrown out. Well, you know what? It's on," Blain barked, smoothing his large hand over his shiny head and heading for the door.

"The only thing on is my tape recorder and video camera," Roman growled, holding up the small remote device and aiming it toward his hidden camera.

"Whatever. All your little movies will show is who the criminal really is here."

"Yes, yes they do." Roman smiled wickedly.

Blain stormed out.

The next day, Rashawn's class was lively, quite surprising for a Friday. Usually by the end of the week, they were ready to break the door down and get out. Today, however, they were cooperating with her, or at least pretending to. She enjoyed her classes when the students learned, or at least appeared to. Besides, she needed to get her mind off the weird dream she'd had the night before. It had disturbed her all morning. Although she'd slept like a stone, the dream came through, disturbing her. Dinner with Davis hadn't helped either. It only gave him the leading role.

She'd stopped by her office before heading home. She wanted to finish the quiz questions, but instead, awoke to find herself napping on her desk with an empty water bottle still in her hand. She figured it was the heavy meal she'd had that knocked her out that way. Needless to say, her apparent exhaustion had cost her, and she had not been able to complete the class's quiz.

Rashawn thought it strange that after getting home, showering and jumping in the bed, she went directly to sleep and didn't dream again.

What did you expect? To dream about sex all night? she asked herself, feeling a smile creeping to her lips.

She was smiling to herself when Davis entered her class.

"Now that's what I like to see. A biggo smile on a pretty face," he said, sounding flirtatious. Rashawn wanted to balk at the statement, but finding Davis's dimple irresistible, she just grinned wider.

"Ready for lunch?" he asked.

"Sure," she answered, sounding impulsive.

Gathering up her papers, together they headed toward the door. As soon as they'd started out, they ran into Blain on his way in.

"Dr. Ams, I wanted to personally return this to you," Blain said, holding out a gold tennis bracelet. Rashawn's eyes widened.

"Where did you find this?" she asked, looking at her wrist, unconsciously double-checking to make sure it was indeed hers. She'd only now realized it was missing.

Tension grew on Davis's face, but she missed that, too.

Yes, the bracelet was gone, and instead, her wrist bore a slight bruise. She hadn't noticed that earlier either.

"It was in my pocket, must of snagged on my jacket or something. I have no idea really," he answered.

"How did you know it was mine?" she asked. Davis could swear he heard flirtation in her tone.

"I'm very observant that way, Dr. Ams." Blain smiled, pouring on the charm.

That was another thing Davis noticed.

"Good job there, Officer Tollome. Now, if you'll excuse us, we were on our way to lunch," Davis said, sounding ruder than he intended while slipping on his hat.

Rashawn looked at Davis with a slight scowl. "We're just going to the sandwich shop. Join us. Is that okay, Davis?" she asked. Davis all but grunted his answer.

"No," Blain reneged like a gentleman, smiling diplomatically, which only bugged Davis all the more.

"Great, let's go," Davis said, reaching for Rashawn's arm. She pulled away slightly with eyes widened in shock at his childish behavior.

"Rashawn, I'm sorry. I didn't mean to . . ." Davis stumbled as he groped for professional language.

Just then, one of Rashawn's students approached.

"Dr. Ams, can I see you for a minute?" the girl asked.

Rashawn, still glaring at both men, didn't even excuse herself from their company as she walked away with her student.

Davis waited until Rashawn was out of earshot before he moved in front of Blain to speak. His body language read irritated; however, Blain just held a blank expression, no doubt wondering why Davis was up in his face.

Davis had to wonder what he was doing up in this man's face, too, besides making an ass of himself.

"Blain, if I'm in your zone, just let me know," Davis began.

Blain looked around as if Davis were speaking to an invisible person standing behind him.

"Your zone?" he asked.

"Rashawn . . ."

"I don't know what you're talking about. Zones, Rashawn, the two don't compute," Blain said, immediately making Davis feel crazy.

"Forget it," Davis huffed, storming off frustrated.

Three men met. Under the shadows of the night and the cover of their disguises, they met in the open, unnoticed and unmolested.

The same laws designed to keep people like them out of society had sheltered them, protected them.

"I can't believe you used it for your own purposes," said the head man, the one they called Doc.

His depth defying eyes often gave the appearance of a gentle soul, but that was an erroneous deduction. This man was nothing more than pure meanness. He had little patience for rule breakers—*especially those who broke the rules he had made.*

"Yeah, well, how was I to even think she would get knocked up?" Red balked, refusing to go along easily with the reprimand.

Red didn't respect Doc, feeling that he was just a bully, and Red hated that. To Red, Doc was just a man, just like him. Yet, for some reason, Doc acted as though he was more. He acted as though he were some kind of demigod.

"I guess curiosity got the best of me," Red chuckled, running his fingers through his thick crop of bright red hair. "I know we're supposed to be ever so thankful you allowed us to sell some of your shit for money, but ah, trying it out, seeing what it does, I felt that was like . . . research," Red explained, sarcasm tipping his words.

"But now you're in it," Leon snapped reprovingly.

"Now you're not only a damn drug dealer, you're a fuckin' rapist." Leon was a bit of a loner, and a newcomer to their little 'arrangement'. Yet he too was someone Red had a hard time with.

"Who's gonna know?" Red added in his defense.

"That's not the point," Doc interjected.

"We're supposed to be in this together, and so we can't be all going in our own directions, seeking each his own interest," Leon went on.

"You know, you are really starting to bug me with your self-righteous bullshit. You're as bad as Doc," Red growled, as he stood. He was nearly as tall as Leon, who jumped to his feet, too, both giants in their own right. However, neither intimidated Doc. He just sighed heavily at the overgrown children—his partners. The young men had a lot to learn about discipline and working together.

"Stop it, both of you," Doc snapped, holding up his hand to end what was yet to start—another fight.

Leon had a bad temper and never backed down once he got going. Doc didn't like him much. He reminded him of someone from his past, someone he had been having foul thoughts about lately.

"Let's get on with the business at hand," Doc decided, taking the lead, feeling as though he was not only the oldest, but also the wisest of the *'gang'*.

The gang.

This was a reluctant partnership at best. Each man in it for his own reason, and those reasons were not for the betterment of the other. However, money, greed, sex, power, and excitement figured into each of their plans.

Red and Leon sat down. Although resistant, they gave in to their lack of experience and know-how in the world of drug peddling. Those two men who sat in the booth with Doc, talking low and reticently, knew they were in over their heads, dealing this potentially dangerous drug around Moorman University. Both of them wanted out, but they knew '*out*' was no longer an option.

They'd heard rumors about Doc and his punishments given to those who he felt betrayed him, or got in his way. Once you got in with him, you were in until the end, or until he ended it for you.

It was amazing to both Red and Leon that he was allowed to hold the position he had at Moorman U—truly amazing. However, knowing that fact did let Red and Leon know, whether they wanted to accept it or not, that Doc had some kind of power and they'd better tread lightly.

A lot of important, prominent people in this city were going down if the operation went south. Doc had assured them of that.

Red and Leon were not true criminals, not really. However, they were greedy, and with that admitted, they couldn't resist this offer when Doc put it before them. Who better to move drugs through Moorman than the two of them, trusted men who could use their positions there as campus security to move about the campus freely?

There was nothing that could go wrong, right?

Who could resist a tasty setup like the one they had? No one.

Doc didn't consider himself a criminal either. He didn't have much of a choice in regards to this drug, in his opinion. Not having it, was not an option for him. He had to have it. He was more like a victim from where he sat.

"What if she remembers you?" Leon asked Red, bringing up the sensitive subject that had gotten their meeting off-track to begin with. He was still angry with Red for getting up in his face.

"She won't," Doc said coolly, answering for Red.

"But what are you gonna do if she does?"

"Hopefully, Yvette Furhman won't remember. I

wouldn't want to have to do anything 'else' to her," Doc smiled eerily.

"She won't remember, so you just stay away from her," Red said, his voice almost pleading in its tone.

"Anything else I can get you guys?" the waitress asked. She appeared suddenly and smiled at them, falling prey to their disguises, giving them the credit they did not deserve.

"No thanks." Doc smiled sweetly, handing her ten dollars to cover the drinks and her tip.

"We're just gonna finish up and get outta here," Doc went on, holding up his iced tea, showing her that he was nearly finished.

The server smiled at his handsome face and nice physique, his strong arms and thick, long legs that hung out from under the table.

What she wouldn't give to have just a little bit of his time.

She smiled at his tip, too, and then at the other two strong, strapping young men at that table.

Where did they make guys like them? Every time they came in, she would just stare, wondering what their wives looked like. She imagined them with little petite girls who probably bossed them around on Saturdays, filling their weekends with 'Honey Do's'.

How wrong she was with her thoughts.

Just then, she noticed that Red was staring at her hungrily.

"When do you get off, honey?" he asked.

"Let the woman work," Doc snapped.

Friday night at the Furhman's house, the air was thick with tension.

"Mr. and Mrs. Furhman, I believe Yvette when she says she was raped. What I also believe, is that she has been a victim of the vice going around our campus, the . . ." Davis groped for the right words, ". . . the virus, as it were, that's caused a near epidemic of date rape cases," he went on.

Yvette's father was a large man with burly eyebrows that resembled a handlebar moustache above each of his eyes. He squirmed slightly with the thought of something so terrible as rape happening to his little girl. The thought disturbed him very much.

"I want to help, and that's why I brought with me, Juanita Duncan," Davis said, introducing his ex-wife as if she were a mere colleague. He felt Juanita's eyes on him, castigating him.

'Claim me!' her eyes pleaded, but Davis said nothing more about Juanita in connection with himself.

Juanita was a psychotherapist who specialized in hypnotherapy. This form of therapy seemed to help many of her clients whose progress was perhaps blocked by past traumas. She had a thriving practice and Davis was hoping that maybe Juanita could help Yvette remember what had happened to her the night of the party.

Yes, help Yvette. That's all Davis wanted Juanita to do for him.

At least that was what he had explained to Juanita when he'd called her the other day.

"Business, Juanita, that's all. I really need your help," he said.

"You need me?" she asked, smiling wickedly on her side of the phone.

Juanita enjoyed teasing him when she could get away with it. They had been married a long time before he'd finally asked for the divorce, and the last couple of years had been filled with mere contrivances, at least on her part, to see each other again. She felt that in his heart, he missed her, too. Even now, this issue with Yvette, it was merely a ploy to get them together again. That's what she believed.

While listening to his heavy sighs of annoyance, she tapped her pencil against the gold-framed wedding picture that sat on her desk—their wedding picture. Sure, Juanita was remarried, but still.

"Why wouldn't I want to have my cake and eat it, too? Who wants a cake, just to leave it sitting there?" she often could be heard saying.

Juanita knew she was sick, crazy, greedy, obsessed, and laden with a good number of imperfections. However, during the divorce, and after, even as recently as her birthday six months ago, Chance could still be enticed into her bed.

In Juanita, he got maturity, brains, talent, beauty, and an insatiable sexual appetite. Juanita was petite, with sinuous, perky breasts. Her full lips and exotic eyes could drive any man mad with desire. There was something about her style, too—her full Afro, sitting several inches from her head, and ethnocentric clothing, bright with color. She was a vamp in the purest form. She sat herself apart from any woman he had ever met, that is, before Rashawn Ams.

Juanita never asked for forgiveness, as it didn't matter to her one way or the other, as long as he came to her when called. Now, suddenly, Chance was acting differently toward her—distant. He was acting as if he really didn't want her anymore, as if he was tired of her trifling ass.

What's up with that?

Maybe he's actually found somebody.

She often wondered how long she could have both Chance and her new husband in her life. And now, all she wondered was if she had possibly lost her *chance.*

However, today at the Furhman's house, Juanita was a subdued professional.

"So you see, Mr. Furhman, Yvette's trauma of losing her virginity under the influence of this drug may simply be blocking her ability to remember. But by using my relaxation therapy, she may be able to come to grips with it all, and release the truth, telling us all what happened, as well as the police. I will document all she tells me, and as a licensed and certified hypnotherapist, my word will hold up in court," Juanita explained.

"How much will this all cost me?" Mr. Furhman asked. He sounded a little tired, although he reached over to take Yvette's hand in his.

Yvette had sat in silence the entire time until now. Now, she wept.

"Nothing, Mr. Furhman. This will not cost you anything," Davis assured him.

"When do we start?" Mrs. Furhman spoke up, showing her eagerness to get this whole nasty mess behind them.

"One question," Juanita began, knowing that she was piquing Davis's curiosity as to what she wanted to ask the Furhmans. Thankfully, he had not butted in during her explanation of the therapy. Still, Juanita wanted to know something.

"Yes?" Ms. Furhman replied.

"Why not just allow Yvette to abort this baby?"

"Abortion? Oh no, we don't believe in that, not at all," Mrs. Furhman answered quickly.

Juanita glanced over at Yvette, and in her eyes, she could swear she saw total surrender, even if just for a second. Juanita felt sorry for the young girl, trapped in her parents' world, bound by their values and beliefs. She wanted to speak up, to show Yvette's parents how wrong they were for forcing their daughter into unprepared motherhood. Juanita wanted to explain how she herself had aborted three times while in high school because of not being ready to deal with the situations her '*illness*' had brought on. However, Juanita's eyes met Davis's, and they told her it was none of her business what the Furhman's believed, so she would just have to let it go.

The Session

"I've missed you lately. I thought for sure you would have come in before now."

"I've been busy."

"Busy doing what?"

"Following that woman."

"Ahhh, so you've decided to become a stalker."

"You think I'm joking."

"Yes."

"Well then listen to this if you want to hear something funny. I have this plan see, I'm going to go into her house at night and I'm going to watch her sleep, too."

"Pardon?"

"I might even get in bed with her and sleep with her."

"Like she's not going to notice that?"

"Oh she won't, because I'm going to be as quiet as a ghost. She won't even know I've been there."

"Ah ha. A man your size . . . you really think you can pull something like that off?"

"Watch me."

"I would love to, but then I'd be an accessory to the fact."

"What fact?"

"The fact that you would be breaking the law."

Laughter.

"I wouldn't be breaking the law. Remember she and I have a love that transcends your understanding."

"I guess. Because that sounds very illegal what you just told me you plan to do."

"No, remember I'm fantasizing. You said so yourself."

"So I did."

Chapter 8

Maceba hesitated before knocking on the door of Blain's office. It had been a long time since she'd spoken to him. The attack at Danton College had taken her out of commission and she used that to finalize her decision on their relationship.

She'd teetered on her thoughts about Blain Tollome for many months, hating him one minute, drawn to him the next. He was a different sort of man, almost like two men in one. Maybe that's what she found so exciting, besides his love of police work. He had a passion for getting involved with things, like this case. He seemed just as driven to find the head of the drug ring as she did. Maybe that's why he was always in her way, always one jump ahead of her.

Admitting that he might have actually cleaned up the campus had been a hard pill to swallow however, and she still wasn't sure if she believed it.

"Come in," he called from inside the office. She hadn't even realized she'd knocked until then.

When she peeked her head in, he barely smiled. She was a little put off by the lack of enthusiasm. But then again, time passes, people change, maybe even Blain Tollome.

"I wanted to talk to you about the situation here at Moorman," Maceba directly started in.

"I thought you said you were taking classes," he answered her, again cutting to the chase.

"I am, but you know, I can't help but notice."

"You're undercover, aren't you?"

"No."

Blain chuckled and shook his head, "You people," he sighed, "and your lies."

"I don't think I like you calling me a liar, Tollome," she snipped. He turned and looked at her. The gaze was a long one, one that made her shift her position.

"I don't think I like you calling me Tollome," he responded.

"Look, let's cut through the bull . . ."

"Yes, Maceba, let's." He folded his papers on his desk, sliding them into the top drawer, and then folded his hands as if he was now giving her his full and formal attention.

She noted him using her full name but didn't comment on that either.

"I guess this is your time to see how it feels to have someone riding your ass on a case that you feel you have under control."

"Is that what you plan to do, ride my ass?" he asked, his lips curving slightly as if he fought a devilish grin, "Because, I mean, if that's what you plan to do, I can surely give you some lessons. You know, make sure you do it right."

"Blain, don't go there," she commented sharply.

"Don't go where?" he asked, sounding innocent before he glanced at his watch.

"Am I keeping you from something?"

"Or somebody," he answered.

"You keep making a point of letting me know you're involved."

"Or you just keep getting that point, one or the other." He stood and shrugged into his jacket, "Now if you want to go through all my stuff, have at it, but I can't give you a tour, cuz I've got somewhere to be."

"I'm not gonna . . ."

"Don't lie, Ceba," he interrupted, touching her chin as he moved closer to her. She moved her face, pulling it quickly from his touch. She wasn't ready for this.

Maybe she would never be ready for Blain to touch her.

Or maybe she was always ready, and that was the problem.

When he walked out, she felt herself breathe again.

Rashawn and Qiana entered the mall. Although the two of them had gone out every week since Rashawn's return, the difference in their friendship was apparent.

Neither wanted to address either the past or the riff, but it was obviously there.

"I need some new lingerie," Qiana announced, veering them toward Beatrice Drawers. It had been their favorite place to shop in the past.

"Let's stop in here first," Rashawn all but insisted, pointing toward the mall's large department store. Qiana, seeing her obvious avoidance to visit their once choice haunt, smacked her lips.

"Shawn, since when do we shop there?" she asked.

"What are you talking about?" Rashawn asked defensively.

"Ever since you've been back, we've not done any of the things we used to, and I'm like . . . what's up?" Qiana asked.

"Qiana, first, I don't know what you're talking about, and secondly, we've done everything we used to do," Rashawn lied. Qiana rolled her eyes, unconsciously twisting her large wedding ring around her finger, as had become her mannerism.

The two of them stood silent for a moment.

"Forget it," Qiana said in a huff, heading now for the department store. Rashawn pulled her arm.

"No, wait, you wanted to say something," she challenged.

Qiana wanted to tell Rashawn exactly how she felt about this façade she was putting on, the silly way she was acting while trying to cover up what she was apparently feeling.

Why was Rashawn avoiding the issues that the two of them needed so badly to address?

The past, the attack by Rufus, the loss of the baby and the way Rashawn had abandoned her in her worst time of need; those were the issues Qiana felt they had.

Qiana squirmed, slightly parting her lips, and then, changing her mind, she just sighed.

"Forget it. Let's go. I need my ring cleaned anyway," Qiana said, trudging forward through the large automatic doors.

As soon as she entered, Rashawn noticed a familiar-looking woman heading toward them, coming from deep within the store. As the woman got closer, the widening of her blue eyes told Rashawn that whoever she was, she knew them, too.

"Qiana!" the woman greeted with a high-pitched voice.

"Sherry," Qiana returned the greeting.

Sherry was Qiana's husband's ex live-in girlfriend. They had been together for three years, parting only after finding out about Nigel's donation to the sperm bank that Qiana used to get pregnant, and Sherry's affair with her coworker. Sherry hadn't taken the breakup well and openly blamed Qiana for everything, even the affair. However, Qiana never felt responsible for Sherry and Nigel's relationship ending and, therefore, carried none of the guilt Sherry had tried to heap upon her.

Now, without the baby that had become the focal point of everything, Qiana felt awkward and somewhat embarrassed.

It was obvious that Sherry was looking around now for Nigel, as it was obvious to Qiana that she didn't know for sure what had happened since the last time they'd run into one another at this very same mall. Suddenly, Sherry's eyes rested on the large diamond in Qiana's wedding ring.

"Have you seen much of Nigel?" Sherry asked tightly, flipping her thick, blonde mane over her shoulder.

Dressed in a sharp, tailored grey pantsuit that hugged her shapely frame, accessorized with a floral scarf that played with the blue in her eyes, Sherry was still an intimidatingly beautiful woman, Qiana felt.

"Yes, Sherry, I see him every night. Nigel and I are married," Qiana answered without hesitation.

"Married?" Sherry managed to choke out, after clearing her throat slightly, her face stiffening. Beautiful or not, Qiana knew she now had the upper hand in this game, and quickly decided that she didn't want to play anymore. Sherry could care less about the baby. It was Nigel she was interested in.

"Well, I suppose that was the best thing, with the baby and all," Sherry said, no doubt justifying things in her mind.

"Yes," Qiana answered, looking back at Rashawn, signaling that this confrontation was just about over. "I'll tell Nigel I saw you, Sherry. Have a nice evening," Qiana said as she grabbed Rashawn's sleeve and led her on into the store.

"Why didn't you tell her you guys didn't have the baby?" Rashawn asked under her breath after they had cleared Sherry's earshot.

"None of her business," Qiana answered quickly.

"But you lied," Rashawn went on.

"No, I didn't," Qiana went on as she sprayed on a sample of perfume from the counter. "She said marrying Nigel was the best thing, and it was," Qiana answered.

"You really feel that way, don't you?" Rashawn asked now, sounding sincere.

Qiana looked at her for a moment. How could she explain what Nigel meant in her life? How could Qiana say to Rashawn that Nigel had filled the void that she had left?

"Yes," was Qiana's answer.

An evening at the mall had not been in his plans but, that's where Rashawn was and so he would make the best of it.

She was there with her friend.

He didn't know why he felt the need to follow her there to the mall, but he felt the need to be around her tonight, to be a part of her life.

How he wished he could hold her hand, walk with her from store to store.

Maybe one day. Maybe one day they would be a real family.

The more he thought about it, the more he grew determined to make it happen.

Back at home, Terrell and Rita nuzzled on the sofa, whispering in each other's ears and giggling like newlyweds while their children slept on the floor in front of them. Apparently, Terrell had gotten over the shock of Rita's pregnancy and was enjoying a newfound sexual freedom within that fact.

"And why shouldn't he? It's not like he can keep his nasty hands off of her," Rashawn mumbled under her breath, pouting while sitting in the kitchen dusting the breadcrumbs from her palms. She dusted Reggie's face, clearing it of crumbs too. He grinned at her.

"Stop it, T." Rita could be heard playfully resisting Terrell's advances.

Rashawn groaned at the sound of their love play. All of this was truly getting hard on her.

Just then, she heard their bedroom door close.

"I can't take it," Rashawn admitted now, downing her glass of water as if it were something stronger. She looked around as if wanting a way out, yet finding none. Who could she call, where could she run? Within seconds, it seemed, she could swear she heard the headboard to Rita and Terrell's bed hitting the wall. It seemed never ending now since Rita's pregnancy had become known to all—their lovemaking.

Just then, the phone rang. Rashawn hesitated before answering it, perhaps dazed at hearing her sister having sex with Terrell and for the first time feeling disturbed.

Perhaps?

"Hello," she answered. The line was silent. Rashawn looked at the caller ID, but it showed that the number calling was blocked.

"Hello," she repeated.

"I hope you found what you wanted at the mall."

"Who is this?"

"Sweet dreams," the man whispered before hanging up.

A chill shivered her body. Suddenly, all Rashawn could hear was the headboard against the wall, all she could see was Reggie smiling at her. The tear ran down her cheek before she could catch it.

Later that night, on the other side of town—way on the other side—a young white boy waited impatiently on a dark corner. It wasn't the type of neighborhood where a boy like him should be waiting, but he wasn't concerned about that element. He wasn't concerned about the prostitutes walking past, nor the drunks hanging out in front of the liquor store hoping someone would hand them just enough to make up the difference for another bottle.

Andy was disappointed. The drug he had bought didn't work right. Sharon woke up right in the middle of it all and pitched a fit. She cussed him. She even spat on him for what he had done to her. She accused him of horrible things and said she would cry rape if he didn't pay her off.

Yes, Andy's only concern was the big red-head dope dealer and how he was gonna fix this situation. But instead of Red, another guy came. It didn't matter, they were all the same—dope dealers, right? What made one any worse or more intimidating than the other, right?

"A hundred bucks," Andy snapped quickly.

He wasn't intimidated by this guy either. He was angry.

"She made me give her a hundred bucks. She said she knew what I gave her and that I was probably the guy who did Yvette. I had to give her a hundred bucks or she was gonna tell everybody that I did Yvette! I didn't do Yvette!"

"Did you do the girl?" the drug man asked, with a creepy wickedness in his tone.

"Well, yeah, but . . . well, at first she didn't even get a buzz from it, then she just . . . well, I thought she was dead. Scared me shitless. I almost couldn't do anything. It's not s'posed ta go like that, is it?" Andy asked before continuing in his attempt to explain why he should get at least a portion of his money back.

"Anyway, right as I was, you know, getting off she woke up. Said she would cry rape if I didn't give her some bread so I gave her all I had in my pocket. This is bad," the boy said, looking over his shoulder nervously.

He turned back to the drug man. "You wanna know what I fig'r?"

"Yeah, punk. What do you fig'r?"

"I figure Red did Yvette," Andy accused with a pointed finger.

The drug man laughed.

"That's what you fig'r, eh?"

"Yeah, that's what I figure," the boy answered, trying to hang on to his nerve, suddenly feeling the cold. He'd left his jacket in his car.

The drug dealer stood silent for a moment, and then, after sucking his teeth, he rolled his toothpick to the other side of his mouth.

"So, you about to cry rape?"

"No, no. I was just thinking I could get my money back." Andy squirmed just a little now as the cold air hit him, as well as the reality of the man's mass. Was it possible that he was even bigger than Red?

"You do, eh?" the drug man said calmly, with a tone that told the boy, fat chance on seeing any of your money—sucka. You got off, now step off.

The drug man started to climb back into his SUV, and that's when Andy made a big mistake.

He didn't know that it was a mistake. He had simply grabbed the drug man's arm. He wasn't trying to make a big deal out of it or anything like that. He just thought he should get his money back. He sure didn't think he deserved any broken bones, but that's what he got.

"Next time, just deal with what comes. Don't fight it. Don't make things so fuckin' hard on yourself. When you fight, you make it hard," the drug man explained, speaking close to Andy's ear so he could hear between his pain-filled groans.

Doc left him right there, on the ground, in the cold.

Suddenly, it became painfully clear that neither the drunks, nor the prostitutes walking past, were too awfully concerned with Andy, either.

* * *

Rashawn's walk ended about midnight at the twenty-four-hour Denny's. She went in. Maybe a cup of coffee and a piece of pie would soothe her troubled mind.

"Why can't I just be happy? Rita and Qiana's lives aren't perfect. God knows their men aren't prefect, yet they manage," Rashawn said under her breath, carrying on a one-sided discussion on the matter.

Just then, Blain entered the restaurant and spied her in the booth. He wasn't in uniform, but all the same, she hoped he was on duty. She hoped he wouldn't have time to come near her. She was wrong.

"Hey." He grinned, setting his take-out on the table. He'd apparently called in his order. It appeared to be waiting for him.

"Hey," she answered back, giving him only half a glance as he slid into the cramped booth next to her. She overtly tightened her jacket around her and pulled her purse onto her lap.

"I'm not tryin' ta jack ya," he chuckled, curving his lips into a smirk.

"Don't you need to be out there catching some bad guys?" she asked

"As a matter of fact, I just got off. I was gonna grab me a bite before heading over the bridge," he admitted.

"Over the bridge? Where do you live?" she asked.

"Showing some interest, Dr. Ams?" he asked.

She smacked her lips.

"No," she answered, sipping her coffee.

"Why do you just so happen to always be where I'm at?"

"Don't flatter yourself."

"I'm not."

"Well, then in that case, none of your business where I live," he answered smartly. She looked at him and rolled her eyes, hating the mixed feelings that Blain gave her—one minute a rush of heat, the next, a sensation bordering on nausea.

"Where do you live?" he asked. Rashawn chuckled.

"Forget it, Blain. I'm not gonna have you stalking me," she said. His eyebrow went up.

"Why in the hell would I do that? Me thinks one doth think too highly of oneself," he said, surprising her with the comment. Rashawn felt the heat rush to her cheeks. Blain slid from the booth and shook his legs for circulation.

"See ya 'round," he said, slamming his heavy hand on the table before walking out.

Chapter 9

Monday, back in her cramped office and filled with distraction, Rashawn looked over her lesson planner. Today she'd met with Roman to discuss the condominium. He couldn't wait to drive her over there.

The condominium was in a secured neighborhood, complete with an encoded, gated entrance and maintained landscapes. It couldn't be more sophisticated, or more perfect.

Now to ask Rita and Terrell for the money.

Buy me out, she was going to say to Rita.

"Two hundred and fifty thousand," Rashawn said aloud to see how it felt. "Things aren't cheap here," she went on, practicing her speech. "I mean, I could move out of state, and take Reggie," she added. "No, no, I won't threaten." Rashawn shook her head shamefully. "Well, unless I have to." She smiled wickedly.

She and Rita had bought out their other sisters a long time ago for next to nothing, but market values had gone up, and surely Rita could understand that. Truthfully, Rashawn was more concerned about Rita having a cow baby over the mere mention of her moving out. Just then, her phone rang. The caller ID told her it was Rita.

"Yeah," Rashawn answered, trying to sound nonchalant.

"When are you coming home?" Rita asked.

"When I get ready," Rashawn smarted off, sounding very tongue-in-cheek.

"No Shawn, it's Trina," Rita began, her voice deep and sad. Rashawn's stomach tightened.

What had happened to Trina? They had not made peace. *Please, God, let it be nothing!*

Her mind raced.

"What!" she exclaimed, louder than expected, shocking Rita.

"Man, you're tense," Rita said.

"What," Rashawn repeated.

"Oh, Trina's walked out on Jason. She's over here crying her eyes out. She needs to stay with us for a while," Rita said.

"Shit. Shit," Rashawn growled, "Shit," she added again for emphasis.

"Shawn, don't," Rita began.

"I told you she hated me," Rashawn could hear Trina say in the background—her voice full of sniffles. "I'm sorry I said she didn't know her 'Baby Daddy.' I know you're not a ho, Shawnie! You just don't wanna be with a man. You just . . ." Trina continued.

"She doesn't hate you," Rita assured, cutting her off before she made things worse.

"You don't hate her, do you Shawn? Here, tell her that," Rita said, leaving the phone before Rashawn had a chance to say anything.

"I'm so sorry for what I said, Shawnie. Man, I'm sorry. I was just jealous. I am jealous. I love you. You're my baby sister. You're beautiful, you're slim, you're . . ."

"Don't be up in my bed when I get there!" Rashawn barked, cutting her short, unconsciously looking around for her favorite stress toy—two small gold magnets. She would pull them apart and allow them to slap loudly back together.

"Where are they?" she mumbled under her breath as she pulled open her desk drawers searching madly for them.

"I won't," Trina said, sniffing loudly.

While sliding from Rashawn's plush comforter, Trina had to wonder if perhaps Rashawn could see her through the phone.

"Here, Rita," Trina said, her voice trailing off.

"Shawn," Rita began, "Are you okay with this?"

"Oh, yes," Rashawn answered, thumbing the furniture brochure she'd picked up on her way back to the campus. She'd given up on looking for the trinket.

"As a matter a fact, I was just being mean to my sister. You tell her to get back in my bed, since I know she had her fat tail up in there already. You tell her to get on back up in there. And when I get home we're all gonna talk," Rashawn said, hanging up and looking around her small office, debating how comfortable it would be to sleep there that night.

Deciding against it, she gathered up her books and prepared to leave. Just then, her phone rang again.

"Hello!" she growled.

"Excuuuuse me," Davis remarked, using his best Steve Martin impression.

"Oh, Davis, I'm so sorry. I'm sooo pissed. I'm just sooo angry!" she shrieked.

"Well, I can't have that, kid. What can I do? You want to talk?" he asked.

Rashawn simmered for a second before answering, "Yes. You can meet me at my car. I'm in the far lot. You can meet me there in like five minutes," she said preparing to synchronize her watch with his.

"You can meet me, and take me out for coffee or pie or something!" she requested in a demanding tone.

"Yes, ma'am!" he agreed, his voice sounding as if he had saluted her while speaking.

The man watched her walk to her car. It was very late. Why was she always out here so late? It was as if she was waiting for him, as if she was asking for it.

She had fought him the first time he met her here, and he'd hit her because of it. He felt bad about that. He hadn't wanted to. She was his queen, but she had made him do it. It was her fault that he had to do what he did that night—she had the kind of effect on him. And since that night, he'd wanted to make up with her, and now he had. The memory of her lying on that desk, open and receptive to him, made him smile.

It was time to reveal himself to her, so that she could reciprocate the feelings he had for her. She needed to know the man who worshiped her, who wanted nothing more than to please her. He had waited a long time for her to come back to him, and finally, she had.

She must have missed him.

Maybe tonight he would show her again how he felt, and this time he wouldn't need any help from the drug.

What if she fought him?

The man hated when people fought him.

"I'm not a violent man," he mumbled.

While he was watching her, he grew excited, aroused. Now, with the lights in the parking lot, he could see her clearly. Her long neck and smooth lines, thin waist and thick, strong legs—how he longed to feel them around his back. How he couldn't wait to caress her, to stroke her hair, maybe she would even let him kiss her. It hadn't been long since the last time he'd touched her, but still, he missed her. He missed the way her body felt, so perfect, so accommodating. He'd not given himself emotionally to another woman since falling for Rashawn.

How could he? He was hers and she was his. They were a couple, even if only in his mind.

The man started to move from his hiding place when suddenly his rival thwarted his plans.

Rashawn was meeting Chance Davis. It was at her car that Davis approached her. He had been sitting in his own vehicle, waiting for her. The man hadn't noticed him.

Davis and Rashawn spoke for a moment before he put his arm around her shoulder, and together they walked off in the direction of the coffee shop.

What the hell! the man's inner voice screamed after he stewed over the situation for a few minutes. Finally, unable to comfort himself, and in full rage, he grabbed up a large stone the size of a small boulder, no doubt a part of the campus' landscaping, and smashed it into the windshield of Rashawn's car.

"You belong to me!" he screamed, his bellows sounding like a wounded animal in the forest.

The man was angry now, and she would pay for that. Chance Davis, too!

Thank goodness for car insurance.

Thank goodness for wood.

Thank goodness for chocolate. For without those three things, Rashawn would have no peace that night.

As if coming back to her car to find the windshield busted out hadn't been enough, by the time she finally made it home, thanks to Davis, Jason was there pleading with Trina to come back home. The whole scene was a mess, and it was way after midnight.

"How embarrassing," Rashawn mumbled under her breath upon entering the house and seeing the sight.

Normally, in most neighborhoods, it would matter what the neighbors thought, but not here in the Palemos. Here in the Palemos, the neighbors all wanted to get involved.

"Wake me up! Let me get in on it!" Rashawn's cousin Jodi from across the street all but said, as she sauntered into the open house dressed in her robe.

"Just in case that boy tries to get all crazy," she went on, jerking her neck, all the while getting an earful of Jason and Trina's private matters.

"Ohhh Jason, it's all a sham! Next you'll be using all the pressures of writing a book for a reason to cheat on me!" Trina yelled full-voice from the kitchen.

"Well, my dear, you're using it to pack away all the friggin' groceries," Jason said with a sneer in his voice.

Rashawn noticed Rita's body jerk as if she, in just that instant, wanted to slug Jason herself for saying something so mean to Trina.

"How could he say something so cruel? With his ugly ass . . ." Rita mumbled under her breath, turning away as if trying not to hear anymore.

"Ohhhh no, he di-n't just say that!" Jodi said now, feeding the fire.

"He needs his ass kicked," she went on, rolling up the sleeve of her large, tattered robe.

"Jodi, stay out of this. Go on home, now," Terrell managed to say while pulling the drawstring tighter on his sweats. Apparently, all this loud stuff had just started when Rashawn arrived, because not everybody in the world had been awakened yet.

"Where's your car, Shawn?" Terrell asked, noticing briefly that she had to be dropped off, having seen Davis's taillights when he made his U-turn in front of the house.

"Somebody broke my windshield," Rashawn said calmly, between the hateful words flying full-voice from the kitchen.

"I left it on campus," she added quickly.

"Ah," was all Terrell could answer, as he now headed toward the kitchen to break up the heated argument between Jason, Trina, and Rita, who had made her way in to help, and failed. Rita was screaming obscenities at Jason now, and Jason's innocent mama, who wasn't even there to defend herself.

"Your windshield? Who'd you piss off?" Jodi asked calmly.

"Nobody, Jodi," Rashawn answered, her words curt and a little patronizing, "Uh, why don't you go on home? It's kind of wet out, don't you think?"

Jodi wrinkled up her nose at her.

Since they were kids, Jodi and Rashawn had never gotten along. Perhaps it was their closeness in age, or maybe it was Jodi's ways. She was a troublemaker from way back.

"My man is sleepin'. He don't need me right now. Besides, maybe there's some beer in the kitchen," Jodi said, starting for the kitchen with a lilt in her step. She stopped abruptly and looked back over her shoulder.

"Why don't you go check on yo' boy if you want something useful to do?" she remarked smartly, and then disappeared into the loud kitchen.

Rashawn rubbed her forehead, thinking about her car. It wasn't like a Corvette's windshield could be fixed for pennies. Plus, with the move coming up, she was feeling the pull on her purse strings already. Her savings had thinned out considerably during her sabbatical in Atlanta.

Who would do something like this?

Just then, the volume in the kitchen grew, and Terrell crept out and back into the bedroom he and Rita shared. The door closed with intent.

"I didn't mean for it to happen, Trina! I didn't! Every now and then, a man needs a woman to understand him, to appreciate his work! Every now and then a man needs a woman by his side," explained Jason, just before the cracking sound of flesh smacking against flesh was heard. It was getting violent.

Even Jodi hurried from the kitchen. Beer in hand and wicked grin on her face, she chuckled at what she had witnessed.

"Gurl, Trina just slapped the shit outta him. Knocked them damn contacts smooth outta his head," Jodi chortled.

"Trina, no!" Rita screamed. Her screech colliding with the noise of breakage and Jason's woman-like screams.

"Ohhhh, honey, sounds like expensive stuff," Jodi giggled now, popping open the beer.

Just then, in full uniform, Blain walked in. Rashawn's stomach tightened. She had called the campus police when she got to her car and saw the damages. She got a recording. It was policy to call campus police before calling city police. Why? No one quite understood, but that's what she did. Rashawn and Davis only waited a half hour out there trying once, twice, even three times before Rashawn finally left a blazing message and had Davis take her home. Maybe they had just gotten her message and had gone ahead and sent one of their own to her house. Either way, she was surprised to see Blain.

"Hello," Rashawn greeted him gruffly. He wore a concerned frown. "Are you here about my car?" she asked. Jodi smacked her lips and shook her head as if Rashawn's question was insane.

"Gurl, don't nobody give a damn about yo' car," Jodi smacked, Ebonics coming out loud and clear. "Terrell! The cops is here!" she yelled out now, her voice being followed by the bellows of Rita's children and Reggie being awakened. Terrell came quickly from the bedroom, fully dressed now, as if ready for legal business.

He was such a chameleon, Rashawn thought while watching him clear his throat, acting as though he hadn't a clue to what was going on.

The scene was one straight from a soap opera. Trina

was crying loudly in the kitchen, informing God that her life was over and requesting that he take her now. Jason was screaming about the loss of his sight while Rita was threatening to 'take out his other eye'. Yes, Terrell was looking truly innocent, as if he had slept in his clothes and didn't have a clue as to what was going on his house, and Jodi was cackling like a hen about all of it while slurping on her beer. Rashawn wanted only two things—her car back and the keys to her new condominium.

She went into her bedroom and slammed the wooden door behind her without saying anything more to anyone.

Spying an opened box of chocolates on her nightstand, no doubt Trina's leftovers, Rashawn kicked off her shoes and climbed into her bed fully dressed and began to consume them while making a note to call her insurance company in the morning.

She had to get out of there.

"He's barely survived this," the doctor informed the agent from the Bureau for International Narcotics and Law Enforcement.

"I understand that, but if I could just ask him a couple of questions," Maceba insisted.

"I would rather you not."

"I'm sorry, but we have to," the male agent, her partner, pushed.

The doctor sighed heavily. He hated the pressure he was under here. This kid Andy Simmons was barely stable, and already they were here wanting to ask questions.

The boy didn't look all that bad, considering what he'd been through. And if her thoughts on the matter were correct, it could have been worse.

"Hello there, Andy," she greeted, flashing her badge

as soon as she entered the room. "I know you are not feeling your best so we're going to be quick." Andy nodded.

"Do you know who did this to you?"

He nodded again.

"Who?"

His mouth opened slightly and she leaned in close to hear, but his voice did not carry.

About that time, the doctor walked in, and Andy pointed at him. Confused, the agents said nothing, hoping that Andy's sign language would become clear to them.

"Your doctor did this?" the female agent finally asked, showing her confusion. Andy shook his head growing instantly agitated, pointing again at his doctor. His mouth gapped over again, but no words came out.

The Session

"What's on your mind?"

"I'm very angry."

"I gathered that."

"She's moving further away from me emotionally. I think I've been more than patient with this woman."

"Or not patient enough."

"Don't make me laugh. You have no clue as to what I'm feeling."

"I'd like to understand. Help me understand."

"Help you how?"

"I was thinking that perhaps we should try another type of therapy, one that involves a relaxation technique that . . ."

"There is no way I'm going to allow you to get into my head like that. You must think I'm stupid."

Standing, he glared angrily. "There is no way I'm stupid enough to allow you that kind of invasion."

"I didn't mean to . . ."

"Look, this has been fun but I think I won't be back."

"I didn't mean to insult you."

"Well, you did."

"Can we start over?"

"You sound as if you're begging me now?"

"No, I would never do that."

"Of course, not unless I gave you reason."

The touch.

"Don't ever touch me again."

"Or what?"

"Or you'll be sorry."

"I seem to be sensing a little fear."

"This session is over."

Chapter 10

The next morning Rashawn took a deep breath, hesitating before heading into Professor Roman's classroom. As she entered, his students rushed out. She could almost feel the heated air following them, no doubt the result of another impassioned debate.

Rashawn stood quietly, watching the debonair man fill his briefcase. With his well-groomed, thick mass of shiny, loose curls lopping carelessly over his creased forehead, he was tall, maybe six foot, four or five, lean, and a rather handsome black man in his mid to late forties, but aging well. His well-known vegan lifestyle had aided, no doubt, in his nearly ageless appearance and healthy, strong physique. His smooth skin, bright eyes, and broad, excited smile gave him a cool manner and aura of confidence. Sometimes Rashawn wondered about his past life, what he'd done before settling into this nearly sedentary career.

Was he married? Was he someone's father? In his past life, before Moorman University, had Allen Roman been just another handsome cad, breaking hearts and wreaking havoc among his certain bevy of admirers? Possibly a rebel, defiant to authority, bucking the system? What had happened in his life to make him so cynical, so damned opinionated?

She watched him a while longer before realizing that she was staring, and then shook herself free of her thoughts.

Right now she didn't care about Roman's past. She needed him to be in the present. She needed to beg him to save her life. Actually, she just wanted to buy his condominium.

Same thing.

Just then, he noticed her, and she could have sworn she saw warmth come into his eyes and a look of tender affection cover his face. Her mind flashed back to her dream, and then, poof, it was gone.

"Dr. Ams," he said in his usual cool manner.

"Dr. Roman," she replied, greeting him in the same way.

"I'm glad you were prompt," he said, looking at his watch.

"I'm always prompt," she replied.

"Good thing, too," he said, ending the brief volley.

She could tell by the way his eyes suddenly sparkled that he was a man used to unnerving his 'prey'. Rashawn knew his words were said just to put her on the defense. She wouldn't give in to it, wouldn't fall for it. She wouldn't be eaten alive by this man, not today.

Be strong, Shawn. You know he will mess with your head if you let him, Rashawn urged her inner child, her curious being. But to no avail.

"Why?" she asked, following him out of the classroom after he brushed past her standing in the doorway. The body contact between them was mild, but noticeable.

"Why, what?" he asked dryly, with a very nonchalant air in his tone.

"Why is it a good thing?" she asked, easily keeping up with his quick strides.

They had agreed to talk in Hillthorn Hall. It was across the campus, and Allen was walking as if they had only minutes before the hall locked up, which was not the case.

"What?" he asked, only side glancing at her.

"Why is it good that I'm prompt?" she asked. He smiled, but only for a second.

"Everyone should be prompt," he answered, sounding sly and evasive.

She knew in her heart that he meant more by his comment, but heaven forbid she ask more and admit to her paranoia.

They reached Hillthorn Hall and entered through the heavy glass doors, which he held open for her. She moved past him, feeling his eyes drop and quickly come back up again, as this time their body contact seemed planned. She actually even felt a little heat on her rear as she passed him.

Is he checking me out? she asked herself.

"Let's sit near the windows," he offered, leading her to a quiet place near the back, beyond the tables filled with students cramming for finals. Rashawn glanced around, looking to see if perhaps any of her own slackers had made their way to a study group.

Of course not.

"I want to buy your condo," Rashawn said, getting to the point before he even had a chance to get comfortable in his seat.

"My agent said you seemed eager." He smiled.

"No, not eager," Rashawn needlessly defended herself. "Just interested," she cleared up. Roman smiled at her, his eyes again showing warmth. She turned away, catching herself before giving in to his friendliness.

"Why are you so defensive?" he asked.

"I'm not," she answered, giving his eyes a good gazing into, to prove her statement. She would make eye contact with this man if it killed her. Even if her skin crawled off her body, Professor Allen Roman, Ph.D., would not intimidate her!

"I was hoping to go through the place with you. Maybe add some personal input, you know, flavah," he said, sounding somewhat loose and hip.

"Flavah?" she asked.

"I had a lot of happy times there. I lived there for many years before going on sabbatical in Negril," he went on, sounding reminiscent.

"Wow, wish I could afford . . ."

"It was family business. My mother was dying," Roman interjected quickly, smiling tightly. "I'm much happier here. Yes, I've had lots of happy times in the condo here," he added.

"Then why are you selling?" he asked.

"Just moving on," he said, as if she were 'tipping near' the subject of something personal to him. "While dealing with my mother, my wife Jasmine died there, and when I came back, well, it just wasn't the same," he confessed.

"Did you two have children?" Rashawn asked, thinking of how lonely she would be without Reggie.

Allen Roman stared at her for a moment before he suddenly became very abrupt.

"I'll have the papers drawn up if you're certain you want it."

"We're not going to haggle?" she chuckled slightly. His brow wrinkled slightly, as if the mere thought of negotiating over his memories hurt even more than selling them.

"Did you not like the quoted price?" he asked.

"It's fine. I was just sort of joking," she said with a sigh. He stood and looked down at her and then his watch.

"Fine, then. I'll contact my agent and you and he can take care of the rest," he said and walked away.

Rashawn sat watching Roman as he left Hillthorn

Hall. He seemed suddenly filled with mixed emotions though he held his head high, not looking one way or the other.

The rest of the day, thoughts of Rashawn filled Roman's brain. Why had he mentioned Jasmine to her? He couldn't believe he had even said her name. Surely Rashawn sensed his lack of closure, the guilt he still felt over what he had allowed to happen—the unfinished business surrounding her

"But I am over her. I'm over all of it," he said, taking out the picture from the top drawer of his nightstand. He'd tucked it there months ago during a moment of denial. He refused to face the resemblance between the two of them—Rashawn and his late wife, Jasmine. He refused to accept that his residual feelings and lack of closure were driving him insane. Roman refused to accept a lot of things.

He looked at his watch. "Rashawn is probably having dinner now," he thought aloud and then chuckled at his schoolboy crush.

Gathering up his running shoes, he headed out to relieve some pressure.

By Friday, Rashawn had signed promissory notes for a bank loan and looked over confusing real estate contracts drawn up by Roman's real estate agent. She knew she should have Terrell look them over, but she wanted desperately to move out on her own.

Forget Terrell's money. Forget everybody!

"Besides, how hard could this all be?" she asked herself aloud while finishing her lunch in the campus cafeteria.

"I don't know. How hard to do you want it to be?"

She heard a familiar voice answer. Just the crudeness of the comment made her brow wrinkle. It was Blain.

He sat, uninvited, at her table. She unconsciously moved her seat away from him. He smiled, noticing.

"I'm sorry. I didn't mean to be rude," he said.

"Well, it was rude," she said, sounding as snippy as she could.

"I thought you had a better sense of humor than that," he went on.

"Well, I guess I don't," she remarked stiffly, and then closed her lesson planner that contained more than just class notes.

"I never get to talk to you alone. I mean, it's nice to have you back on campus. Where were you?" he began.

Rashawn looked around for a possible escape and saw none.

"Uh, I spent some time with family in Atlanta," she answered.

Why be so rude, Shawnie? What did he ever do to you?

"Look, let me buy you dinner tonight, welcome you back. You look tired and in need of some pampering. And you know I'm good for it," he said, pouring on the charm. "I mean, I wanted to talk to you the other night, but it seemed like Davis had you pretty hemmed up. Am I right? You two seeing each other or something?" he asked. Rashawn said nothing, allowing her eyes alone to give him a blazing response.

"Come on, just one date. Let me make up for the last time. What can it hurt to give me a minute of your time?" he requested. However, Rashawn wasn't having it. He had blown it big time the first time they attempted an evening together, and again today with that nasty remark when he approached the table.

Yes, it was nasty. She could tell.

"No," she answered flatly, watching the frown crease his brow as he sucked his teeth, probably unconsciously.

He then seemed to regain his composure before speaking, "Look. I'm not here on campus today just for you. I got a lot of stuff going on. This place is a cesspool. So much crime going on. You know there's a drug problem here. These snot-nose kids they've got for security don't know sh—nothing," he corrected just in time, as if any of his words impressed her anyway.

"Oh, yeah, tell me about it, Mr. Supervisor Campus Cop guy," Rashawn began. She was gonna tear into him now. He had it coming. "My car was vandalized as you know, and we called and called. Nobody was even in the office. You guys are way understaffed. Are you trying to tell me we don't even have twenty-four hour help?" she questioned, charging and accusative.

"Well, I see he got you home safely." Blain snapped, not intimidated in the least.

"He?"

"You said we. I just assumed . . ." he said, suddenly looking around as if he now wanted an escape.

"You know what they say about assuming, Officer," Rashawn snipped sarcastically.

"Now you're being rude," he retorted coolly, his eyes locking on hers, "By the way, you need to thank me for coming out there and getting that guy out of your house," he went on.

"Yeah, whatever," Rashawn said with a smirk and a shrug.

Suddenly, he smiled, his eye winking ever so quickly. Just talking to Blain disturbed Rashawn. He was an attractive man, who was so sexy that he actually took her breath away. However, there was something about how he looked at her that was bothersome. There was so much want in his eyes. No matter what she said to him, there was always a hint of lust for her in his expression, in his words, and in his body language. Sometimes the ruder she was, the more he seemed to be 'turned on'.

Any other man who looked like him would be gone by now, on to bigger and better, yet he was still sitting here.

"I saw your car, Rashawn. I care about what happened to your car," he said with sincerity in his tone. There was a long silence between them. "And that's what I'm here to talk to you about."

"I made a report to the city police, and . . ."

"Remember Rashawn, I'm no rent-a-cop, I'm one of our city's finest. I know who you talked to," he said flatly, then broke into a smile again. "I know everything you do. You just can't get away from me. I'm always there," he said, and then grinned widely, showing her he was teasing her. She rolled her eyes.

"Well, then you know that my insurance company is taking care of things for me, huh? Not the campus police," she said smartly, thankful she was fully covered. "You guys did absolutely nothing. I believe the proper term is shit. You guys didn't do shit for me," she glowered.

Just then, Davis walked into the cafeteria. Spying Rashawn, his face broke into a wide grin. She hadn't seen him since the night her car got vandalized, and she was happy to see him today. She smiled back. He approached the table where she and Blain sat. Davis didn't notice or care that Blain now grew uncomfortable.

"Say, kid, what's goin' on?" he greeted teasingly, with his light-heartedness showing. She wondered why his mood was so good today, but instead of asking, she glared at Blain and then turned her attention back to Davis.

"Nothing. What's up with you?" she asked.

"Just feeling good about that matter concerning my student, Yvette Furhman. I'm helping her with . . ." he paused and glanced at Blain, "With some problems she's having," he said. "In just a few days, it looks as though she might be having a breakthrough. She's getting hypnotherapy," Davis divulged.

"Yeah, Davis here can bring his students to tears with that math stuff. Drive them straight to the couch," Rashawn said to Blain brightly, although she was totally in the dark as to Yvette's true problems.

Blain stood, no doubt noticing how her mood had changed since Davis had arrived.

"You leaving?" she asked, sounding surprisingly sincere.

"Yeah, I'm gonna go check on some other pressing matters," he answered.

Rashawn frowned.

"I thought my car was pressing. I want to know who busted my windshield. I mean, I want to know if someone like, has some kinda problem with me or something. I don't want to be looking over my shoulder," she said. "I mean, it's not like I can just call you guys and you come running," she went on. "I don't want to be scared. I . . ."

"Maybe you should park somewhere else then! It's very dark at that end of the parking lot," Blain interjected, snapping Rashawn into silence. "Maybe you shouldn't wear such short skirts and high heels. Maybe . . ." He stopped speaking abruptly when Rashawn's golden eyes widened.

"I'm just saying. You never know what can cause someone to become fixated with you, a good lookin' woman out that late at night," he went on, his tone calming considerably.

"Are you implying she's being stalked? From one incident?" Davis asked.

"I'm just saying that this campus is dangerous, and she needs to look out. And it's more than one incident," Blain went on. Rashawn noticed he was speaking to Davis as if she wasn't even sitting there.

"She's got a gun, ya know," he told Davis, who now looked at Rashawn out of the corner of his eye.

"Wasn't some guy named Rufus stalking you a little over a year ago?" Blain asked. "Before you left?"

"Hey, I remember that guy!" Davis exclaimed, joining in with Blain with a head nod.

Rashawn couldn't believe what she'd just witnessed. In just a second or two, Blain had distracted Davis from his possible intentions of asking her out.

"She almost shot me one night when she thought I was him. She thought he was following her," Blain made known.

"Yeah, Shawn, I remember one day he was accosting you at your car, back when you used to park in staff parking," Davis went on. "Why don't you park in staff parking anymore?"

"Look, uh, guys, I'm not being stalked and I'm not worried about anything like that. Besides, Rufus, Russell Thompson is dead," she snipped, not wanting to verbalize her thoughts on the matter.

"Dead?" Davis asked, his voice reaching a high pitch.

"Did you shoot him?" Blain asked with the same concern showing.

Rashawn stood and excused herself from the two men, gathering up her papers and walking away.

It was six o'clock and already dark out. Rashawn was ready to go home, but she was stuck in her office. She was stricken with panic, and nearly weak with fear. She had called and cancelled her four o'clock class, though she was already on campus. All she wanted to do now was go home, climb into her crowded bed, put her earplugs in, and go to sleep.

Other than buying a home, a day that should have been very exciting, had been, basically, a disaster. Blain and Davis dredged up horrible memories for her. *Thanks, guys.* She was scared out of her mind, feeling no guilt for canceling her thinning class. Surely they got Dr. Roman to conduct it.

Besides, he's a better teacher than me anyway. Why did I bother to come in at all today? Why did I bother to come back from Atlanta?

Her thoughts were all over the place as her panic grew.

Every semester, the closer they got to any vacation of length, the thinner the classes got. The other day, in a more lucid moment, Rashawn had been thinking about giving her class a meaty topic to chew on before they left for Thanksgiving break, or she would lose them for sure. With winter break falling right after, the students would have three weeks to do nothing but drink and play. Their brains would be molasses when they got back come January. But tonight, Rashawn didn't care about her class or their brains. Tonight she only wanted to get out of her office.

Rashawn sat staring out her window, down onto the campus. She couldn't get what Davis and Blain were saying this afternoon, about stalkers and obsession, out of her mind.

It was an interesting topic.

When you're not the one stalked, of course.

The gift box and roses crossed her mind, giving Rashawn an instant chill.

The clock audibly ticked away the minutes.

Just then, there was a knock on her office door. She jumped.

"Yes," she called loudly through the thick steel.

"Professor Ams, it's Officer Tollome. I'm here to escort you," he called out.

Swinging open the door, Rashawn knew her face was covered with fear and confusion.

"Why are you here?" she asked.

"I knew you were still on campus, and I also knew the last bus going to your house had run. Plus, I got to thinking about today and how scared you looked when we were talking about the prospect of you being stalked."

"Stop it, Blain! I'm not being stalked!" she snapped. "Now just stop it." She raised her hand to silence him.

Blain chuckled while looking around her small office, the room where she had just barricaded herself.

"And you're not scared either, eh? Well then, I guess, professor, my services aren't needed," he said, reaching in to close the door. Rashawn blocked his efforts, clearing her throat. She then grabbed her coat.

"You know, that little .22 you carry isn't gonna stop anybody who really wants to get at you," Blain explained while they walked together across campus.

"I don't carry it anymore. I told you, Rufus is dead. I don't need to carry a weapon anymore," said Rashawn, her voice low, nearly growling. She didn't want to talk about this. She wanted to get a taxi and get home.

"You don't?" he asked.

"No. I told you, I don't need to carry it," she said, and then stopped in her tracks. Blain walked only a couple of steps before noticing she had stopped walking.

"Look, I don't like to be scared, Blain. I'm not some timid, little missy, missy Sister Mary, a la sissy girl."

"Whew, that's a long title to just say typical female," he laughed. Rashawn felt the heat of anger rising.

"Women aren't all just walking around afraid," she added.

"Oh, come on. Then why do you all give in to a man putting his arm around your shoulder, or holding your hand? A woman will hold anybody's hand when it's dark," he insisted, outstretching his large one for her to take hold.

"I'm not holding yours," she smarted off.

"But you're with me. Same thing," he said, smiling victoriously. "And you wouldn't have left that office if I hadn't come to get you."

She scowled and started walking again. Blain laughed aloud, his voice echoing in the dark of the nearly empty campus. Rashawn hated him right then, but was oh so grateful this giant man was by her side. She hated what was going on in her life, the lack of strength and esteem. It seemed that so much had been taken from her that day and she had no clue how to redeem her loss. Did she need a man in her life—a protector? Who knew for sure? She needed something, that was for sure, because now she believed someone was actually following her. She was experiencing self doubt . . . the worse of obsessions.

"Blain," she began, "I'm beginning to think . . ." Rashawn hesitated now, before deciding that Blain would not be the one with whom she shared her fears. She would not weaken her resolve, or admit to paranoia. "Nothing," she said, reneging.

"Tell me," he urged.

"Never mind."

"You are so stubborn." He shook his head, smirking. "Your stubbornness is gonna get you hurt one day."

"Is that a threat?"

"No, a warning," he answered flatly.

Blain pulled up to the house. He offered to walk her to the door, but she insisted she didn't need an escort.

"Are you sure, I mean, in a neighborhood like this, well, you just never know," he said again, getting on her bad side.

Nobody says nothing bad about the Palemos.

Even if she was planning to move away, this was still '*her*' neighborhood he was talking down.

"We have a lot of security in this tract. Not much happens here," she defended.

"I understand that a woman was nearly murdered here not long ago. Right on her front lawn," he went on.

Rashawn, not wanting to go into the incident surrounding Qiana, and the attempt Rufus had made on her life, climbed out of the car.

"Goodnight, Officer Tollome, and thanks again," she said coolly before walking to the door without looking back.

Inside, Trina was making herself comfortable in her bed, snuggling deeper into the plush linen. Just the sight of her sister looking so comfortable made her sigh with mixed feelings. Rashawn missed sleeping with Reggie. Now, since Trina had moved back, Reggie had been moved into Rita's boys' room to sleep.

Sometimes it was hard to accept that Trina was four years older than she was. She was like such a big kid sometimes.

Kicking off her shoes, Rashawn, without her usual nighttime primping, quickly changed into her pajamas. When she turned back to the bed, Trina had moved just enough for her to get in, which she did, and then quickly went to sleep. She missed seeing the single red rose lying on her vanity—another *gift* from her secret admirer.

The steps behind her quickened as she looked over her shoulder, time and time again, willing her legs to move faster. But they felt like lead.

Suddenly, the man was on her, slamming her to the gravel. With one sweep of his large hands, he ripped her clothing from her, leaving her bare and shaking. This time she was able to remove the mask. This time she saw his face.

She began to scream hysterically.

"Rashawn, wake up! Wake up!" Trina screamed, too, shaking her.

Rashawn's eyes opened and she burst into tears, jumping quickly from the bed and tumbling to the floor as if she'd seen a mad man instead of Trina. She began scrambling toward the door as if being chased by a wild animal. Trina jumped up and ran over to her, wrapping her arms tightly around her. Rashawn, coming to, began to shake from her hysteria.

Just then, Rita burst into the room.

"What's going on?"

"It's Rashawn. She had a bad dream," Trina explained, while stroking Rashawn's hair.

Rashawn quickly dried her tears and pushed Trina's hands off her. She looked up at Rita standing over them and then she looked back into the eyes of her other sister, Trina. Both of them were frightened and waiting for an explanation of what had just happened, but she said nothing about the dream. Looking scattered, Rashawn then attempted to cover the situation over with humor, "I'm just not used to sleeping with anybody but Reggie. Trina's old crusty feet musta made me think I was in the jungle or something," Rashawn lied, laughing it off now.

Trina looked at Rita, who didn't crack a smile, and then back at Rashawn who was settling back into bed as if nothing out of the ordinary had just occurred.

"Whatever, Shawn," Rita said with a scowl and walked out. Trina, a little more concerned, hesitated before climbing back into bed. Rashawn quickly clicked off the light, leaving her sitting on the floor in the dark.

"Sorry," was all she said.

"It's okay," answered Trina, making her way back to the bed.

Chapter 11

The next morning Rashawn sat at the table sipping coffee. She had risen earlier than anyone else that morning.

She needed to talk to someone before she started going crazy. She needed to put an end to the nightmares before they started getting worse again. She needed her life back, her real life, not this made-up, half-assed recovery that she had made for herself. Rashawn knew she needed to regain her full confidence, her ease with life, a clean conscience.

Glancing at the clock, she debated on a call to her best friend.

"Hey, what are best friends for?" Rashawn said aloud, reaching for the phone.

"Wait, I need to get something for Nigel," Qiana said, stopping in at Sees Candies. They had decided on an early afternoon mall date.

The mall, filled with pre-holiday shoppers, was bustling. Rashawn held her hand out to receive her sample from the candy store counterperson, and then waited while

Qiana picked out several pieces of her favorites and a few pieces to take home for Nigel.

"How are you feeling these days? Planning another baby yet?" Rashawn asked, not thinking about the timing of the question. Qiana glared at her and then went back to the counter, continuing to choose her candy. Rashawn then realized how her question must have sounded.

"No, no. I was just asking because . . ."

"I know I'm big, Rashawn. I know this," Qiana snipped. "The doctor says because I got pregnant again so fast after the incident, and then miscarrying the baby, my body still thinks it's trying to be pregnant," Qiana explained, sounding sober and strong, though Rashawn knew she hurt deep inside. How could she not?

"But Nigel and I are gonna wait before trying again," she added, and then started in on the piece of candy that had the cherry filling.

"Nigel's mother said that would give her more time to get things in order for her grandson," Qiana added with a chuckle as they walked out. Rashawn tucked her sample pieces in her bag to take home to Reggie.

She smiled at the implication that Qiana and Nigel's mother were developing a friendship. It must be nice to have a mother, even if it was someone else's. She missed having that for Reggie—a grandmother.

They walked on through the mall.

"Do you ever think about it, or him?" Rashawn asked then, cautiously. Qiana nodded without hesitation, knowing immediately what and to whom Rashawn was referring.

"Yes. I do. But he's dead, and so I just, I just get over it," Qiana said, sitting down on the bench in front of the jewelers. "Besides, thanks to Rufus, I have Nigel now," Qiana said, and then outstretched her hand to look at the big diamond in her wedding ring.

"Don't even think about getting that cleaned again.

You clean it every time we're here," Rashawn snapped, sounding playful. Qiana grinned.

"No, I don't," she lied.

There was a pleasant moment of silence between them before Qiana noticed Rashawn's distant demeanor.

"Why did you bring him up?" she asked.

"Oh, I guess I just wanted to know how you were feeling about all that," she said, her words hanging. Qiana tried to look at her directly, but Rashawn's face was not squaring with hers.

"Because . . ." Qiana prodded. She knew Rashawn too well.

"Because . . ." Rashawn hesitated. "Because I think he raped me," she said, finally getting it out. Qiana sat silent for a moment, the candy in her mouth just resting on her tongue.

Suddenly her jaw began to move as she mashed the soft center around and then swallowed hard.

"When was this?" she asked, her voice cool and controlled. Rashawn tried to read her face, but couldn't. Qiana was better at hiding her feelings than she was.

"I was coming home from a board meeting. You know, the ones we always have at the beginning of the semester," Rashawn went on, sort of rambling. She couldn't believe she was talking about it, telling someone, telling Qiana! But she knew that she had to go on now, or she would never be able to. She paused to make sure she was still calm.

Yep.

"Rufus had been messing with me, you know, saying things, nasty things," Rashawn went on. "I was gonna tell you, but I couldn't. The time was never right, ya know?" Rashawn sighed.

"Anyway, I was walking through the parking lot one night, and you know we didn't have the lights back then," she said, without realizing that Qiana had never been on campus. She didn't know they had lights now. However, she was nodding, listening. Her small hands gripped her bag of candy, tight.

"I knew someone was following me, but I slowed down. I don't know why . . ." Rashawn shook her head, sounding guilty, feeling guilty. She looked at Qiana with burning eyes, fighting emotion.

"And he grabbed me from behind. He picked me up off the ground," she went on, her arms rising just a little, trying to remember that night and the man behind her—Rufus aka Russell Thompson—Qiana's ex live-in boyfriend, lifting her off the ground.

"And he said, oh my God," Rashawn exclaimed as she, for the first time, remembered clearly what the man had said.

"He said, 'Smile for the camera, baby,'" Rashawn said, touching Qiana's arm. "He then said he would kill me," she added. "That's what he said. And then he raped me," she nodded with her eyes closed, her memory of the night, vivid. "God, he just seemed so huge, I mean, just all over. I've never . . ." She stopped speaking, letting the words hang, hoping Qiana would understand the rest, because she was finished talking now. Her eyes were burning.

"Rashawn, why didn't you tell me? Why didn't you . . ."

"I couldn't. It was like a dream. I mean, even when I found out I was pregnant, I . . ."

"Rashawn, Russell didn't rape you," Qiana interrupted suddenly.

Rashawn grew instantly angry.

How dare she defend that man! How dare she!

Here she was attempting to fix what was broken between them, and Qiana was defending the very person who had messed everything up!

"And why do you say that, Qiana?" asked Rashawn, her tone snippy and short now.

"I'm not saying he wasn't capable of raping you. God knows Rufus, I mean, Russell, had his issues. I'm just saying he wasn't capable of impregnating you. Russell was sterile. That was why I went to the sperm bank in the first place. That was why he got so mad that day I told him about the baby," Qiana said, touching Rashawn's trembling hand, watching the tear roll down her cheek.

"Are you sure?" was all Rashawn could ask now, quickly wiping away her tears, hoping no one was watching. Qiana nodded sadly while handing her a tissue.

"He was sterilized when he was younger. I don't know the how's or why's, but I know that he did some time in juvenile hall back in the South where he was from, and I think that's when it happened. He never really talked about it, or why he was there. But he had to wear a hormone patch, because he was pretty-much mutilated down there. He sometimes needed an apparatus to perform," Qiana began to explain, nodding her head in confirmation of her own thoughts on the matter.

"We really only used condoms for safety, not contraception," she added.

"Oh man, Qiana, I never knew you were living like that," Rashawn gasped.

"I mean, that's why I was so shocked when he cheated on me. But then, like I said before, he wasn't born that way. It's like in his mind he hadn't really accepted that he was, you know, not fully a man anymore," Qiana went on telling Rashawn about Russell Thompson's deficiencies. "Besides, it's not like you could tell just by looking at him that he was different down there. Sometimes he was fairly normal, except that he was sterile," she added, popping another chocolate in her mouth without thinking or choosing.

Rashawn sighed heavily and the two women sat silent for a moment. Qiana thought about Rufus and his anger, no doubt caused by his loss of manhood. Rashawn's thoughts were only of the man who raped her. He was still out there.

"Shawn," Qiana finally said. Rashawn looked at her straight on. "Is that why you left me like you did?" she asked. Rashawn, unable to hide her shame and guilt any longer, broke down.

"I am so sorry," she sobbed. Qiana put her arm around her shoulder to comfort her.

Roman's eyes met the reflection in the stainless steel front of his refrigerator. It was almost humorous seeing himself this way, so needy. Who would have thought a little white powder could buy his soul?

He would have laughed if his heart had allowed it; however, the emotions that stirred his beating organ tonight caused nothing more than stone cold hatred to come up for the man he saw in the reflection.

Jealousy.

Murder.

That's what filled his heart right now.

Roman sneered at the reflection, growling under his breath and remembered all the bad that lay in the history he had with the man who stood behind him, glaring at him, no doubt feeling the same things—blackmail, addiction, slave, trade, bought, sold, trapped, bound— somehow in this miserable, sick relationship they had.

One day there would be an escape, even if it had to be over one of their dead bodies. Many times Roman had sworn to that.

And so be it, he thought, feeling his teeth grinding.

"You'll be sleep in about five minutes, so you besta get ta ya bed," he heard the man say, mocking the accent heard on the island of their upbringing.

"I know, I know," Roman mumbled, sounding old

and cantankerous, showing his age. "Get out," he added with a little bite in his tone.

"Now, don be given me no back talkin'" Doc snipped sarcastically. "I don' wanna be curryin' ya up dem steps," he went on. "You don't want somebody getting your arse," he teased, implying vulgar innuendo that lay behind the use of this particular drug.

"Go da hell," Roman fussed, heading toward the staircase, stopping suddenly to catch his balance. The man stepped up to him.

"Don' cha touch me. Don' cha eva touch me," Roman snarled, holding out his hand to distance the man from him, his accent slipping out, more reminders of his past.

"Fall on yur ass den, stupid bastard," Doc said, walking out.

When Doc closed the door, he could hear Roman hitting the floor.

Davis took a chance when he decided to call Rashawn that night. For weeks their signals were more than a little mixed. He needed to get them going one way or the other. Davis needed to make a decision.

Again, he'd fallen for Juanita and her tricks. Again, he had made a trip to her bed. She was like a drug and he was like a crack head—strung out. Intervention, that's what Rashawn would be for him, could be for him—salvation, a new lease on life, clean, sober, and healthy. For surely what he and Juanita had was sick.

"Rashawn, I was hoping that perhaps we could take this thing slow, but fo sho," he said, attempting light humor. He waited, listening to the silence that came from her end of the phone.

It was hard to explain what was going on in her life. There was no way she could tell him that she had lost her edge. She felt weak and with that feeling came shame. She needed something—someone and at this point she was fighting the urge to grab at the first man that came along—Davis.

"I've had a bad day, Davis. It's not you. I've had a bad day," she said, covering her true thoughts.

"Perhaps then it would make sense, it would add up that you and I could work through our . . . our stuff together," he stammered.

"I don't want to work through my stuff," Rashawn lied, yet tried to sound firm and resistant.

"Look, Reshawn, I'm not perfect, but I am interested in you. I'm not asking for a lot . . ." he began, and then paused to gather his thoughts.

"I just want a friend, Davis. I think I need one," she said, sighing heavily.

"Friends will work . . . for now," he conceded.

Chapter 12

November had come in cool this year, and was going out even cooler. The rains that had started back in October had only gotten harder and more constant. November came in with changes all around, some good, some not so.

With the revelation at the mall pushing its way to the front of Rashawn's mind, she was growing more and more suspicious with each passing day. Every sound sat her on edge. Every unfamiliar car in her neighborhood had her inches from dialing 911.

"When did I get so paranoid?" she asked Roman after finally giving in and reluctantly visiting his office.

"I wouldn't say you were paranoid—overly careful, but not paranoid. But then again you've always been so easily upset."

"Why do you say that? You say it like you know me or something. I'm not *easily upset*, and I resent you saying that," she balked. He held his large hands up in surrender.

"Fine, have it as you want. However, you must admit it's been a long time since your attack and well, I think it's time you start letting it go. Perhaps dating again, perhaps . . ."

"How do you know I'm not dating?" she asked.

Their eyes met in an intense stare down before he finally broke the tension, "You're dating?"

"Well no, but," she admitted, certain that he sighed, with relief.

"Why does that make you happy?"

"I'm not happy." he denied.

"Yes, yes, I saw your expression change when I said I wasn't dating."

"You're being para . . . no, overly careful again." He chuckled.

She smacked her full lips in instant irritation.

"So you're saying to let it go, huh?"

"Yes, Rashawn, let it go. You've got a life to get on with and I suggest you start getting on with it, like maybe tonight. Maybe we could go to dinner," he suggested.

"No," she answered quickly.

"I was merely suggesting as an experiment . . ."

"No. I've already experimented and I don't need to go out to dinner with my therapist. Thank you," she smarted off.

Roman's eyes asked the question his voice could not. However, Rashawn felt she heard him speaking loud and clear. "And you as a man, well, Roman, I just don't think it would be appropriate," she answered. He simply nodded, showing a little embarrassment.

The situation on campus was continuing, which, when translated, meant getting worse. Nothing could stop the drug traffic it seemed, and students were dropping out like flies. Classes were thinning out long before the exodus that the holidays normally brought.

Because of the increase in erotic dreams, Rashawn

had tailored some of her class time to discuss issues such as addiction, compulsions, obsessions, and fixations..

With students leaving for back-to-back breaks starting in just a few days, many professors wanted to make sure their young minds had something for stimulation, something other than indulgence in the aforementioned vices and Rashawn, with what was filling her mind and disturbing her peace, felt it would be good to incorporate a little of her personal issues in her curriculum.

"So now the essence of obsession lies in one's fixation," Rashawn said, using her laser pen to stress the point of her discussion. She wanted to reiterate some things before dismissing the young adults. She wanted to give the students some food-for-thought, and a starting point for their papers.

"And these can be?" she asked.

Hands flew up. She pointed at one of the more energetic students to comment.

"Like, if you are really into, like, toes. You just can't pass up a person without looking at their toes. You have a fixation for toes."

"That's a fetish, not a fixation," another student interjected.

"No, that's just plan freakish," another student called out, bringing laughter with his comment.

"Okay, okay," Rashawn smiled, bringing her class around.

"You get what I want. Two pages on fetish and fixation, including the difference, and then your opinion on where they fit into today's society. Also, just a little on what you think obsession is," Rashawn instructed. "Where the laws of the land should draw a line," she added. There were a few groans, nonetheless, an overall acceptance of the assignment.

As the students poured out, Davis made his way in.

He was smiling. Rashawn looked at her watch. It was lunchtime and they did have a date.

Together they drove to what was fast becoming their favorite restaurant. The ambiance of the place was charming, quaint—romantic even. This was their third lunch together since deciding they would be *friends*. As much as Rashawn hated to admit it, she liked him a little more than that. If only she could work through the barrier that kept *them* from happening.

"Seems like you've got your class back," Davis said, noticing the high energy coming from the exiting students.

"I hope so. I mean, after next week they leave and it's over, man," she said, giving in to the reality.

"Well, that's what's good about math. Once you got it, you got it," he grinned.

"Or you don't," she chuckled.

"Yeah, or that." He smiled.

Suddenly, he laid his hand on hers. She didn't move it, but instead gave in to the moment between them.

"Come to my house for Thanksgiving?" Davis asked.

Rashawn knew she was in true form today. She was charming and beautiful, if she had to say so herself. Especially since Davis hadn't. She had even spent a fortune on her outfit.

She'd even bought flat shoes to cover those inches that kept their eyes from really, fully locking on each other's. She wanted to get into him completely. She wanted to see where it all might go. So far, it was only going—slow. But she was partly to blame. She knew that. She hadn't even told him about Reggie.

Rashawn listened to the soft jazz playing in the air of the restaurant. It was the newest by that jazz group that Nigel and Qiana listened to all the time—GrooveWave. *They have a good sound*, she thought to herself.

Her inner voice growled at her, snapping her back to attention. *Answer the man!*

"Thanksgiving . . . ? Oh wow, my family gets together that day. I mean, it's really big doings," Rashawn smacked, wondering at the same time if Carlotta would even notice if she wasn't there. Everyone was so preoccupied with their own lives lately.

"Can't you get out of it?" he asked, his dimple again showing up. Rashawn was finding him truly irresistible. Where had he been all this time? It was hard to believe they had been coworkers for so long, and yet, it was only now that the sparks were flying.

Maybe it had been her snobbery, or maybe his wife. Who knows? But whatever the barrier had been, it was down now, and she was indeed ready to move this thing forward.

"But you don't know my sister," Rashawn attempted to explain.

"You sound like you're afraid of your big sister," he laughed, being the oldest of his siblings.

"Oh man, you haven't met Carlotta, or Trina, or Rita, Ta'Rae, and now that Shelby is married, she's even got a little attitude problem," Rashawn chortled.

"I'd like to meet them," he said. Her eyes widened.

"No. Oh no. Trust me; you are not ready for the Ams women. Nope," she stressed. Davis chuckled.

"I'm ready for one of them," he said. Rashawn felt tickled and giggly inside.

"Besides, we'll see how ready you are for my family," he added.

It was settled. Rashawn was going to tell Carlotta she would be missing Thanksgiving dinner. The first one since their father had died.

But come on now, times were changing.

"Hey, Carlotta," Rashawn began, after calling Carlotta at work. She started talking immediately. There was almost no room for Rashawn to jump in, what with all the orders Carlotta was slinging out, to her employees, to Rashawn, Rita, and Trina via Rashawn. Carlotta was just so bossy.

"Hey!" Rashawn finally yelled into the phone. Carlotta stopped speaking abruptly.

"Who you yellin' at?" she asked, after a regrouping moment of silence.

"You! Man, you act like we are in the military. Lordy! Okay, listen. I'm not gonna be there for Thanksgiving," Rashawn said, squinting her eyes, waiting for the retribution. There was only silence. "I mean, not the whole Thanksgiving," Rashawn amended. "Okay, okay, I've met this man, see, and . . ."

"Gurl, why didn't you just say so? Do yor thang," Carlotta guffawed, loudly snorting. "Just bring him over later for some sweet-potata pie," she said, making it sound more like an order than a request.

Now she'd gone and done it. Rashawn was heated now, sweating even. Carlotta could be so intimidating.

"Uh no, see, Carlotta, we're not there yet," Rashawn reneged.

"Where are you . . . at, then?" she asked, wanting to delve deeper.

"Nowhere. We're *friends*," Rashawn said finally. "He doesn't even know I have Reggie," Rashawn admitted, not giving into the instant shame she felt.

"You haven't told him about your child? What kind of man is he for you to lie like that? "

"A friend, I told you," Rashawn went on, working hard to keep the whine out of her words. "And I didn't lie," Rashawn added.

"You gonna miss tradition for a friend? Ain't that some shit?" Carlotta said, taking a long drag off a forbidden cigarette that she pulled from the lips of Flossy, her head cook.

"Here," she said, sticking it back in Flossy's waiting

lips. She and Flossy had been friends for years. It was like that for them.

"Look Rashawn, you're a grown-ass woman and it's about time you started acting like one. I heard about your buying that condo. And frankly, I'm proud of you. I mean, you've made some dumb mistakes, having Reggie was one of them, but he's a doll and we love him. But don't make another one, okay?" Carlotta lectured.

"What are you talking about?" Rashawn asked, her patience growing thin.

"I'm saying, don't get carried away behind this man and get yourself in trouble again," Carlotta fussed. "Don't be acting like you don't have any responsibilities, like you're carefree. You're not!"

Rashawn bit her tongue. She had forgotten the lie she had told her family, the lie about Reggie's conception being due to a careless one-night stand. Realizing what Carlotta must have been thinking, Rashawn now had to hold back.

"You're right, Carlotta. And I'm hearin' you on this. Tell you what. I'll bring him by after dinner, okay?" Rashawn conceded. She was going to have to get all this straightened out one day . . . maybe soon. Maybe her life of lies was the root of all her other issues.

Carlotta huffed.

"Okay, talk to you later," came next, and then a dial tone.

Chapter 13

Clearing out her office, Rashawn gathered up all her loose files to toss in the recycle bin on her way off campus. After she returned from vacation there would be finals, and that's all there was to it.

She had to admit the last few months back in the classroom had been as easy as riding a bike. It felt good to feel in control of her class, to have a handle on everything in her life. And that's how she felt, in total control. *When she allowed herself the lie. Rashawn felt tampered with and violated.*

Her trip to the dumpster was a blur as she worked with all her might to fill her mind with pleasant thoughts. When she reached the large receptacle, she realized the lid was heavier than she anticipated.

"Damn it," she cursed, looking around now as she attempted to figure out her strategy. Just then from the darkness stepped the tall security guard with flaming red hair. Catching her off guard, she gasped. He smiled, which gave her no comfort at all.

"Hey there teach, need a hand?" he asked.

"No," she answered quickly.

Cocking his head to the side, confusion covered his face, before he opened the lip of the large dumpster.

"Sure you do," he said, grabbing at the arm full of papers she had.

Just the feel of his hot breath against her face as he closed in on her made her instantly weak, and she dropped the load she had.

"I'm sorry . . . sorry," she stammered, diving for the paper.

Red held her off as he attempted gallantry. Rashawn pulled from his touch and stood quickly, only to have Red look up at her, showing even more confusion now.

"Why you so jumpy?" he asked.

"I'm just tired," Rashawn chuckled nervously, while Red began to dump the papers and files.

"What you need is some sleep, some sweet dreamin'," he added.

"What did you say?" she asked.

Just then, Blain appeared from the shadows. "Problem?" he asked, snapping Red to attention. Blain being his supervisor commanded his respect if only for that reason.

"No. I was just helping Dr. Ams here with her trash. She was having a hard time," Red explained.

"Well, you're off your post," Blain said flatly.

Red smacked his lips in irritation and walked off without argument. Rashawn stood silently until the young man left the area. It was then she realized she was holding her breath.

"Scared?" Blain asked then.

Rashawn's eyes locked on his pools of blackness. He neither smiled nor flinched as they stared at one another for what seemed like timeless moments.

"Why would I be scared?" she asked, trying to hold on to a voice level that hid her true feelings. Blain's face broke into a smile. He slammed the top of the dumpster closed. Rashawn's tension caused her to jump with the loud crash. He noticed.

"That's right. Professor Ams is never afraid. She just pulls out her trusty piece and starts blasting," Blain teased, referring to the time Rashawn had pulled a gun on him, back when she thought Russell Thompson was following her. She felt the heat come to her face.

"I told you I was sorry about that, Blain," she said, her voice coming in a low whisper. Blain chuckled.

"Yeah, yeah, Tex, I know." he teased taking on a Southern accent, "Officer Tollome, I didn't know the gun was loaded,'" he added in high falsetto, keeping the joke going. Rashawn couldn't resist now, and burst into laughter. Blain could always bring her to laughter despite how she felt about him most of the time.

"Trina," Rashawn said into the darkness, hoping that her sister was awake. She hadn't heard any snoring so it was safe to assume she was.

"Yeah," Trina answered.

"Haven't you ever wondered who Reggie's father is?" Rashawn asked.

"I figured you didn't want to tell me so it wasn't any of my business. I did think it was strange that you haven't even told Rita."

"How do you know that I haven't told Rita?" Rashawn asked, turning toward her voice.

"Because, you know Rita. She can't hold water. If you had told her she would have told me," Trina admitted.

Rashawn chuckled, after quickly accepting that fact.

Silence came over them.

"I don't know who he is," Rashawn finally admitted. "You were right. I don't know."

Trina sighed heavily.

"I'm sorry, Rashawn. I'm sorry I said what I said to you and I'm sorry . . ." Trina began, before Rashawn heard her sobs.

"Girl, why are you crying?" she asked.

"Because, I aborted my pregnancy back in college because I didn't know who the daddy was," Trina cried. "I wasn't brave like you. I . . ." Trina explained.

"Trina, stop," whispered Rashawn loudly, trying to keep their voices at a secret level. "It's not like that," Rashawn attempted to explain.

"Yes, it is. I've never finished anything I've started, and now Jason. What is my worth?" Trina asked, sounding now as if speaking to God instead of Rashawn.

Rashawn listened on as Trina's sobs slowed to snivels.

"You are worth everything to me, Trina. I rely on you for more than you know," Rashawn admitted now.

"Yeah, I'm sure you do. I'm so good at what I do."

"You know that you are my favorite sister, right?" Rashawn said.

"Well Shelby is mine, but you come a fast second, girl," Trina replied and then chuckled, sniffing loudly, showing that her moment of self-bashing was over.

Rashawn laughed too.

Roman had been sitting for hours on the floor of the condominium, trying hard to release the old memories that came with the place, the place that was once his home. For a while, he could still hear Jasmine's laughter within these walls, see her smile as she descended the staircase—smell her scent. Sometimes when he would stand near Rashawn her aura would fill his nose, causing him to have a similar libido reaction. The sexual thought made him smile.

He was supposed to give the realtor all the keys to the condominium, as Rashawn would be taking over occupancy by the end of the month, but Roman wanted to visit this place one more time, he wanted to remember the good times one more time.

But the good times were short lived. It all went bad so quickly.

One day there was love and the next it was gone.

One minute you have people you can rely on, the next you don't. Betrayal is funny that way. One moment there is trust, the next none.

Rashawn—back when she needed his comforting words, she was there in his office begging for succor. But now, now that she had come back, falling into the arms of the first man to look her way, a man like Chance Davis, not only didn't she need him anymore, she often acted as though she despised him.

Roman gathered up the roses he had brought to pay homage to the woman he loved. It was time again to say goodnight to his memories. It was time to let Jasmine go. Just as he had told Rashawn to do, he too had to make that move forward.

Red roses were something Jasmine treasured. Even when the police found her body, they said she still had the roses in the backseat of the car.

"One day, one day you too will be in need of someone like me, Rashawn. One day you too will wake up and see me in a different light," Roman said aloud, before standing.

Chapter 14

Rashawn had always liked Pacific View. It was surely the fog capital of the world, but it didn't matter, because it was a place she enjoyed spending time. *Besides, Davis lives here,* she snickered to herself, feeling seventeen again. The last few days away from the office had her feeling better, brighter, and not too heavy burdened. Maybe she was more stressed than she realized because since having the last few days off, even her dreams were less perverted and dark.

His apartment was in a large complex at the top of a hill, just off highway 101-South. It was easy enough to find.

"You'll have to find parking across the street at the grocery store. I know that sounds ghetto, but that's just how it is," Davis had assured her.

While she drove through the supermarket parking lot across from his complex, she could see she wasn't the only one using this lot as overflow parking. With this being a holiday weekend, the lot was tight for parking and the people—nearly vicious.

It worked out. She took advantage of the store still

being open and went in to grab some Tic Tacs, her and Davis's private joke.

The parking lot, however, was nothing compared to the maze of apartments once she entered the complex on foot. Now she remembered why she enjoyed living in a house.

This was crazy living—too closed in, she thought.

Just then, she heard her name. It was Davis. He had seen her from the window and come down to the bottom of the stairs to show her the way to his front door. Taking his hand, she followed his lead to the stairs.

Inside, there were about seven or eight people, with more coming in behind her. A couple of them looked a lot like Davis, the same freckled, fair skin and soft, wavy hair.

"This is my mother, Mrs. Carmen Davis," Davis introduced respectfully. Rashawn had been correct in her assumption, having noticed her from across the room as soon as she entered. Davis looked a lot like his mother. She was a Creole woman, of that Rashawn was certain.

"My father is over there." He pointed to the corner of the large living room where his father sat playing a little boogie woogie tune on the keyboard for a couple of attentive guests.

"He thinks he's a pianist," Davis's mother said. Her voice was soft and her words articulately delivered.

Rashawn could feel her shoulders squaring off, knowing that she would have to stay on her toes. None of that ghetto stuff she was used to at parties. She was sure of that. These people were uppity, so she would have to remember who she had to be and not who she was, that was what she figured.

"My baby sister, Dera," Davis said, nearly dragging her over to a beautiful woman, completely aglow with pregnancy. She reminded Rashawn immediately of Qiana. She glowed during her pregnancy too.

"Davis, this isn't show-and-tell. Let the woman fin

her own way around," his sister scolded. She then smiled at Rashawn. "We only bite when we get really hungry, so I'm about the worst of 'em, but it's only because I'm hungry for two," she teased, obviously noticing Rashawn's tenseness.

Davis had told his sister that Rashawn wasn't shy, so it was obvious to Dera that she was nervous.

"So, who is this figgity-fine fox?" Davis and his sister groaned as cousin Cedric came through the crowd loudly inquiring about Rashawn, with an open beer in hand.

"Nobody, foo', now get on." Davis playfully pushed him away from Rashawn, who he feared would grow uncomfortable with his aggression.

"Ahh man, don't do me like that," Cedric stumbled off disappointedly.

Dera leaned in close to Rashawn. "There's always one," she said, with laughter in her voice.

The stereo came on and Davis ran over to where his father was. The two of them attempted to *Get Jiggy Wit It* along with the young folks, two or three little children about five or six years old. Just then, a teenage boy stepped up and stole the show, with unbelievable breakdancing moves, seemingly inconceivable for such a small space, but he managed them with style and a near elegance that was unmistakably *fame-in-waiting*. Dera let out a loud cackle at Davis and her father's attempts to keep up with the boy, adding to her earlier comment and comparing them to cousin Cedric.

Rashawn's first impression had been way off. She liked his family, and they seemed like they were going to like her.

Dinner was fabulous. Rashawn had never had Thanksgiving Louisiana-style. She could definitely taste the difference.

"You had some pretty slick moves there, for an old dude," Rashawn flirted with Davis while washing the last of the dishes.

He leaned in close. "I'll let you in on a secret. That's my kid brother."

"Oh, the little kid that was doing all the great dancin'?"

"Nooo, the old dude," Davis joked, letting out a cackle that matched Dera's. She could tell that when Davis was around his family he was very relaxed.

"No, seriously, the kid that was really dancin' is my little brother, Dallas," he said. "Late life thing with my parents," he went on in almost a whisper, as if the young boy's birth was a bit of an embarrassment, him being no older than fourteen or so. "But they did remember to stay with the Ds at least," he added.

"But you're not a D," she noted.

"Yeah, and that's a Chance they took, huh," he smarted off playfully. Rashawn giggled, though she had no idea what he'd meant by that statement.

"That's cool, though I think. Your brother Dallas shows your parents are still, you know . . ." Rashawn shrugged and hinted.

"They're still what?" Davis led. Rashawn winked and nodded.

"You know," she giggled.

"Ohhh, having sex," he said loudly. Rashawn looked around hoping none of the lingering guests had heard him.

"Can you stop embarrassing me?" she laughed, shoving him hard.

"I'm just giving you a hard time," he teased.

"Who's in here having sex?" Cedric, of all people, asked, barging his way into the kitchen.

He always walked as if bursting through a crowd, even when there was no one around him or in his way.

"Well, nobody now, thanks to you," Rashawn teased

catching both men off-guard. Rashawn had been re-served most of the evening, so an off-color joke was not what either man had expected. After a sharp silence, all three of them broke out into laughter.

"I'm so glad you came," Davis said to her, standing in his doorway. He was going to walk her back across the street to retrieve her car, but he had been saying good-byes to his family and guests at the door for the last fif-teen minutes, and had been stuck standing there.

"I had a wonderful time," she responded, looking out at the fireworks sunset bursting in the sky, coloring up the heavens. When she turned back, Davis was wait-ing with a warm kiss. This one was full of passion. There would be no rejection of his lips tonight. Tonight she gave in to it, moving back into the apartment. She heard the door close. Her heart was pounding, but she wasn't sure if it was just panic building, or maybe . . . just maybe . . .

Before she could decide, they were in his bedroom, tumbling onto his bed, still intertwined in passion-filled kisses. Davis's hands were all over her, caressing her, squeezing her, causing feelings all-too-forgotten to rise up. Without warning, his hands had gone under her blouse, cupping her lacy bra, filling his palms with her breasts. She froze. Her dreams came quickly to her mind and she froze. So many times in the dreams Davis had ravished her while she cried and pleaded for him to stop. Because they hadn't so much as kissed, it had been easy to reason them away when in his presence, but now the look in his eyes and the feel of his hands actually on her skin . . . it was all too much. What if this all took a bad turn, ending up like the sex in the dreams—dark and nothing less than rape?

"I can't," she blurted, her voice just above a squeak. She jumped up from the bed. "I'm not ready! I'm not ready!" she panicked. Davis, too, jumped up from the bed and quickly wrapped his arms around her in a comforting embrace.

"I'm sorry, Rashawn. I'm sorry," he pleaded. It was too late. She had gone beyond panic now and was nearly hysterical.

Davis held on tight as Rashawn gave way to all her pent-up emotions, held in since the rape. Heavy sobs racked her slender frame. So much grief over all she had lost the night the heavy stranger had violated her.

So much pain she had felt. Surely, she was damaged goods now, anyway, although the doctor had assured her she was fine—intact.

Davis could feel her anger, the angst in her fists, as they beat against his chest. He could see it in how she stomped her feet and cursed bitterly. He had to know. He had to know what was causing her pain.

"I'm sorry, Rashawn," Davis finally said, watching her sip the tea he had made once he had gotten her calm.

They sat now in front of the fireplace. The season on the bay brought the night in cooler than where she lived. It was well after midnight.

Rashawn looked at him through puffy eyes.

"I know that," she said, noticing, too, her stuffy sounding words. She grabbed another Kleenex and blew her nose hard. "I'm a philosophy major for crying out loud," she sniveled. Davis pretended to get the correlation and then just nodded.

"And I teach math," he said, handing her another Kleenex.

"What I'm saying is that I don't think I'm capable of loving anyone, not anymore."

"Why, because you don't want to have sex?" Davis asked, thinking now of Juanita. Juanita always wanted to have sex, but that wasn't love either.

And that right there truly was another story.

"I, uh . . ." Rashawn began. "I have, uh . . ." she stumbled and failed. "I've got to go," she finally said, standing.

"Rashawn, that's not fair," he said, forcing her back down to the pillows they were sitting on.

"I have some issues," she said.

"Apparently," he chuckled nervously. "But, hey, it's still very early in our relationship," he admitted. "I was just using your words against you," he said.

She was confused and it showed.

"When it's right, you show it right off," he said, smiling. Rashawn felt the heat come up to her face.

"Davis, I . . ."

"Take a chance, Rashawn," he said, using his name as a witticism to his statement. She smiled weakly and fell into his arms, feeling safe.

Something bad had happened to this woman and he regretted that. But whatever it was, it wasn't his fault. However, he would sure like to find out whose fault it was and pop his face inside out!

"Tonight could have been really bad for our relationship," he said, leading her to his guest room.

"What do you mean?"

"Let's just say that I'm shooting a bit higher than sex for us," he admitted. Rashawn, who was still blowing her nose, was caught mid sniffle, staring now into Davis's caring eyes.

Yes, Chance Davis was turning into quite the find.

"I need to call my family," she sniveled.

"The phone is over there," he said, pointing to the cordless.

Davis hadn't meant to eavesdrop, but hearing Rashawn through the door of the spare room, hearing her doing all that sweet-talking to that Reggie person, well, he didn't have to be hit with a rock.

Apparently, Rashawn had a lot of unfinished business.

Rashawn wasn't home.

He'd called twice.

How could she just not have Thanksgiving with her family?

What's happened to her sense of loyalty?

Doc had waited until way after midnight, way after all had eaten dinner and left to go home.

All of Rashawn's family, he felt he knew them. Carlotta, her husband and their kids; Ta'Rae, her husband and kid; and, of course, those friends from down the street, the white guy with the black wife and their little boy—what a cute kid he was, tall and lanky. Even for a toddler you could tell he had football or basketball written all over him.

Doc found himself smiling at the thought of fatherhood.

His half-imagined life with Rashawn and a baby, a family taking over his thoughts.

"Yeah right," he said, giving in to the reality of his solitude.

"Me? A family man? Not hardly, but I do want that woman," he went on in his one-sided conversation, referring to his lust for Rashawn. He'd wanted Rashawn for a long time . . . long before he actually accepted it. There was something familiar about her. Perhaps it was just her resemblance to Jasmine that set him on fire . . . and Jasmine had set him on fire. Hell, Jasmine had burned down his whole world. But Rashawn was different, he could tell—or maybe he just wanted her to be.

He looked in his rearview mirror again at the little family heading down the street—the white man and his black wife, along with their child. He finally shook his head free of those silly thoughts and, against his better judgment, took a drive out to Pacific View. He drove around the crowded complex and then through the parking lot across the street.

Doc had only gone to the parking lot to see if they had an all-night coffeehouse or liquor store he could hit before staking out Chance Davis's place. He wanted some answers and figured that by watching Davis for a while, he might get some. But instead of finding an open market, he saw her car. Rashawn's car!

Rashawn's car was in the parking lot across from Davis's place.

Now Doc knew for sure that she was inside Davis's apartment. What would a woman be doing in a man's apartment at three in the morning? What in the hell would 'his' woman be doing in Chance Davis's apartment—period? Just the thought of it enraged him.

He was getting tired of Davis and his backstabbing ways, moving in on *his* woman when, in fact, Davis was still bumping his ex-wife.

"Just plain ol' greedy," Doc said under his breath.

You see, there wasn't much that went on, on that campus that Doc wasn't aware of. It was his job to know everything. Perhaps misdirected, but albeit a reality for Doc, Rashawn Ams was his business too. And she was making his job difficult.

Doc was her self-appointed guardian and her rebelliousness and insistence on breaking the rules was really starting to tick him off.

Maybe if she would just agree to be his woman, keeping track of her would be a lot easier. But no. It was almost as if she enjoyed the little cat and mouse game.

The way she was acting, Doc believed that she truly did deserve all that had happened to her.

No, he didn't feel sorry for her trifflin' ass at all. "Bitch," he mumbled under his breath as two snorts of cocaine went up his nostrils.

He stepped out of his car and started into the complex. The drug now gave him intentions that went beyond his thoughts. He figured he would know what to do when he got to Davis's door. Perhaps he'd drag her out by her thick hair. She deserved that much at the very least for playing with his emotions.

However, before reaching the middle of the complex, Doc saw something afoul going on near the back dumpster. He just couldn't ignore it.

After all, he was a decent man.

He approached the young men. "What's going on here?" he asked.

"What's it to you, ol' dude?" asked one of the boys, stepping forward boldly.

Doc grabbed the boy off his feet, slamming him into the side of the dumpster, holding him by the neck. One of the other boys bravely took a step forward to help out his comrade only to be stopped by the rush of heat coming from Doc's nostril's as they flared. "You want some of this?" he asked the boy, to which the boy quickly shook his head in answer and ran off, on the heels of the first deserter.

Blood covered Doc's fist as he took out the frustration he felt on the boy's face.

Perhaps, in the darkness, the boy had miscalculated the man behind the voice, or maybe he just thought a little too highly of himself. Either way, there could have been no way the boy had bargained for what he got.

Rashawn barely slept. Davis's spare room was not as comfortable as she had fantasized it would be. She found herself wide awake, listening to the sirens and commotion going on, all of what seemed to be right outside the window.

Chapter 15

The weekend was spent making up to Reggie. Rashawn felt guilty over neglecting him, and her family, on Thanksgiving. She felt guilty about a lot of things where Reggie was concerned.

"What was I thinking trying to have a relationship?" she confessed to Qiana as they walked the mall with Reggie, riding along in his stroller. Rashawn had just finished telling Qiana about the disastrous Thanksgiving spent with Chance Davis.

"Rashawn, I just think you have been trying to get your old life back, and well, frankly, your old life is gone," Qiana said bluntly. "You need to just wipe your slate clean and just start over from today. Be Reggie's mother and forget all the rest."

Rashawn turned them into the Disney store, instead of their usual haunt—Beatrice's Drawers.

"I saw something in here I wanted to get for Reggie," Rashawn admitted. Qiana giggled under her breath—lingerie vs. Disney Store. Yes, Rashawn had changed and she didn't even realize how much.

"I'm not saying you're not a good mother. I think you are. But I just think when you got back here, you thought everyone was expecting something from you that we're not," Qiana continued to analyze. "I think you were trying to live up to being who you were and you're not."

"I'm not? By the way, who was I?" Rashawn asked, sounding tongue-in-cheek, while eyeing the toys, waiting to see which one Reggie would go for first.

"Rashawn, the uh . . ." Qiana looked down at Reggie and then mouthed the word Bitch, ". . . Doctor" she went on full voice.

"Oh my God, Qiana," Rashawn gasped, bursting into laughter.

"I never knew you felt like that," Rashawn went on, trying to contain her amusement at Qiana's boldness.

"You were always so sure of yourself, so in control about everything. I mean, yeah, sometimes we wanted to see you fall. I did at least," Qiana admitted. "And then when you came up pregnant from your," Qiana made quotation marks in the air, "one-night-stand," she whispered. "I was like, ah ha, a weakness," Qiana went on.

"But then instead, I'm still the Joan of Arc," Rashawn sighed, realizing something deep about herself.

"I'm not saying all that. I'm just saying you need to stop shutting people out. You need to get up off that high horse of yours and start letting people in. Quit acting like you can handle everything, when it's more than obvious you aren't handling anything very well," Qiana said, taking a duplicate of Reggie's toy choice and showing it to the counterperson so as not to cause Reggie to have a fit by taking his new 'best friend' from him. "You are gonna have to let us in."

"Well, you lost me there," Rashawn said after paying for the toy. They had walked out of the store, headed now for the food court.

"You are gonna have to let the past go so we can have you back. Talk to somebody about it, besides me. Get some help letting it go," Qiana suggested, showing a little caution in her words. Rashawn caught it. "I mean, now that I know there really is something to let go of, I can see you haven't let go of it."

"Let it go?" Rashawn asked.

"Yes, let it go. I can tell you are not letting the past go. You are just letting it ruin your life and I'm here to tell you this, girlfriend of mine, if I can do it, you can, too," Qiana said, without looking at her, taking her tray from the counter and sliding it along the Panda Express serving line.

"That's so funny you say that. My shrink told me to do the very same thing."

"Your shrink?"

"Yeah, the school shrink. I've tried not to see him . . . ever, but after you told me about . . ." Rashawn paused, "you know who not being Reggie's father, well."

"I can understand. But if he told you to move on and get past this, then he's the man with the right information."

Rashawn shrugged reluctantly.

"I talked to Nigel about what happened that night. More than once, I talked about it, and he talked about it, too. We cried and got it out of our systems. Wow, that was a life saver," Qiana sighed heavily. "A relationship saver, too," she went on.

Rashawn thought about Qiana's words all evening. Tomorrow she would be moving into her own home. She and Reggie would be living alone for the first time. Maybe Qiana was right and she didn't need to be emotionally alone as well. Perhaps she should bring someone into her world. Maybe Carlotta was right and Reggie did need a father. This entire attempt at acting like the strong, untouchable, invincible woman she used to be was making things worse than even believable. Finding a balance was going to be the key.

Looking at the clock, Rashawn decided to call Davis and ask him for another chance. He wasn't in.

Juanita added the final touches to her look. She knew she looked absolutely delicious. And not a moment too soon either, as the doorbell sounded telling her that Davis had arrived.

Once more, she passed a glance at her fabulous reflection.

"Gurl, you sho 'nuff got it like that," she whispered, blowing herself a kiss, and then changing her expression to a downtrodden one, she went to the door.

"Thank you for coming over," Juanita sighed heavily.

"Well, life and death and all that," Davis said, walking into what had once been his home.

He looked around, noting her new husband's presence there—tennis rackets, exercise equipment, etc. It bugged him to no end that Juanita was with this punk kid, but he would never tell her that. "I still can't believe I'm here," he said, settling in on the sofa, his sofa. She handed him a drink before making herself comfortable as well.

"I can't believe you never changed any of the furniture," he finally said, unable to keep his curiosity under wraps.

Juanita was sitting in the corner of the large piece of furniture. She always used to sit there. She enjoyed the way the sofa caressed her.

Such a sensual woman, Davis thought now, looking at her, small, helpless, and lonely.

STOP!

He ordered himself to shake off the trance her gray eyes were placing on him as she pulled her knees up to her chest. Davis glanced at her freshly painted toes. She saw him looking and stretched out her shapely leg as if it was an unconscious movement. Her foot brushed against his thigh.

"I was alone for Thanksgiving this year," she sighed again, overly dramatic this time.

Davis wasn't fooled at all. He sat down his drink and adjusted himself on the comfortable sofa. He didn't want to get too comfortable. She was crafty and he knew he needed to be on guard.

"Now, about Yvette, I wonder why she wasn't home when I went over there."

"Dunno," Juanita purred, fighting his attempts to avoid her obvious allure. It was a full out war—Davis of the 'Northern Plane' against Davis of the 'Southern Extremities'. Her foot, now in his lap, inched its way higher. He went to push it off.

"Nita, come on. I want to talk about this thing with Yvette. I mean, she's given you permission to discuss it with me, so let's discuss it," Davis argued weakly, noticing his hand around her small ankle.

Out of reflex, or maybe juju, he kissed her small tattoo—a sexy Spanish Rose tattoo—there on her ankle, and then pulled her closer to him, kissing his way up her leg until he had her sarong hiked up high enough to reveal all he had been missing on an everyday basis these last couple of years.

This hit it and then miss it stuff needs to stop.

"Make me cum," she requested bluntly, her voice heavy with sexual intent.

Davis's mind said 'no' but his lips, filled with hers, could not utter the words.

Soon Juanita had Davis out of his shirt, massaging his chest and shoulders. She was urging him to reciprocate her chest and shoulders as well.

What a comfortable piece of furniture, Davis remembered as he pulled the naked Juanita under him. She was more than ready for him, and he was way past ready for her. It'd been over three months since Davis had fallen for this ploy of hers.

Juanita's birthday.

His mind ran across Rashawn for only a second before Juanita's sexual magic upon his body emptied his head of everything except her performance beneath him.

At the pinnacle of his climax, she moved upward on the sofa. Masterfully, and with full control, she guided him into her, working him over until she began to cry out in her own ecstasy.

It wasn't unusual for her to experience multiple orgasms before he released, but tonight was different. Tonight she screamed out his name as if he were literally her last chance. Tonight, she acted as if she could not continue unless he pumped air into her—hard and fast. Tonight, Juanita had Chance believing she truly did love him.

Flipping her over, Chance pulled out all the stops. He was like a kid enjoying a once in a lifetime trip to Disneyland. There was no ride he wouldn't try. And Juanita had strapped him in tight.

Finally, while on the floor, Davis's body could take no more, and the relief he felt was tremendous.

In his failed attempt to pull out before the explosion, he now finished his ejaculation on Juanita's chest as she squeezed his pulsating member between her firm breasts.

She was freaking him tonight, and he loved it all. Sliding him, still half-erect, into her mouth, she worked him until he was hard again. Davis could only feel now as his voice had been taken by Juanita's bewitching magic. His thoughts too were taken by her evil sex. She was casting a spell as she scratched and purred.

Biting him and digging in her nails, she climbed on his back, humping him as if roles had been reversed and she was now the man. Davis knew, deep inside, that Juanita would have given anything to be a man for a day—to have the sexual power and prowess of a man. Juanita would give anything to have the upper hand right now, to make him scream out her name as she had her way with him, as a man.

She then rolled him over and climbed on top, moving over his body until she hovered over his lips, lowering herself until he could barely reach her molting cauldron with the tip of his tongue. She would gasp with each quick flick and eager lick she would allow him to have. Finally, half-insane with passion, he grabbed her hips, pulling her down on his waiting 'kiss'. Never had Juanita tasted so sweet. Never had he been so crazy for her.

It had never been this way for them as husband and wife, so why now? Why now, when he was at the pinnacle of a new life, a new love with Rashawn? He began to wonder this as he then cursed her, slamming her onto the thick shag carpet, mounting her, and with nothing less than primal passion, driving his thick, hot hardness into her. Her eyes rolled back in her head as she arched upward, giving him his way, which he took.

Together they climaxed this time, holding onto each other for dear life. Davis did not attempt to pull out, and Juanita didn't care.

He began to think, while listening to her heavy breathing as she rested on his chest. *Why now?*

Without answering himself or asking Juanita to explain her superior display of gratification, he moved her from him and quickly dressed. Something uncomfortable stirred in him, urging him to get out of there.

Juanita tied the last knot in her sarong only moments before the door opened and her husband walked in.

Any sooner and the three of them could have qualified for the next reality TV show, Davis thought, catching the wicked grin come to Juanita's lips before she kissed her husband's cheek.

Any other man would have sensed that his woman had just thoroughly been sexed, but not this guy. Perhaps the flush on her cheeks was a common condition for her, as young as he was. Perhaps the smell of male sex on her breath and hands were commonplace.

"What an idiot," Davis said out loud as he stepped off the porch. He was referring to Juanita's young husband and the rest of the evening spent at that house, the house that used to be his home, with the woman who used to be his wife. Davis could not believe that Juanita's husband could not smell the masculine lingering that was not his own.

"What an idiot! Couldn't he tell?" Davis went on, before bursting into laughter at his next thought. "Unless Juanita bottles that shit and sprays it around everyday." He chuckled.

Reaching for his cell phone as he walked out to his car, he called Rashawn. As her number rang, his conscience pricked him and he hung up.

What kind of a playboy was he turning out to be? Had he really excused his indiscretions with Juanita as acceptable behavior? What kind of man was he? What kind of devil woman was Juanita?

"I am so not worthy, Rashawn," he sighed now, giving in to the fact that he indeed had an illness, a disease possibly an incurable case of the *Juanitas.*

Just then, Davis was hit with a shocking sight, worse than Juanita's husband. All four of his tires were slashed.

Her blonde hair was shiny, even now, as it lay spread out in a silky fan around her head. Flakes of red were speckled throughout. *What a bright red*, he thought now

He wasn't a violent man. This whole thing had gone against his nature.

At first, the sight of her moved his stomach to near nausea, but within minutes, he had recovered.

Looking at his hands, he wanted them to cry out innocence. He wanted them to save him from the truth. However, he knew he'd come here to kill her.

She was ruining everything.

Her screaming over the phone-threatening exposure, shouting and blaming everyone for the responsibility of her pregnancy, had only fueled the fire.

Now Yvette Furhman would never blame anyone again, especially someone with so much to lose.

Bending over her, he called her name softly, hoping, hoping deep inside that she truly saw him through those open eyes that stared so blankly. But she said nothing. She was dead.

Actually this was going to work out just fine. This was going to make things better.

He left her there in a pool of her own blood.

Chapter 16

The next morning was moving day. It was a day filled with mixed emotions.

Davis was unavailable to help. He sent his apologizes via an early morning phone call. Rashawn was both embarrassed and irritated at her new 'boyfriend' being a no-show.

"We'll just do the best we can," Trina said bravely, hoisting the large box onto the truck. "Just pull ya thong up and let's go," Trina smarted, giggling all the while.

Too much radio, Rashawn thought, shaking her head at her offbeat sister. Trina was getting worse everyday.

"I cannot believe everybody got tied up this way," Rashawn pouted now, thinking of Nigel and Terrell working at their office—on a Saturday.

They were interviewing a female attorney they wanted to take on as a partner. Rita had smirked at the mention of her and the possibilities of her being with Terrell and Nigel in that tiny office they had.

"Why she got to be female, the heffa," Rita had barked, sounding harsh and ghetto, while following Terrell around fussing at him after he got off the phone. The love shack was changing. Over the last couple of weeks, the only sounds coming from Terrell and Rita's room were the sounds of Rita's barking, about everything and everybody.

Speaking of Rita, she suddenly walked out to the truck in her house shoes, robe, and hair in rollers. She was carrying with her a brimming cup of hot coffee.

"I can help!" she fussed. Rashawn and Trina eyed her up and down.

"You can go back in the house," Trina snickered.

"Quickly," Qiana chuckled, stepping onto the ramp, trying to get some kind of leverage so Rashawn could hand her a box.

"Rita, I need you to watch Reggie," Rashawn said to her, hoping to absolve her of any guilt she might be feeling for not lending a hand in the move. Everyone always chipped in when there was a move. This was Rashawn's first one, and no one was there. The irony was obvious.

"Why is everyone treating me like I'm handicapped? Ugh!" Rita growled, tossing her coffee into the bushes and storming back into the house.

Just then, Rashawn felt Qiana tapping her on the shoulder.

"Who's that?" she asked, drawing Rashawn's attention to a Cadillac Escalade pulling up in front of Auntie's house.

The shiny SUV looked fresh from the showroom, as it pulled up slowly and parked.

Rashawn's chest tightened when the door opened and Blain stepped out.

"Oh my God," Trina gasped. Rashawn could clearly see that she was impressed by Blain's bulk. Maybe Qiana was a little, too, because she just stared in silence as he approached the truck with his slow, commanding strides, while taking a toothpick from his breast pocket and tucking it in his cheek.

"Hello, Professor," he greeted, smiling broadly while removing his dark glasses and running his hand over his smooth head. Trina gasped again, no doubt falling prey to Blain's dark eyes. She apparently missed seeing him the night he 'aided' Jason in his hasty exit from the house.

"Hello, Officer Tollome," Rashawn greeted coolly.

If the others didn't know how Rashawn felt about this man before, the brisk chill that suddenly filled the air should have made it instantly very clear.

"What the heck are you doing here?" she asked bluntly, holding back any stronger language that wanted to come out.

"Just happened by," Blain answered, giving Trina a quick wink.

"How did . . ." Rashawn began, interrupted then by Trina's flirting body language, nudging her slightly, moving her forward.

"Don't be rude," Trina whispered.

"What's going on here?" Blain asked, tucking his shades in the top button of his well-fitted Polo shirt, rolling the toothpick to the other side of his mouth.

"Nothing we can't handle. Thanks," Rashawn said, turning back to the truck.

"She means nothing you can't handle," Trina said, pointing at one of the larger boxes on the lawn. He quickly and effortlessly picked it up, cradling it in muscular arms.

Trina burst into a coquettish giggle when he, in three steps, took the ramp with the box. Rashawn caught Qiana's eye as she watched the massive figure brush past her.

"See, this is what I'm talking about," Rashawn mouthed and then followed Blain up the ramp.

* * *

Rashawn knew she would have to explain the statement later as she had never mentioned Blain to Qiana.

"Look, Blain, we really do have a handle on this. I mean, I'm sure you were on your way somewhere," Rashawn pleaded, hoping he would get the hint and leave.

"Nope," he answered, flashing his beautiful smile. He then asked with sarcasm showing heavily, "Where's your man, by chance?"

Rashawn was instantly irritated.

Just then, Rita burst from the house, still looking raggedy.

"Shawnie, Reggie is calling for you!" she screamed, using no tact. Rashawn's stomached tightened. "He won't get outta the bed unless you come in here," she went on, failing to notice Blain's reaction to the announcement.

"Reggie?" he asked. However, Rashawn ignored his inquiry. She simply bounced from the truck with no further conversation.

When she returned about fifteen minutes later, her large bedroom set that Terrell and Nigel had managed to get as far as the lawn before abandoning, had been loaded along with the larger boxes, and Blain was gone.

Trina was sitting behind the wheel of Rashawn's car, and Qiana was in the passenger seat of the U-Haul truck. Rashawn looked up and down the street for Blain.

"Oh, honey, he's gone. He wanted to go with us, but after you blew up his boat, I was like, 'sorry, baby, but you got to take the next one,'" Trina said, chuckling at her made up euphemism. "The gurl blew it up!" she repeated, starting the car.

Rashawn just smirked, sucking the air through her teeth.

* * *

Nigel, Terrell, and a good friend of theirs, Smithy, wrestled the last piece of heavy furniture into the condominium. They had kept their promise and hurried over to Rashawn's to finish moving as soon as they'd ended the meeting with their potential new partner.

"Where do you want this?" Terrell huffed, giving the roll-top desk a slap—just punishment for it being so heavy.

"Over there," Rashawn pointed.

The men looked at each other and frowned.

"What's in this?" Terrell growled now, pulling hard on the locked top drawer, forcing the small lock to become detached. "Oopsy," he snickered, embarrassed at his brutality toward the piece of furniture. That was when he noticed the gun.

"What is this?" he asked, pulling it out quickly. Rashawn hurried over and grabbed it from him.

The room was silent as everyone and everything seemed to stop moving and focus on the weapon in Rashawn's hand.

"What is that, Rashawn?" Terrell asked again, firmer this time, sounding like the big brother Rashawn didn't have.

"It's a gun, T, what does it look like?" Rita blurted, stepping forward and taking the gun from Rashawn's frozen grip. She looked it over.

"And not a very big one either. Didn't daddy teach you anything? If you gonna get a gun, get a real one," she smarted off. Terrell looked at Rita.

"And what do you know about guns?" he asked.

"You jump bad with me, Mr. McAlister, and you'll find out," she barked.

Smithy burst into laughter, which broke the growing tension.

"I say Rita may be correct, however," Smithy began, his words already deep and sounding full of wisdom.

Everyone now focused on him as he stepped forward, taking the gun from Rita.

"This .22 wouldn't stop much, unless you were right there. I mean, right up in his face," Smithy went on, holding the gun flush against his own chest. At that point, Rashawn had heard and seen enough. She quickly excused herself and went into the kitchen.

She could hear them all now discussing the type of gun she should purchase to replace the one she had. No one bothered to ask why she had it in the first place.

Finally, Trina came into the kitchen where she was. Neither of them spoke, for the sisterhood between them said it all. Rashawn just looked at her and smiled weakly.

"I love you, Shawnie. And whoever it is you're scared of, you don't have to be scared anymore. I'll kick their ass. Tae-bo," Trina said winking, after a swift low kick. Rashawn, fighting emotion, just grinned and gave her a tight hug.

Chapter 17

The drug was getting out of control, even from where Doc sat. It was being used in ways he had not intended, and by people he hadn't expected to use it.

There were many addicted to the drug. That he knew. But he was hearing more and more reports around the campus of this drug being used, misused, and things were going to be ugly. Yvette Furhman was a good example of things getting out of hand. "And now look . . ." he grumbled.

He'd halted sales of the Get Ass drug until things blew over a little, cooled off a little with this Yvette thing. Now he just had to get Red and Leon under control. He'd been neglecting his *partners*, chasing behind that *woman*, Rashawn . . . he needed to get focused again.

That's going to be fun, he added to his list of distressful thoughts. "Those fools are gonna make me have to hurt them," he confessed.

"Why do you always have to hurt people, Doc?" Blain asked. "Why is that the first thing you come up with as a solution?"

"I can't believe you asked me that. Since when have we ever been able to reason with someone without force, without just a little power behind our words?" Doc explained, holding out his large hands to emphasize his point. Blain looked down at his hands and shook his head.

"Still, there's got to be another way to reach people, to get their attention."

"Like you've managed to get Rashawn Ams' attention," Doc snickered wickedly.

"Why you gotta bring that up?"

"I don't know, just felt like the right thing to say at this juncture," Doc smarted.

"Well shut the fuck up and mind your own damn business," Blain growled.

"Testy," Doc teased and then with all seriousness he asked, "Have you thought any more about the boy?"

"What about the boy?"

"He's your family. You have a right . . ."

"It's not that easy."

"It would be that easy for me."

"You let me handle Rashawn, and you just mind Maceba. She's riding your ass like she's your new playmate or something."

"She don't wanna play with me," Doc assured and then burst into wicked laughter. Blain just shook his head.

"Just be careful, Doc."

"No, you be careful."

Maceba didn't expect to see Blain when she got to the bar. It had been a local hang out for many on the force, however, Blain wasn't one to socialize with the Feds or the INL agents. He barely hung out with other cops. He spotted her immediately and fanned her over to his table.

It took a minute for her to realize that she was in fact, smiling. He was like a drug.

"What brings you here?" she asked.

"I realized I was rude to you the last time we spoke. I acted badly during our last encounter."

"Yeah, but then I mean . . ."

"No now, I acted out for no good reason and I want to apologize to you," he explained, holding up his hands in surrender.

"And you plan to apologize, how?"

Blain touched her hand gently. She didn't pull away.

"I just did." He smiled.

Maceba chuckled, feeling the heat on her face.

The waitress brought Blain's drink and took her order, which he quickly paid for.

"So, what do you want to talk about?"

"Why do we have to talk about anything?" he asked.

Maceba looked around at the couples talking and the other agents relaxing, drinking . . . taking the edge off. She had to wonder about her lack of balance where her job was concerned, or maybe it was more than that. Maybe it was her obsession with finding the man who had attacked her that had her thinking about work after hours.

"I just don't think I'll ever be happy again, well until I find him," she admitted after sipping on her second drink.

"Maybe he's dead," Blain suggested, shrugging slightly. Maceba chuckled.

"Yeah, right. I could only hope."

"You hate him, don't you?"

"Of course I do. Wouldn't you? I mean someone attacked you and tried to kill you," she explained. "If what that person did to you was so evil that the memory of it controlled all your thoughts, invaded your dreams, if every waking minute you thought about them and what they did to you."

Blain's eyes glazed over as if her words were beyond his understanding. "But then I guess you can't relate," Maceba said, noticing.

"It's not that I can't relate. I can totally relate. It's just, I mean, my job is to serve and protect, so no, I don't ever think about someone hurting me, controlling me. I mean . . ." he shrugged again, "I mean, I'm not easily controlled," he joked.

"You think you're sort of . . . uncontrollable?" she asked, almost teasingly.

Maybe it was the alcohol.

Their eyes met for a moment. "I'm human," he then answered, showing offense at her sarcasm.

"I didn't imply you weren't."

"I'm not a freak. I'm a man," he grumbled, downing his drink and fanning the waitress over again.

Maceba looked at the large man. *His soft eyes cried out to be loved.*

Blain was a lonely man. Maceba knew loneliness when she saw it. The two of them were very similar in a lot of ways. Of this Maceba was certain. No one understood her drive and ambition, her quest for knowledge. And she was certain that no one understood Blain at all. How could they? He was a confusing man. *Hard to read.*

The dim lights and mood of the room lent itself to relaxation, and Maceba wanted to give in to it. She wanted to end this sparring with Blain. She wanted, just for a moment, to get to know him better.

"Let's dance," she requested, sounding totally impulsive.

Blain was a good dancer—smooth and surprisingly full of rhythm.

Or maybe she had just stereotyped him and assumed the worst. Anything was better than what she had imagined from the big 'white boy'.

The guys from the agency there didn't seem bothered at all by his presence, as if it was almost natural for them to be together, at least that's what Maceba wanted to think.

God I hate being lonely, Maceba admitted to herself, feeling Blain's large hands on her neck, and massaging just the right places. She allowed him to touch her breasts.

It had been a long time since she'd allowed him to get this close, since she'd allowed anyone to.

And now they were in her apartment. "I thought you were seeing somebody," Maceba said, her words coming breathy and barely showing control. Blain didn't answer as he now nibbled on her earlobe, creeping closer to her lips. "I thought . . ."

"You think too much," he mumbled, covering her mouth with his, his tongue and hers volleying for control. He groped her more now as she grew moist and eager, despite the inner fight to resist. She didn't know why she allowed it, but for a moment it felt right and now she felt nearly out of control, and she couldn't have that.

"I have to keep sharp. This case is driving me crazy," she admitted aloud, unbuttoning his shirt, trying to fight her growing passion for him. He was like opium— one taste and she was going to be hooked. Yet, just like the flower, he was beautiful, irresistible.

"Why you letting it? The answers are right in front of you." He closed his eyes as if giving in to her growing enthusiasm as her hands ran up and down his back.

"Why do you say that?" she asked, allowing his hands to wander a bit more, catching her breath as he reached between her thighs, separating her legs wide.

"Why are you asking me questions when I'm trying to take care of some more pressing matters?" he asked, tearing her quickly from her panties, inhaling her scent before tossing the torn fabric to the floor.

When he turned back to her, the darkness of his eyes caused fear to course through her. He slowly wrapped his large hand around her neck, squeezing slightly. She grabbed his wrist tightly.

"Feel the power, baby?" Blain asked while unbuckling his belt with his free hand.

She swallowed hard, her pulse rapidly beating, lightening her head slightly.

"Tell me what you know," she begged her voice just about a whisper.

"I know I'm about to fuck-you-blind," Blain chuckled, readying himself to take her.

"No, tell me what you know about Doc."

Blain's grip on her neck tightened just a bit before he suddenly released her. She couldn't help but sigh in relief.

"You sure know how to change a man's mood," he admitted with a frustrated chuckle.

"You brought me here to question me, didn't you? You wanted to catch me off guard to get information, huh?" he asked, putting himself back together while shaking his head in disgust.

Maceba too showed the end of a 'mood' between them, sitting up on the couch, smoothing down her short skirt, and crossing her legs tightly.

"I just figured that if we were in a more comfortable setting you would feel more relaxed. And since you did say you wanted to make up for . . ."

"Such a cheater," he laughed, standing quickly and gathering his jacket.

"Let's talk, Blain. We're on the same side."

"No. And for the record, I'm on my side, unlike some people I know."

Doc found the whole thing funny and laughed all the way home, despite Blain's misery.

It was hell living with such a maniac like him, but Blain didn't know what else to do.

"You're stuck with me. Now about Rashawn . . ." Doc started in.

"I don't want to talk about her."

Chapter 18

The week crept by slowly. Living alone was becoming a fast disappointment for Rashawn. Every night she was unnerved by the new sounds of her home. She was constantly looking in closets and pantries, finding herself jumping at the slightest sounds. She'd even gone so far as to change the locks, but it hadn't helped much in easing her mind.

Getting home from the university, she unlocked the door with her new door key. It felt unfamiliar and ill-fitting to the lock. She missed the Palemos already; however, there was no way she was going to admit that to Rita, Trina, Qiana, or anyone else. She had her pride.

The condominium was comfortable. She had to admit that. It was surely private, and that's what she wanted. But still she felt watched.

Reggie ran inside. He had adjusted quickly to his new surroundings. Rashawn envied that quality in children.

"Maybe it's just me," she thought aloud. Even in Atlanta, she had felt a little uneasy, unsettled. There had continued to be a dark clouded feeling hanging over her head, a watched feeling. Every piece of unusual mail that came set her on edge, and she would toss it in the trash without even opening it. No one knew she was in Atlanta, except for family. Therefore, she questioned her reason for receiving mail from anyone except family. Then again, who would be looking for her? Who cared?

Just then the doorbell rang, Rashawn noticeably jumped. She chuckled at her nervousness and then went to answer it.

"Dr. Roman!" she exclaimed upon seeing Allen Roman at her door. Dressed casually in a dark turtleneck and black slacks, he looked relaxed, yet his eyes danced nervously.

"Hello there, Ms. Ams. And please, call me Allen. I wanted to stop by to see how you're enjoying the condo. I'm sure the realtor has called and all that, but I wanted to give you a personal . . ." he stammered while searching for the right words, "Hello . . . I guess you could say." He smiled.

From behind him, he pulled a bouquet of fresh flowers—red roses. It was a beautiful arrangement, which immediately affected her. Suddenly, however, her loosened guard tightened when Reggie ran into the living room where they stood. Roman's eyes were immediately transfixed on him. With raised cockles and bulldog reflexes, Rashawn grabbed Reggie up, dropping the flowers in the trade off. She had intercepted Roman's reach for him, and with almost a growl, the word *no* came from her lips. The moment between them grew tense for a second or two before both of them, clearing their throats and the air, decided to speak.

"No, go ahead, I'm sorry . . ." Rashawn began. Roman, shaking his head, just smiled, still gazing lovingly at Reggie.

"It's just that he's such a lovely child. I had no idea," he said, outstretching his large hand to touch him. Rashawn pulled Reggie slightly outside his reach.

"I don't take him out very much. I mean, he's just a baby," Rashawn excused her overly protective ways.

"Oh, I perfectly understand," said Roman forgivingly. His body language invited him further into the condominium. He picked up the flowers and started toward the kitchen to put them in water. Caught off guard by his forwardness, Rashawn hurried behind him.

"I can do that," she insisted. He fanned her on.

"Not a problem. Roses always looked so nice in this kitchen. Where did you put the vases?" he asked, looking around as if she had come into 'his' kitchen and moved things around.

"I don't have any vases," she admitted.

Reggie began to laugh at the conversation they were having. Again, Roman seemed mesmerized with him. Rashawn wanted him to leave.

"Why are you here?" she asked.

"I told you. To check on you," he answered flatly while improvising a holder for the flowers out of one of Rashawn's glass containers.

"Well, thank you, I guess," she said, trying hard to relax. Seeing Roman off the campus was hard for her to get comfortable with. Having him in her home was nearly impossible to accept.

She sat Reggie down and he ran off toward the den where his toys were kept. When she turned back, her eyes met Roman's. He was standing in her space, her comfort zone. So close, in fact, she could feel his body heat, smell his cologne, and sense his growing passion. For a split second, Rashawn thought he might kiss her. She stepped back an inch or two.

"Do you know who his father is yet?" he asked, his voice low and covert. Rashawn's stomach tightened.

"I told you he's dead," she answered quickly in the same tone.

"Oh, so you did," he responded, throwing caution to the wind. Rashawn's distress came quickly.

"Look, I'm not comfortable with this conversation," she snapped, turning away from him.

"Of course you're not. How thoughtless of me," Roman admitted, looking everywhere but into her eyes.

"I would like for you to leave," she requested now.

Her words came out softly, but her meaning was clear. He nodded, showing shame and embarrassment. Rashawn led him quickly back into the living room, to the front door.

"Rashawn, I do know your pain and I want you to know that anytime you feel like talking, my door is always open," he offered. Rashawn opened the door, and without looking at him, gestured for him to leave.

"Well, mine is not. And please, please don't call on me again," she requested. He agreed with a nod of his head.

After closing the door and bolting it, Rashawn went to the roses in the kitchen. The card was from the same florist as the others that were delivered to her over the last couple of months.

"At least these crazies have some good taste," she sighed, taking the roses from the jar and shaking the water from the bottom. She opened the trash receptacle, prepared to toss yet another beautiful arrangement, when suddenly she stopped herself.

"Shawnie, come on now, what did he ever do to you?" she asked herself. Then, with a shake of her head, she put the roses back in the water and took Reggie upstairs to get him ready for bed.

Nothing much had gone well over the last two months. That stupid white boy getting the bad dope, Red going wild, terrorizing the college campus, bringing the unwelcome attention from Maceba Baxter and this whole Yvette Furhman thing, and last but not least, his personal life. All of this had Doc in bad humor.

He hated when his world was disturbed. He tried hard to be a positive person. Working constantly, trying not to overreact when people refused to do things his way. However, he hated when people fought him, talked back, rejected him, or just plain 'got on his nerves'. Doc hated when people had the audacity to question his power.

Way beyond tense, he could barely manage a 'normal' day in his 'normal' world.

Normal life? How did I let this happen? he asked himself. *And these idiots, these stupid people are driving me to drink. How in the hell did I let myself get surrounded by so many idiots?* he thought, watching Leon and Red while they argued again.

"But you didn't have to go back and clean up after me. I told you I took care of him," Leon said.

"Yeah, but your way of taking care of him was kinda, you know, sloppy," Red said, smirking.

Doc then moved his toothpick to the other side of his wide mouth, closing his full lips around it.

"Not smart, dude," Red teased.

"Like beating him up was. Asshole," Leon griped.

"Fuck you, prick!" Red snapped, raising his voice a little, his words causing a sharp silence to radiate.

Leon then spoke, "And then you go and cut up that girl!" Leon snapped, raising his voice.

"I didn't kill her. I keep telling you that. When I left, she was alive," Red defended.

"Save it for the jury, man," Leon said, sounding flat. "The cops are already starting to investigate this shit. You can't just go killing people without cleaning up after yourself. Didn't your mama teach you that?"

"You both are really stupid," Doc reprimanded coldly.

Both men stared in the silence that again covered them before Red spoke. "Yeah, like slicking your wick on that chocolate bunny while she's drugged out of her head isn't, like, totally illegal," he said, his words flying out with apparent impulse behind them.

Doc's eyes were all that moved now as he rolled them over Red, sizing him up—shutting him up.

"Don't you ever fucking mention her to me," he said, with menacing finality in his words.

"Sorry, man," Red recanted, gulping audibly at the sight of Doc's angry face.

The air got thick around them as Doc's glare showed him there was no area of equality between them.

"Hey guys, now we're all in this together," Leon said, attempting to slice the thickness.

Doc stood and walked out.

Around midnight the man had come into the condo and quietly switched out all Rashawn's water bottles. He gave no thought that she might ever have company and decide to be social with her remaining bottled water one of these days. All he wanted was for her to drink it. All he wanted was for Rashawn to go to sleep so that again he could have her without a fight, like he had the other nights in her office.

It was difficult to be patient, difficult to wait, but soon she would come down.

Deep inside, he had to admit that he was a bit angry with her.

Keeping Reggie from me like this.

But then again, what else was she supposed to do? Blurt it out to everyone?

"I suppose she doesn't actually know that I'm his father," he said in an undertone while looking around at the baby toys.

It was hard to imagine Rashawn being the motherly type. She flirted too much. He'd been watching her for months, dare he even say it, years. She flirted with everyone, even people she didn't like.

Sure, she was sexy-hot, and watching her giggle while talking to Chance did kinda turn him on.

But that Davis was just an annoying bug. He had to be squashed soon. Somehow, he'd have to find a way to eliminate his competition.

The more he thought about the connection he had with Rashawn, the more he wanted to touch her, right then. But no, he couldn't risk being discovered that way. He had too much to lose if he was caught. He would just wait.

When he'd come by the first few times and hid inside her pantry, he watched her turn up the untainted bottle of water and chug it like a beer. She drank it so quickly that she sometimes knocked down another one right after.

She drank water the same time every night—about one a.m.

Surely not enough water, clearly not her eight glasses a day. And he had planned to talk to her about that, because staying healthy was important to him. But, anyway—

It was always the same time every night. She would come down those stairs, drink water, straighten up a little, glance through a periodical, and then head back upstairs.

This was surely going to be easier than that refrigerator in her office. However, he did notice that she didn't seem to sleep as well in the condo as she did when living in the Palemos.

But it was understandable.

He missed the Palemos, too, sometimes.

Her family hadn't even come over for dinner or anything since the move. Surely, she was lonely living here in this 'biggo' condominium. Perhaps one day, when they married, this place would become a home again.

The thought made him smile.

When had he switched from wanting her dead to wanting her for a wife and mother to his child?

It all boggled his mind.

Betrayal was a funny thing to chastise. How much, how little discipline does one dole out to the guilty.

"And you are guilty, Rashawn. Just like Jasmine was," the man declared. He often had to remind himself of that fact. This was no time for love to cloud his thinking. He'd been watching Rashawn push him further and further away; just the same way he had watched Jasmine resist the love he had to offer.

He just hoped he wouldn't have to punish Rashawn similarly.

Around one, like clockwork, Rashawn came down the stairs for a drink. She was a creature of habit, and he loved that about her. It made his plan so easy to carry out, he thought, as he watched from the tight quarters of the pantry.

Before she left the kitchen, she was flat on her face. He came out from the pantry and hurried over to her, examining her, relieved to hear her light breathing. She was his queen after all, his possession, basically, his wife.

It wasn't as if he had gone through any channels to make a statement like that. However, that was the way things were. To him it was a fact, and the thought of her with Davis . . .

Or anyone for that matter.

He fought to hold back emotion while lifting her limp body, carefully carrying her to her bed.

Keeping his eyes on her, he undressed, and then climbed in with her.

Raising her gown, he lay there beside her, naked, skin-to-skin. He felt so much love for her. Just holding her, feeling her smooth, flawless body, it was hard to contain himself. He closed his lips on one of her nipples and then watched it react, rising and hardening at the light flick of his tongue.

Her breathing was shallow and soft.

Just then, he noticed the vase of flowers on her nightstand.

Why couldn't she just love him as much as he loved her? Why did their affair have to be so one-sided, so close to perverse?

Mounting her, he began to feel strange. Never before had he thought this hard about what to do next.

"I just want to make love to you," he whispered in her ear, as if he needed to explain his actions to her.

As he entered her, he thought he saw her eyes open and lock on his. He pulled out.

He was only imagining it, wishing for it. For she just lay there limp and dead-like beneath him.

Again, he listened for her breathing. Yes, she was alive.

Moving down on her, he kissed her belly, amazed at the smoothness of it despite childbirth. He kissed the insides of her thighs.

Unable to resist, he lingered there between her legs until he felt her body responding, growing wet and ready for him, and he was more than ready for her. But as he was about to take her, he heard her call out, "Blain," in a breathy pant.

Growing tension and sudden confusion scattered his thoughts. Sliding his hand around her throat, he squeezed slightly, but knew he couldn't go through with it.

Love had indeed clouded his thinking.

He got up and dressed, leaving her there, indecently exposed.

Chapter 19

Rashawn locked her office and headed down the stairs. Although her mind should have been on her students, it was far from them. All day she could not get last night's confusing dream from her mind. The sensations she'd felt still tingled her body.

Her scattered thoughts were upsetting as well. She felt almost hung over.. Once again the sexually filled dreams had dominated her slumber. It was as if she'd partied all night, instead of simply sleeping restlessly. The dreams were less violent now as if her rapist were now a lover, yet they still disturbed her . . . maybe even more now considering he held the staring role.

When the alarm clock buzzed, she woke to find herself sprawled out on top of her bedding, shivering from the morning chill. Her bedroom door was shut.

"I never shut my door," she mumbled while heading out the building. She was still trying to sort out the events. "How can I hear Reggie if the door is shut?" she asked herself.

Fortunately, Reggie slept hard as a rock most nights. When she went in to him, he was out like a light, tucked in tight just as she had left him.

In the shower Rashawn had noticed a new bruise on her thigh. Again, she had hurt herself.

"And that's got to stop, too," she added to the self-reprimand, while unconsciously quickening her pace.

All she wanted to do was get off the campus without seeing Davis. Such dreams she was having, such naughty dreams.

Suddenly, while shaking her head free of the thoughts of him, she heard her name. It was Roman. She wanted to pretend she hadn't heard him, but she had already looked his way.

"Can I have a word with you?" he called out, while hurrying toward her. She noticed his physique. Roman was put together nicely, as much as she wanted to deny it.

"Get your mind out of the gutter," she mumbled under her breath, reprimanding herself again.

"Yes, Dr. Roman," she answered, purposely formal. He simply smiled, though she could tell he wanted to correct her formality.

"Rashawn, yes, I uh, I wanted to simply wish you happy holidays," he said. "And if there is anything you or Reggie need to make this Christmas more pleasant, please don't hesitate to call on me," he added, touching her arm. She fought not to pull away, as his dark eyes caught hers for a moment, causing her stomach to flutter.

"Yes," she responded, and quickly turned to leave.

Suddenly she felt the tug on her jacket as Roman pulled on her slightly. She looked at him sternly before she pulled free.

"Anything, Rashawn, anything," he repeated, his dark eyes burrowing into her, revealing so much desire and want. It was apparent.

The tension she was already feeling, mixed with the sudden aggravation by Roman, had caused her stomach to all but turn over completely. She simply nodded and walked away.

Later Rashawn found herself fondling the phone while deep in thought of Davis . . . and the dreams too, she had to be honest about it. She was only human and the dreams were getting to her. Despite her fears and celibate resolve, the change in the dreams had brought about a new thought pattern for her . . . a promise of pleasure unlike she'd ever known. Finally, she sighed heavily and hung up. The phone rang under her hand.

"Yes," she answered quickly.

"It's Chance," he said, sounding out of breath.

He'd gotten her message.

"I'm glad you called. I, uh . . . wanted to talk to you . . . about Thanksgiving," Rashawn stammered. She sounded shy and unsure of herself.

"Would you like me to come over?" he asked quickly. She looked at Reggie sprawled out on her bed. He was a sleeping angel.

"No," she whispered. I'll meet you somewhere," she suggested.

"How about the Radisson on First Street," he suggested.

Her mind spun for a second.

Why at a hotel? Why a place with beds? Get over it Rashawn, grow up . . . this was your idea after all.

"They serve a nice crab salad there," he went on. "Are you hungry?" he asked.

Yes, Davis, hungrier than you could ever know, she thought, moving the phone to her chest, hoping that maybe he could hear the beating of her heart.

"Sure, dinner is fine. Give me a little bit to get myself together. How about seven?" She suggested, giving Reggie plenty of time to get his nap out.

"Dinner it is, then," Davis said, smiling on his end.

* * *

Qiana was always so happy to have Reggie stay over, and now that Rashawn knew that Reggie wasn't conceived by her ex, it was easier to leave him in her care.

Qiana didn't ask a lot of questions about Rashawn's date tonight, and it was a relief for her because, frankly, she didn't have any answers . . . none she wanted to share anyway.

As she pulled into the hotel's large parking lot and allowed the valet to take her keys, Rashawn glanced around for Davis's car. He was there all right. She looked at her watch.

"And early, too," she said, feeling the heat coming up to her face.

"I ordered wine," Davis said as soon as she sat down.

He was dressed casually, yet preppy. His burgundy shirt looked good with his complexion.

"Thanks," she said. Her voice was a little shaky. He noticed and smiled while pouring her glass. While she was taking a long sip, the waiter came over and took their order.

"So, you wanted to talk?" he asked after the young man walked away.

"Yes, I wanted to talk about . . . Thanksgiving," she said, her voice coming weakly.

Davis sipped his wine and then tenderly touched her hand over the table. "Shawnie, we're both adults here. Let's have dinner and then decide where and how we'll talk about Thanksgiving."

Rashawn was falling in love, or lust. Whatever it was, it had Chance Davis's name written all over it.

She nodded slowly and smiled, giving in to the ambiance of the restaurant.

* * *

The elevator let out on the third floor. Rashawn watched Davis's hands while he opened the door, sliding the flat card through the electronic opener. Inwardly, she prayed for a red light. But no, it was green. All systems were a 'go'. They walked into the clean room. The scent of recent maid service filled her nose. Davis immediately checked the thermostat.

"Are you warm?" he asked, before pulling her into a soft kiss. She returned his affections. Davis was a wonderful kisser and she wished they could kiss all night, but as he moved from her lips to her neck, and as his hands wandered down her back, ending with a squeeze on her backside, she knew he would want more than kisses from her that night.

The bed was large and firm as she quickly slid naked under the covers. Davis smiled at her and immediately pulled her close to him. Rashawn attempted to relax, to give in to his fondling, his petting, his intimate probing, but she couldn't. This wasn't a dream this was real . . . too real. He pulled her under him now and started his downward journey.

If one thing didn't work, there were other ways to wet a whistle.

Her breast, her stomach, her thighs . . .

Thinking now, about her dreams, and how far off this was, Rashawn stopped him short of his aim.

"I don't know if I can do this," she said, now realizing that she was shaking all over. Davis held her there under him.

"Then why are we trying?" he asked, kissing the side of her face as he rolled off her. She turned to him.

"I want to feel normal again. I want to feel whole again," she said. "I mean, I have these dreams about . . . well maybe they're about you, I don't know," Rashawn began, rambling, sounding foolish. "I'm starting to think that I'm going crazy."

What a time to talk about this, she thought.

"Tell me about the dreams," he requested.

"Why? You get off on . . ."

"No . . . no," he chuckled nervously, holding her a little tighter, hoping to confirm trust. She snuggled closer, once again feeling good in his embrace.

"Well, the last dream I had was the worst. I was at my new place. Oh, and my move went just fine by the way." She looked at him accusatively. She was hoping to make him feel bad for standing her up.

"It did?" he asked. "Then why aren't we at your place?" he asked with play in his voice. She grinned.

"Because, I don't do nasty things in my house," she giggled, and then thought about the last dream she'd had.

These dreams were no laughing matter, though. They were nasty.

"Well, I see we are kinda stymied on the hotel nasty stuff, too," he teased, thumping her nose playfully.

"Like I was saying," she went on, with a giddy looking smirk, "It was, like, a few days ago. I got home and I climbed into bed. I heard something downstairs and I, like the dumb women in the movies, went downstairs to see what it was. I have a gun, but it's downstairs. I keep forgetting to move it upstairs," she said now. "I mean, I think I went downstairs," Rashawn knew she was sounding confused.

Davis seemed to be unconsciously massaging her arm. No doubt having a beautiful naked woman in his bed 'just talking' was kinda strange. His hands, apparently, didn't know what to do about it, so they wandered, just a little. Rashawn didn't mind.

"Anyway, when I got downstairs there was nobody there. I went into the kitchen and got me a drink, or else I got the drink first. I don't remember, but next I knew, I was waking up back in my bed all . . ." she began and then giggled, "undone," she finally admitted.

"Were you drunk?" he asked tactfully.

"No, a drink of water," she giggled.

"How strange. I'll have to ponder this for a moment," he said, closing his eyes and lying back in the bed. Rashawn looked at his face. He looked like a boy. Forty looked good on him. She remembered his family, how youthful they had all looked. It was a blessing to age so well. Of course, he looked nothing like Reggie, and there would be no way anyone would believe Reggie was his son if they married.

Married?

Nobody is even talking about that, Rashawn, she mentally reprimanded herself. *You can't even be a woman with him. How in the world are you gonna be a wife to him?* she asked herself.

Before she realized it, Davis was staring at her. Her stomach fluttered. They silently assessed the situation before he pulled her to him and held her close.

"Rashawn, this isn't a game," he said in her ear.

"I know," she whispered back. "And I'm not trying to play with your feelings," she admitted.

"But it feels like you are," he said, hoping the words came out right. He looked at her face, softened by the dim light of the small lamp.

"You understand that, right?" he asked, again in a half whisper. She closed her eyes tight, holding back her tears.

"Yes," she answered.

"I'm not trying to pressure you," he said, now in full voice.

"I know," she replied, giving in to the moment, moving her hands to his intimate places. She felt his readiness.

Trying not to show her apprehension, she kissed him.

Closing her eyes, she heard the plastic tear away as he opened the condom.

The once tender moment that had now become an obligation. She sensed he felt the same way.

This was bad.

When he entered her, she felt nothing. It was as if she had turned her switches off and given in to the physical element of the act. Though he seemed to be attempting affection, sex with Davis was merely sex. How she regretted allowing things to get this far, how she wished she could turn back the clock and put this night off for another time, a readier time. But it was too late now.

Maybe he wasn't the one, the man from her dreams, the one who brought fire to her body.

If not Chance then who?

Davis knew this wasn't going well, and he wished he hadn't pushed the issue. Rashawn lay under him like a CPR dummy.

Ol' Resessy Annie, they called her.

Davis thought about those days in gym class when the guys would hump on Resessy, getting their kicks on the pseudo-porn toy as soon as the coach was out of the gym. He had resisted the urge to participate in the 'fake sex' then, and wished he had resisted the urge to participate in it tonight.

Within a few minutes, his erection was gone. He pulled out.

"I'm sorry," he said, while discarding the condom in the trashcan by the bed. He then followed the light into the bathroom. When he returned to the darkened room all he heard was Rashawn's heavy sighs. He knew she was crying.

She wasn't home. The man had waited until way after midnight. He had even gone through the trouble to take the dying roses from the vase on her nightstand, replacing them with fresh ones.

After giving up the wait, he drove through the Palemos. She wasn't there either. He didn't even want to think about Davis and Rashawn being together. He couldn't put himself through that mental angst. How could she cheat on him this way?

Hadn't she learned anything since they'd been together? When would she get it?

"Why don't women like you get it?" he called out.

Slamming through the living room in the dark after returning to the condominium to wait a little longer, the man noticed Reggie's toy sitting on the sofa.

"Abandoning your child to chase after a man? What kind of mother are you?" he barked.

The immediate mixed feelings coming up in him sent him nearly over the edge.

"People die over actions like yours, don't you realize that?"

"All the time wasted," he went on in his diatribe. Finally giving way to tears, he growled, "I'm not a violent man, Rashawn, but you are taking me there."

Carrying the bear up to her room, he threw it on the floor, and then taking the roses from the vase on the nightstand in Rashawn's bedroom, he threw them, water and all, onto her bed. Then he smashed the vase against the wall.

Rashawn pondered the call for what seemed to be hours. Finally, after giving in, she called the police.

The phone call had been the cincher. Perhaps she could have gotten over the mess in her bedroom; however, when she heard the breathing on the other end of the phone, the angry breathing, her heart raced and she knew then she needed to call the police.

"I came in tonight and I think someone has been in my condo," she explained again.

"And you think this because of a vase being knocked over in your room, on a windy night, a night that you happened to have left your window open?" the woman asked, sarcasm heavy in her tone. Rashawn sighed, realizing the call was a mistake.

"Yes," she answered. "And someone called me," Rashawn added to the nebulous report.

"Well, ma'am, we can send out a couple of squad cars to look into it. I mean wrong number, heavy wind, no problem. The officer can dust for prints or whatever," the woman went on, sounding bored and bothered at three in the morning.

"You know what? Don't bother, okay!" Rashawn snapped.

She looked again at the broken glass on the floor and the mangled roses strewn on her bed—this was no dream.

"No, you listen," Rashawn continued. "Wind? Wrong number? I think not," she snapped.

There was a long pause.

"Okay, ma'am, we'll send out an officer," the woman said, sounding condescending now.

"Thank you," Rashawn said tightly.

The female officer looked around the condominium with a notepad in hand. She wrote down many things while the male officer asked Rashawn questions.

"Have you noticed anything suspicious?" the male officer asked.

"No, I just moved here. I bought this place from . . ."

"Dr. Allen Roman," the female officer interjected. Rashawn and the male officer looked at her curiously.

"I've been out here before. Seems that Dr. Roman

had some problems here," the officer said now, smoothing back her already immaculately neat hair, in what appeared to be a nervous mannerism.

"What problems?" Rashawn asked. "Phone calls? No, of course not, we have different phone numbers," Rashawn said then, answering her own question.

"I was just saying that Dr. Roman had some problems here, and well . . ." she added, looking harder at the roses and then glancing around the room, "So you're saying that those roses were in that vase?" She pointed from one thing to the other. Rashawn looked at the roses on her bed. They appeared fresh and new.

"Well, yeah. I mean, I know it sounds crazy, but I want to say that those are even new roses." She chuckled nervously. "But what intruder leaves roses? So, I would say yes, those roses were in that vase," she affirmed, sounding more confident than before. The female officer wrote it all down.

Before they left, the female officer handed Rashawn a card. "Maceba Baxter?" Rashawn asked while making sure she had it right. The name sounded familiar.

"Yes. Call her if anything else strange or funny happens. And, I mean anything else," she said.

Her words gave Rashawn an eerie chill.

"Sure," Rashawn agreed.

Shutting the door behind the officers when they left, Rashawn headed back upstairs, only this time to Reggie's room. There was no way she was up to cleaning the mess in her room. After the evening she'd had with Davis, there was no way Rashawn was up to anything.

Chapter 20

"So you're telling me that you know who's behind all this drug trafficking?" Maceba asked him.

"Of course I do, but catching him is another story."

"Why would it be hard?"

"Because you can't just walk up to him and arrest him. It's not that easy of a thing to do. You're working with a sick mind."

"And you know this how?"

"By the fact that I've had dealings with him and I happen to know how sick and crazy is."

"Is it Blain Tollome? Is that why you follow him from campus to campus?"

"Or the other way around? Haven't you stopped for a moment to think that maybe he's following me, waiting for just the right moment to kill me?"

"That's insane. Why in the hell would he be trying to kill you?"

"Because I know his secrets, I know the truth about everything. I also know for a fact that Blain Tollome and this Doc person you seek are on close personal terms."

"Now how do you know that?" asked Maceba, growing instantly agitated. It was bad enough that after reading over the files from Danton University, there were suspicious gaps in the reports that led her to wonder about Blain's possible involvement with the infamous Doc. It was bad enough she'd managed to find a possible connection between the security guards there at Danton and the movement of drugs through the campus—and that meant the involvement of Blain. But now she was dealing with Allen Roman, another man who bothered her. In her opinion, Roman was an insidious mind controller who she felt used his talents as a psychiatrist to get into people's heads, minds, maybe even their hearts.

He was wicked, but Maceba couldn't prove that either.

She couldn't even find the man who had tried to kill her, and if she did, could she prove it? She once felt so close to discovery, yet back then, before she could question her suspects, she was attacked, attacked by the big man who, without a doubt, was trying to kill her.

Something always seemed to stop her right before she could accomplish what she needed to accomplish in this case. It was almost as if she was dealing with magicians here, masters of 'slight of hand'. It was as if she was living a normal life and then 'poof,' suddenly she was part of some macabre stage act.

"I'm not sure I should be talking to you like this. I think maybe I've already said too much," Roman said now, pulling back from further discussion of Blain.

"How do you figure?"

"Well, I'm sure by now you've grown to suspect our Blain Tollome. And I'm not sure if you had put it in your mind that he could have been the man who tried to kill you, in order to cover up his involvement with Doc. However . . ."

"Why are you playing games with me, Dr. Roman?"

Maceba asked, moving uncomfortably in the seat. She could feel him controlling her, moving her thoughts. He was a true puppeteer, a master of mental manipulation. She'd seen his type before.

But there was no way she would accept that her attacker was Blain. A dirty cop, yes, a drug dealer, sure, but if he was the one behind all of this violence, *that would make him an animal*, she reasoned, shuddering with the thought, remembering their last encounter and what had almost happened.

"Why are you trying to implicate Blain Tollome in my attack and the rape and murder of Yvette and . . ."

"I never said that. I said . . ." Roman quickly blurted.

"I heard what you said," Maceba snipped, knowing instantly where she would have to put her thoughts from this moment on.

She was a professional and she knew what an implication sounded like. She knew what a reluctant witness sounded like, too. Roman was a reluctant witness, and she was going to get to the bottom of his story.

"What's he got on you?" Maceba asked.

Reggie sprung into Rashawn's arms as soon as she entered Qiana's home that Saturday morning to pick him up. It wouldn't take a psychic to tell Qiana that Rashawn was disturbed, and to be honest, Rashawn hadn't tried hard to hide it.

"I'm going nuts, I think," Rashawn said, after a little prodding from Qiana. "I finally called the cops," she went on. Qiana was intrigued.

"What did they say?"

"That the intruder was probably some leftover perp from the days of when Roman lived there. And the call, coincidentally the same wrong number that used to call me when I lived in the Palemos. Yeah, right. Qiana, I'm not crazy. Those were fresh flowers. I know it. And who would call me just to scare me, who would do something like that?" Rashawn asked now, finally giving in to the acceptance that someone had been in her condominium and calling her with intent to frighten her.

"I think something freaky is going on. I think someone is trying to scare me," Rashawn said.

"Scare you? Or are you just getting scared? There's a difference," Qiana stated simply. "I mean, you got a gift that hits you wrong, and some flowers from a secret admirer, who is probably this Blain guy, in which case I'm sure he's not trying to scare you. Maybe he's just overdoing the secret admirer thing," Qiana explained.

"But coming into my house?"

"I know. I know what you're thinking and I do think you need to talk to him, but still, this might just be an extreme case of misunderstanding," Qiana elucidated further. Rashawn's face twisted with reluctant acceptance.

"Okay, I'll assume that for a minute. But the panties? They were just like the ones . . ." Rashawn paused, glancing briefly toward Reggie. "They are just like the ones I wore that night," she whispered, "How would he know that unless . . ."

"Shawn, I've got a pair like that. They're very popular." Qiana smiled, trying to say something to soothe Rashawn's brow. Instead, it rose slyly.

"I bet you do, Miss Nasty," Rashawn giggled, causing a light blush to rush to Qiana's brown cheeks.

"Nigel wants to try again for a baby, I think," Qiana said now, her words rushed as if held in for a while, changing the subject abruptly.

"But the doctors . . ."

"I know . . . I know," Qiana went on, shaking her head and wringing her hands a little.

"Not to get graphic, but he's been neglecting the ol' raingear these days," Qiana divulged.

"Maybe he thinks you're taking the pill," Rashawn attempted to reason.

"He knows I'm not," Qiana went on.

"Well . . ." Rashawn sighed, letting the sentence hang. Qiana sighed, too.

"At least you can have sex," Rashawn finally said, after making sure Reggie was onto something more interesting to him than their adult conversation.

"And you can't?" Qiana asked, attempting to make eye contact with Rashawn who was avoiding it.

"Apparently not," Rashawn admitted.

"Shawn, talk to me," Qiana said softly, before standing up and heading to the kitchen. "Let me get us some tea."

"Girlfriend, you know me too well," Rashawn laughed quietly, letting a little sadness show. "I can't talk to anybody else about this."

"You know I'm always here for you, Shawn . . . always," Qiana called from the kitchen.

Rashawn toyed with the idea for hours before finally picking up the phone and calling campus security.

"If there is no answer and this is important, you can reach the campus security supervisor—Police Sergeant Blain Tollome at . . ."

Rashawn wrote down the number of Blain's pager quickly and called it before she could talk herself out of it. Her phone rang within seconds of her hanging up.

"Tollome," he answered. His phone voice was deep and rumbling. Its effect surprised her immediately.

"Tollome," he repeated, during her silent regrouping.

"Blain, hi, it's me, Rashawn Ams," Rashawn stumbled. There was a long silence before he spoke again, softer this time.

"Yes, Professor Ams. How may I . . ."

"Rashawn, you can call me Rashawn. I was wondering if I might meet you for coffee. I really need to discuss a little problem that I'm having," she requested quickly before chickening out. She couldn't believe herself—asking Blain Tollome out.

Fear—Rashawn hated it. It made her do things out of her nature.

"Definitely. Where do you want to meet?" he asked, sounding serious, yet polite.

Sometimes Blain was harder to read when he was being normal.

"I can get to the Palemos in about five minutes. I'm not far from there," he suggested.

"Why there?" she asked, sounding full of suspicion.

"You live there," he answered.

"I don't . . ." she hesitated. "Yes, that would be great. There's a Denny's on the corner by my house and we can talk there," she said. "Give me about twenty minutes."

"Not a problem, baby, I mean, Professor Ams," he quickly corrected, but not before Rashawn caught the slip. Yes, he was indeed the Blain she knew.

Denny's was quiet for a Sunday evening and Blain wasn't hard to spot, sitting in the back booth, head shining, clothes well fitting, diamond stud sparkling in his ear, and his eyes dark and shining like onyx stone. He smiled as she approached the table. Wanting to turn and run, she sat—instead.

"I think someone is following me," she said quickly. His eyes dipped down to her hands and then crept up to meet her eyes. So dark was his gaze, through to her bones, and then beyond to her soul. She fought the urge to squirm.

"Do you have any idea who would want to?" he asked. Rashawn paused to order her coffee. Blain did the same.

"No, of course not," she said, sounding snippier than she wanted to.

"What gives you the idea that you're being stalked?"

"Could you stop calling it that?"

"What . . . stalking?" he asked, smiling wickedly. Rashawn looked away and then turned back to him sternly.

"Is it you?"

"Is it me what?"

"Trying to scare me. Is it you?"

"What the fuck kinda question is that?"

"I guess what I want to know is, do you do any body-guard work in the private sector? You couldn't do it if you very well are the one following me, now could you?" she asked, looking around nervously. When her eyes came back, they met Blain's again.

"You want me to guard your body?" he asked, raising one eyebrow. Rashawn's lip twisted in irritation.

"Why do I try, Blain? Why do I try?" she asked, start-ing up from the booth. He grabbed her hands with one of his larger ones. Her eyes fixed on his grip and then at him again. He quickly let go.

"I'm sorry. I was just messing with you. But check it, first you insult me, and then you, in the next breath, you have the nerve to get all testy," he said, licking his full lips before sliding in a toothpick from the holder that sat on the table. She sat back against the seat.

"Okay, let's review. First, you are being stalked by someone who is not me," he began pointing at himself dramatically. "Then you want someone who is me to start stalking you. Are we on the same page?"

"Look I have a . . . I have reasons for not wanting to be molested by a follower . . ." she said, avoiding the word stalker.

"Stalker," Blain said for her and then spelled the word for emphasis.

The waitress brought their coffee now. Rashawn noticed his eyes dance over the woman as she walked away.

What am I thinking, treating Blain this way? He's a single man. It's part of his lifestyle to flirt and be full of himself. And why not? He apparently had no ties to anyone.

"No Ms. Ams, I don't do bodyguard work. Being big doesn't always mean that guys like me wanna put our asses on the line for the private sector. I'm a cop, a public servant, I put my ass on the line for the public," he now answered.

Rashawn's face showed her embarrassment. She knew it did because her cheeks were on fire. She'd overestimated his attraction for her. She'd inflated her appeal and left herself open for this humiliation.

"I'm sorry," Rashawn said, sounding sheepish. He leaned in close to her.

"Don't be," he responded. His voice was warm and caring. "Personally, I think you might be in danger. And with that said, I plan to stay right on top of you, Rashawn. You never have to worry about being left open—exposed," he said now, winking at her ever so quickly.

"But I thought . . ."

"I'm not your bodyguard. I hope over the years I've become your friend," he explained.

Rashawn didn't know what to say. Blain had never been on her list of friends, and she wondered how he could have felt that he was.

"Oh, and by the way, you don't have to thank me for getting that troublemaker, Red, off you," Blain said now, emptying three sugar packets into his cup Rashawn tried to remember the incident.

"Oh that, yes, thank you," she said. He looked at her shaking his head and smiling.

"You are the most stubborn woman I've ever met," he said now.

"How is that?"

"As soon as you're told not to do something, that's when you seem to go out of your way to do it. Life is just one big confrontation with you, isn't it?" he asked, gulping the coffee with his toothpick remaining in place.

"I wouldn't say . . ." Rashawn began. She was gonna set him straight on a few things.

"I swear, women like you . . ."

"What about women like me?" Rashawn asked, growing irritated.

"Your mouths always say one thing to a man like me, but you know, deep inside you all want something else—from a man like me," he said, smacking his full lips shaking his head again.

That was it. Blain was impossible.

She stood, and reaching in her pocket, she pulled out a dollar and slammed it next to her untouched cup of coffee.

"You leaving? Our date over already?" he asked, his words dripping with sarcasm.

"Fuck you, Blain," she growled.

"Yeah, see what I mean?" he responded sarcastically, before bursting into laughter. She spun on her heels and walked out, hearing his laughter in her ears all the way out the door.

Chapter 21

"Nobody wants to give him up."

"After Danton, they wanted to believe he was dead. Yeah, like I ever thought that," Maceba said with a smirk, sipping her coffee. "Besides, one bullet," she chuckled sarcastically, "One bullet would only make him mad."

There was a moment between the two of them before Maceba asked, "So, do you know who Doc is?"

"You're kidding right? I think . . ." the redheaded officer began, before suddenly looking around nervously. "Did I say something?" He chuckled again, only this time with more nervousness behind it. "I meant to say . . . I have no thoughts on the matter."

Despite the fact that he held his coffee cup in solid hands, his fear radiated, causing Maceba to look around, and then shiver slightly from the chill that came over them.

"Tell me what you know," Maceba pleaded.

"Look, you figure it out. You're the one on his tail. All I came to tell you was that I want immunity when this is all over with. That I'm willing to confess to what I did, and that's all I'm gonna say."

"Are you scared of him?"

"Yeah, he's gonna kill me. I know he's gonna kill me if you guys don't stop him soon. He's crazy and he could be anywhere. He could be watching us right now," Red said, shaking his head as if realizing that his days could be even shorter than he first thought.

"Why is he gonna kill you? I thought you guys were partners," Maceba asked, sounding a little cynical. Red stood suddenly, indicating that the meeting was over. He had done his part. He had rolled over, now he needed to get out of there. He had a bad feeling about all of this.

"Apparently you don't know Doc very well."

"And I guess you think you are just supposed to walk up out of here after what you did to Yvette Fuhrman?" Maceba asked him. Red's green eyes blazed as he stared at her a long time. His thin lips pursed tight.

"Yeah, that's what I'm thinking, because I didn't kill her. I had sex with her, but I didn't kill her," Red explained frankly, before shrugging his jacket more assuredly on his shoulders and hulking out. He reminded Maceba of an overgrown boy.

Rashawn had not heard from Davis since the hotel fiasco. Today, however, she saw him entering the cafeteria. She smoothed her lap and unconsciously ran her hands over her hair, waiting for him to notice her. But he didn't. He spoke quickly with the Dean and then hurried from the cafeteria as if on a mission. Embarrassed, Rashawn cleared her throat and went back to her salad.

"Well, it's not like you look your best," she admitted to herself, honestly assessing her physical appearance. The dark circles under her eyes had her wondering what was going on inside her body. She'd be seeing her doctor soon if she didn't start feeling better. Her sleep over the last few weeks had been rough. Every morning she awoke feeling drained and worn out. Between the weird dreams of sex and bizarre conversations with inanimate objects in her home, she would awake feeling often displaced. It was all taking its toll on her. But at least she wasn't feeling stalked anymore, and she had to admit, that feeling of violation was a relief to get rid of. Yet, still there was something foreboding and it made life a little less than fully *good.*

It's always something, Rashawn sighed.

Roman came in for a salad, and he, too, looked every way other than at her.

"Now that's really bad," she said to herself, after watching him give not so much as a glance in her direction. After finishing her lunch, she headed back to her office to pick up some papers, and noticed Blain on campus. He too seemed preoccupied.

"So much for the sex appeal, Shawnie. You might as well retire," she mumbled under her breath.

When she entered her class later that afternoon, many of her students looked solemn, as if they had all lost their best friends.

"What is up in here today?" Rashawn asked, thinking now that aliens from the planet *Distraction* had replaced possibly everyone at Moorman University.

The class settled in their seats, everyone looking at the other to see who would speak up first. Finally, one of the girls from the swim team did.

"Yvette Furhman's body was found," she said, her voice hollow and full of moroseness.

Rashawn knew of Yvette. She was on the debate team. She was a bright girl. She was also in Davis's math class.

Thinking now of Davis and the night she saw Yvette running away, Rashawn asked as calmly as she could, "Okay, anyone know what happened? Is this something we need to talk about as a class? I'm sure it's hit some of you hard. I can tell . . ."

Rashawn opened the floor for discussion.

"She was raped," one of the quieter girls bravely blurted out.

"No, she wasn't. I don't buy that. She knew what she did and then she just couldn't handle it," one of the boys jumped in.

"Oh, and you know this . . . how?" a girl who had dated Andy once, snapped, pointing her finger accusingly.

"Look, I only know what I know," the boy went on.

"Okay, okay, hold on," Rashawn interjected, raising her voice, calling them to order. Just that little bit of conferring on the topic of rape had shaken her.

"Yvette was raped. She got pregnant and now she's dead. Those are the facts," the girl from the swim team said coolly as if she truly was the only one who really knew. "And now the cops are questioning everyone who knew her. They think whoever gave her that Get Ass, or whatever you call it, drug at the party in the beginning of the semester, killed her," she added.

"I hear she was found without her locket," another girl said..

"I hear the killer stole her locket," someone said.

"She always wears that locket. If they found Yvette without the locket, then the killer has it," another voice said, following a melodramatic gasp.

"The date rape drug?" Rashawn asked. The girl from the swim team nodded.

"I took her to a party with me at the beginning of the school year and she got raped there, had to be because she came up pregnant. Yvette had never, you know. She wasn't like that."

"The locket thing is just for drama. There's no locket," another boy commented.

"How do you know what Yvette was like?" someone else commented back.

"Yeah, she told me that she got slipped a mickey. She's not stupid. Well, she wasn't stupid," someone added.

"There's no locket," the boy said again.

"Are there any suspects?" Rashawn asked.

Just then from the back of the room, the normally quiet girl jumped up and ran out of the room in tears.

"She's just upset. Her boyfriend, Rogelio, got beat up at the last frat party. They pulled his life support this morning," someone said.

Chapter 22

The final report was in.

"Murder, and in the first degree, I'd say. Shame, too. She was a pretty girl." Homicide Detective Cookie Maxwell sighed.

Retirement was just around the corner for her.

Cookie liked working. It was a measure of her worth, she would say. It was a strange thing to stay for a woman who had single-handedly raised all three of her children while still a beat cop, but working was what she loved.

Today, however, she was feeling tired, which wasn't hard to feel at fifty-two.

"No matter how gooda shape you're in," she would say to her partner, Rachel Perkins. Rachel was nowhere near ready for retirement, and that was okay with Cookie.

Rachel was a good listener, and never threw Cookie's tired complaints back in her face. She never said anything about Cookie's often-morbid references to death, as if the Grim Reaper often met her at her door at night when she arrived home, swapping with her another day, on the promise that if possible she would put some useless scumbag's lights out.

Rachel would say nothing when, at a moment's notice, Cookie was prepared to take down a runaway suspect twice her size, slapping cuffs on him as if he were her own delinquent son.

Yeah, Cookie Maxwell was tough.

"And I just hate when people call me Kooky. You know what that means right?" she asked Rachel, who was only half listening today.

"No, what..?"

"Crazy. Kooky means you're missing a few crayons in your box," Cookie said, letting out a chuckle, which was followed by coughing sometimes—*the residual of years of smoking, long time quit, but every day, haunting.*

She patted her chest.

"So what do you think happened? Who do you think would butcher that girl like that?" Rachel asked, looking over the photos, a gift from the guys in forensics.

"Well, she was pregnant. So my guess is it was the sperm donor," Cookie answered, sounding flat while reading over the file.

"So, who was that?"

"That's what we're gonna ask Dr. Davis," Cookie said without a smile. "Her parents said he knew her, so we need to go see if maybe he did in fact, ya know, 'knew' her," she added with a wink and quotation marks made in the air.

Davis ended his sparse class early. Yvette's death had spread around the campus like the news of war, just like the news of Andy Simmons' little mishap as well as Rogelio Brown's.

Andy had gotten himself beat up pretty badly, and ended up in the hospital with a broken arm, lacerated liver, and ruptured spleen. Rogelio was bleeding from the brain, on life support last he had heard, and Yvette was dead.

Yvette's parents called him after having been summoned to come down to the coroner's office to identify her body, although time spent under water had changed the once pretty Yvette into a monster of deformity.

"A mother knows her child," Mrs. Furhman said, showing bravery while speaking.

On Davis's way out of the classroom, Blain intercepted him.

"Tollome," Davis said, greeting him solemnly. It hadn't been a cheery day.

"Hello, Davis. I need to talk to you," Blain began, sounding quite official. Davis slipped on his hat.

"I hear they're investigating the death of a student of yours, Yvette Furhman. Do you know her?"

"You just told me she was a student of mine," Davis answered coolly.

"Yeah, well, I guess what I'm asking is, did she know you outside of school?"

"Who really knows anybody, right?" Davis answered vaguely.

"You never saw Yvette Furhman outside of here, off the university grounds?"

"And my reasons for doing that would be?"

"I'm just ax-in' you some questions, Davis," Blain snapped.

"And ax-in' some pretty stupid ones, I might add," Davis snipped sarcastically before turning and walking away.

"I was just trying to help you out," Blain called after him.

"What are you getting at?" Davis asked, spinning on his heels to look at him, his eyes glowing with rancor.

"But then again, I guess you're not worried about it because you have an air-tight alibi, right?" Blain asked, moving his toothpick to the opposite side of his mouth. The air around him was one of confidence. It was as if he knew the answer. "Yeah, I'd say air-tight," he smacked, while clasping his hands together tightly, obscenely.

Davis contemplated the moment when Yvette wanted to tell him what she remembered about the night she was raped and became pregnant while under the influence of the newest date rape drug, crudely referred to around campus as Get Ass. Yes, she had said over the phone that afternoon, she remembered the 'who,' the 'where,' and maybe even the 'why' parts of this entire situation, and that she wanted to tell him, even before telling Juanita, even before telling the police.

Yvette had done some investigating on her own, she said. She had some theories on the incidents surrounding Andy and Rogelio, too, she said.

"You're gonna be surprised. It's only about three degrees of separation on this one," she had said on the phone.

That was the last time he'd spoken to Yvette before she died. She was found nearly a month later with her throat gapping open, floating in the bay after her water logged body, along with the help of hungry sea life, freed her from her weighted-down ropes, allowing her to float to the surface.

Chance Davis was a concerned man. He cared about Yvette. This whole thing had bothered him. It especially bugged him knowing where he was during the time she was murdered.

Oh, how he had let Yvette down, and her parents. He'd let a lot of people down lately.

He contemplated the moment, his life, and his integrity. He then looked at Blain, standing there, implying that he knew about his *visit* with Juanita. But how could he? How could Blain know any of it?

Suddenly Chance remembered his flat tires, the jagged cuts. He thought about Blain's knife that was now missing from his belt. He wanted to ask Blain where it was. Davis wanted to see it, as if he could tell by looking at the blade that it had cut rubber, or a throat. The thought was foolish and he knew it. But he wanted to blame someone, and end this mess quickly.

"Unless you're taking me downtown to book me, Dano, I'm through talking to you, Ace. I'm going home," Davis said with a sneer before again walking away.

"Yeah, you do that, *Chance*," Blain called out, saying his name as if it meant something obscene.

Davis wasn't worried about the detectives showing up during his class the next day. He was more irritated than anything, and he knew it showed. However, showing irritation to the cops in the middle of a murder investigation was not wise, not at all.

"You seem a bit tense, Dr. Davis," Cookie said, noticing the way he tapped his pencil against the palm of his large hand.

This Chance Davis fella is a handsome man, Cookie noticed. *Maybe five foot, nine or ten, about a hundred and ninety pounds, built solidly with thick legs, like maybe he had run track in school. However, school had been some time ago. He's showing just a little gray at the temples. Maybe young girls make him forget about that gray and think about the days when he crossed that finish line first. Maybe the young girls still cheered him on.*

Maybe Yvette was his number one cheerleader.

"So what was your relationship with Yvette Furhman?" Cookie asked.

"I was her teacher," Davis answered, not stumbling over the fact that all references to Yvette were now past tense.

"Was she a good math student? I mean, did she make good grades?"

"No. As bright as she was, she was terrible in math," Davis admitted, again with the 'was.'

"When was the last time you saw her?"

"She called me the night she was, apparently, killed," he answered plainly, to the surprise of the detectives. "She called me because she wanted to tell me something important. She wanted me to come to her house, but when I got there, she was gone. And now, now she's dead," he said.

"Well . . . uh, Dr. Davis, you don't sound too . . ." Cookie groped for the words to describe the cool man.

"Too what? I'm very upset that this has happened. I'm upset about Yvette, and Andy Simmons, and also Rogelio Brown—all the kids in this school whose lives are being cut short or otherwise affected by some damned drug dealer selling them sex in a pill," Davis said, snapping his pencil before he could control himself. Cookie and Rachel's eyebrows rose considerably. Certainly breaking a pencil didn't make the man a candidate for a cold-blooded murder, but still, it did show he had a few buttons that could be pushed. And maybe, just maybe, he had the 'I don't want a baby,' button, and Yvette had pushed it.

"How often did you meet Yvette at her house—alone?"

"Never. I usually spoke with her when her parents were present, unless we talked over the phone. I was helping them deal with the fact that Yvette was pregnant, and that she didn't remember how she got that way."

"And how were you doing that?" Rachel asked, suspicion still showing.

"My ex-wife is a hypnotherapist. I arranged for Yvette to have some sessions with her in her parent's home. was hoping that through the therapy, Yvette would be able to reveal something to her parents about that night, settle their minds about this whole thing. The don't believe in abortion, so Yvette was going to have the baby, but still, they wanted to put some closure o this matter, gaining some redeemed trust in their daughter,"

"Did it work?"

"You'll have to ask my ex-wife. I only went once. But I am beginning to think it must have, as Yvette did call me, and she did say that she remembered who it was that had raped her," Davis said.

"Rape?"

"You're the cop. The girl was drugged out of her mind. She goes to a party, has a soda, and wakes up pregnant. Sounds like rape to me," Davis said now, giving the two detectives a tight and forced, finite smile that told them he had said all he was going to say on the matter of Yvette.

"Can we have your ex-wife's number and address?" Cookie requested, opening her pad to a fresh page.

"Yes, certainly," Davis answered.

"One more question, where were you on the night of the eighth?" Cookie asked.

Finally, the dreaded question. Davis knew today he would have to admit it, and he felt foolish. He wasn't ashamed, but he sure was filled with regret. If this was an alibi, he sure wished he had a better one.

"I was with my ex-wife," he said, his voice unconsciously lowering. All he needed was for Rashawn to hear him, to find out.

God, it was a mistake! Can't we just erase the whole thing? He wanted to scream.

"With her?" Rachel asked, wanting more clarification of the statement.

"Yes, we were together at her house . . . my house, hell, we were together," Davis stammered, showing his discomfort. His blush brought a smile to Cookie's face.

"I gather your wife will corroborate this?" Cookie asked. Davis sighed heavily.

"Ex-wife, and yes, I have no doubt she will. She'd be glad to," he said with a smirk.

* * *

Standing, he paced the room. He knew his way around that room in the dark by now. Every piece of furniture was in its place at all times.

Rashawn was an immaculate housekeeper.

"Except for Reggie's toys," he snickered, picking up the stuffed lamb and inhaling its baby powder freshness.

"I'm not a violent man," he mumbled under his breath, glancing over at her asleep on the sofa, her magazine fallen to the floor. The man could hear her soft breathing; smell the scent of her body. Taking a deep breath, he sucked her in through his nostrils. *Just determinately in love.* He smiled at his thoughts.

He'd come in late tonight. Later than usual, and she had been asleep awhile now. Surely she would awaken at his touch. He couldn't risk it. He'd only taken a moment to visit Reggie's room. Normally he spent longer with him.

The house was silent except for the ticking of the clock.

He looked at his watch.

"It's probably time to get going anyway," he said, grabbing up his jacket from the back of the chair.

Later that same night, Doc entered the bar. He needed a drink.

The clock struck midnight as Doc sat at the counter thinking about things. How wrong things were going. Red was getting out of control.

"He's getting outta hand."

Red pushing the limits was making him do things he didn't want to do. He was going to mess up everything.

He was gonna go down, and Doc knew he wouldn't

go quietly. He was going to take everyone with him. He was a coward.

"A big goofy-ass fuckin' coward," Doc growled in an undertone. "He's gonna get his self killed," he went on, mumbling.

"Well, they can't really link Red to me anyway," he said to himself, still speaking in an undertone. "So I'm not going to worry about it," he added, finalizing his thoughts.

"What'll it be?" the bartender said with a smile.

She was a pretty woman. Her complexion was that of rich, dark chocolate. Doc always liked dark-skinned women. Jasmine's skin was dark.

Jasmine was a woman of hypnotic beauty, addictive beauty. Her laughter was like a song, and her kiss . . . her kiss was like . . .

"What'll it be?" the bartender repeated.

"Gin and tonic," he requested.

She winked.

"Ya know, gin'll make ya sin," she flirted, her eyes dancing all over him, sitting for a moment on his broad shoulders, dark eyes, and large hands.

"Then change that to some Cold Duck." He smiled.

Her eyes locked on his for a moment before she handed him his gin and tonic and he took a sip. The moment between them lasted a minute or two longer before she was summoned to the end of the bar to serve someone else.

Doc watched her as she giggled and flirted now with that man and then again with the next man whose order she took. After a time she came back to him.

"Want something else?" she asked, biting her bottom lip as she held in her laughter, which had started while she was with the last customer. Doc looked at her. He didn't know what to think of her. It wasn't like he had come to meet her, nor had they made more than a flirtatious connection. His eyes rested on her ample cleavage, peeking out from her tight, low-cut sweater.

"You seeing somebody?" he boldly asked. Her smile left her face suddenly, and then returned quickly.

"Yeah, sure I am," she answered.

An obvious lie, he could tell.

"Why are you lying?" he asked. She grinned wide.

"Look, I don't see guys like . . . uh . . . you," she answered bluntly.

"Why are you so shallow?" he asked.

"I'm not shallow," she answered, showing snippiness.

"Yes, you are, because you don't even know me, and already you judge me by my appearance," he said.

"Well obviously, you're judging me by mine," she said, wiping the counter so she could appear to be working, her bouncing breasts entertaining him just a little before he set his empty glass in front of her, tapping the rim and sliding it toward her. She refilled it, and then slid it back to him. He took a long draw on the glass.

"You're a fine lookin' woman," he said, before pulling out a thick money clip. She noticed.

Suddenly this man was interesting.

"So, you from around here?" she asked, looking down the bar at her other customers. None of them seemed to need her attention just then.

"Yeah," he answered.

"You seeing someone?" she asked. Doc laughed now.

"Yeah, as a matter a fact I'm married, to someone just like you," he answered, allowing sarcasm to come into his words. Her eyes widened just a little before she showed her irritation.

"You know what . . ." she began, only to get Doc's hand in her face.

"Save ya breath, baby," he said, reaching over the bar sticking a rolled up twenty between her tight breasts.

She pulled it out, quickly throwing it in his face.

"I'm not no damn trick."

"I was just paying the workers. I mean, they seem to be working as hard as you," he chuckled, pointing at her bust line before walking out, leaving the money on the floor.

After leaving the bar, Doc thought about what he had to do now. He felt good about it all. He felt good with the choices he was about to make regarding Red, regarding Chance Davis, and regarding all the other people interfering with what he was trying to get done. Speaking his thoughts made them clearer in his mind. He knew now what he needed to do.

The Session

"*I don't like it when you just drop in on me like this.*"

"*Why? I thought you said I could stop by any time.*"

"*That means with an appointment . . . any time.*"

"*I think I make you uncomfortable.*"

"*No, you don't make me anything.*"

He moved closer by sitting on the other side of the desk.

"*You aren't comfortable on the sofa any more?*"

"*No. I feel very vulnerable over there.*"

"*This isn't combat, we aren't at war. We are equals here.*"

"*I never thought we weren't.*"

He laughs, gets up, and walks back over to the sofa.

"*Come sit by me here.*"

"*No.*"

"*Why?*"

"*I just think it's better if I stay over here and you stay over there.*"

"*Are you still upset about our last session?*"

"*I've nearly forgotten. Tell me what happened again?*"

"*You remember. You claimed that I came on to you.*"

"*I claimed no such thing.*"

"*You said I scared you?*"

"*I've told you time and again, I'm not afraid of you.*"

"*If you aren't afraid of me, you would have no problem sitting near me.*"

His challenge is met, and he is joined on the sofa.

"*Now, isn't this better.*"

Silence.

"I think I should get back to the desk. It's more professional, better for us."

The kiss.

"I think this is better—for us."

Another kiss that is surprisingly returned.

There is more kissing until he has gained advantage, pinning her under him.

"And your intentions?"

"I think you know my intentions."

"Don't you think I should stop the tape?"

"No, I may want to see the reruns," he chuckled.

Chapter 23

Juanita thought about the session she had just had. What a problematic man he was, and such an angry bitter man too, driven by jealousy and his need to share his anger with a woman who clearly did not want him. Soon she would have to get him to tell her who the woman was. She was pretending to know, but in actuality, she had no clue.

"I think he's going to do something to her," Juanita said into the small tape recorder.

About that time, the two female officers walked in. Juanita was caught off guard by their presence, yet she hid it well.

Maybe Davis was having her arrested for rape. It would be just like him to do that.

Or some other impropriety, she thought, reflecting back on her last session. The bizarre thought brought a smile to her face.

Now that man is quite disturbed. No qualms about that observation, she thought.

She wished she had never taken him on as a client. This time things went too far and now she was involved. The last session got way out of hand. They had sex.

I hate when that happens, she mentally reprimanded herself.

"Mrs. Davis?" The older officer spoke, bringing Juanita's attention back to them.

"The former," Juanita corrected.

Cookie looked at her notes and nodded in affirmation that 'Duncun' was indeed her last name now, not Davis.

She clearly has a thing for Davis, Cookie reasoned.

"We're here to ask you a few questions about the eighth of last month,"

Juanita thought back and then smiled.

"What do you want to know?"

"Where were you on that night?"

"I was at my home. What is this all about?"

"Alone?"

Juanita looked at the pretty younger officer and smiled even broader, allowing her wickedness to come through.

"No, I was there with my ex-husband, Chance Davis."

"All night?"

"No, he was there for a few hours. He got there around like, eight or so and stayed until we were finished, like ten thirty. Then my husband arrived," Juanita said, pulling her fingers through her tangled hair.

"So you, and your husband, and your ex were all there together until around eleven?"

"Don't make it sound so obscene, officer. My ex was at my house. We spent some time together before my current husband arrived. My ex and I are close like that."

"I see. Do you know Yvette Furhman?"

"Yes, she and my ex and I were working together to find out how she got raped."

"Are you aware that she was found murdered?"

Juanita's loud gasp told her answer. "My God, no! I

hadn't been able to reach her and so I figured my ex . . . that she didn't need me anymore . . ." Juanita covered her mouth in her growing despair.

"You stopped your sentence. You figured your ex, what?"

"That he'd gone back to help her out, and her parents, like he was doing before. My God, what happened to the poor girl?"

"She was killed. Her throat was cut."

"My God, how horrible. She was raped you know. She was pregnant. I've been hypnotizing her in order to get to the root of her problems. I'm a hypnotherapist," Juanita went on.

"Do you think your ex could have had anything to do with . . ."

Just then, her phone rang. Out of reflex, she answered it. "Hello," she panted.

"You still heated?" the man asked.

"My God, I can't talk to you right now," she spat.

"What's wrong?"

"Another client of mine has been killed. She's been murdered. It's absolutely horrible. The police are asking questions," Juanita explained.

"Do you want me to come over there? I can come and comfort you."

"No, please, no. I have to call my ex-husband," she divulged without thinking and then hung up.

The two officers stared at her.

"I have to call Chance," Juanita explained. "I can't believe he didn't tell me."

"Ms. Duncun, are you going to be all right?" the officer named Cookie asked before looking at her pad. But by then Juanita was on her feet, pacing the room, antsy like a caged cat.

* * *

That's what she reminded Cookie of . . . a cat—wild and untamed. She could see why Chance Davis grew so flustered when forced to talk about this woman.

Even her office gave off the air of something primal. She was a sensual being, used to having what she wanted. Cookie felt all of this emanating from the exotic looking woman.

Cookie believed Davis's alibi. There was no way that if he had seen this woman at all that night, he had been able to get away quickly.

"I need to call Mr. and Mrs. Furhman, please, if you are finished questioning me. I really would like to do that," Juanita requested.

The two officers agreed.

Chapter 24

"Just a little too much information today," Rashawn said aloud, thinking about all that filled her head—rape, assaults, drugs, murder. She glanced at her reflection in the stainless-steel refrigerator door.

"Ugh, and me. Look at me," she said, smoothing her hands over her face. She rubbed her forehead and turned back to her desk for an aspirin, but before she could get a bottle of water from her small fridge, there was a knock at her door.

"Who is it?" she called.

"Officer Tollome," Blain called out. Rashawn sighed heavily and shut the refrigerator door.

"What is it that you want?" she asked him after opening the door and letting him in.

"You realize there is going to be an investigation into the death of Yvette Furhman as well as the attempted murder of Andy Simmons and Rogelio Brown?" he stated matter-of-factly, as if the two of them had been discussing it all day.

"Andy Simmons . . . attempted murder?" Rashawn gasped. She was unaware that anything had happened to one of her students. Or maybe she had heard something . . .

She could be so obtuse sometimes.

"Oh yeah. I personally have my hunch about the whole thing, but you know cop business. I have to follow procedure," he said, sounding sincere.

"And what is your hunch, Officer?" Rashawn asked, again reaching in her small fridge and taking out a bottle of water. She had just replenished her supply.

Just then, Blain looked very anxious.

"Thirsty?" she asked. He seemed to hesitate before answering.

"Yes, yes I am," he answered. "Let's go get a soda," he offered.

Rashawn thought about the offer.

"Where?"

"Cafeteria."

"It's closed," she smarted off.

"It's never closed to me," he retorted with a smile, jingling his large chain of passkeys.

Again Rashawn noticed his nice smile.

"Okay . . . this time," she agreed, grabbing up her jacket. Blain took it from her and assisted her in putting it on.

"You see, I can be a gentleman, too, Dr. Ams," he said, close to her ear. His words were soft and tickled her.

"Rashawn," she said, giving in to the moment.

Together they walked toward the dimly lit cafeteria. Blain's hands were deep in his pockets, and he did not attempt to hold her hand or even flirt.

"I think it was one of the teachers here. I think Yvette had a crush on one of her teachers. I think it was the wrong teacher. I think he drugged Yvette, had sex with her, impregnated her, and when she refused to get rid of the baby, he killed her."

"Why a teacher and not a student?"

"I have my thoughts on the matter. Also, I have a suspicion that if you find the locket . . ." he continued.

"I heard something about this mysterious locket," Rashawn interjected.

"And I believe, once we get our hands on that, we'll know who killed her," Blain answered.

"Oh, so you already have your suspect in mind?"

"Yes, and that's sort of why I wanted to talk to you," he began.

Now don't be startin' up again on my Davis, she was about to say. *You're crazy if you think he had anything to do with this, because I know my Davis and he's no . . .*

"Now, you don't think it's Chance Davis, do you?" she heard herself ask. Blain's lips curved into a little smile.

"Oh no, no, no, he's got an airtight alibi for the night she was killed," Blain went on. Her mind went blank for a second before she spoke.

"Alibi, why in the hell would he need an alibi?" she asked, her question taking on a biting edge. Blain held up his hands in surrender before using his campus passkey, opening the cafeteria door.

"But I do think it's someone on this campus," Blain went on, ignoring Rashawn's question.

"Why would Davis need an alibi?" Rashawn asked again.

"He's a playboy. He used to date one of the students here before he broke her heart and she quit school," Blain went on, trying to sound nonchalant. "Everybody knows he's trouble when it comes to women. I mean, he's still involved with his ex," he added making quotation marks around the word 'involved.' "You know, you might want to reconsider seeing . . ."

"Ridiculous. You're crazy," Rashawn snapped, holding up her hand to silence him. "They are involved, yes, but they were helping Yvette with some, some problems she was having," Rashawn went on, sounding naïve and full of blind belief. She wished she knew more about Davis and Yvette's little secret. She wished she knew more about Davis.

"Always the last to know, eh, Shawnie," he said, taking the liberty to call her by her family's pet name. He had blown it now.

"My ass," she snapped, and turned to leave the cafeteria.

Out of reflex, Blain grabbed her arm.

Rashawn's heart jumped nearly out of her chest as Blain's strong hand grabbed her tight and pulled her into an embrace.

"Let me go," she voiced. The volume of her words came lower than she wanted them to be. She wanted to scream, to scratch, to bite, but instead, the moment passed like an hour as they gazed into each other's eyes—Blain's dark eyes gazing into her pools of molten lava.

The sexual tension was high, higher than she wanted it to be. She couldn't help but feel it. It was there, and her body was reacting to his touch. Maybe it was the dreams again. Damn her crazy mind.

He loosened his grip on her. She pulled away, rubbing her arms where he'd held her tight.

"Why are you seeing Chance Davis?" he asked. "He's using you."

Rashawn's mind was still spinning wildly.

Who was this man, and why was he trying to get in her world this way?

She said nothing as he circled her slowly.

"Davis is gonna hurt you. He's playing you for a fool. But a guy like Blain Tollome would never hurt you like that. But can you see that? No," he said, moving up behind her slowly. Rashawn could do nothing but shake. She was terrified. Her thoughts were garbled. She could feel her head shaking in response to his accusations against Davis, yet her heart was pounding and her belly quivered. Just the sound of his voice so close to her was causing far too many emotions to come up. It was familiar, and yet so strange, so foreign.

So much want.

So much revulsion.

"What the hell is going on here?" The big redheaded campus cop asked, exploding into the cafeteria. His reddened face nearly matched his fiery red hair.

"Nothing," Blain answered quickly, moving past Rashawn and on to the soda machine. Using his key, he opened it and handed her a Coke.

"I need to talk to you," the redheaded cop growled

"In a minute," Blain answered.

"Now, dammit!"

Doc gave Red a blank stare before turning back to Rashawn. "Here, Dr. Ams," he said, sounding formal and unfamiliar, as if they had just met.

"Thanks," she whispered, walking out of the cafeteria, past the two men.

Despite the ill feelings Blain had left her with when she walked out of that cafeteria, visions of him filled her sleep later that night.

She felt her eyes open. They had to be open, as she watched him close the door of her bedroom and then undress; she saw his muscular body and the definition of his firm thighs as he climbed into her bed.

This wasn't a dream. It couldn't be.

He was all over her, causing feelings all too wonderful to deny. The way he touched her, his large hands, intimately probing, his full lips on hers, the way he orally pleasured her—though she wanted to fight what she felt, she couldn't. And soon found herself engulfed in an orgasm that left her breathless.

She awoke calling out his name, but when she opened

her eyes, it was morning. Feeling tired and worn out, she looked around for him, but he wasn't there—of course. She looked around for traces of him, but there were none. This morning, as late as she slept, Reggie had awakened before her and called to her.

Chapter 25

Allen Roman was sitting in his office having lunch when Rashawn entered. He immediately stopped eating and, wiping his face, he quickly jumped to his feet. She smiled.

"Rashawn, hello," he greeted, gesturing for her to take a seat, which she did. He, too, sat back down.

"I would like to talk to you," she said, her tone a little sheepish.

"Yes, go ahead," he began, tucking his lunch into the top drawer of his desk.

"Do you have time to talk to me?" she asked.

He nodded his head vehemently, "Of course . . . of course."

"I'm having very disturbing dreams," she began.

"Dreams?" he asked.

"Yes. I'm falling asleep and having these . . . dreams," she answered.

"Tell me about them," he said.

The silence between them was deafening as Rashawn took in the moment, listening to her heart, her breathing, the sound of the birds outside, the tick of Roman's clock.

"Gimme a second here," she began. Roman moved forward on his desk. Rashawn looked into his eyes, his dark eyes. They began to dig into her. She turned away.

"I think my dreams have something to do with my rape," she went on now.

As usual, Roman didn't flinch.

"The dreams seem to come when I'm deeply sleeping. I can't wake up, no matter how hard I try. And this man . . ."

"Do you know the man?" Roman asked.

Rashawn felt the heat come to her face. She hoped her complexion covered it, but could tell by Roman's expression that he had seen her blush.

"Yes, I do," she said, readjusting herself in the seat. "But the point I'm getting at is . . ."

"Who is it?" he asked.

"I don't think that's important," she answered.

"I think I can help you if . . ."

"I don't think that's important," she said bluntly. "I'm not here to tell you my pornographic dreams. I'm here to ask you if perhaps they mean anything? Should I be afraid?" she asked, gesturing wildly.

"I wouldn't know. I'm a psychiatrist, not a soothsayer," he said, chuckling now, to her surprise.

Rashawn thought about his words. She wanted to be angry, but deep down inside, what he had said was indeed humorous, and very true. She had asked him to interpret a dream as if wanting to have her premonition read.

"I'm sorry, Roman," she said, standing now, shaking her head in embarrassment. He stood quickly.

"Rashawn, I'm sorry. You're upset now, aren't you?"

"No . . . no, I'm not. I just realize now how silly I must sound," she sighed, smoothing down her skirt and then her hair.

"Nothing is silly," he retorted, his voice caring and soft.

"I mean, they are just so real, though. I can almost feel his skin, smell his cologne," Rashawn added, her brow creasing as she spoke. Her disturbance was showing. "It's like . . ." she started, before suddenly the door opened and Blain stepped in.

He realized his own intrusion.

"Oh, excuse me," he said. Rashawn cleared her throat nervously as she quickly brushed by him on her way out.

After a moment of silence between them, Blain spoke.

"So, what the hell was that all about?" he asked.

Roman attempted to ignore him, taking his keys out of his pocket and starting for the door. Blain blocked him.

"I asked you a question," he growled. Roman looked at him with hate showing in his eyes.

"Move your hand or I'll break it," he threatened.

Roman couldn't fight the anger he felt . . . the rage. For more years than he wanted to remember, he'd gone rounds with Blain, and soon it would have to end. There was a time when Roman tolerated this kind of thing, being accosted and accused of the ridiculous, but he and Blain were getting too old for this, and it was time for their crazy game of jealousy to end. Kindred sprits is what they were, one black, one white, both passionate and determined, both in love with the same woman—again. Roman could see it on Blain's face that he too was a man desirous of Rashawm Ams.

"I'm not going to let you do this," Blain said now.

"Do what?" Roman asked.

Both men stood silent, allowing the tension in the air to speak for them. Roman and Blain were about to repeat history, however, it was time he planned to 'flip the script' so to speak, on all this madness. Blain had long thought him weak, but he wasn't. He had more power than Blain Tollome could imagine.

"Stay away from her, or I'll . . ." Blain finally began, breaking the silence.

"You'll what?" Roman glowered, getting up in Blain's face, showing no intimidation. "You'll kill me?" he spat.

"Don't push me, Roman," Blain growled. Roman laughed, pushing his way past him.

"You are a very troubled man," he said, simplifying what he felt were Blain's bigger issues.

"No, you're gonna have trouble. You keep creeping around Rashawn," Blain went on, giving Roman a shove with his two fingers, poking hard into his chest. Roman slapped his hand away.

"You're gonna give me trouble? What is this, the pot calling the kettle black, so to speak?" Roman snickered, knowing the color of Blain's skin was always a sensitive point for him. Being white would not have been Blain's choice of color had he been given one.

"You had your day, now stand down," Roman said, sounding full of confidence, control, and superiority, as the older of the two.

"So, it's war, is it?" Blain asked, taking Roman's military expression to heart. "How many more wounded, Roman? How many more lives?"

"God, you're full of melodrama today, aren't you?" Roman asked, with a wicked smile curving his lips. "By the way, I'm not responsible for my adulteress wife's death, if that's where this conversation is going," he added, finishing that conversation before it even started. "As if I need to tell you—again," he smacked, and then quickly pulled open his door. "Now, get out," he insisted.

"You won't get away with that crime either. Don't be responsible for another," Blain said, nodding in the direction in which Rashawn had gone, his nostrils flaring in anger.

It was taking everything Roman had to resist the building fight that was way past overdue.

"Your brain and how it works will always amaze me." Roman let out a sardonic hoot. "I had nothing to do with Jasmine's murder. You know that. I was . . ."

"Drugged out of your mind, and don't know what the hell happened," Blain finished the sentence. "I've read the report a million times," he barked, fanning his hand, uninterested in the excuses for Roman's claimed innocence. "Next you'll have everyone believing in a mysterious masked bandit."

"Don't make me put you out," Roman threatened.

"In your wildest dreams, old man," Blain said, bursting into laughter before leaving.

Chapter 26

Maceba's heart raced as she watched from her car. She'd been stalking Blain for over a week now. His being off work due to the school break gave her plenty of time to track his comings and goings.

All she wanted was to catch him with Doc engaged in something even remotely illegal. Just one good time and she would bust them both. But it never happened. Never did the elusive Doc make a showing. It was almost as if they were both on to her and Blain had Doc hiding out.

She'd tried to get a tap on Blain's phone; however, she couldn't prove any connection with him and the drugs on campus.

After the fiasco of trying to seduce him, she knew better than to try anything else like that.

"That was humiliating," she muttered, before suddenly seeing Blain coming from Red's apartment building. He looked different somehow—angry, wickedly mad.

"Maybe another date gone wrong," she said aloud, her jealousy showing just a little. She heard herself and shook her head free of the thoughts she had about Blain and his 'love life'

"Focus Maceba, God! What is your problem?" she asked herself, watching, as Blain walked quickly to his SUV, climbed behind the wheel, and peeled off, breaking the neighborhood speed limits without question. Maceba followed him.

The two officers hesitated before heading up to Red's apartment. Red was a drug dealer.

They didn't want to believe it. As a matter a fact, no one in the precinct wanted to believe it. But the captain had said to bring him in for questioning, and that's what they were gonna do.

Sometimes these young cadets just were not ready for law enforcement. It happened.

At the door, one of the officers noticed that it was slightly ajar, and the television was on full blast. He looked at his partner who shrugged and gave the door a little shove.

"Red!" he called. There was no answer.

They both called again when they entered the apartment and looked around for the young man.

Splitting up, one of the men went toward the bathroom. The sight there was alarming. It was Red. He was slumped over on the floor, his throat cut; his lips were blue, and his eyes wide-open. His face was a strange hue of misty green, contrasting wickedly with his fiery red hair. He was dead.

Blain showered—a long hot one. When he finished he heard his doorbell ringing. He looked at his watch, out of habit more than anything else.

Looking through the peephole, he was shocked to see Maceba there.

What the hell does she want? he asked himself, opening the door after giving his living room a quick glance for neatness.

"Hi," she said, sounding shy and a little sheepish.

"Here to screw more information out of me," he greeted rudely.

Her face blushed but still she moved past him into his home, looking around suspiciously as if hoping to catch him in some kind of 'act'.

"What are you looking for, Ceba?" he asked her after following her around the living room, kitchen, and finally ending up with her standing in his bedroom.

"I . . . I just don't trust you, Blain. I think you know something about this case. I know you know who Doc is. I know you know he attacked me, and I know . . ." she began, but found herself unable to finish speaking as Blain stopped her words with a kiss.

"Why you playing games with me, Ceba?"

"I'm not. I'm . . ." she began, only to have Blain stop her words again with another passionate kiss.

"You don't play fair . . . you don't," he told her, kissing her neck, unbuttoning her blouse, filling his nose with her scent.

Quickly he undressed her before she could remember how she truly felt about him, how much she hated him.

"You saying I cheat?" she asked, quickly helping him with his zipper.

"Yeah. You're just a damn cheater."

"Cheaters never win."

"Your words, not mine," he said, staring at her for a second before lifting her from her feet. Together they tumbled onto his bed while groping and kissing each other with a passion resembling horny teenagers.

Blain couldn't go back in time, he couldn't change what Doc had done to her. But maybe somehow through his actions he could make it up to her. Maybe he could make things right, just like he wanted to make things right with Rashawn.

So much guilt he carried, and was it truly all his?

He couldn't imagine being the animal Roman had convinced him that he was. The growing anxiety over Doc and his actions began to ache at his head. Doc began to ache at his spirit.

"No, not now," he begged Doc, pleading with him not to come, not to ruin this, not to kill her.

"Yes now," purred Maceba, begging, speaking with words of blind passion, not realizing whom she was calling to, summoning—not realizing how she would lament the beckoning.

Maceba received Doc with the result of the inner battle with Blain coming forth in the form of a violent entry that caused her to cry out.

Doc cursed her while sexing her wildly and with an unbridled passion that left her breathless, gasping for air. "You want to know about Doc, bitch?" he asked her, pulling at her hair. "You want to know?"

"Yes! Yes I do," she screamed, not realizing for one moment how she would one day regret those words.

Doc stood with her, wrapping her legs around him, pinning her to the wall, where he, without tiring, made her moan for at least another hour.

"Maceba, you need to get off this case," Blain said softly, stroking her hair as she lay on his chest. The room was dark and filled with their aura. It was sensual and sultry, relaxing to his senses.

"Why does everyone keep telling me that? I thought you of all people would understand my need to catch this man," she explained, looking up into his eyes. He closed them, as if that way she would not see him— through him. Maybe if he closed his eyes she would not able to see the demon who lived within him.

"Do you love me?" he asked her after a moment of silence. She said nothing.

Of course not, Doc taunted. "Do you love me?" he asked again.

Still she said nothing.

"Woman, the man asked you a question. Just answer!" He growled suddenly as Doc, pulling her by the hair, snapped at her.

Fear rushed through her before she felt the grip on her hair loosen and the rise of his nature. "Maceba," Blain whispered into the darkness of the room, stroking her hair gentler now. His voice, strange and distant, moved her.

Mounting him, she slid down on his hardness.

His eyes closed as his tension seemed to ease and his troubled brow smoothed. She examined his body, his broad chest, scarred with healed over wounds, keloidal and raised, marked his conquest in battle. His muscular arms were tattooed and strong, his hands, thick and large.

He pulled her to him, holding her tight as together they worked out their forbidden feelings for one another.

It was late by the time Maceba left the big man sleeping like an innocent baby. Her head spun with the confusion she now felt. All she knew to be rational thoughts banged around in her brain.

She refused to see the troubled man in him.

She refused to see guilt in him.

She refused to see the evidence of the crimes Blain had committed earlier that evening.

Hot tears ran down her face as she crossed the San Rafael Bridge that took her back to the city.

Chapter 27

Rita called Rashawn and asked her to come over for Sunday brunch that weekend.

When she walked into the house in the Palemos, it felt good to be home, although Trina's decorating efforts were everywhere.

Marriage to Jason confused Trina—a lot. That was all Rashawn could figure.

"You like it?" she asked, noticing Rashawn looking at her abstract art on the wall.

"Uhhh, sure," Rashawn stammered.

"Thanks, sweetie," Trina answered, sounding perky. "I painted it," she admitted, and then began humming as she went back into the kitchen. Rashawn then noticed the looseness of her jeans, and knew exactly why Trina was sounding so happy. She was losing weight.

On the other hand, Rita was huge. It seemed like she'd blown up like a balloon overnight. But then again, she was expecting another set of twins.

The news was so shocking that Rashawn had all but blocked it out. However, seeing Rita now had brought it all back. She looked so miserable and tired. Rashawn hugged her tight, hoping good feelings would pass through to her.

Rashawn's other sisters showed up shortly afterwards. Qiana was invited to join in the festivities as a fill in for Shelby, the youngest sister who was out of the country. Conversation was lively as the women sat in the kitchen enjoying rich biscuits with heavy gravy, eggs benedict, sausage, bacon, and fresh winter melons. It was getting on that time of year for the Ams girls— Christmas without their parents.

"Is Shelby gonna make it back in time this year?" Trina asked.

"I think so. She made it last year," answered Carlotta, not bringing up the fact that Rashawn had been the one missing at the table last Christmas.

"Are we gonna have any new men at the table this year?" Trina asked, directing the question toward Rashawn, who frowned.

"No," she answered quickly.

"What about that beefcake who was helping with the move?" Rita asked, loading up her plate with slices of cantaloupe.

"Oh yeah, Rashawn. What about him? Damn, he was phoine . . ." Trina squirmed with ecstasy at just the thought of Blain Tollome's broad shoulders. "He's white, too, or else just really, really high yella—hard to tell with them juicy lips." Trina glanced at Carlotta, who raised an eyebrow at Rashawn.

"No, oh, hell no. I don't like him. He's creepy. Plus we make a bad rhythm, ya know what I mean," Rashawn responded to the inquiry. "I have to admit, though, that lately I have been having some hot dreams about him, howeverrrr . . ." she cackled giving into the mood of the morning.

For the moment, Rashawn felt safe with her sisters

and Qiana, enough to admit to the dreams she had been having. They were just dreams after all.

A dream can't hurt you.

But then, there was no way she was going to discuss her true feelings of disturbance.

"What do you mean 'a bad rhythm' You two already . . ." Carlotta asked.

"I thought you were dreaming about Chance Davis," Qiana's sudden interruption divulged.

"Oh, there're two men on the horizon," Rita teased now. Nobody noticed Carlotta's growing disturbance, her seriousness.

"Two, shoot, call me the playa of the year, even my therapist is kinda, hitting my dream button," Rashawn chortled further, allowing her sentence to broach onto the dream conversation but stop just short of the details.. Trina let out a howl.

"The *bitch* is back amongst the living," Rita laughed loudly.

"Gurl, I was beginning to worry 'bout yo ass."

"Two men. A therapist. Shawnie, what the hell is going on with you? You're seeing a therapist, why?" Carlotta interjected, sounding stony and cold. Rashawn flashed a glance at Qiana and then swallowed hard.

The laughter died away.

"You know, it's funny, I always thought when the time came to get all of this off my chest, to put it all behind me, it was gonna be hard. But it's not, it's not gonna be hard at all," Rashawn began, flashing a wide grin at Qiana who audibly gulped as she prepared herself for the results of Rashawn's revelation to her sisters.

"Why you lookin' at Qiana? What is it, Shawnie?" Carlotta asked, unconsciously gripping the edges of the table where she sat at the head.

"Carlotta, Shawnie is trying to tell you. She . . ." Qiana began, only to receive the palm of Carlotta's hand in her face silencing her immediately.

The hush fell heavy among them and stayed for what seemed like hours, although it was not more than a moment.

"I was raped," Rashawn said, speaking only to her eldest sibling. "I was raped and I didn't tell you. I hid it. I . . ." Carlotta's loud emotional outburst interrupted Rashawn's confession. Ta'Rae grabbed her arm tight to help her maintain her composure.

"When?" Ta'Rae asked Rashawn, taking over the questioning since Carlotta now was beside herself. "Was he caught? When did all this happen?"

"A couple of years ago, well," she nodded toward Reggie and said nothing more.

"Oh Lord Jesus, his daddy is a rapist?" Carlotta moaned, weaving just a little. Ta'Rae tightened her grip.

Trina and Rita said nothing. Both of their minds had gone quickly back to the nights filled with Rashawn's nightmares and sweaty dreams. Rita didn't even ask why she hadn't said anything. She knew. Trina grabbed Rashawn's arm tight while she held back tears behind a tight smile.

"It's okay, sister, it's over now," Trina said, kissing her cheek. "And we're here for you," she added.

"No, it's not all right what I did. I nearly ruined my friendship with Qiana," Rashawn said, taking hold of Qiana's hand. "And I lied to my sisters, my refuge, my family. I thought I could find my strength in my lies but I can't."

"Shawnie, I think we understand," Rita began, only to have Carlotta begin again.

"No, no, we don't understand," Carlotta growled, tears draining from her pools of melting copper.

"Carlotta, don't," Trina snapped, coming to Rashawn's defense.

"Don't start on her. We've all had secrets. You've had secrets, too," Trina added, apparently putting Carlotta in her place, as the anger seemed to ease from her face just a little.

"Trina . . ." Ta'Rae bit now, showing that Carlotta's secret was one she knew about too. "Rashawn, look, we're just emotional and this news is shocking. You have to know that. Did you see a doctor, did you even . . ." Ta'Rae was attempting to get the conversation back on track now.

"It's okay. I get AIDS tested regularly. So far, so good. I'm not really worried about that too much, though. I was more worried about . . . you know, feeling whole again," Rashawn said, directing her comments toward Rita, whose eyes seemed to demand that comment. "I worry about feeling sane," she admitted, tipping slightly into the feelings she had been having lately.

"Well, sweetie, that's gonna take time. I mean, it sounds like you're doing okay," Rita said, with a smile coming slowly. "We Ams women can do anything. We's scrong heffas," she added with a light, nervous chuckle.

"Besides, I've met someone I really like. He's very nice," Rashawn confessed, directing the comment to Carlotta who still looked at her as if barely recognizing her. "The man I spent Thanksgiving with. He doesn't know about Reggie yet, but I'm gonna tell him, and it's gonna be okay," Rashawn explained and then raised her glass of juice. "Now come on, let's enjoy the rest of our brunch and think about Christmas," she added.

Carlotta nodded slowly, sniffling and wiping at her tears before they fell. She held on to strength the best she could while glancing over at Reggie every now and then.

For the rest of the day, Rashawn's sisters could be caught giving Reggie a closer than normal look, searching for any clues as to what his father could look like.

* * *

Leon dropped his backpack in the seat next to the wall. He didn't want to risk the contents falling out. He was nervous, and knew he was not at his best. It had been a long, sleepless night. He looked around at the other patrons in the small restaurant enjoying their Sunday suppers.

He'd never been here, but from what he saw of it, it was nice. If this was that female Fed's idea of a pay off, he was all for it—so far.

She wanted information about Doc.

Everybody is scared of him.

"Not me," Leon said in an undertone.

Doc was a big deal when it came to drug dealers. He was far from small potatoes. Although he may not have been on the America's most wanted list, he surely had made the INL's top ten for many years apparently, according to Maceba Baxter.

Importing an often-lethal narcotic from his native island of Jamaica, Doc had manufactured it several ways over the years, peddling it around the city. On this stop, Moorman U, under a new name—Get Ass. Of course, Leon happened to know that Doc's personal drug of choice was cocaine.

Funny how he wouldn't touch the Get Ass with a 10-foot pole.

Rubbing his forehead, Leon noticed cool moisture on his fingertips. It was nearly freezing outside, yet here he was perspiring.

Okay, maybe he was a little afraid of Doc, but not enough to turn down a chance like this—immunity, pure and simple. Doc had moved into murder and Leon wanted no parts of that. He knew, however, if Doc were to find out that he was here, selling him out this way, he would be added to Doc's death row. No second chance—just like Red. The death of Red had scared Leon witless.

Leon wanted out of this mess. He wanted out now. How hard could it be to take this man down? He was only human, right?

Leon looked at his watch. Maceba Baxter was late.

"Maybe I need to get up outta here," he said aloud. Even though delicious aromas wafted out from the restaurant's kitchen, and he was a little hungry, he decided he'd have to meet with his connection another time. Maybe he could grab a bite from the burger joint he passed on his way there.

Just then, a tiny bit of a woman slid into the booth across from him. "You're a Fed?" he asked, surprised to see such a small person behind the commanding phone presence.

"I work for the INL," Maceba answered flatly, not attempting much by way of a trivia exchange. There was no time to shoot the breeze.

Leon's eyes darted back and forth now.

"You scared?" Maceba asked.

"Shit, yeah," he admitted now.

"Well, don't be. Just answer my questions. I'm trying to help you."

"Like you helped Red, right?" Leon asked, sarcasm dripping.

"Red didn't do what he was told," Maceba answered, showing no guilt or regret.

"Well, do I need a lawyer?"

"Are you under arrest?"

"Am I?"

"Not yet, but I can arrange it."

"Not yet? Not ever, bitch!" Leon snapped, standing now.

Maceba tugged at the strap of his backpack urging him to sit back down.

"Calm down, Leon. You help me, and I'm gonna help you," she assured him.

"I just can't believe Red is really dead," Leon sighed, finishing dinner at Maceba's expense. The tension between them had lessoned immensely and now they conversed openly about the situation to which they both found themselves a part of.

"Well, believe it."

"Doc did it, you know. I know he did, and the girl, too. And . . . and he's doing other stuff too," Leon explained, feeling more relaxed and liberal with information.

"Like what?"

"He's using that Get Ass drug on the faculty members."

"Using it?"

"You know, for sex," Leon explained, lowering his voice slightly.

"Who told you that? I mean, rape doesn't sound like Doc's MO," Maceba said, thinking aloud. Doc was not a sexual predator, despite his crimes.

"Well, he musta changed it a little. Red told me that's what he's doing. Red said one night he went up to that teacher's office, Ams is her name—the one that Doc's got the hots for. He went up to lock up. Anyway, Red said that he listened at the door. He heard the sex. Had to be Doc, cuz the guy was loud and gross . . ."

"It was obvious she was sleeping. No woman could have possibly stayed quiet being sexed the way Doc was going at it," Red explained, sweat appearing on his top lip as he spoke.

"Red also told me Doc killed that girl too . . ."

"I didn't kill her. When I got there, she was already dead. She called the office screaming at me, so I agreed to meet her. I don't know what I was gonna do when I got there, but man, I

tell you when I got there she was dead, throat cut," Red said, slicing his hand along his own throat. *"I got outta there with a quickness. I wasn't trying to stick around."*

"Doc is the only one I know who carries a knife like that," Leon went on. "Sure, Red did the college girl and he felt bad about that, but he didn't kill her. Doc did it," Leon told Maceba, who sighed heavily after hearing it all. "I know he did it. Who else would have? You can say all day he's not a rapist but I know damn well he's a murderer."

"What about Blain Tollome? Why not him? I mean, he is in on all this mess, isn't he?"

Leon stared at her for a long time before bursting into laughter.

"What the hell is so funny?" she asked him.

Leon again stared at her a moment before speaking. "You can't be serious?"

"I'm very serious."

"Who in the hell do you think Doc is?"

Maceba sat for a long time behind the wheel of her car. She could barely breathe. Her journey to the truth had ended now, with her feelings dashed against a brick wall in the discovery. It hurt like hell. She hurt like hell. But at least it was all clear now. She knew clearly what needed to be done. Doc had to be stopped, once and for all.

Realizing she had him in the palm of her hands all of this time troubled her, but in all actuality, his words made sense now, the game he accused her of playing with him. He'd all but told her to her face what was going on between them.

But he had called her a cheater. That part she still didn't understand.

"But I'm sure I will soon," she mumbled under her breath as she started the ignition.

Maceba gave Leon a plane ticket to get out of town, departing in two hours.

He had just enough time to make it if he left now, but when he stood to leave, he bumped right into Doc. Leon's heart raced as if the devil himself stood there smiling wickedly.

"What 'cha doing here, Leon?" Doc asked.

"Ta . . . I . . ." Leon began to stammer. His words cut short as he felt the tip of a blade under his ribs.

What a surprise Juanita had for Chance that New Year's Day—the biggest one Chance ever thought possible.

"Pregnant?" he asked, although he really didn't want to hear Juanita say it again.

"Yes," she answered.

"I don't believe you," he snapped, looking out toward the sound of the waves, which drew him to the sliding glass door. He stepped out of the apartment onto the balcony. He soon heard Juanita behind him rustling paper. He turned to see her holding up her pregnancy test confirmation.

"I knew you would say that so I brought this," she said, dabbing the tissue to her red nostrils. "And my husband is sterile, I can bring his medical records too if you want. He's going to divorce me you know, as soon as he finds out." Chance just groaned and snatched the paper from her, tossing it into the sea below without looking at it. The paper floated down slowly.

He then stared at Juanita for a long time—her face, her eyes, her small hands. Pulling her to him, he held her tight.

"Juanita, this is crazy. Why now?" he asked.

"That's what I get for taking a chance," she whimpered, burying her head in his chest. He smiled to himself, stroking her fuzzy hair.

* * *

Lying in her big bed, Rashawn stared at the clock. It was nearly 1:00 A.M.. She hadn't slept a wink. She felt discordant and her body clock was totally off.

She'd been feeling *different* for weeks. Even her cycle had gotten out of whack, "and I know I'm not pregnant," she mumbled under her breath, listening to the night sounds of her house.

Suddenly there was a noise that rang off key. It was the sound of her door opening, had to be. Even though she heard no key turning, the sudden resonances of outside sounded closer as if . . .

She sprung up in the bed.

Immediately thinking of Reggie, she jumped from the bed, and ran from her room into his, slamming the door and locking it. She felt foolish for not having her gun closer to her. She felt panic stricken that her crazy dreams had driven her to the point of not being able to distinguish them from true life.

Climbing quickly into bed with him, she held him tight until his mild disturbance caused by her shaking hands and loud beating heart, subsided.

She strained to hear anything more, but the house again grew familiarly quiet. Soon she, with Reggie tight in her arms, dozed off to sleep.

Blain sat in his car staring at Rashawn's condominium, waiting. He wanted to see for himself if it were true. If what he imagined to be was truly the way it was.

"There, are you satisfied?" Doc asked after giving him the answer to his burning questions regarding Rashawn and what was really going on inside her bedroom in the middle of the night.

Blain buried his head in his hands.

Chapter 28

Gray days followed more gray days. The year left with many wondering how the New Year would come in.

Davis knew he'd find Rashawn in the cafeteria today. He'd seen her eating lunch there every day this week, and he hadn't even stopped to say hello. Between the disturbance with the Yvette situation still unresolved, the total distraction caused by the Andy Simmons and Rogelio Brown incidents, and then the disappearance of the two security guards, and Blain's eerie silence, coupled with his guilty conscience from this 'Juanita thing', Davis didn't know what to think, let alone *say* to Rashawn. Nevertheless, here she was, wearing burgundy, her hair in an up-do off her shoulders and exposing her long, supple neck. How he longed to kiss that neck and nibble on those earlobes.

Fat chance of that now, Chance, you screwed that up royally. Juanita's words were still ringing in his ears, her scent still in his nose. His life was a mess, he was a mess. What had he turned into? If he had asked a preacher . . . which he did not, they would have surely told him to repent, turn around . . . seek absolution. He believed all those things would come from Rashawn, he just didn't know how to go about earning them.

How about starting with some honesty?

Davis shook off the thoughts in his head as he approached Rashawn at her table. She looked up at him, but didn't smile.

She knows.

Davis's guilty mind told him she already knew.

"Can we talk?" he simply asked.

"This sounds like it's something serious. Let's go somewhere quieter, a little more private," Rashawn said, gathering her things immediately as if she too burned to tell him something.

"It's been a long time, Davis," said Rashawn while they strolled along the edge of the man-made lake.

Moorman University was a beautiful campus. The layout spoke of vision. Somewhere in some architect's mind, they had to have figured that a person could learn so much more when surrounded by trees, water, and flowers. Perhaps they were right, because right now, Davis was learning that he really did care for Rashawn and wanted another chance.

Rashawn was learning, too. Maybe she should throw love to Davis.

"So what's happening?" she asked him.

"You want honesty or bullshit?" he asked, looking over the lake. Rashawn was shocked at his frankness.

"Uh, sounds like I might want a little bullshit," she chuckled.

He loved her smile.

"No, you want the truth. I have . . . been having . . . had some unfinished business with my ex-wife," he stammered, in a way that told Rashawn exactly what he meant.

"Did that have anything to do with . . . ?"

"No . . . no," he said, taking her hands in his. "Look,

this is not the right time to talk," he said, looking at his watch. "My last class ends at four. Meet me there, and we'll talk more," he said.

"Let's go to your place to talk," Rashawn said. Davis smiled warmly, tempted to kiss her cheek.

But not here, not now with so many people watching.

The fire rose high in the fireplace. He joined Rashawn on the sofa to watch it for a moment before speaking.

"Days ending early are good, especially when you like to watch fires," he said. She agreed, sipping the Chablis. The silence grew between them until Davis broke it with a kiss. He was surprised that she accepted it.

"Juanita, my ex-wife, she's what you might call 'a player,' I mean, she played me," he chuckled nervously, letting his mood hide his true feelings.

"Are you sleeping with her?" Rashawn asked flatly.

Why not ask? They were friends, right? She had no claims to this man. *Right.*

He nodded.

Her heart sank.

"It wasn't planned," he said. "Maybe it was . . . who knows." Davis sounded flustered.

"You still love her?" Rashawn asked.

"Hell no," he answered flatly. "Now that, I do know." Rashawn curled her lip and looked at him.

"Hey, you're the one who said sex is not the same as love and all that," he smiled.

"I never said that," she said, folding her arms and pouting playfully.

"Then trust me on this, it's not," he said.

"Then why?" she asked. He looked away and then back at her.

"Why you all up in my business?" he asked jokingly. She burst into laughter.

"She played you!" Rashawn laughed. "How much money did you give her?" Rashawn laughed again.

"Nothing. Thank goodness, she's not like that."

Suddenly, he grew serious.

"She's pregnant," Davis now confessed.

Rashawn's eyes widened.

"Yours . . ?"

"She says it is, but I'm not so sure," Davis answered quickly, as if pushing the words from his lips, admitting it to himself for the first time.

"So what does this mean?" Rashawn asked, her heart aching just a little, while her brain tried to keep the confusion from clouding out reasonable thoughts like forgiveness and understanding, worked over time.

"Now . . . what about you?" he began.

"Me?" she squeaked.

"Yes. I've shared my dirt, now you share yours. You wanted to come here for a reason," he said. "Why did you drive me to the arms of a Jezebel by rejecting me," he teased. She fanned him on.

"Yeah, well I did sorta want to talk," she began, clearing her throat. "I feel suddenly as if we are in this, like, relationship, ya know," she chuckled.

"Yeah, I knocked up my ex and you're avoiding me like the plague. It's a great . . ."

She slapped his arm playfully, "Stop."

"Just kidding," he laughed, leaning in to kiss her.

"I was raped," she blurted. He froze with his lips still puckered.

"It was on Moorman's campus, back before they installed the new lights."

"Did you report it? I never heard anything . . ."

"No, I didn't. I was . . . I was scared . . . and afraid. I just wanted it not to have happened to me," she said, holding strong. Once again, she felt calm. Maybe talking about it was the best thing for her to do. This was only the third time she talked about it, and she wasn't panicking or hyperventilating. This was nothing like when she attempted to talk to Dr. Roman.

"Do you remember anything?"

"Yes. He had an accent of some kind, and his cologne . . ." Rashawn closed her eyes as the memory came in on her full force now.

For the first time in almost two years, Rashawn allowed her mind to fill to the brim with the memory of that night.

"It was a night I will never forget." She sighed. Davis pulled her closer to him. "I was walking to my car. It was after one of those boring meetings," she began. Davis nodded his understanding.

"Wesley Hawthorne had asked me to meet him at the campus. We were going to go for dinner after, but that was a total bust in plans. That was when he was running for Dean. Anyway, I was leaving for my car and I thought someone was following me. I had no idea who it was, but after it all happened, I thought it was my best friend's ex, Russell Thompson. You remember him?"

"Yes, I do. The weirdo from the parking lot, that day he was being all rude . . ."

"Yes, well, he ended up attacking my best friend and killing her unborn child," Rashawn continued, her eyes burning from the building emotion she had held back for so long.

"Oh my God," Chance exclaimed.

"The police killed him, so I thought it was over. I even sought out therapy from Dr. Roman to talk about my feelings. I told him about the rape," she confessed.

"You did?" Davis asked.

"Yes, I did."

"What did he do?" Davis asked, his question sounding strange. Rashawn leaned back a little to see his face. She was wondering why he asked.

"Nothing. I left before we could really talk about it. However, I did let it slip about Reggie," she said, slipping again.

"Reggie?" he asked.

"My son," Rashawn said flatly, and then listened as her voice reverberated in the silence.

"You had a child?" Davis asked, his body language speaking for him. Rashawn frowned.

"Yes, I have a child," she snipped. Davis noticed how he had moved away from her and again pulled her back into him.

"Okay. You have a child," he sighed. "Reggie."

"Yes, I named him after my father. Anyway, I just found out that Rufus was sterile, so I know that someone else raped me. I got pregnant from the rape, so . . ."

"So did Yvette. I think that's why someone killed her," Davis blurted out. Rashawn's brain spun from the instant overload of interjected information.

"She was pregnant?" Rashawn asked, as if she hadn't been hearing about it all day.

"Yes, that night you saw us talking, she was telling me. I got Juanita, my ex, to hypnotize her and help uncover what she remembered about the night of the rape. Juanita is a psychotherapist. I'm beginning to think that might be my problem. Anyway, Yvette had been raped by using that Get Ass drug—I'm certain. Now the police are questioning me, me, of all people. Tollome even called himself questioning me," Davis said with a scowl.

"Blain? What is it to him? It didn't happen on campus, did it?" Rashawn asked, wondering immediately about the possible connection.

"No, it didn't. He needs to be investigating the stuff that does happen there. The drug deals, your car being vandalized, your rape," Davis said, showing true concern in his eyes.

They sat quietly for a moment allowing the silence to speak for them.

"So what happened between you and Blain?" Davis asked, digging for further information. Rashawn rolled her eyes.

"Why do you ask?"

"I think I need to know. I . . . I just feel the need to know," Davis stumbled, his face reddening a little.

"Trust me; you don't have anything to worry about with Blain. Am I to worry about Juanita?"

Davis shook his head.

"Then you're not to worry about Blain. He's got some serious control issues but . . ."

"Well, I think he's dirty. I think he's involved in all the stuff going on at the university. I'm watching him with both eyes open," Davis admitted.

"Do you really think you should get involved with all that . . . with him?" Rashawn asked, showing concern.

"You don't think I can handle Blain Tollome?" Davis asked, pushing up his glasses. Rashawn didn't answer out loud; however, her silence said what she thought of his physical abilities if he ever came up against Blain in hand to hand combat. Chance just chuckled, accepting the facts without them needing to be spoken.

"You know, I want to meet your son. I want to be in your world, all the way," Davis told her, nuzzling her neck. Rashawn accepted his affection. "But I've got all this stuff on me right now. I shoulda been honest with you about Juanita from the start," he confessed without looking at her, sighing heavily on her shoulder.

"Well, I didn't tell you about Reggie," she too, confessed. He looked at her now and smiled.

"I'm gonna break it off with Juanita for good, ya know—soon. Like, yesterday," he admitted.

"I'm sure you are, but until you do, we can only be

friends, Davis. I can't confuse Reggie like that," Rashawn finally said. She could feel him sigh into her shoulder again and then nod slowly. Her heart ached a little.

She was so close to love and yet . . .

Chapter 29

Again, he couldn't resist. Rashawn was too sweet, too beautiful. The memory of her body encasing his, was nearly too vivid. He couldn't pass up the chance, especially considering how stressed he'd been lately. Maceba's presence in his life was causing him more stress than anyone realized.

He'd tried to stay away from Rashawn for a few days but it was impossible. He knew he was killing her slowly but sometimes that was the price for love, right?

He'd taken his time to love Rashawn tonight, right there on the floor in front of the sofa, even lighting candles for the occasion.

She'd had nearly two whole water bottles tonight, and slept like a stone. He tried to keep his control, yet he still got at her twice. He could have had his way with her all night if he wanted, "But then that would be greedy," he told himself, smiling at the memory.

He'd finished making love to her the first time and had started cleaning her up with a warm towel. He'd washed her thighs and her intimate places, removing all traces of his love for her. Yet, tending to her on such an up close and personal basis had only aroused him again. "But you didn't seem to mind," he snickered, inhaling her scent, which remained on his fingertips.

Suddenly he thought about Reggie. What if he had come down the stairs and seen his parents that way—entwined, conjoined, copulating.

"Well, it's only natural. The show of tender affection is a natural thing," he said into the camera. "And besides, if I play my cards right, she'll give me a daughter next time."

The next morning while Rashawn sat staring aimlessly from the window, Maceba hesitated outside her office. What she had to tell her was not going to be easy, and all she could hope for was that along with the difficulty of the news, there would be accuracy in what she was telling. Maceba was disturbed about this whole thing. What Doc was doing to Rashawn Ams was very different, even for him. Nonetheless, Maceba was about to stop him cold in his tracks. She was about to end his reign over Moorman University.

She was about to purge herself of guilt.

Doc was the man behind the drugs, which led Maceba to believe he was raping Rashawn, using the drug on her to knock her out while ruthlessly taking her dignity.

The drug dealing and even the possibility of murder made sense to Maceba; however, rape wasn't up his normal street. Normally Doc was just a brute, a vicious drug dealer who cared nothing about his victims and even less about what he stood for in society's eyes, however, when it came to women, he was more of a ladies man, charming and all that.

"Whatever . . ." Maceba shook her head of the thoughts that were creeping in.

The sounds of his voice close to her ear, the strength of his hands, the heat their bodies made while working out their for-

bidden lust for one another. How could Doc be her lover . . . the thought gave her chills.

Rashawn was a confident and beautiful looking woman. Doc's desire for her made total sense. He was a very primal man who loved beautiful, black women. Maceba knew that much about him.

He was coaxing, enticing, exciting even, until . . .

"Now, how can I explain all this to Rashawn without sounding like a jealous idiot?" Maceba asked herself. She thought about her former partner's words.

"Get out of this Maceba. Let it go, let the cops do their job. You're taking this too personal."

But she wasn't going to go out like that. Doc had tried to take her life. No Blain—Blain had tried to kill her. It was personal. She had trusted him, worked beside him for crying out loud. Maybe even loved him.

Such betrayal! Such . . . Maceba's eyes burned with the thought of it. She shook her head.

"The point being, Maceba, is that now you are on some vigilante mission," Phil explained. "You need to give the information you have to the chief," her former partner went on, trying to convince her to turn over what she knew about Blain Tollome to their superior so the agents assigned to the Moorman case could do their jobs.

Phil knew even his loyalty to her could only go on so much longer before he would have to roll over on her and give up what she was telling him. "I want to work with you. Hell, I want to be a hero too, but the way you're going about this is kinda . . ."

"I didn't intend to sleep with him. I told you that! I didn't know . . ." Maceba blurted out, her voice full of shame. She couldn't stop the tears from welling up in her eyes.

Phil wrapped his arm around Maceba's shoulder and gave her a brotherly squeeze.

"You act like I'm going to tell anybody about that. I wouldn't," he promised.

She nodded sadly, full of humiliation and embarrassment.

"I wasn't talking about that. Actually, I was talking about you taking on this case undercover, flying without an agency net like this. It's dumb."

"I know, but it's something I have to do. Doc . . ." Maceba paused. *"Blain has hurt so many people."*

"Come in, Maceba." Rashawn smiled weakly.

"Your name is so familiar to me, beyond the class," Rashawn admitted, smiling past her tired, drawn out looks. Having just pulled out a water bottle from her small fridge, she sat it down on her desk, unopened, giving Maceba her full attention instead. "Are you here about the quiz? I know the questions were a little convoluted, so I'm grading very loosely because of it. I . . ."

"Actually Dr. Ams, I'm here on another matter, a more official one," Maceba said, reaching into the inside fold of her jacket and sliding out the card that identified her in the capacity of a working INL agent. Rashawn's eyes widened at the sight of the badge.

"I'm a little confused, which isn't very difficult for me lately, but anyway . . ." Rashawn chuckled, attempting to hide her nervousness. She'd been feeling shaky all day, worse than ever before, perhaps it was the flu . . . who knew.

The seat by the door—the hot seat—was where Maceba now sat. She took a deep breath before speaking.

"As you know, Moorman U. has a drug problem—a very big drug problem. I've been on this case for nearly three years now, and I think I'm about to break it; however, I need your help."

"So you're saying someone is actually stalk . . ." Rashawn hesitated and then closing her eyes, she swallowed the words.

"Possibly," Maceba answered.

"How can I help you?"

"Dr. Ams, I have reason to believe that you and possibly other instructors, have been a victim of the drug that is commonly referred to here around this campus as Get Ass. I have reason to believe that you are somehow being drugged, for reasons I would rather not jump to conclusions on . . ." Maceba paused, hoping Rashawn would say something, but there was no response, so she went on.

After filling Rashawn in on all she had regarding Doc's activities thus far, and the Moorman University's crime spree caused by his dirty work, Maceba sat quietly watching Rashawn assimilate what she had heard.

Rashawn, gripping the water bottle, slowly turned the top, cracking the seal. She pulled it up to her lips and thought about her hidden stash of Johnny Walker Red, hidden deep in her filing cabinets. She quickly twisted the cap on the water and tossed it back in the fridge. "Wanna drink?" she asked Maceba, her voice sounding odd and her thoughts scattered. Maceba just shook her head as Rashawn quickly retrieved the alcohol bottle and poured herself a stiff drink, gulping it down quickly holding the paper cup tightly to her chest as she relished the burn.

"Don't play with me. I'm in danger, aren't I? Why?"

"That part I had hoped you could tell me."

"I don't know why. I'm a nice person, I mean . . ." Rashawn's mouth hung open, but the words faded.

Maceba shook her head in full understanding. She didn't want Rashawn to start panicking.

"Yes, Dr. Ams, you're a wonderful person. People like Doc don't care about all that. That's why I thought you could help me figure out why he's doing this? Why you would be a target?"

"I have no idea why this Doc person would want to follow me or . . ." Rashawn paused thinking about Yvette and what the kids in her class were saying about her being raped under the influence of that drug. Just the thought of it made her swoon.

"Will you help us?"

"How can I help?" Rashawn finally asked after a moment of absorption of both the drink and the words. "You've been nothing but vague. I don't even know what I would be helping you do?"

"It's very similar to a sting. You know what that is, right?"

"Sting? Like a set-up? You want me to be stool pigeon?" Rashawn asked, her voice peaking a little on the high side. "And you don't even know who you're looking for?" she squeaked.

"I'll be right there, Dr. Ams, all the time . . . if not me then another operative. You will never have to be afraid."

Rashawn felt panic building and this time there would be no stopping it. Her hands shook uncontrollably as she poured herself another drink.

"I can't . . . I." She gulped her drink. "When and where are you saying this has happened to me . . . how?"

"From what I'm gathering right here in your office . . . but we can't be sure and we sure don't know how."

"If I decide to help you, I gather I can't tell anyone?"

"No. However, soon this whole thing will be over. I promise you that," Maceba explained, hoping to get out all she had to say before Rashawn became unable to comprehend any more due to her alcohol consumption. "We'll find out how he's doing this to you."

"You won't tell me who this Doc person is, will you?"

"No, I can't just yet. It will put you on guard and tip him off. With your innocence you will be acting normally and we can use that to our advantage. You have to trust me, you'll be perfectly safe."

"Who will contact me?" Rashawn asked.

"If not me, the other agent assigned. Whoever it is, they will tell you what you need to do, and I want you to follow their instructions, Dr. Ams, to the letter. I know

I'm sounding very mysterious, but for now I have to keep you on a need-to-know. Do you understand?"

Rashawn nodded her head. Maceba stood now and reached for Rashawn's hand, pulling the third drink down from her lips.

"Please don't be afraid."

"Shit, that's easy for you to say. You've got a gun," Rashawn nodded toward the holster that Maceba wore under her jacket.

Mentally, Rashawn's mind went in search of her own weapon.

Maceba chuckled slightly, hoping to ease Rashawn's worries a little, hoping to appear lighthearted. However, there could be no easy way to deal with this matter. Doc was not an easy man to deal with. His quick dispensing of Leon and Red told Maceba that she had to stay close to Rashawn. Trusting that he might feel something human toward her could easily be an overestimation of the animal he'd shown himself to be.

This case was about to break.

Leaving the office, walking down the stairwell, Maceba passed Roman on his way up. She smiled at him and he returned the greeting.

Rashawn's mind was scattered. She quickly gathered up her papers, needing to get home to put the gun in her purse. She slung her bag over her shoulder and dashed from the office, brushing quickly by Roman without so much as a greeting.

The bartender from Doc's normal haunt turned back to the dresser. Despite her insistence on virtue, here she was in his bedroom, naked. Her smooth, brown skin was flawless except for a couple of silly tattoos. He could look past those, however.

Nice ass, he noticed.

"I don't normally do cocaine," she said, sniffing the line up her nostril.

Like a pro, Doc thought. *Why can't women just tell the truth?*

Looking up, she saw his reflection in the mirror and smiled slyly, the light dancing off her eyes.

"I thought you were so married?" she asked.

And what difference does it make? Obviously none, bitch. You got your ass up in my house, he thought, but did not say. *Now hurry up so we can get to this. I'm ready.*

Turning to him, she noticed his erection.

"So much for the 'other' myth," she said with a wicked giggle. "You don't look like no white boy I've ever seen. What's that, a baker's dozen?" Her question teased.

Thought you said you'd never been with a white man before. See how you lie, Doc thought, shaking his head slightly, growing tired of her voice. She'd been talking non-stop since agreeing to come home with him.

"I don't know if I can work with all that," she said, attempting now to renege.

Doc moved closer to her and placed his large hand on her head, aiming it downward.

"Oh, hell no. No, I don't do that," she squirmed until finally her knees hit the thick carpet. She received his hardness in her mouth with intent, gagging slightly until the drug began to take effect.

She began to moan, taking him now, nearly to the shaft.

Doc suddenly lifted her off her feet, closing his teeth on the tenderness of her breast.

"Ouch! Stop, shit," she whined, wrapping her legs around him while pushing him off her. Doc impelled her then upon his stiffness. She screamed out with the suddenness of his entry, and then again as he continued to slam her downward. Her head jerked back wildly as she now hung on for the ride. Stepping over to his bed with her clinging to him, he then pulled her off and threw her on the mattress, flipping her over. She attempted to scramble onto her back but Doc was on her. She attempted to cover herself but he moved her hands, spreading her legs wide.

"Don't hurt me," she begged.

Yeah, real nice ass, he thought as he too gave in to the drugs and alcohol filling his blood stream.

Ignoring her cries, he entered the woman again with no less energy than he'd shown when this all began twenty minutes ago.

"You're hurting me," she claimed, as her back arched upward, willingly offering herself.

Shut up, Doc thought, closing his eyes again blocking out the woman's voice as he rode her hard and fast with no end in sight.

"I'm tired . . ." she finally cried.

Bad thing about coke, takes you so damn long to get a nut, *he thought now, looking at his watch.*

He pulled out and rolled the woman onto her back. Her eyes were at half mast, her hair all over her head. He caught her glancing at his still swollen organ.

"Damn," she groaned inching upward.

I know she is not trying to get away from me, Doc thought to himself.

Pinning her down with his body weight, he entered her with two fingers, and then three, until he felt renewed wetness coming from her. She groaned now upon his entry, to which he barely replied with a grunt.

Finally he began to feel the building eruption. He knew she could feel it too as she began to quicken her receptive pace, receiving him with a fervor that matched his own—panting, gasping, grunting . . .

Oh, now she's gonna try to get hers, Doc realized, the thought causing him to smile.

Suddenly the woman began to push against him screaming, "Don't cum in me, don't cum in me, I said."

As he exploded in her, his face twisted with the confusion that her comment had caused him to feel.

Too bad . . .

He pulled out.

He could feel the woman's eyes on him now as he climbed from off her.

What? he wanted to ask as she glared at him relentlessly.

"What about me?" she asked.

What about you, bitch? Get out, his eyes told her.

"I wanted to cum, too," she whined.

What the fuck, woman? You snorted all my blow, drank all my drink! Doc's mind screamed as he rolled his eyes while sliding into his pants. *Get the fuck out!*

"I see why your wife musta left you. Your ass is crazy," she sneered, mumbling under her breath.

He smiled while deciding if he would give into his irritation or not. Deciding, he grabbed and pulled her up from the bed, whispering in her ear while sliding his hand around her neck. "You know what, baby? You wanna know how crazy I really am?"

Her eyes widened as she tried hard to shake the drunken stupor, grabbing for his large hand.

"What are you gonna do?" she asked, closing her eyes tight, feeling his grip tightening a little.

His laughter sent a deep chill through her that he now felt. The fear she displayed far from aroused him. She far from aroused him.

Finally, in his frustration, he tossed her like a rag doll onto the mattress, along with a hundred dollar bill and her dress, and pointed towards the bathroom. She quickly climbed off the bed and ran in, slamming the door. Doc went to the dresser and snorted the last line of white powder.

Chapter 30

"I can do without tonight," Roman told Doc, who, red-eyed and high, pushed his way inside anyway.

"Why you have me all out here in the dark for nothing?" Doc asked while looking around. "What, you gots company or something?"

"Oh, like Rashawn?" Roman asked.

"You know what? You keep playin' with me, and you are gonna get hurt," Doc, shoved his finger hard into Roman's chest.

"Look, there are things we need to talk about. I should have told you this sooner. It's about Maceba and Rashawn," Roman began.

"There's nothin' 'bowt either one of dem I don't know," Doc said, walking into the kitchen and pouring himself a drink. "Or da boy. Didn't think I knew about him, huh?"

"And why shouldn't you know about the boy?" Roman said flatly. "He's your little reminder."

"Shut up." Blain smashed his fist into his palm, coming to the surface.

"She told me all about it, in one of our sessions . . ."

"I said shut up."

"I'm sure that must have frustrated the hell out of you," Roman taunted. "So you're trying to finish the job?"

"Didn't you just hear the words that came out of my mouth? I said shut the fuck up. You must get some sick thrill hearing about folks' private matters, or is it just that you're pissed you weren't there to recor . . ."

"Now who is being sick?"

"So how do you feel about the boy?"

"I don't feel anything," Blain admitted, cutting him off. It was clear he was lying to cover his trust feelings.

"Then how do you feel about Chance Davis?" Roman inquired, pushing the buttons of irritation harder.

"Chance Davis is a dick."

"Yes, I agree. He surely wouldn't make the boy a very good father—but then, neither would you. No, I think that, considering all things, I would be a perfect fa . . ." Roman began, only to find himself ducking from the flying tumbler that was hurled at him.

"To hell wit chu," Blain screamed, overturning the large butcher-block table, causing Roman's vegetables to go everywhere. "You always do that to me. You always try to take away the woman I love, who loves me."

"How can you even think she would love you? How can you think she would want to live with you and your issues?"

"I'll kill her before I let her live with you and yours." Blain's nostrils flared like those of a bull. He was beyond angry.

Roman spoke on, throwing caution to the wind. "Like the way you allowed that monster to kill Jasmine . . ."

Upon Roman's unspoken request, the monster arrived, grabbing at his burning eyes, holding back the hot tears.

"You did kill Jasmine, didn't you Doc?" Roman asked, his voice straining hard to cover the growing emotion that came with watching the metamorphosis of the man who stood before him. He was good at bringing Blain's psychosis to the forefront. "When they found her body, it was your knife that had cut her throat, wasn't it? Why? I knew you two were having an affair, so why did you feel the need to kill her?" he asked, pushing further. "I know you wanted my wife, Doc," Roman went on, tugging at Blain's alter ego, urging him to confess.

"I didn't kill Jasmine. She killed herself. You killed her. It was your fault," Doc screeched. "Don't start your *stuff* on me Roman. I'm not your patient today!"

"I'm just trying to help you Blain, you need help . . ."

Blain came back in a flash, and out of reflex charged him, and the two men smashed violently onto the counter, causing everything on it to fly off, crashing to the floor. Cursing angrily, the men, meshing size and bulk, slugged and pummeled one another all around the kitchen.

Roman never relented, even when the taste of blood came up in his mouth. "I wish my father had killed you, too," Roman, seething with ire, spat, while he gripped onto his nemesis, spewing hateful words that dug deep and cut sharper than the blade that now touched his throat.

"What did you say?"

"My God, look, you need help. Let me help you," Roman pleaded now, his tone changing, as Doc's crazed expression filled him with fear for his life.

"You're high. Stop what you're doing, Blain. I want only to help you."

"You, help Blain? That's a laugh. You're just a dope fiend who can't even help himself. You're gonna help, Blain? Now that's funny," Doc howled.

"All I want is for you to leave Rashawn alone," Roman pleaded. "She's not Jasmine. She doesn't want you. Just leave her alone. Stop hurting her, stop hurting yourself," Roman spoke, inching himself away from the blade's point. "Let's get this all out in the open, confess what you've done to the police."

"You need to stop talking." Blain spat, shoving him back. The push caused him to stumble to the floor and after giving him a swift, hard kick, he then reached deep in his pocket and tossed Roman a small bag of white powder.

"Here, take it."

Roman stared at the bag, filled with relief. It was the Get Ass drug—his salvation. He wanted relief more than anything at that moment, yet his pride prevented him from reaching for it. He wanted to maintain control over this situation.

"Take it!" Doc screamed, returning in full fury to replace Blain once again.

Roman looked up at him. "You've been drugging Rashawn with this, haven't you?" he asked, looking around as if for something.

Blain wasn't sure if it was a weapon or a tape recorder he sought. He wasn't sure about the answer to the question either.

"You drugged, Jasmine, too, didn't you?" he asked. "You drugged her, and then cut her throat. Just like you killed that young girl. Tell me and I can get you some help."

Blain listened for a second longer before he raised his hand to silence Roman.

"Shut the fuck up and take the damn drug. You're hurt. Take it," Blain insisted, seeing the blood forming in the corner of Roman's mouth.

"Do what the doctor says. Isn't that what you say to people?" Doc then snickered, sarcastically.

"I cannot believe the same blood flows through our veins," Roman said, in an undertone, his voice hindered by the ache in his ribs.

Doc's dark eyes, as dark as his own, blazed like onyx stone.

"Don't ever call him your brother again. Quit mess-ing with his mind," Doc threatened. "Do you realize how angry I am right now?" Doc screamed. "I'm angry enough to . . ." He paused, and then slammed his fist through the cabinet door.

"I just want you to stop . . ."

"I could kill you," Doc growled through gritted teeth. Then with a sudden change of demeanor, he smiled. "I'm sick and I'm tired of this game you play with my mind. If I didn't know any better, I'd say you were trying to drive me crazy. As a matter a fact, this is the last time you'll get any help from me or Blain," Doc said flatly, al-most with an air of arrogance in his tone before, sud-denly, he aimed the knife, letting it fly. It stuck in the linoleum, only inches from Roman's thigh. "The last time," he said, then grabbing up a toothpick from the holder that was knocked to the floor during his tirade, he stuck it in the side of his mouth.

Blain then smiled wickedly, taking on the familiar re-semblances Roman often refused to see.

"You heard the man. Now, take that shit and be done wit it," Blain said after looking around the thrashed kitchen. "Clean up this damn mess," he added satiri-cally, jerking the knife from the linoleum, and shoving it back into the sheave.

"I've gotta go. I've got another stop to make to-night," he said.

"Just leave her alone," Roman simpered.

"Yeah, whatever," was all Blain said before walking out.

Rashawn couldn't sleep. Maceba filled her mind with unforgettable things. Glancing at the clock, it was nearly one a.m. She went downstairs for a bottle of water. To-morrow she would request another leave of absence. The thought of someone she might know stalking her, or some mysterious crazy known only as Doc drugging her, well, she wasn't going near that school.

Passing Rashawn's condominium more than once, and wandering around the complex, he felt so many mixed emotions. Tonight would be the night he forced her hand. He would come out from hiding and offer Rashawn and Reggie his love. What if she didn't accept it? What if she turned him down for Chance Davis?

"Well, she won't. If I have to, I'll kill him," he said, feeling his heart beating suddenly faster.

Not caring if Rashawn might be awake, he turned the key in the lock. Upon entering the condo, he saw Rashawn on the kitchen floor. He quickly picked her up and carried her to bed.

Walking out to the hall, he stood for a moment gathering his thoughts. For the first time, he wasn't sure of his next move. Then he noticed that the door to the second bedroom was open.

His mind went to Reggie. The boy's dark eyes and crooked grin, it was like looking in the mirror, only Reggie was the boy he should have been—happy, loved, and content. The man was brimming with jealousy, an emotion he could not handle.

His emotions were all over the place. One second he loved Rashawn, worshiped the ground she walked on, and the next second he hated her with all of his dark heart, swearing to take her life the next time he laid eyes on her.

Reggie was sleeping soundly when he entered his room.

"How beautiful you are, my son," he said under his breath as he smoothed back the curls that rested on the boy's smooth brown forehead. "No matter how much I want to deny it, or what I am about to do to your mother, I love you. I truly do."

Taking a deep cleansing breath, he soon found himself back in Rashawn's room. He watched her sleeping, so soundly and peacefully, so unaware of the crimes he had previously committed on her and those he was about to.

"All you had to do was love me. I would have kept you safe," he whispered in her ear before kissing her cheek.

"All I wanted was for you to love me with your eyes open," he said, glancing over his shoulder, again he thought about Reggie. "All I wanted was . . ."

Closing the door, he glanced at his watch. "Never mind," he grumbled, sounding disgusted.

He looked at her. "Look at what you've done to me," he yelled. "You are ruining my life," he explained to the sleeping beauty. "That's my son in there, my son. No, I didn't intend for it to happen, but it did and now . . . now you are messing everything up."

Stepping over to a small, barely noticeable button in the closet door jam, he pushed it off. "Tonight, I'm going to teach you a lesson. I guess you're just gonna haveta learn the hard way that I'm the man you need."

Undressing her, he hoped he had plenty of time.

The phone rang in the office of Clinical Therapist Juanita Duncun. It was after hours and there was no one there to answer; however, the machine picked up the call on the third ring.

The sound of weeping was heard, heavy and filled with remorse.

"I went too far this time," the man with the deep voice said between sobs.

Chapter 31

The phone's ringing woke Rashawn the next morning. She shot up in the bed like a rocket, grabbing for the receiver.

"Hello," she answered. Dean Morgan's secretary was on the other end of the phone.

Rashawn covered her bare breasts when she answered the phone, before even realizing they were bare.

"Where are you? You're not here . . ." Dean Morgan's secretary started in.

Glancing at the clock, Rashawn realized she'd missed the staff meeting.

Where are my pajamas? she asked herself.

"What is going on?" she asked aloud.

"That's what I'm asking you, Dr. Ams," Dean Morgan's secretary said.

Suddenly, Rashawn realized that Reggie had made his way into her room and was asleep on her throw pillows tossed on the floor beside her bed. He was holding an unfamiliar toy, one she had not purchased for him. Just then, she looked around at all the roses in the room, dozens and dozens.

Pulling her blanket back seeing now that she was

completely naked, brought a wave of heat over her, making her head spin. She looked around her tumbled bedding, her soiled sheets—soiled with her blood and the obvious emissions of a man. She felt faint. Glancing down at Reggie, she felt a wave of nausea. She ran her fingers through her tangled hair. Throwing her legs over the bedside, she then noticed her bruised thighs and arms. Then she saw the typed note.

"Sweet dreams, Rashawn.

Love, Blain," it read.

Bounding from the bed, she ran into the bathroom to vomit.

After quickly stripping her bed, she balled up the linen and shoved it in a garbage bag, immediately taking it to the dumpster outside. She carried her cordless, cradled in her neck as it rang to Rita's house. Trina answered.

"Look, I need you to come over right now," Rashawn's tone commanded into the receiver.

"No, you look. I've got my karate class in an hour. I . . ." Trina began to explain.

"I need you to get your ass over here now," Rashawn screamed, as she slammed down the lid of the dumpster.

Rashawn rushed out as Trina arrived at the door to watch Reggie.

Trina had a billion questions, the main one being why she was summoned to the condominium, but Rashawn had no time to answer. She had to see her doctor right away.

On the table, while verifying that she had indeed had sexual relations within the last twelve hours; old memories came back—the painful examination, the accusative eyes of the nurse, and the concerned expression of the doctor. "We're going to want a full blood screening also, Rashawn," her doctor explained, "including a pregnancy test . . ."

Rashawn's head spun. She felt perspiration coming to her face.

It was all too much.

Rashawn headed out to find the animal's house. Today she carried her gun.

Her heart raced and she felt nearly faint, but not so weak that she was unable to take care of business. Today she would kill a man.

It was on her list of things to do.

Today she was going to kill her rapist—Blain Tollome.

Surely I can find his address in the school records. I'll just break into the office if I need to, she thought to herself while pulling into the Moorman University parking lot. Suddenly she spied Blain's SUV and slammed on her brakes nearly hitting the large vehicle. She jumped from her car and opened her trunk. Taking out the crowbar, she ran up to the car, smashing the windows, and scraping the metal bar along the paint, sending the alarm into a loud screech.

"Come on bastard. Come on!" she screamed, hoping Blain would hear her and come into the open where she had planned to shoot him—dead. Perhaps he was lurking in the bushes, watching. "Come on," she screamed, beyond reason, beyond thinking.

Just then, Roman appeared instead. "Rashawn," he called to her.

Dropping the crowbar, she ran over to him and fell, weak, into his arms.

"I need you to help me," she said, sounding out of breath. He gave her his undivided attention.

"It's Blain. It's really Blain. I know it now . . . I mean, I don't know for sure, but . . ." she paused. Roman wrapped his arms around her and for the first time, she gave in to his embrace.

"Say it, Rashe, talk to me. You have to face it to fight it. You know that, don't you?" Roman requested, lifting her face to his. Rashawn's heart tightened.

Of course, Roman knew the mantra that had once meant her salvation. Roman knew everything about her without her even needing to explain.

"I came to kill him but I can't do it. I need to go to the police," she said finally, giving in to her feelings of total betrayal. She was overwhelmed with emotions. "He raped me again last night, he . . ." she sobbed. "I don't know how he did it this time, but . . ." she simpered, "I know he did . . ." she continued weeping hot, bitter, angry tears. "All this time, all this denial . . . my God, I'm so angry . . ."

"No, Rashawn. Now listen to me. I need to tell you something," Roman said softly. Rashawn looked up at him.

"He told me what he did to you," Roman said. Rashawn pulled away. "I've known everything for a long time."

"What?"

"He's been using a drug on you, Rashawn. I don't know how to tell you this any easier way."

"Oh my God, Roman, you're kidding, right?" She continued to snivel, unable to pull it together.

"Being that I'm his therapist, I've been prevented from telling you anything. But I regret that now, and I want to help you catch him, but the right way."

"You're my operative? You work for the INL?" Rashawn asked. Roman paused.

"Of course, I'm helping Maceba Baxter put him away . . . yes," he admitted, smiling, as he rubbed her shoulder, comforting her while she laid her head against his chest.

Rashawn wiped her eyes, "You're my operative?"

"Yes. Look, you're not thinking right," he explained taking her hands in his. "Let's go to your house. You'll lie down, and get some rest," he said, holding her now, by the shoulders. "Then we'll talk. I'm going to tell you things that are going to frighten you, and upset you. I know how easily you get upset, but you need to hear them out, okay?" he requested. "And then it'll be okay—because I'll be there for you . . . to protect you."

Rashawn was ready for anything and nothing all at once. She nodded as he pulled her closer to him and directed her toward his car.

"But what about Blain?" she asked first, reaching in her bag, pulling out her gun. Roman quickly grabbed it from her, looking around the nearly empty lot. "Put that away. As a matter of fact, give it to me," he demanded, taking the gun and shoving it into the front of his belt.

"First, you need some medical attention," Roman suggested.

Feeling mixed with emotions, she looked back over her shoulder at the SUV, and then back at the man standing there before her—Roman.

How wrong she had been. She had trusted Davis only to feel betrayed by him. She'd even trusted Blain only to have him devastate her life. But Roman had turned out to be her unexpected hero. He was about to save the day, even save her life.

Rashawn climbed into his car and allowed him to take her home.

"I was worried about you," he said, when finally Rashawn came down the stairs after an hour or two. She had invited him inside, then at his urging she went upstairs to lie down. Of course lying down in her bed was the last thing Rashawn wanted to do.

"It took me forever to get through to my doctor," she began explaining. "I go back in Monday. I can't believe I'm gonna go through all this again," Rashawn sighed heavily.

"Going through it again?" he asked.

"Yes, again. If I'm pregnant again, I'm going to abort this time. I . . . I just can't handle it, ya know," Rashawn explained flatly, shaking her head and wringing her hands just a little.

Roman wore his normal expressionless face as he moved over and sat next to her on the sofa, putting his arms around her shoulders. "You think you might be pregnant?" he asked. Rashawn stared at him for a moment and then turned away.

Just then, Trina walked in the living room with Reggie.

Trina looked surprised to see Roman and Rashawn looking so comfortable on the sofa. Rashawn had not shared this little secret with her either.

"Trina, you met Allen Roman, right? I mean, you two have been talking, right?" Rashawn introduced quickly, unconsciously moving away from him.

"We've met," Trina said, glaring at her. "We've been talking and all that," Trina said, with added innuendo in her words.

Rashawn picked Reggie up and held him close, despite his squirming.

"No," he squealed, holding her face in both of his small hands as he often did when attempting to reason with her. He wanted Allen Roman and he wanted him, now.

Rashawn and Roman's eyes locked just as Reggie reached out for him. It was something he had never done before. Rashawn looked stunned by Reggie's unusual actions.

Apparently, Roman was too, as he instantly recoiled.

"Rashawn, I just came in to tell you that Maceba Baxter just returned your call. She said to call her back when you woke up."

"Oh yeah, I called her too. I hope you don't mind." Standing quickly, he looked at his watch.

"Well, I better let you go make your call," he said.

"My call? Don't you want to make it together?"

Rashawn asked, sounding a little surprised at his hurry
to leave.

"No. I'm sure you two have business to take care of,"
he answered, smiling warmly and turning his attention
to Trina, who simply smirked and went back into the
kitchen.

"I think the good doctor is a nut," Trina said, coming
back into the living room after she heard the door
close.

"Trina, stop. He's not. He's . . . eccentric yes, but
he's . . ." Rashawn began, before turning her attention
to Reggie who was at the window, looking forlorn, as if
he was missing Allen Roman's presence.

"He's just trying to help me. He's had to keep this
terrible secret from me about his maniac patient."
Rashawn nodded towards Reggie slightly. "I mean,
think about it . . ."

"I thought about it. All the while he was flapping his
lips, I was thinking about it."

"What was he saying?" Rashawn asked, glancing at
Reggie again.

"He told me all about his childhood and shit, like I
care about that. He was talking about how he and his
brother saw his father kill his mother's white lover, his
brother's father," Trina gestured, trying to keep the
story straight.

"Then after that happened, his father was executed
in the electric chair for that and his mother decides
then she can't raise the bastard son—his brother—because of the people in the community giving her a hard
time because the kid was white skinned and looked too
much like his father. He was like, 'All my life I have
hated my brother for what he did to my family.' He's all,
'But I'm in therapy for that.' I was like, umm, and I care
about all this, why? I mean, who isn't in therapy these
days right? Am I right?" Trina asked, sounding rude
and careless.

"Oh man, then he started talking about his wife who was murdered and how he blames that on his brother too because they always fight over the same woman and then bad stuff always happens to the woman, blah, blah." Trina's arms flailed in the air as she spoke.

"Why was he telling you all about his brother? What in the world does that have to do with Blain Tollome and all this mess?" Rashawn asked, still a little confused.

Trina stared at her intensely for a second as if trying to mind meld with her, "Blain Tollome, the big white boy with the lips . . . that's his brother, duh. Rashawn, what is wrong with your mind lately? You haven't been thinking real straight. I mean, I get the point that you've been going through some things but come on, let's start thinking here."

"He's a nut who is in love with you," Trina stated flatly. Rashawn simply stared at her, stunned and speechless. "I'm telling you, that statement right there scares the shit out of me. I finally had to tell him to stop talking to me. I wasn't trying to be rude, but come on, just a little too much info comin' down the pipe line. I just walked out, hoping he would just get the hint and leave," Trina added, gulping down the Diet Coke. "I can't believe he said all that and then expected me to be okay with him being in this house."

"You need to drink more water," Rashawn said, listening to the odd sound of her own words.

"All your water is gone," Trina explained.

Rashawn rushed over to her refrigerator.

"That's crazy. I had at least three bottles in here last night," she gasped, looking deep into the back.

Chapter 32

Blain wasn't stupid. Something was going down. He hadn't seen Maceba in days. He'd called her and left messages, but she hadn't returned his calls. They had gone from being the newest couple on the block, to her being nearly invisible—overnight. Blain hadn't seen Rashawn either in a couple of days, and now there was this thing with his car being vandalized at the university.

He remembered how he felt upon finding the windshield smashed. Of course, it could have been anybody. *That was so bizarre.*

"Maybe it's time you got the hell outta here," Doc whispered, looking around the garage, taking stock of the places where evidence was well hidden. "All of this is getting tired, real tired."

"What about Maceba?"

"Fuck Maceba," Doc spat.

"What about Rashawn?"

"What about her?"

Blain knew the power within him needed to see Rashawn. He'd even been compelled to drive out to Pacific View to see if perhaps she had gone there. He started to ask *Chance* if by *chance* he had seen her.

What kind fucked up name is Chance, anyway? Doc thought now, laughing internally at the thought.

Suddenly, his phone rang.

It was *HER*. His pulse quickened, he could feel his heart beating in his chest.

"Hi Blain, it's me," she said casually, as if calling him was something she did everyday.

"What do you want?" Blain asked her.

"I want to meet with you. I need to talk to you."

"About what?"

"About what?" Rashawn gasped, before remembering Maceba's instructions.

"He might not remember what he's done—so just go along with whatever he says," Maceba told her.

"I've been thinking, about what you said to me before," Rashawn said now, after swallowing hard, regaining her nerve.

"I've said a lot of things to you—before."

"Yes, I know, and I'm finally hearing you," Rashawn said, adding a seductiveness to her voice, trying to keep her stomach from turning. "After last night, I'm finally hearing you."

"You're such a tease. You're a damn tease, Rashe'," Doc said after taking her words in—tasting them.

Her voice had gone to his head, made him nearly weak.

"I know, and I'm sorry," she went on. "I got the note and I know what it meant."

"What note?"

Rashawn allowed him his pretense at innocence. Maybe Blain really didn't know what Doc had done.

"Listen, I'm trying to give you what you want."

"Do you really know? Do you have a clue what Blain wants?"

"Yes, I think I do," Rashawn said, trying not to be affected by Blain speaking in the third person. He was crazy—of this she had been made painfully aware. Maceba too had reinforced that fact.

"*So you figure he raped me?*"

"*To be honest, that doesn't sound like something Doc would do, but strangely enough, it adds up that way. With what Roman told me. He told me all about Blain and his multiple personality thing. Roman describes it as like, Blain has both an emotional, primal self and an intellectual, more controlled, pre-meditated self,*" Maceba explained, her emotions growing by the moment. "*Apparently the childhood trauma of seeing his father murdered and then being 'punished for it' . . .*" Maceba went on, making quotation marks in the air, "*was just too much for his little mind, I guess. And then, having a brother like Allen had to be hard on him . . .*"

"*No doubt. I still can't believe they are brothers. Roman is so brilliant and Blain is well . . .*" Rashawn said with a smirk, while allowing her distain for Blain to come out along with her residual surprise at learning the truth about Allen Roman and Blain Tollome and their relationship to one another.

Maceba frowned slightly. "*It's not like it was his fault. I mean . . . sure Blain had choices. Everyone has choices, but . . .*"

Rashawn couldn't help but notice how personally involved Maceba seemed to be, glancing at Reggie's picture the way an 'other woman' would—as if she had been forced to accept something about the 'man' in her life.

"*Is this your boy?*" Maceba finally asked.

"*So, which one did you end up involved with?*" Rashawn asked her, instead of answering her, putting her own philosophy degree to work.

Maceba's eyes widened and she jumped to her feet. "*Doc attacked me. He tried to kill me at Danton when I got too close to his little drug operation. Blain, well, let me just say, I got sent on a wild goose chase, misled by thinking that Blain was trying to help me. But of course, there was no way he was trying to help me catch Doc." Maceba looked around, avoiding Rashawn's eyes.*

"So I guess that means you've had the worst of both."

Maceba nodded and then sighed heavily, her sigh filled with acceptance. "And now they both have to be stopped before they hurt any more people."

Rashawn agreed.

"Fine, meet me at Shoreline restaurant. It's near Alameda where I live. We're gonna do this on my turf for a change," Doc barked.

"No, come out here."

"To your place?"

"My place," she repeated, and then hung up.

Surely he was dreaming now.

Doc knew if he played his cards right, she would come around, eventually. He just didn't expect it to be so easy, so fast. "I told you they all come around. Even Jasmine finally came around," Doc said out loud, taking on a braggart's tone.

When Jasmine had come to him, Doc had never been happier in his life. He had even convinced Blain that there was true love in his heart for that woman, and maybe there had been. But in the end Jasmine was just too stubborn to make it work. So many times Doc had asked her to run away with him and she had refused, cowering to Roman and his *control-freak* ways.

She took so long to make up her mind that the night she finally agreed to leave with him, she never made it to the meeting place. She was killed—found in a rented car with her throat cut.

Blain had no alibi but neither did Roman for that matter so Doc was left to wonder which one was more at fault despite the fact that they both immediately blamed him.

"Why would I kill the only woman I've ever loved?" Doc asked Blain, who said nothing in response. "I will never forgive you or Roman for taking Jasmine from me."

"Is that why you are torturing yourself over Rashawn?" Blain finally asked.

"You sound like Roman right now. You don't know what you're talking about either. Can't you see she called me . . . she called me."

Blain knew Doc would never get over what happened to Jasmine and knew his infatuation with Rashawn had a lot to do with that whole situation. He didn't need Roman to tell him that, adding salt to the already gaping wound that Doc made sure he felt. Blain knew it was Doc's hurt feelings that made a normal relationship with Maceba impossible. Blain knew it was Doc's troubled soul that caused him to take to cocaine for succor. Blain knew it was Doc's broken heart that had him making a fool of himself over Rashawn Ams. What Blain wasn't sure of was how far Doc would go to win Rashawn over—or how far Roman would go, for that matter.

Rashawn was Jasmine and Jasmine, Rashawn, in Doc's mind, and maybe Roman's too. Blain didn't know what to do about Roman's sick mind; he was too busy dealing with his own. Having a man like Doc as a part of him was causing him enough trouble in life—as well as other people's.

"So what about Chance Davis?" Blain was thinking aloud.

"Dr. Davis is just an unfortunate soul who is in the wrong place at the wrong time, messing around with the wrong woman, and he is gonna get hurt if he doesn't back off soon. That's a fact."

"Come on, man, let it go."

"No, you let it go," Doc mumbled under his breath, while he knocked at the door of Rashawn's home.

His fist rose to knock a second time.

Unexpectedly, from the side of him he felt the cool steel of Maceba's gun against his temple, felt the click of a gun safety being unlatched.

"Hold it right there, Doc," Maceba said, her voice low and even.

Blain's hand went up as he stepped back from the porch. His mind spun as he cleared his head of thoughts about love and togetherness—Rashawn. His head instead filled completely with only the cold, hard thoughts that controlled the persona that was completely Doc.

The skinny white boy and the petite chick—that's who Doc saw holding the guns on him. That's who he summed up his contenders to be.

Doc hated Maceba with all his dark heart. She weakened Blain, almost to the point of betrayal.

"You sure you don't wanna hold it, Ceba?" Doc joked, cutting his dark eyes at her. "You used to want to hold it."

She flinched.

God yes, she flinched.

With a one-step action, Doc had grabbed the 'skinny white boy' around the neck and with one quick jerking motion, he drew blood from his face with the tip of his blade.

"Blain, let him go," Maceba growled, still holding the weapon.

Her eyes danced off her partner. His eyes darted to the knife as his face dripped blood from the fresh cut. Doc had freed him of his gun and held it now on Maceba.

"Blain? You sure you guys don't even know who the bad guys are. And you're in law enforcement?" Doc sarcastically taunted before nearly rendering Phil unconscious with a blow to the side of the head. He dropped at Doc's feet like a sack of potatoes. Without further hesitation, Doc fired at Maceba, missing her by obvious misaiming. It all served his purpose as she ducked. In her avoidance, he made his escape.

The chase was on.

"I need back up," Maceba yelled into the radio as her partner struggled to put the siren on the top of the car. She glanced over at him.

He was hurt bad.

Racing through the traffic, she never took her eyes off the SUV driven wildly and recklessly by the man she both loved and hated. The man who at one moment could seduce her to his bed, and in the next, attempt to break her in half with his bare hands. What a demon he was—a Nephilim revisited on this planet.

How could someone so beautiful in appearance be so evil inside? How could I have not known? How come it took me so long to figure it out? Maceba wondered.

The turn off was a sharp one, a windy way leading up to the cliffs. Maceba saw the vehicle dart off the road and she followed. Spying his SUV on the side of the road with the door still open, she knew Doc was on the move—on foot. Her partner was still bleeding.

"I'll catch up," he said to her, receiving a half-nod as she dashed into the thick greenery after Doc.

There was nothing on the other side of this plush forest except for the cliffs. She had him now, no doubt.

She had to get him this time. It was a war for right-eousness—*David and Goliath.*

Creeping slowly through the brush Maceba skulked, her eyes scanning the darkness. Just then, she heard the gun click behind her head.

She froze, dropping her gun.

"Ceba, why don't you ever learn? You are the most stubborn woman I've ever known, well, you and Rashawn. Blain will never learn how to choose women."

"And you do?"

"You know, Ceba, if you still wanted me, alls you had to do was . . ."

"I never wanted you—never!"

"That's not what you said the last time we . . ."

"I don't have time for this shit," Maceba yelled before swinging around with a high kick that both shocked and stunned the giant of a man. He stumbled backward. She had drawn blood from his lip.

"Okay, so you wanna play rough," he declared, charging at her. Maceba drew her second weapon, stopping Doc in his tracks. He smiled wickedly.

"Even if I just shot you now, nobody would care," she threatened.

"Keep your focus, girlie. Do your job. Don't let your little personal problems affect your judgment," Doc taunted. "You have to put the past in the past. All's fair in love and . . ."

"Shut the fuck up!" Maceba screamed, her hands visibly shaking now. She called out to the injured Parker.

"Oh, he's dead," answered Doc nonchalantly. Maceba's blood ran cold as she noticed the knife missing from the sheath that hung on Doc's belt loop.

"Doesn't matter, back up is on its way. We'll just stand here all night," she said, attempting to regain her nerve while blocking out the traumas he had already caused her in the past. The concussion, the broken bones—she almost died at his hands once.

In addition to her anger, she was terrified.

"All night, I like the sounds of that," he grinned, stepping toward her. She visibly jumped.

"When will you people ever learn?" he said calmly, lowering his hands now, his voice deepening to a growl that rumbled deep in her belly.

It all happened in slow motion, Doc reaching for the gun and turning it. Maceba struggled but didn't stand a chance against the massive giant. The smell of gun smoke filled her nose as his eyes peered deeply into hers, until there was only a haze. He stepped back from her. He wasn't smiling anymore. In his eyes she suddenly saw Blain. Just for a flash of a second she saw him in the madman's eyes. He almost looked regretful over having killed her this way.

She fired at him twice before everything went black.

Chapter 33

Walking back from the corner mailbox, Roman noticed the sharply dressed men standing on the sidewalk in front of his home. They were more than obviously waiting for him—the stiff look, the conspicuous inconspicuousness.

He chuckled.

Finally the day had come—a day of judgment, of just due for being related to Blain Tollome, a day of retribution for allowing his younger sibling to walk around being a menace to society. "I should have pushed him in front of that gun," Roman thought, as the sounds of the bullet leaving his father's rifle still shook him, still did a quick freeze on his heart.

Vivid was the memory of the blood that exploded out of the tall white man's back.

He didn't fall right away. Instead the man turned and looked at the two of them, Blain and him, while they stood stone-like with fear watching the entire act play out as if on stage, as if unreal.

They were boys, yet at that moment they were thrown into manhood, forced to become onlookers of life in its rawest form.

Blain cried out first, as if his little mind had processed his loss within seconds. He screamed and broke free from their mother's arms, running toward the man whose life was rushing away, the man who was his father.

Dying . . .

That's when Roman saw it, the look in his own father's eyes as he slowly moved the aim of the rifle toward the bastard child, the boy who he had blamed for the loss of his family, the boy whose existence told everyone that his wife, the love of his life, was a whore, the boy whose white skin would always mark the betrayal of his wife and the weakness on his part to control his property—Blain.

The next memory was nothing but painful as Roman flinched, almost feeling again his father pushing him out of the way. He had stood between his father and the boy, but his father pushed him out of the way and, with the butt of the rifle he slammed the boy to the ground, cursing him while attempting to crush him with the end of that heavy gun.

Grabbing at his groin, the boy moaned in agony as Roman's father slammed him with that weapon there and in the belly, until finally, he hit him in the face and head, rendering the child unconscious.

Roman shook his head, clearing it of the sounds of his mother's screams, pushing back again the memory of the day that changed his and Blain's lives forever.

"What can I do for you gentlemen?" Roman asked, approaching the men before they could approach him.

"We were told you were quite astute," one of the men said, showing his intelligence. Roman liked that.

There was nothing worse than stupid people claiming to be law enforcement.

"Can we step inside?" the other agent said, flashing his INL badge.

"Certainly," Roman agreed leading the men inside his immaculately clean home.

Chapter 34

Rashawn stood at the counter. Her mind was scattered and unable to hold a thought.

"Before I realized what happened, I had become an accomplice to one of the largest drug dealers in the city," the voice said on the television.

"As a respected member of the medical community, I compromised my position and abused my power, allowing this crime to continue in exchange for my selfish needs. I am guilty by my silence. I'm guilty of drug addiction and allowing a criminal to live among your children in order to have that addiction satisfied. The actions of the authorities in this matter were justified, although I've received several sanctions from prosecution for turning states' evidence. I will be punished for my illegal drug use. As for allowing my brother to remain free among the innocent members of society, a higher source will judge me. I have been deport . . ."

"Turn that shit off!" Carlotta yelled out, suddenly the sound of cartoons filled the air.

Just then, Trina came into the kitchen where Rashawn had been hiding out, trying to find some peace.

"You need to lay down a while, sweetie," Trina said, in consideration of Rashawn's weakened state.

Finding that she had again been made pregnant by a rape, Rashawn aborted her pregnancy, immediately starting a detoxification program that utilized a dialysis technique to clean the drug out her system. It had been rough on her. Unfortunately, no such machine existed to clear her garbled thoughts.

What had she done to deserve this? How did she become a target for such a sick man as Blain Tollome?

"Maybe he just needed love. Everyone needs to be loved," she told her herself before quickly shaking her head free of any sentimental thoughts of the demented demon who had destroyed all she knew to be normal in her life. Having his child did not demand love or understanding on her part, right? Not with all the hurt he'd caused. Although she felt a part of that responsibility, and it was a heavy weight—why hadn't she seen the signs, paid closer attention to the clues and hints . . . reported the dreams that often had him in them?

Well for that matter, her dreams had Davis and Roman in them too . . . were they guilty somehow?

To add to her stress, everyone in the house was being so secretive.

There was a conspiracy going on for sure.

Rashawn was certain she had seen Terrell coming from her bedroom after snooping around, as if looking for some kind of clue that the police had missed. Let's not forget the police and the 'search' they had done on her home before finding whatever it was they were looking for. It took all day to clean up the mess they left, and still there was structural damage to her walls where they had removed the hidden surveillance camera. Rashawn was at her wits' end.

Why in the hell were there cameras in the bedroom?

And now, Allen Roman . . . deported.

Why? He was nothing other than a victim of Doc's, just as I was, right?

* * *

Ta'Rae had taken her blood pressure one time too many for one afternoon.

True, she had fainted when receiving the report regarding Doc's SUV ending up found in the bay, bullet holes in the driver's window with bloodstains on the seat.

"Presumed dead, a body has not been discovered," the report said.

Unfortunately, Maceba's death left no guesswork. She was found dead with a bullet from her own gun, having taken her life. It was all so ugly and overwhelming. The guilt . . . so much of it to go around. How much of it was hers would take years to figure out.

When is everybody gonna leave? Rashawn wondered. The condo had been crowded for weeks, it seemed.

"It's that Chance Davis on the phone," Carlotta's daughter called.

"Hang up! Auntie Shawnie doesn't want to talk to no man!" her other daughter answered.

"No, wait," Rashawn called out, grabbing up the closest extension.

"Chance?"

"I'm at the gate," he said, sounding cool and controlled.

"I think I need to see you," she confessed.

Rashawn didn't notice Trina's smile creeping onto her lips as she eavesdropped.

The front door opened.

"What the hell is that?" Carlotta asked, her voice heard above the already commotion-filled living room. Rashawn followed Trina from the kitchen to hear what all the hubbub was about.

Qiana came in, followed by Nigel, who was carrying a large potted plant.

"Oh come on, get that out of here," Rashawn balked.

"I think it's nice," Ta'Rae commented, grabbing Rashawn's flailing arm and taking her pulse. "Don't worry about it," he ordered. She pulled away from her.

"Stop, everyone just stop," she yelled, before running toward the stairs. She turned back to search for Reggie, who was busy playing with his cousins and the toys within his reach, unconcerned with all that was going on around him, except the twins and Ta'Rae's daughter, Precious. Reggie . . . perhaps the biggest victim of them all, Rashawn felt the tears leave her eyes as she ran up to her room.

"My life is a mess once again," Rashawn said to Davis, who was now sitting at her vanity looking at her. His face appeared stiff for what seemed to be an hour, as he listened to her tale, the story of her life over the last few years.

He had no idea the extent of everything—the far-reaching effects of the rape, her job, the drugs at Moorman University—he didn't know what to think about Rashawn and the negative things she'd endured. Had she been the epitome of strength or just another victim? And now that it was over, she was suffering. He could tell. Her family was out in full for her—supporting her, standing by her. Davis wanted to be there for her too. He wondered if maybe he was perverted somehow, because right now, all he wanted was to hold her, stroke her, make love to her, soothe and comfort her the only way he knew how. His sexual views had never been tested to this degree. All he wanted to do was console her and frankly, he knew no other way. But what Chance wanted went beyond the flesh. He knew that. He loved Rashawn Ams. Only now, with what she'd been through, he had no idea how he would ever show her without seeming like just another rapist.

* * *

Doc had made it to Allen Roman's second house nestled in the cliffs of San Simeon.

He'd often harassed Roman for owning two homes when he could only live in one at a time. However, tonight, after more than two weeks on the run, he was thankful for his brother's showy display of his excessive means. He'd have to thank him one day, considering he was out—free, and according to the press release, innocent of all crimes.

"Higher source," Doc grumbled. "Yeah, I'll show you a 'higher source," he fussed on, making his way toward the house in the shadows of the night.

Inside, Doc clicked on the television only to, again, hear the report about his own death, given in an updated report on the Moorman U. drug debacle.

"Greatly exaggerated," he chuckled wickedly, throwing back a tall glass of bourbon, his eyes met the reflection in the glass's bottom. For an instant, he thought he saw Maceba's eyes. He'd always remember her eyes.

Noticing a picture of Jasmine on the dresser, he slammed it face down, smashing the glass in the frame. His thoughts ran to Rashawn. It had been forever since he'd seen her. He couldn't believe how much he missed her.

But . . .

"It's a shame, Shawnie, a shame you did me like that. Now, I've got to teach you a lesson. It's a damn shame too," Doc said. "You lied, you cheated. You betrayed me—just like my mother. And why?" Doc went on, grumbling as he headed to the shower. "Like I have time to deal with all this mess. I don't have time for this. Where is a shrink when you need one? Oh well, I've always liked my way of solving problems anyway—simple. Either you're with me or ag'n me," he joked, still finding humor even at this dark time. "None of that psychobabble shit for me." Suddenly he turned to the mirror, pointing accusatively at the reflection—the reflection of a man he could no longer trust.

"With me or against me . . . right?" he asked the man in the mirror.

It'd been days since he'd had a warm meal, clean clothes, or a hot shower.

"This being on the run shit is for the birds," he chuckled, while waiting for the timer on the dryer. He had redressed his wound. The gunshot had barely grazed him; still he bled like a stuck pig.

He had taken the longest shower of his life. He almost felt like himself again, but not quite, considering he wasn't really sure who he was anyway.

This place was no everyday hideout. It was modern and fully equipped. It was obvious Roman still used it regularly.

"Must be where he comes to think . . . or . . ." Doc went on talking while looking through the drawers noting feminine accessories.

"Oh, oh, you go boy," Doc laughed, sniffing at the nearly dead roses to see if they still had any scent left.

Just then, there was a knock at the door.

"Allen . . ." he heard a woman calling.

Doc thought a moment before heading to answer it. Surely, the woman had seen the news, read the paper, knew. Before he rationalized the situation out in his head, he had opened the door.

Standing in the dark was a petite, blonde woman— cute, yet very book-wormish, in Doc's opinion.

"Figures," he mumbled almost audibly.

The woman looked up at him, smiling warmly.

"Oh my goodness, you're not Allen." She grinned.

"No, I'm not," Doc answered, watching the little woman's eyes drop the length of his long frame and then settle for a second on the towel wrapped around his waist.

"Wanna come . . . in?" Doc asked, suggestion riddling his words.

The woman blushed, clutching her jacket tightly, pulling it up under her chin. She smiled, apparently flustered.

"What happened to your arm?" she asked, finally allowing her eyes to move upward.

Bet this bookworm could spin a good . . . tail, Doc thought, the pun bringing a smile to his face.

"Nothing. Wanna come in and talk about it?"

"Oh no, I just thought Allen was here. I saw the light," she said, pointing behind him to the dim living room lamp that he had turned on.

"You and Allen, friends? I mean, me and Allen are friends," Doc explained.

"Oh well . . ." the woman's head dropped shyly, "I'd say we're . . . friends," she giggled, sounding coquettish and youthful. There was a moment between them before she spoke. "Guess I am a little curious about what lays under that . . ." Her eyes wandered again, "bandage."

Doc snickered. He too put on a shy act, pointing his finger at the woman playfully. "Oh, that Allen, always keeping secrets. And I guess you two have a lot of secrets." He chuckled while thinking of yet another woman of Roman's at his access.

"Well yes, Allen and I do talk a lot. I mean, there's not a lot out here and Allen's got the most modern cabin around, but you know, still, you just don't know who to trust with your business," the woman continued.

"That's for sure. Even out here in the boonies, you just don't know who might be lurking, trying to ya know . . . get in your . . . uh, business," Doc mocked, continuing to let out innuendos while wondering if the woman was game for a little romp—testing. It had been a while, and he was way past tense. And besides, it was obvious the woman didn't have a clue who he was.

"My name is Wanda," the woman introduced herself, outstretching her hand, watching it disappear into his palm. He could feel her pulse quicken.

"Well, Wanda, I'm freezing my arse, ya know," Doc chuckled now, tugging at the towel, causing it to loosen a bit.

"Oh sorry, I'll just . . ."

"So why not come in? I was just going to have some cocoa. I'll uh . . . slip into something, and we'll visit until Allen gets back."

Wanda pondered the moment.

When will my brother ever learn to spot a ho? Doc wondered, regarding Roman's choice in women. *Jasmine, and now this,* he mused, as Wanda wriggled past him into the cabin. *But then, Blain, you're no better,* he snickered sarcastically, catching Wanda's attention. She too giggled—foolishly thinking she was about to spend the evening with someone sane.

"I'm going to stay with you," Trina fussed after everyone except for Davis had finally gone.

For a minute there, Rashawn thought she'd have to add on a room or two.

"No . . . you're not. You're gonna take Reggie and leave. I'm gonna go to bed and get some real rest. All this *help* has exhausted me. Please . . . I'll see you in the morning. Just one night, okay? Let me have my space, just for one night," Rashawn begged them both. Trina sighed heavily and Davis just folded his arms, saying nothing.

Rashawn looked at him as he simply walked into the kitchen and poured himself a fresh cup of coffee. She smacked her lips in irritation.

"Don't send him away, Rashawn. That man cares about you. He's been here for you," Trina told her. "Fix this *thing* now."

Rashawn smiled slightly.

"I know what you're trying to say, but I'm so unsure,"

"I'll take Reggie but you let him stay."

"But I'm only gonna let him stay a minute longer. I'm serious. I need some time alone," Rashawn insisted.

"Fine," Trina said before she then grabbed her large bag, looking around to see if Reggie was watching her. Reaching deep into the bag, Trina then pulled out a familiar looking Smith & Wesson.

"Oh shit, Trina!" Rashawn gasped before Trina shushed her quickly.

"Now, you keep this here, baby girl, and if you have to, use it like daddy taught cha to," Trina said, sounding her age, for once. Rashawn gulped audibly and nodded, taking her father's *old trusty* in her shaking hands and placing it in the roll top desk.

She hadn't thought about the need for protection. Her predator was dead and she was safe, right?

After Trina left, Davis moved behind Rashawn and pulled her into an embrace. She turned and with a surprising response, gave into his affections.

"I love you," he whispered in her ear.

"I love you too. I know I do," she answered, holding on tight, "and I want to forget everything bad that's happened and start over fresh and new . . . with you."

"I need to show you. I want you to know. I . . ." he began. She shushed him.

Taking her outstretched hand, he led her up the stairs to her room.

She looked around at the bed. She had not touched

it since the morning of her revealed violation. She'd been sleeping on the sofa downstairs.

"Are you okay in here?" he asked, noting her scan of the room. She looked at him and smiled.

After undressing, he pulled her comforter off the bed and spread it on the floor, tossing a couple of her bed pillows there too.

His kisses were soft and her body reacted to his lips as they touched her skin.

"I'm gonna love you until you've had enough, Rashawn. You say when," he whispered in her ear. "I would never hurt you."

Wetting his two fingers, he slid them into her, urging her lubrication to come. She gasped slightly at the new sensations caused by his technique. Again he tasted his fingers, only now her scent lingered on them.

He smiled at her. His surprising sexiness instantly aroused her, taking her mind off reality.

"You taste like heaven," he said.

"Then take me there," she answered.

Mounting her, he entered her slowly, cautiously at first until she arched upward, begging for more. He gave it to her happily, plunging deeper with passion-filled expressions leaving his lips. Words that called to her, begging her to join in song—*which she did.*

They were a perfect fit as together they moved and created, singing together love's chorus. She never wanted to come back to the darkness of her world. Being with Davis now, right now, was all she needed, as his explosion sent tingles down her thighs.

He lingered inside her, waiting patiently for Rashawn to share in what he had just experienced.

"Come with me," he whispered in her ear.

"I don't think I can," she cried.

"Don't think, just fall," he told her, his voice barely audible, his eyes closed as he rocked his body against hers, hitting all of her pleasure spots with just the right amount of pressure.

Cupping her breasts, he felt her nipples rise and harden. He grew firm inside her with quick strokes, followed by long, deep thrusts and heavy pants filling the room with sounds of their commitment. Soon they, together, brought their pleasurable trip to a satisfactory end. The intensity of Rashawn's orgasmic cry could be heard by anyone listening nearby.

"I'm starving," Davis exclaimed after a few more moments of euphoria. Rashawn could only giggle, as she too had to admit that her days of not eating were now being felt.

"How 'bout some fried chicken? Davis joked, reaching for his clothes.

"Chicken?" She giggled.

"You know how we do."

Rashawn, pulling her pajamas from the bed and quickly dressing, could only chuckle at Davis's ethnicity coming through.

"I'll hit Popeye's down the way and head straight back, okay?" he asked, patting his pocket for keys and making sure he had his wallet.

"Okay," Rashawn answered, sounding shy, still under the influence of his passion.

"You gonna be okay? I mean, you wanna go?"

"No, no . . . you go," she agreed, fanning him on.

"Tell you what. Let's eat, pick up Reggie, and then head out to my place," Davis offered now. Rashawn looked at him, smiling warmly—in love.

"Yes, let's," she agreed. He grinned.

"I'll be right back," he said again without moving from his spot. Suddenly he pulled her from the floor into a deep kiss, "I'll never leave you. I'll never hurt you . . . I'll . . ."

"Go get the chicken," Rashawn said, pushing him away playfully.

"I'll be right back."

She could hear him singing Stevie Wonder's "Signed, Sealed, Delivered" all the way down the stairs.

Doc headed back to the city. He needed to see Rashawn. There were things he needed to get resolved with her. There was some finalizing of matters that needed tending to.

"What a bitch you turned out to be," Doc said. He then sucked his teeth and moved the toothpick to the other side of his mouth. A wicked grin curved his full lips.

"You don't even know what a wicked woman you are!"

His mind drifted back to Wanda.

"Cheating comes so easy for some," he sighed heavily, remembering Wanda's eagerness to be a part of betraying Roman. "And in the man's bed, too," he said, blowing off his disgust with the innocent looking woman.

"Undercover whore," Doc said out loud, thinking of Wanda's sexually freaky ways and wants, her untamed antics, and wild, verbal response to his performance.

Wanda stayed the night with him. During their time together, between the sessions of unbridled sex, they talked—about a lot of things, too many things. Perhaps more things than Wanda should have talked about. However, it was right after breakfast while they visited Roman's library that Wanda finally said too much.

"Yes, he's a genius," she told him. "We've worked together on a few projects including this last one on sex . . . the thin line between love, passion and violence."

"Reeeeeally," said Doc looking with amazement at the shelves filled with video and audio tapes of the many sessions Roman held with his clients. So many tapes, so many hours of mental abuse his elder brother had dished out to the unknowing, and more than likely—if they had known what he was doing—unwilling participants to his little 'study'.

Suddenly Doc's eyes ran across a tape that caught his attention. It was flagged with a red sticker. He pulled it from the shelf.

"His research is magnificent," Wanda said now, sounding awestruck and impressed. "At first I was a little put off by the topic, however, once you get into it and get a full understanding of . . ."

"Have you seen any of these, like maybe, this one?" he asked, holding up the tape that had caught his eye, dated just a few weeks ago.

Wanda looked away, her cheeks blushing red. "Yes, I've seen some," she confessed.

Doc realized then that Wanda did indeed know him—very well—as a matter of fact, too well.

"And what do you think about what you . . . saw, Wanda?" Doc asked, his voice deep and rumbling, frightening.

Wanda shook. She was instantly terrified.

"Nothing. I didn't think anything."

"Uh-huh," he grumbled, thumbing through the rest of the tapes on that shelf, and their titles.

"Don't tell him about this," she begged.

"I won't," he promised.

Right before he strangled her.

Climbing out of Wanda's jeep, Doc punched in the numbers that opened the secure gates leading into Rashawn's condominium community.

He hated the thoughts that filled his mind—so confusing, so jumbled. It was as if Blain and Doc struggled with their emotions. For the first time it was as if the two of them just could not come to any type of agreement on how to handle things.

There was no room for forgiveness of Rashawn in this matter of betrayal.

Before reaching his car, Chance saw a familiar figure step from the darkness into the light of the street lamp. That distinct chiseled jaw line was one Chance recognized from even that distance.

"My God, I thought he was dead," Chance said aloud. "I should have known it would take more than a few bullets to kill that Devil."

That lunatic was on his way to Rashawn's condominium—had to be.

Chance had to stop him. He had to intercept this psycho.

Dashing through the complex, Chance was covered in a nervous sweat as he cut around back so that he was heading toward the man, who strolled, unconcerned and confident. Rethinking his approach, Chance looked around for a possible weapon.

Eying a broom leaning against someone's door, Chance grabbed it and readied himself to confront the man. His breathing became erratic as a mixture of emotions and thoughts swept through him.

I could die tonight, was one of the thoughts that tore at his belly.

"Well, well, well, and who might this be—by chance," he heard from behind him.

The man apparently saw him and backtracked himself. The big man was truly a solider. Chance knew he'd been out-maneuvered, but he still held tight to the broom. The man laughed almost as if he sensed that Chance felt the broom becoming immensely inadequate in his hands while staring at the hulking figure in front of him.

"Don't you have a life?" the man asked, smiling that crooked grin of his.

"Yes, I do and I'm about to do whatever it takes to save it," he said in reference to Rashawn, holding on to his voice and nerve.

The broom snapped like a toothpick in Doc's hands.

Chance watched the splintered ends of the broom fall to the ground and then looked up to see that smug grin spread out on Doc's chiseled face. His left hand shot out before he realized what he had done. The lightning fast jab caught Doc in the chops.

"Good shot," Doc said, wiping the blood that formed at the corner of his lip.

Chance was aware of his pounding heart at that moment. Fear made the palms of his hands slick with sweat. It was then that he realized the immensity of the situation. As the monstrous man loomed before him, his smile slowly stretching back into that sadistic grin that promised Chance a beating that would leave him praying for death, Chance realized that he actually might die this night.

"Don't do this, Chance—" Doc began, but his words fell away as he stared into Chance's eyes. There was something missing in that sudden cold, calm stare. Something that Doc knew should have been there, and indeed had been there only a moment ago—fear.

The two men faced off in silence. Chance's fear of death had made the transition into pure, unbridled rage. Every moment of memory burned through his mind, every wistful breath he had ever taken, every sunrise he had ever witnessed, every raindrop that had ever fallen upon his skin, came down to this one moment in time. The fear of death is the pinnacle of emotion. It lends strength to the weakest of men, it provides hope when all that remains is despair, it turns a sniveling coward into a fierce warrior—and that is what Doc saw when he looked into Chance's eyes.

The world no longer existed for Chance. No sound registered to his ears. There was no pain; there was no happiness, there was nothing. Even Rashawn was now a mere dust mite beneath his bed of worries. No, for Chance there was only survival.

Doc could feel his own heart rate increase as the nearly foreign emotion, named fear, tried to pry into his veins. But Doc was too stubborn to accept it, too acclimated to his history of dominating other men. He would crush Chance just like all the others.

With a low growl of annoyance, Doc lunged at Chance, seeking to grab him up in his powerful arms and snap his small body like he had snapped the broom.

Doc was not accustomed to pain. So it was that his face contorted into confusion when he felt the fire suddenly burning in his left knee. He fell forward to his hands and knees, his world becoming a blur of bright lights and more of the strange sensations of pain as Chance followed up his kick with a series of lightning fast punches.

Chance's knuckles were quickly bloodied and he did not know if it was his own blood, or if it was Doc's. Nor did he care. The adrenaline rushing through his system forced his arms to continue pumping as he danced around the prone and injured beast, just out of reach, his fists crashing down over and over again.

Doc crawled after the swift moving man, growling away the pain and disorientation as blow after blow fell down upon his head.

Chance could feel the adrenaline slowly giving way to fatigue. His breathing was labored, and he panted heavily. His arms felt like tree limbs, and his muscles burned. He swung less frequently now, stalking over Doc, timing his shots carefully, seeking to knock the big man out. Whenever Doc seemed to be making it back to his feet, Chance would kick him back to the ground. Growling angrily at the stubborn beast, Chance stomped at his head, his right shoe striking Doc in the temple. Instantly Doc's body flopped to the ground and Chance moved in. He straddled the beast, grabbing him by the ears.

Doc teetered on the edge of consciousness, feeling his head being forced back and then slammed forward into the cold concrete once, twice, three times.

Chance's expression shifted as he stared down at the bloodied man, like a pit bull that had tasted blood, it infected him, and his eyes seemed to fill with madness. Grunting as he struggled to pull Doc over onto his back, Chance began to pummel his face. He had to kill this beast, or be killed himself.

Again Doc lapsed into unconsciousness as Chance's fist caught him in the temple. Chance reeled back in pain as he felt his wrist fracture from the impact. Obstinately, he pulled the injured limb close to his body and continued his assault with his left hand.

Doc groaned, his arms waving in an instinctive, yet feeble attempt to protect his face and head. Again he felt the blackness flash over his consciousness and his arms went limp. Then he felt something smooth beneath his fingertips—the broken broomstick.

With a growl, Doc fought away the darkness and slammed the splintered end of the stick into Chance's shoulder.

Chance howled as the pain rolled over him like a black wave on a moonless night. The splintered wood dug deep into his flesh, rending muscle and tearing cartilage. He fell over from the force of the blow, his hand wet with blood as he felt at the wound where the broomstick remained.

Doc groaned as he forced himself to his feet, limping after the wounded man like a vulture. He stood in Chance's path, ignoring the hand that clawed desperately at his legs. He sneered, spitting out blood and tooth as he kicked Chance in the head.

The force put behind that hit caused Chance to writhe on the ground in pain, barely conscious. "You do not understand what is going on. You do not understand what I have to do," Doc managed through labored breathing.

Chance didn't want anymore to do with Doc, but suddenly his eyes caught the light in Rashawn's window, and he remembered what this fight was all about. Scrambling to his feet, he grabbed the shaft still protruding from his shoulder and ripped it free, lunging at Doc in one last frantic attempt to take Doc out.

Doc caught Chance's hand before the blood stained wood could pierce his flesh and the two men crashed heavily into the side of the condominium. Ripping Chance from him like a bug, Doc slammed him to the concrete.

Chance stubbornly attempted to get to his feet when suddenly, he felt the air rush from his body as Doc's boot made contact with his gut again and again, until the toe of the boot came back covered with the dark liquid that was now flowing from the wound he had earlier inflicted with the shaft of the broom.

"All you have to do is stay down. Quit fighting me . . . stubborn, damn people!" Doc's voice boomed, echoing through the quiet complex. He continued to kick at Chance, alternating from his body to his head, until Chance laid completely still, his clothes saturated with blood.

Finally Doc ceased his onslaught and stood in the thick silence, his eyes staring down at Chance. Growling, he spit out another tooth that had worked its way loose as he clenched his teeth in anger. Then he turned and headed off in the direction of Rashawn's lighted apartment window.

*   *   *

Rashawn heard the loud voices outside. She'd heard the scuffling and sensed that Chance was in trouble, but fear had taken over and she was paralyzed as to what to do next. She hated being afraid, and she'd been nothing but afraid.

Suddenly, she heard the front door open.

Why did she have to be so damn stubborn? Why did she let Chance leave? Why did she send Trina home?

To make matters even worse, why did she leave the gun in the desk downstairs?

Rashawn looked around her room for another form of weapon, something that would hold off the intruder if he happened to make his way into her room.

A thief would surely find all they needed downstairs. There really wasn't too much more up here that anyone could want.

Except maybe her.

"Honey, I'm home," the deep voice called out, vibrating in its baritone, radiating as she hear his heavy steps coming up the stairs, "Come to Doc," he called

"Hey, where's Reggie?" she heard him ask loudly before slamming Reggie's bedroom door.

"Where's my little buddy?" she heard the man ask again—the familiarity of his voice spinning in her head now.

She knew that voice.

But how?

He was dead.

She audibly gulped at the sound of the familiar voice. There could be no more hellish life than enduring a rape again by Blain Tollome. *It can't happen again,* she thought, her mind spinning with the growing panic.

After all of this, for it all to end this way . . .

"Babe, you'll never guess who I had to kill on the way

home. Guess. I'll give you one *chance*," he said, with a sickening chuckle in his tone. Then he added, "Your little boyfriend had bigger balls than I thought. Damn shame. The world could use a few more good men like that," he laughed, only sounding half sincere.

Slamming her bedroom door quickly, she locked it. Within seconds, it seemed, he was twisting the knob. Rashawn panicked now and ran toward her bedroom window.

How many times had she climbed onto the roof of the house as a kid and swung like a monkey from house, to tree limb, and onto the ground?

As she shoved the stiff window open, pushing out the screen, she knew tonight would be one of those times.

"Rashe," he called, trying the door again. "Baby, come on."

"Rashawn!" he yelled ."Why you always making things so fuckin' hard—needlessly! You're pissing me off. I'm already having a very hard time dealing with what you and Ceba did to me. I really am beginning to believe you don't want us to be friends." She then heard him laughing wickedly before, with the force of a bull, her bedroom door flew off its hinges.

It was Blain Tollome—or was it.

Their eyes met for just a second.

It was long enough for her to see a stranger. Vacant orbs that held only darkness and evil. His lip was bloody and swollen, his face, sweaty and battered. She could only imagine Chance's condition.

"Tell me this, what does Roman got that I don't got? Well, besides a really cool video camera. Is it on now?" He grinned crazily looking around as if wanting to make sure he was caught by a hidden lens. "He wants to see the difference between love and violence? I got some violence for his ass."

She screamed, scrambling to get out the window before he could grab her with his monstrous hands, dragging her back in.

"Smile for the camera," he said in her ear, sending her into a déjà vu. *The dark parking lot of Moorman University. The gravel against her face. The smell of his cologne.*

His words, though not the ones said that night, forced her mind into the forgotten place. "Oh my God, Blain, no . . . please God. Don't hurt me again," Rashawn begged, as he groped for her, grabbing at her breast roughly and pulling at her pajamas. She was both stunned and shocked, no longer thinking quick on her feet.

Her eyes blurred as they welled with tears, but she quickly wiped them clear. The past violence done to her came back on her like a heavy weight.

"Please don't hurt me," she begged.

"Hurt you? I only wanted to help you," he insisted, still trying to pull her into an embrace.

She fought him, scratching at him and hitting him. "Why are you doing this?"

"I'm angry Rashawn, why does anyone do anything . . . and people call me crazy," he said, chuckling just a little, pulling her tighter to his chest. Rashawn attempted to dig into the skin of his face, but he prevented her. "Look, I have to tell you something. Listen to me," he insisted, turning her back to him, preventing her from attacking further. Suddenly she could feel his hot breath on the back her neck. Instead of speaking he sniffed her neck.

"Damn Rashe' baby, you feel good, you smell good. No wonder my man Chance fought so hard to keep you from me," he purred, sounding suddenly and inappropriately flirtatious.

Her mind spun as she tried desperately to take his hands from her, but he was behind her, tightening his grip, pulling her to the floor.

As soon as he got her there, Rashawn, managed to crawl on her belly away from his clutch, and get to her feet. She ran quickly from the room and headed downstairs.

"Don't fight me! I'm just playin'. Look, I'm willing to forgive you for everything, but you have to stop fighting me," he screamed angrily, coming after her. "I've been through a lot and I'm getting tired of you!" he called, sounding eerie, odd, and even stranger than before.

"Don't touch me," she screamed, tearing down the staircase.

"Oh, I can't touch you? He can, but I can't?" he asked, pausing only for a second.

Rashawn didn't stop to attempt to make sense of his words. Everything was far too clear to her now. Doc was here and she was in danger. That fact and only that fact was very clear.

Before Rashawn could reach the bottom of the stairs, he tackled her and both of them tumbled five or six steps to the hardwood floor below. Rashawn knew her ankle was sprained. The pain surged through her, but she would not stop to baby it. She had to get away.

Doc was on her, attempting to cover her mouth. She fought him, scratching his face. She knew he would hit her. Mentally she got ready for it, and just in time too, as his flat hand slapped her hard.

"Damn it Rashe'. Damn it. Now see, here we go again, roughhousing. How do you think you are worth all this shit?" he cursed, all the while reminding Rashawn of their date, yet another time Doc had forced his affections on her.

Stunned, she lay still for a moment. Fighting this big man would get her nowhere—she knew that. It got her nowhere the first time, and it wouldn't now.

Suddenly, she realized he was kissing her—her neck, her face. He stroked her hair softly.

"I would never hurt you," he whispered. "I think I've always loved you," he said, almost sounding reluctant to admit his feelings. "And not just because he did."

Rashawn turned her head back to look at the beast straddling her.

"I can't believe I just said that." He smiled.

This truly was Blain Tollome. How could she have ever guessed he was the animal whose obsession with her reached the level of inconceivable perversion to where he had drugged her time and time again in order to have his way with her in a macabre intimacy— a spurious marriage, of sorts.

How could he be Reggie's father?

"Blain?" she asked, her voice, a half whisper.

He looked at her and for a second he was Blain, just before his eyes, dark and depth defying, emptied of all warmth and human emotions. He looked strange and suddenly unfamiliar to her as if someone else now possessed his soul. Rashawn's blood ran cold.

"Let me up. I hurt my leg. Let me up," she requested, mustering up all the gentleness she could find amongst the barely controlled panic.

Reason with the man, Shawnie. It's worth a chance.

Chance . . .

There was no time to think about him now.

Watching Doc shake his head, she felt a warm tear run down her cheek. "I won't tell anyone, if you let me up . . ." Rashawn said.

"I don't give a damn abowdat," Doc said, allowing the accent that shadowed his existence to slip out—the accent that belonged to the mother that he and Allen Roman shared. The accent he had picked up in hopes of fitting in with the family of the man his mother destroyed through selfishness—Allen Roman's father.

There was never acceptance for him, only rejection.

The black boy, with the white skin . . .
The outsider no one wanted, not even his own mother.

Rashawn remembered feeling vulnerable, breakable under the weight of the heavy man on that night in the back lot of Moorman University—just like now. Doc could kill her now, and probably would. However, Rashawn knew she would rather die than again go through what he put her through that night. She would rather die than give in to him willingly, whoever this was here—Blain or the maniac Doc. It no longer mattered. She wanted no part of either of them.

She couldn't imagine that somehow in her deep subconscious dreams, she'd given in to Doc's perverse acts, and gotten any kind of pleasure.

"But you do care? You don't want that on Blain's record, Doc," Rashawn continued cautiously in her attempt to keep him in the now.

"Shut up," he said flatly, putting one of his large hands over her mouth. "Don't try that psychoanalytical bullshit on me. I hate that stuff," Doc growled. "Roman already did the psycho thing on me, hey, and you too for that matter," he chuckled, removing his hand.

"What are you talking about?"

"Oh, now you want me to explain. Now you want the answers to life's big questions. What's on the tape? What does it all mean, Doc? What about Reggie?" he mocked in a high falsetto.

"What about Reggie?"

"Yeah, what about Reggie?" he repeated the question. "What a sweet little family we could have. You, me, Reggie, Blain, all of us could . . ." he began before suddenly she spat in his face, catching him off guard. He hadn't expected her to still have so much fight left. It startled him.

That was all it took. Rashawn grabbed the leg of her footstool and cracked it against his head.

The blow stunned him, but Rashawn didn't care. She pushed him off her and crawled to her desk.

Scrambling to her feet, she pulled the gun Trina had given her from the drawer, turning to shoot him, but he was gone.

Familiar with her living room, Rashawn clicked off the lamp. She'd forgotten that Doc no doubt knew her home just as well as she did. He'd spent a lot longer in that condo than she had being Allen Roman's brother if nothing else.

Searching madly, her heart was beating so hard she almost became lightheaded, but still she held firmly to the gun—aimed.

"Don't ever go near my son," Rashawn screamed.

"Blain!" she screamed again into the darkened room, only to get deafening silence in reply.

"Blain!" she called once more before suddenly, she heard a crash behind her.

He had stumbled over the new plant.

Thank God for Qiana!

Reflex got the best of her as she fired in the direction of the sound. There was silence.

"Blain, did I shoot you? If I did, you better let me get a doctor!" she called out, still attempting to reason with him.

She heard him groan slightly, sounding as if he were struggling to get to his feet. She fired again. This time she was sure she hit him, as she heard him take the slug with a grunt, and then she only heard a thud.

"I see you took my advice. What's this now, a .45?" Doc asked, with a heavy pain-filled voice behind the dark attempt at humor.

Quickly she clicked on the light, thinking she would find him on her floor, but instead she saw only blood-stains where he had fallen.

The light went out again. "See Blain, I told you," Rashawn heard Doc say.

"Yeah, you did, didn't you," Blain answered.

"I mean, I tried to help her, like you asked. I tried to love her, but you know how stubborn some women can be."

"I know."

"I tried to tell her about the tape, but she doesn't want to know the truth."

"You're right, you're right."

"So now, I'm just going to have to kill her," Doc whispered loudly.

"Do we really have a choice?" Blain asked.

"No."

The voices in the dark drove Rashawn to a near frenzy. She looked around for him madly while she tried to dial 911. She groped for her cordless which sat on the coffee table. Finally, she found it. "Yes, I have an e . . ." she began, before the phone went dead.

She turned, only to find him, standing inches from her, his face glowing against the full moon shining through the open curtain. He was bloody and smiling, holding up the wall end of the cord, tauntingly.

"Nice piece," he said, before grabbing her. Rashawn pulled the trigger, this time with her eyes closed . . . again and again until she heard the gun click.

She fell, with Blain's dead weight against her.

Epilogue

Eighteen months later.

Rashawn leaned against the balcony, gazing out over the Pacific Ocean. Sometimes she would imagine life on the other side of the water, life far away from the west coast.

But, her life was here—here on this side, in Pacific View—here with Chance.

Sometimes she still dreamed about that night—Blain's wicked grin, the confusing words he spoke before she squeezed that trigger, right before she closed her eyes.

She often thought about how his feelings for her had turned into a mad obsession that rushed him further along the road to insanity. She thought about Maceba and how she loved him, and how that love cost her, her life.

That night, he could have easily taken her, yet he didn't. Why had he drugged her all those months? It just didn't seem to fit with his angry 'gotta have it now' persona. So many things didn't fit when it came to Blain, and ultimately, Doc.

Rashawn wished she could have learned more about his mental illness, how she wished she had known from the start what Blain Tollome was capable of doing. Rashawn wished she could have collaborated with Allen Roman more—maybe to help Blain, maybe even to have cured him. Of course, for some reason it never seemed as though Roman really wanted to help Blain.

"His own brother . . ."

What had Roman to gain by his brother's sickness? Why would he want to see his sibling living such a hell-ish life? Rashawn shook her head at the questions she'd raised in her mind. *I guess no one never really knows all of a family's dirty secrets.*

Yet there were so many loose ends, so many inconsistencies in Roman's behavior. True, he was addicted to a narcotic that no doubt had altered his mind but still, there was more, it was deeper. She felt it. There was something in the riddled words of Blain that night . . . who would ever know?

"And maybe I'll never know the truth. Maybe Allen was a little crazy."

Although she had fully recovered from the drug's effects, Rashawn knew the whole ordeal would always haunt her. Blain Tollome and the mad man living within him—Doc—would always haunt her. She would never be the same. A fact confirmed every time she looked into Reggie's eyes.

How could such a sweet boy have such a sick father?

So many questions left unanswered. Maybe she'd pondered it all too long, it was going on two years since this all started, longer if you count Reggie's dubious conception, maybe it was time to let it all go. Call her weak-minded, but she was tired of thinking about it all now and in all reality, of what good would the answer be at this point in time?

Just then, Rashawn heard her newborn calling out

for nourishment, and Reggie adding to the bellow, bringing her back to reality and the joy of motherhood. The thought of her children brought a smile to her face.

"Hold your little horses, the troops are a comin'," she teased, entering the apartment. "Cuz your daddy is starving us out, with his late behind," she called out loudly.

She could hear Davis's shower ending—finally, and a good thing, too.

For a mathematician, he knew nothing about being on time. They were due in the Palemos in an hour. He moved as slowly as he could most days, always claiming recovery from his injuries incurred that night, which was his attempt to use humor in order to keep the severity of what had nearly happened to him to a minimum.

He'd gone into therapy for his addiction to sex, finally facing the fact that both he and Juanita had some serious issues in that area and if he was ever going to move on and succeed in a healthy relationship with Rashawn he was going to need help, especially with Juanita having the baby and using that as an excuse on every turn to get him over there. So far, even after all this time, she'd not succeeded and after reevaluating his understanding of love and what it really was, while being married to Rashawn, the most trusting, loving and forgiving woman he'd ever met, he knew Juanita would never succeed again.

Carlotta was making her famous gumbo and had called everyone to the table, insisting that no one be late. Chance seemed to enjoy incurring her wrath.

"Hey, what's all the hooey?" Chance called from the hall, in his playfully stern voice while tying on his robe.

"I've got your hooey, mister," Rashawn chuckled, shooing him on toward the bedroom, urging him to finish getting dressed. He resisted and kissed her instead.

The doorbell rang. Glancing at Chance, Rashawn decided to answer it.

"Delivery for Ms. Ams," the boy said, holding a large bouquet of red roses and a small box the size of a VHS tape.

Rashawn's heart raced as she looked quickly at Chance for answers.

Chance accepted the delivery for her. He tipped the boy quickly and closed the door. Rashawn stepped away from him as if afraid to touch the flowers.

Laying the roses on the entry table, Chance looked the VHS box over closely. It was flagged with a red sticker that simply said Rashawn Ams.

There was a card attached.

"I'm writing to thank you for ridding me of the nuisance that was once my brother—Blain. He was such a troubled young man, rebellious, and as you can no doubt imagine, the bane of my existence. He did serve a purpose for a time, but when that time was up, I was at a loss on how to dispose of something so large. In that area, I must say, you helped me more than you could ever know.

With that said, I thought I should give you a gift. You deserve it. I know how you like answers. So here is the answer to the biggest question I'm sure you have—Reggie.

This tape was part of a research project where you were (and I've always been a little sorry about that) an unwilling participant. I haven't officially titled it yet; as my assistant who normally helps me with that kind of thing is dead now, poor Wanda. I must admit this was some of her best camera work. Blain could be such a brute most of the time. My apologies, I digress. Let me get back to the point. I'm sure once you see the film you will give it some simple title like, "The Rape of Rashawn Ams."

However, I was thinking more along the lines of, "The Night I Fell in Love."

The main character in the movie is not who you might think. And if you don't believe me, ponder this fact: due to injuries incurred in childhood, Blain could no more reproduce than a stone, along with the fact that the unlucky young man has never once had sex with you. It's all simple science, my dear.

I know what you must be thinking and you're right, but if this helps at all Rashawn, my dearest one, don't ever think of yourself as a murderer of an innocent man, although Blain never once touched you, he was far from innocent. Think of yourself as an assistant.

I just know this whole thing has upset you tremendously. You're always so easily upset. So I better close here and let you enjoy the movie. Give my love to our son. I must admit, the older he gets the more he looks like me.

Can't you see it in his eyes? I can.

Perhaps one day I can repay you for the favor you did of killing Blain for me. Of course, for now, deportation has me homebound in Jamaica and all I can do is kiss you in my mind until my return.

Until then,
Sweet dreams,
Allen."

Rashawn cried into her hands, inconsolable.

About the Author

California transplant Michelle McGriff now writes using the lush green backdrop of the Great Northwest as her muse. Known to her family as the 'best of storytellers' and with many novels and short stories under her pen, she excitedly joins Q-Boro Books with hopes of entertaining a new audience with her rule-breaking, cross-genre writing style that's sure to entertain the enlightened reader.

Michelle is the author of *Majestic Secret, For Love's Sake, Obsession 101*, and several other novels. She is currently working on her next enthralling tale of mystery, romance, and drama.

PREVIEW
DEADLY TEASE
By Michelle McGriff

Coming soon from Q-Boro Books

The body was found right where the caller said it would be, in one of the empty rooms of the abandoned Madison Hotel, which was atop the Asoki liquor store on the corner of Madison and Mather Way. It doubled as a Victory Outreach church, a meeting place for the religiously misplaced. They gathered there to hopefully one day find their way back to some semblance of normalcy with God as a platform.

"Somebody didn't wanna hear no more preaching, I guess," thought Lawrence out loud. Jim snickered wickedly.

These five blocks used to hold a fairly decent strip of industry. Lawrence remembered being a kid and going through this area with his folks on their way to visit family in the Palemos—a track of homes not far from there. Lawrence's dad would stop in the liquor store not far from where they had found the dead man today. Lawrence's father would buy a few forties to throw back with his brothers while Lawrence, being so much younger than everyone else, would sit inside with the women folk.

Back then, in the seventies, the owner of the store was an old Oriental man named Chi Asoki. He was an oddity to his neighborhood. But not anymore; now, foreigners ruled. Lawrence didn't have a problem with the foreigners coming in. He just hated change. No matter what it was.

Now Asoki's store, now Asoki's Liquor Mart, during

day light hours, doubled as a crack house after dark. And the ice cream parlor across the street was now some kind of dance hall, "What's the name of that place?" Lawrence asked Jim, thinking aloud.

"What place?" asked Jim, his face still twisted up with disgust, as if the foul smell coming from the area where the body was laying was still in his nose. It was an awful scene—and in his mind, nowhere near a random act of violence. Somebody meant for this man to be *really* dead. He'd been sexually assaulted, stabbed and mutilated—his penis removed—who knew which came first. One could only hope he was dead before being detached from his manly member. Blood was everywhere, making the men have to walk on their tip toes to prevent the sticky reddish brown fluids from getting on their shoes. Gloves and masks were quickly passed to Jim and Lawrence.

"Forget it, we're outta here," Lawrence said, backing out of the room. They'd return after the room emptied a bit.

Moving out onto the sidewalk now, Lawrence pointed to the neon-lit building that sat in place of his pleasant childhood memory.

"What's what place?" he asked.

"Oh you mean Queer Land," Jim answered.

"What . . ." Lawrence chuckled.

"The Rainbow Room, s'cuse meeee," one of the apparent patrons of the homosexual bar commented, showing irritation with the way Detective Jim Beam addressed his hangout.

"Ahh . . . Rainbow . . . yeah," Lawrence said with sarcasm showing. He'd been following the fads and trends; he knew what the reference of a rainbow meant now.

The pretty, young man just shook his head in exasperation and then with a nervous drag from his cigarette his attention was brought back to the grisly scene he had stumbled upon. Of course it wasn't easy to come across a body found on the second floor of an abandoned building.

"No, it wasn't an abandoned building. It's was being used as a church. I thought I told you that when I called. I was there for a reason . . . was about to confess some stuff to Father Fox." He smacked his lips and then, still holding his cigarette between his two fingers he bit his thumbnail nervously.

Lawrence stared at the young man for a moment. He could only imagine that dressed up, the young man had to look like Eartha Kitt a little. He was getting ready to ask when their attention was drawn away by a ruckus starting up in front of the Rainbow Room. From the passenger window of a fast moving truck a large rock was thrown, busting the window with a loud crash and the familiar sound of breaking glass. The young man let out a womanly scream.

Out of reflex, Lawrence ran out to the street to catch the license plate number of the vehicle. He only caught a couple of numbers. From inside the building, several drag queens emptied into the street, cussin' mad.

"Are you the police?" one of them finally asked.

"Can't you tell? Got that big . . . ummm gun," the owner, a tall exotic looking woman flirted while moving through the gathering crowd. She wore a kimono robe that exposed much cleavage. Lawrence caught himself staring at her for a second before suddenly, feeling the tightening in his throat, looked at Jim who was smiling—grinning actually. Jim could tell Lawrence was about to panic.

"Okay, ladies," Jim interceded, corralling the drag queens together. "Okay, one thing at a time . . . one thing at a time," he instructed. "We got a stiff in that building and some stone throwers over here . . . so—"

"A stiffy?" one of the drag queens gasped. "That doesn't sound like a good thing—or does it?"

Lawrence couldn't breathe. He quickly headed back over to the dead body being loaded into the coroner's wagon across the street. He could handle that much better.

"Somebody get this placed closed up," he instructed one of the uniform cops, who nodded.

"You need to loosen up Larry," Jim said, while they road back to the precinct.

"What . . ."

"Those gay guys . . . you gotta loosen up. It's not like rap music. Homosexuality is here to stay," Jim said looking at his notepad before looking up at him, grinning again.

"Look, I'm a Christian, man. I just don't believe that men need to be doing that," Lawrence explained flatly, bluntly, and to the point.

"Come on, Lawrence, you're just a damn homophobic; being Christian doesn't even come close to being your main issue with those guys. Besides, one of them was female. Bet you can't guess which one."

"No and I'm never gonna get close enough to even try to guess."

"I'm not saying that I'm like . . . into that either, but you do need to open your mind a little more . . . accept the differences, man," Jim explained. "Differences can be . . ." Jim paused. "beautiful." He was being sarcastic but Lawrence took him far too serious.

"My mind is as open as it's ever gonna be, Jim," Lawrence said with his large hand flying up and then cutting the air on its way down. Jim just shook his head and looked out the window. "What?" Lawrence asked,

uestioning the silence, refusing to acquiesce. This con-
ersation wasn't over as far as Lawrence was concerned.

"What . . . what? I'm just sayin' that you need to get
1 touch. You are gonna have to stop just judging things
ased on what you see up front, or what you think you
ee," Jim explained. Lawrence glanced over at Jim
gain, while maneuvering the wheel.

What was Jim trying to say?

"Are you gay, Jim?" Lawrence finally asked. Jim rolled
his eyes.

"No. Why is it always black and white with you? Just
because I try to get you to think with your mind open, I
have to be gay . . . or whatever. Like when were talking
about politics, I disagreed with you and suddenly I was
communist. And you wonder why you're not married . . . ?
Do you wonder?" Jim asked again—rhetorically.

"Whatever," Lawrence sighed still refusing to see the
correlation between the scene today at the gay dance
hall—the Rainbow Room and why women just didn't
understand him.

He sure didn't get the connection between all of it
and the fact that Jim was communist.

"You need to get out more—you need a life," Jim finally said in summation of the conversation.

Attention Writers:

Writers looking to get their books published can view our submission guidelines by visiting our website at:
www.QBOROBOOKS.com

What we're looking for: Contemporary fiction in the tradition of Darrien Lee, Carl Weber, Anna J., Zane, Mary B. Morrison, Noire, Lolita Files, etc; groundbreaking mainstream contemporary fiction.

We prefer email submissions to: candace@qborobooks.com in MS Word, PDF, or rtf format only. However, if you wish to send the submission via snail mail, you can send it to:

Q-BORO BOOKS Acquisitions Department
165-41A Baisley Blvd., Suite 4. Mall #1
Jamaica, New York 11434

*** By submitting your work to Q-Boro Books, you agree to hold Q-Boro books harmless and not liable for publishing similar works as yours that we may already be considering or may consider in the future. ***

1. Submissions will not be returned.
2. **Do not contact us for status updates.** If we are interested in receiving your full manuscript, we will contact you via email or telephone.
3. Do not submit if the entire manuscript is not complete.

Due to the heavy volume of submissions, if these requirements are not followed, we will not be able to process your submission.